PRIDE & PREDATOR

BOOK TWO

SALLY S. WRIGHT

MULTNOMAH PUBLISHERS

Sisters, Oregon

PRIDE AND PREDATOR
© 1997 by Sally S. Wright
published by Multnomah Fiction
a Division of Multnomah Publishers, Inc.

Cover design by D^2 Designworks

International Standard Book Number: 1-57673-084-0
Printed in the United States of America.

For information:
Multnomah Publishers, Inc., PO Box 1720, Sisters, Oregon 97759

Library of Congress Cataloging-in-Publication Data
Wright, Sally S.
  Pride & predator/Sally S. Wright.
      p.cm.--(Ben Reese mystery series:2)   ISBN 1-57673-084-0
  I. title. II. Series: Wright, Sally S. Ben Reese mystery series: 2.
PS3573.R5398P7   1997
813'.54--dc21   97-15561
                                                                    CIP

97 98 99 00 01 02 03 04 05 — 10 9 8 7 6 5 4 3 2 1

Because of David Munro
who started the book with his stories,
then patiently answered more questions about Scotland
than anyone ought to be able to.

ACKNOWLEDGMENTS

Pride and Predator has been written because a lot of people went out of their way to share their knowledge and experience with me. I was especially helped in Scotland by the Reverend and Mrs. Thomas Dick in Dunkeld, Edward MacMillan at the Blackwatch Museum at Balhousie Castle, Geoffrey Wardell (beekeeper) in Scotland Well by Leslie, Angus Kelly (then at Kinnaird, now at White's in London), Mary Morrison at Kinnaird, Donald MacDonald (solicitor), Andrew McGuire (pharmacist) in Dunkeld, Dr. Jimmie Mackie in Dunkeld, and Ken McKay (Procurator Fiscal's office) in Perth. Chief Superintendent J. A. MacKay of the Tayside Police in Perth was very generous with his time and experience, as was Detective Chief Superintendent Barry Stewart in Newcastle upon Tyne, Northumberland, England (and I hope they won't resent the fact that the police don't solve the murders). Kate Tristram at St. Mary's Hostel on Holy Island and Miss J. M. Backhouse (The British Library, London) were also very accommodating.

I wanted to use Cawdor Castle as the basis for my Castle Balnagard, and the late Earl Cawdor and the Dowager Countess Cawdor showed me the public and private rooms at Cawdor Castle, answered a great number of questions, and fed me an excellent lunch. I modeled Alex's room descriptions on those written by the late Lord Cawdor. Yet I didn't set Balnagard in Cawdor, Scotland. I placed it at Kinnaird in the countryside near Dunkeld.

Kinnaird is an exceptional country house hotel on a huge estate on the River Tay, and its manager, Mr. Douglas Jack, couldn't have been more kind or helpful during both my visits. The grounds I describe around Castle Balnagard (including Castle

Perach and Loch Skiach) are a largely accurate depiction of Kinnaird Estate.

Kilgarth in my book is based on Kinnaird (the hotel-house itself), but I've moved it to the estate at Cromlix House, another very fine hotel, near Kinbuck and Dunblane.

Here in the United States, I was helped with artifacts and fisticuffs by John Reed. I was also assisted by Morton L. Levy (chemist), the late Clyde Craig and Randy Pelc (electricians), Dr. Ivan Valiella (Boston University Marine Program, Woods Hole, Mass.), Rick Lamprecht (mechanic), Deputy Sheriff Antonio Ricciardi, Dr. Morris Weaver (veterinarian), Larry Houck and Tim MacCartney (pharmacists), Dr. Hansen (Pathology Labs of Northwest Ohio), Dr. Brunner (Endocrine and Diabetes Care Center, Toledo, Ohio), Dr. Armando Bautista (Director of Pathology, St. Luke's Hospital, Maumee, Ohio), Dr. Robert Forney Jr. (Director of Toxicology, Medical College of Ohio), Paul Samenuk (pharmacist, Medical College of Ohio), Dr. Kerry Garretson (psychologist), and Ron Sladky (president, Master Chemical Corp.).

Rod Morris at Multnomah Publishers is the editor who fought for my work, and I'll always appreciate his faith and persistence and his vision of what fiction should be.

LIST OF CHARACTERS

Dr. Allan—pathologist brought in by Procurator Fiscal for Perthshire

Mary Atwood—housekeeper at Kilgarth, MacLean family home

Tom Atwood—Mary's son, gardener at Kilgarth

Katherine Burnett—friend of Jon MacLean

Michael Cameron—head keeper, Balnagard Estate

Ruth Cameron—Michael's wife, part-time cook at Castle Balnagard

Lord Alexander Chisholm—writer, owner of Castle Balnagard and Balnagard Estate

Lady Jane Chisholm—Alex's wife, mother of James, Elizabeth, David, and John Chisholm

Edward Creith—beekeeper, farmer, Kilgarth neighbor

Dr. Allen Curzon—chief pathologist, Berwick Infirmary

Alfred Dixon—director of Edinburgh import-export office

Rev. Duncan Donaldson—army chaplain of Jon MacLean

Dr. William Graham—physician friend of MacLean family

Detective Inspector Grey—head of Criminal Investigation Division, Perth

Hamish MacDonald—pharmacist, member of Jon MacLean's church

Martha MacDonald—Hamish's sister in Peebles

Jamie MacIntosh—beekeeper

Harold MacIntyre—employee of Alfred Dixon, son of parishioners in Jon MacLean's church

Roderick (Rory) MacKenzie—editor of *The Daily Scotsman*

Rev. Jonathan MacLean—Church of Scotland minister in Cawdor, owner of Kilgarth (MacLean family home)

Ellie (Elinor) Maitland MacLean—pianist wife of Jon
          MacLean
Hugh MacLean—geologist, Jon MacLean's younger brother
David McGuire—Jon MacLean's solicitor
Police Superintendent Mills—Dunblane police
Sir Robert Morgan—Alex Chisholm's uncle
Gerald Pilcher—mentally disturbed person in Linlithgow
Ian Pilcher—Gerald's father
Jimmy Reed—boy on Holy Island
Ned Sutherland—import-exporter, employer of Alfred Dixon
Agnes and Emma White—women with dogs on train
Marjorie Wilson—Glasgow friend of Alfred Dixon

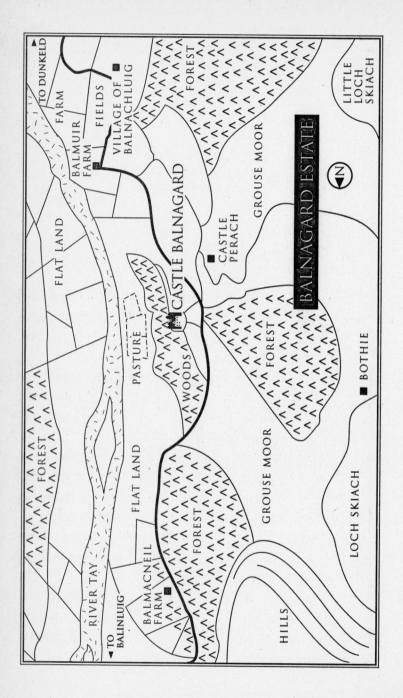

CHAPTER ONE

Friday, May 12, 1961

THE PATH FROM THE RUINS of the priory to the castle wasn't hidden in early morning mist that day, and the sea birds were easy to follow as they glided silently, crying to each other, or the sea itself, while they rode the east wind.

The sun hadn't been up long and it hung low above the water, pale and soft and salmon colored, and yet for the north coast of Northumberland in early May, it was already a warmer morning than most, in spite of the wind.

Few people from the mainland came over to Holy Island that early in the morning, even when the tides cooperated and they could drive across the causeway from Beal. Especially then, in 1961, before tourism had become both a scourge and a saving grace. Yet that Friday, there was a tall thin man in three-piece tweeds with a knapsack on his back walking into the wind toward the castle, swinging a large wicker basket.

He moved easily with long, quick, loose-jointed strides, with his head up and his shoulders back. But he didn't hurry like day-trippers intent on the castle and the priory in less than an hour.

He stopped beside the harbor and watched a cormorant fly past just above the water with a long stream of seaweed in her beak. He smiled to himself and hopped from rock to rock without having to think about balance, breathing in salt air with silent satisfaction, the iodine and the fish and the seaweed he'd loved as long as he could remember.

He set the basket down and stretched his arms above his head while he gazed back the way he'd come, contemplating the ruins of the Benedictine priory, standing like yellowed lace against the sky in empty arches and winding stairs that led up into open air.

His knapsack was hanging unevenly and he adjusted the straps before he started off again toward the castle, his hard-soled shoes sliding a bit on the moss-covered cobbles in the patches that weren't covered by sand. The wind had whipped his hair in his eyes, but he put up with it for a quarter of a mile, before he held it back with his free hand so he could stare at Beblowe Rock.

It would have been hard not to on that path. For it shot straight up out of that flat grassy island like a small volcano, or a giant barnacle, two hundred feet wide at the bottom and half as high, a green mossy dolerite dike, with Lindisfarne Castle crouched like a cat at the top.

It was a strangely haunting place. Striking and mysterious. And Jonathan MacLean stopped fifty feet or so from the high cliff and studied the smooth fortified walls growing from the jagged rock. The castle had been built as a fort by Henry the Eighth, if he remembered his history correctly, and shaped to fit the top of the rock, narrow and asymmetrical, with something like a prow and stern. It had been turned into a country house at the turn of this century, only to fall into the hands of the National Trust.

And that must have been years before the war, because the first time he'd seen it, he was wearing short trousers. Gray, undoubtedly, to match his old school uniform.

He could still remember cold winter rain running down his bare legs and settling in his socks as he climbed the steep cobbled ramp that had been cut up to the castle from the south cliff wall.

His mother had tried to talk him into taking her umbrella, but he was defending Lindisfarne against foreign invaders and couldn't let himself be coddled by any woman, especially his own mother.

And how many years ago was that? Time, evaporating faster every year. Thirty? Thirty-one? He must have been ten at least, because Alex was with them, and they'd met when he was ten and Alex was eight, when they were both still suffering the indignities of chapped knees. The curse of the British schoolboy. Even those from the highlands of Scotland.

He'd come a long way to stand on those stones and stare at that stretch of sea, and he smiled again as he watched the ocean, lying at Lindisfarne's feet, being ruffled by the east wind while the sun burned a hole in the sky.

Still, the wind was wearing on him. Not because it was cold. It wasn't. Living in the desert had given new meaning to terms like hot and cold.

But breakfasting in the midst of such a wind would be no small feat. And he pulled the collar of his jacket together and began walking north, curving left around Beblowe Rock out of the wind's path.

And then Jonathan MacLean looked startled. Apprehensive, almost, as he turned his head to the left and listened. He turned to the right too and closed his eyes so he could concentrate better. And then when he opened them, he examined the ground around him first, before looking away to the horizon.

There was nothing noticeably alarming. A handful of sheep

were a few yards away, waddling across the grassland in their matted winter wool, hardly looking at Jon, when they'd seen so many strangers before. They darted here and there, as they often do for no apparent reason, scattering the lambs who actually seemed to enjoy the excitement, while they watched Jon curving around the stone wall in the short grass and the mossy patches, picking his way through the sheep droppings and the sharp outcroppings of rock.

He kept to the flat ground, and he laid his basket and his knapsack down, and then stood still again and listened.

There was no obvious reason why anything much should have alarmed him. He knew how to take care of himself. He was strongly built, with wide shoulders and big bones. Few men in their twenties could have managed the training he'd been doing ever since the war.

And yet he still looked tense and ill at ease. Until a crosswind swept around the end of the rock and his coat flapped open and his hair lashed back across his face.

Then he shook his head as though whatever he'd been thinking didn't make any sense, and unrolled the army-issue blanket tied beneath his knapsack and spread it on the damp grass. He set the knapsack and the basket on it to hold it down, and then he squatted on his heels on a corner of it and fiddled with the strap on the picnic basket like it was either stiff and hard to work, or he'd never unfastened it before.

As he pulled the top open with his left hand, he looked up at the sky and shaded his eyes with his right so he could watch two terns turn and wheel as they fished off the rocky shore.

His left hand was resting on the edge of the basket, his fingers lying on the thermos inside, his eyes still fixed on the terns— when he jerked his hand out of that basket as though he'd been stabbed.

He was standing in a second, slapping at his hand and swatting at the side of his face. He started tearing at the left inside pocket of his jacket, making a strangling noise in his throat, ripping and clawing at whatever he had in that pocket.

But before he got it free, his legs buckled under him, and he crumpled forward and collapsed on his side at the bottom of Beblowe Rock.

His left arm was under him and his face was turned to the right, and he was staring at a soft round tuft of green moss with empty eyes.

Jimmy Reed was half a mile away dawdling along the harbor, picking up stones and skipping them when he felt like it, or throwing them in when he didn't. He couldn't have explained why he liked the sound of a stone slipping into water, or why a high splash made him feel good. He was male, and ten years old, and it was in his blood.

He'd managed to sneak out before six, but he still thought he ought to check the time, and he pulled his grandfather's pocket watch out of his shirt pocket and consulted it analytically like a businessman on a sales trip. His thin mouth slid into a one-sided grin, and then he opened and closed the lid four or five times, because he liked the delicate click and the feel of the thin gold disk.

He'd slipped the watch off the kitchen shelf to make sure he got back for school, and he didn't want to think about what would happen if he got it wet, so he eased it back in his pocket and buttoned the button before he forgot.

He was on his way to the old lime kilns on the far side of the castle, even though he knew only too well that he wasn't allowed to go there on his own. His mum said he'd hurt himself, and his dad wouldn't say anything to her, not about the kilns, and it wasn't fair. He wasn't a baby. He could take care of himself as well as Freddie could any day of the week. Fred was only three years older and Mum didn't stop him anymore, not Freddie. And anyway, how would she know?

Jimmy's shoes were wet, and his pants' pockets were bulging with small stones and shells, and he was jumping on one foot on the sandy stone path, when he decided to stop at the overturned boats on the hill behind the castle. It was fun to jump from one herring boat to the other and see if you could land on the ridge.

Which meant that just before he got to Beblowe Rock, he turned left off the path and ran north.

There were three sheep pulling at the grass close to the path, and he stooped and picked up a rock, which he promptly tossed in their direction. He wanted to see if they'd scatter. *If* they noticed the stone a'tall. They were silly beasts, really, and frightfully dumb.

Jimmy laughed as they bleated and rushed off.

And then he saw a dark shape ahead of him on the ground.

It was a man lying on his side, half on a blanket and half off. He didn't look like he was asleep. He looked crumpled, sort of, and uncomfortable like he'd fallen. It wasn't at all like he'd lain down to take a nap.

But he wasn't moving. And he didn't answer when Jimmy called to him.

So Jimmy moved closer, slowly, feeling funny in the middle of his stomach, and said, "Mister? Mister? Are you alright?"

The man's eyes were open and they were staring right at Jimmy. They never blinked and they never moved. And there were bits of hair, light brown hair and sort of curly, that had blown across the blue parts. It almost looked like some of it had stuck to his eyeballs.

And Jimmy turned and ran home across the pasture with his arms flapping, and his grandfather's watch slapping against his ribs.

Lord Alexander Chisholm, the Thirteenth Thane and the Eighth Earl of Balnagard, was lying on the grass under a large tree on the edge of Beal with his head on a tartan blanket. He was right at the entrance to the causeway to Holy Island. And his eyes were closed and his mouth was open and he was holding a small worn book propped up on his chest on a folded Mac. The book swayed a bit as he breathed in and out, and then it bobbled and fell, almost pinning his lips against his teeth.

Even so, Alex didn't straighten it and start to read, until a single fly had settled on his nose. Then he opened his eyes, read a paragraph or two, laid the book down beside him, and laced his fingers together underneath his large square head.

That was why he was there, where he could put a book down if he felt like it, and his conscience would leave him alone. It was his one week a year without writing or research. Just walking, rambling, talking with Jonathan, or not, without any demands a'tall.

It was always wonderful, wandering about, arguing about where to stop, and whether there was an inn in the next village, and just where, precisely, that village might be. It set him up for another year, drinking mugs of tea by an open fire, tracing the constellations in a cold sky, discussing the Picts and the Celts and the Romans, not to mention the childhood debacles they'd miraculously managed to survive.

And this time, when they got to Housesteads up on Hadrian's Wall, he was *not* going to let Jon sneak off without discussing his finds with the curator of Roman artifacts. It was time he determined how much the cooking utensils and the old Roman boot were actually worth. Jon left them lying in his front hall, for heaven's sake, and used them for his children's sermons, and he ought to take more care. The truth was that Jon had no interest whatever in worldly arrangements and never had.

Oh? And were his own affairs more judiciously arranged? Hardly. And Jon would never have referred to it.

Still, he'd often thought Jon should have taken up archaeology. It would've suited him down to the ground.

No, that was a shocking thought. Really quite reprehensible. If Jon felt he ought to be a minister, no one had a right to quibble. Nor would one wish to. Not a'tall. Jon did a wonderful job up in Cawdor, and the local people clearly loved him.

Yet even as a child, digging in the pasture at his own country home, Jon was uncannily proficient at unearthing historical artifacts. It was one of the reasons that tramping about with him now was such a delight. Especially in Northumberland where there was so much Celtic and Roman history, as well as that of the Scots, and the English, and the battles they'd fought for the Borders. Not that they would dig, certainly not. But Jon's sense of it, of the reality of earlier times, made rambling this one week a year, without one's family and one's work, a rare treat indeed for them both.

Yes. And where *was* Jon? Surely it was time he turned up.

Alex shifted his small gold reading glasses to the top of his head and peered over his crossed ankles, which lay an inordinate distance away, and discovered that the causeway was completely covered. There was a mile and a half of water where there had been open road, so he must have been asleep considerably longer than he'd thought. Even the wind had died down. Which would certainly make walking more pleasant.

He stood, stretching himself to his full heighth of something over six feet six, and brushed grass out of his thinning brown hair (which led him to discover his glasses and stick them in his breast pocket) before he fished his father's watch out of his brown wool waistcoat.

Yes, Jonathan was terribly late.

And it was very unlike him indeed.

Alex slipped the watch back in its pocket while he stared across the water to the western end of Holy Island. No one could have come across in the last two and a half hours at the very least. And there was no one in the little white hut on stilts halfway across that had been built to accommodate the stranded.

Alex turned, tapping his index fingers on his long thighs, and looked at the tiny village of Beal, while he pondered what he ought to do next.

Jonathan MacLean had almost never been late in the thirty years they'd been friends.

Still, it might be a simple matter of communication. Either one of them could've got the time wrong. And all things considered, it was far more likely to have been him than Jon. Jonathan was known for having a firm grip on the practical aspects of daily life, while he, sadly, was not.

In any event, Jon would have had to come over from the island before eleven because of the tide. And if indeed they were to meet at one, Jon might well have gone off to walk the beach north of Beal, or inland to the west toward Northumberland Park, and misjudged the time it would take to walk back.

On the other hand, Jon could have returned and not seen him, if he'd only looked down the main street, since he himself had been off reading Bede on the far side of a rather large tree. Jon might well have gone on into the village, thinking he was late instead.

Therefore, after one last look at the causeway, Alex started into town, in his old tan tweeds with his rucksack on his back, his long legs whipping ahead as though they had a life of their own, while the entire visible population of Beal watched him with some curiosity.

He was thinking intently, not noticing, really, much of what he passed, trying to put himself in Jon's place.

Jon might well have gone somewhere for a bite to eat. So Alex stuck his head in the tea shop and surveyed the handful of tables, before crossing the street and winding his way through the side rooms and niches of the Wolf and Hare—the only restaurant and the only pub in town.

No. No Jonathan MacLean in either.

And no messages left behind by him.

It was two-fifteen. Jon was an hour and a quarter late. And Alex decided to call Jon's wife on the north coast of Scotland near Inverness.

He ducked his head and held his hat in his hand as he stepped through the door of the small, cluttered post office that sold sweets and tobacco and biscuits, while providing a public phone.

He laid an assortment of large coins on the wooden shelf, while he dialed Jon and Ellie's number. He was prepared for difficulties and delays, like anyone in Britain in the early sixties. And he smiled to himself as he remembered how once, when he'd lived in London, he'd answered the phone, only to find a gentleman in an Edinburgh hotel on the other end calling the concierge.

It was ringing. Finally. That was something. Though no one

appeared to be home, unfortunately. And he was just about to disconnect when he heard an unfamiliar throat being cleared and a very faint voice say, "Hello."

"Ellie? Is that you?... It's Alex here. I've been waiting for Jon for something over an hour, and I thought perhaps there'd been a change of plans. Have you heard from him by any chance?... Ellie?... Hold on a tick, I have to shovel more coins into this blasted machine... Has there been a change of plans and he wasn't able to reach me?... No! Surely not!... Ellie, please don't disengage! Are they certain it was Jon? Perhaps... No, I see... Of course not... I'm so sorry. I don't know what to say. It doesn't seem possible a'tall."

Alex knew he was babbling, but he was afraid that if he stopped, she'd hang up, as she'd started to do more than once. He couldn't let her go before he'd had time to think. For there had to be something he could do to be of help and he had absolutely no idea what. "How did he die? He was so fit... Well, if they don't know, there'll have to be an inquest... No, let me! Please. I shall take the train up to Berwick upon Tweed and identify the body myself... I see... You're certain it has to be family?... Well, Hugh, then. Surely he could do it for you... Aye, I should've known. The season has started with a vengeance. It's an American couple he's driving, is it? So he couldn't very well leave them on their own... Really? Why would you wish to?... Ah. Yes, I suppose one would want to see him again. I would, if it were Janie."

Ellie MacLean had stopped in the middle of a sentence and it sounded to Alex as though she'd had to, as though her voice had started turning into someone else's, an injured animal's or an abandoned child's.

And yet he still had to persuade her to stay on the line. "Ellie, please listen, my dear, just a moment longer. Let me call Jane and get her to meet your train in Edinburgh, and then the two of you can come on to Berwick together. I'll arrange rooms in a hotel, and then meet you at the station, shall I?... Good. I think that's very wise... When will you arrive in Edinburgh?"

They sorted out the timetables and the practical details and Alex told Ellie again how sorry he was and felt like an incompetent fool.

He phoned his own wife next, at Balnagard, and explained the situation, and the schedule, and remembered at the last moment to ask her to bring him a suit.

Shortly after midnight, Dr. Allen Curzon, chief pathologist of the Berwick Infirmary, held the heavy metal door that said "Autopsy" for Ellie MacLean and then followed her into the small white room. Alex came in after him and stood beside Ellie looking like nothing could have kept him from being there, even if he didn't know what to do.

Ellie was holding herself in, very tall and too erect, and she kept her hands in the pockets of her long tan trench coat as though she couldn't trust herself with them without a place to put them. Her heavy dark hair was pulled straight back, wrapped in a wide braided chignon. And her face was stripped of everything but sorrow. Her chin trembled ever so often, and her breath came intermittently in audible sighs as though the act of making an acceptable sound helped control the anxiety, and the adrenaline, and kept her from breaking down.

She did not want to be surprised by anything that was about to happen, and her large green eyes inspected the white walls and the olive green concrete floor as well as the large metal autopsy table in the middle of it. She saw the small wooden block lying at one end of it, and the shiny metal scale hanging above it, and tried not to think about what they might be for, as she scanned the cabinets and the workbench across the back wall.

There was only one place Jon could be, and the thought of it made her flinch. She swallowed methodically, trying to keep herself from being sick, and closed her eyes for several seconds, before she turned toward the long stainless steel refrigeration unit with the two wide horizontal drawers.

There was a metal handle on each end of each one.

And Curzon was reaching for the two on the top drawer.

Ellie wanted to stop him, but she didn't. She just clutched the fabric in the pockets of her coat and watched Curzon's small broad hands as they pulled on the polished handles.

The drawer was hinged on the bottom and opened down from the top to form a shelf, and when Curzon reached inside and slid a body out on a metal tray it rested on the open door.

Ellie froze for a minute with her eyes on the floor, while the speaker in the ceiling crackled and a woman's voice paged Dr. MacClellan. Blood pounded in her ears and her throat, in that small soft hollow between her collarbones. But she forced herself to move. To put one foot in front of the other. Until she stood beside Jon and looked down at his empty face.

It was a husk he'd broken out of. A bone house that had been abandoned. A poorly done mask he'd cast aside like a bad wax model from a cheap museum.

But Ellie nodded at the doctor, with her eyebrows pinched together and her lips pulled in between her teeth, while she fought against an almost uncontrollable urge to whimper. She knew she couldn't. It wouldn't be right to make Alex, or the other one, whatever his name was, any more uncomfortable than they already were.

Alex was standing by Jon's feet looking battered, but like he wished there was something he could do for her.

Curzon looked embarrassed and pretended to read the note he'd already written on his clipboard.

And then he began pushing Jon back inside the cooler.

Ellie put her hand on his arm and said, "Wait. Please. I'd like to be alone with him for a minute." Her voice was dry and brittle and her American accent sounded harsh to her, and far too loud for a small hard room.

Curzon didn't answer right away. He turned and studied Ellie, as he pushed his horn-rimmed glasses up his long thin nose. "I'm sorry, Mrs. MacLean, but I don't think that would be—"

"Please. Just for a few minutes."

"Are you sure?" There were tears on Alex's chin, and yet he was watching Ellie as though what he saw on her face was beyond his comprehension.

"I won't be long, Alex. And then I'll answer the medical questions. I promise."

Ellie waited, tight and silent, till they'd closed the door behind them and she was left alone with Jon. With his beautiful strong athletic body lying cold on a metal tray.

She pulled the sheet back—the way strangers would after she was through—and looked at Jon's whole body.

It was sagging already. And it was bruised underneath. Purple along the whole length of him. Jon. Who'd been so fluid and so full of energy. So quick, so physical, so hard.

The face she'd always thought was remarkably handsome, with its strong bones and the Adam's apple she loved and the incredibly blue eyes, was sunken and disintegrating.

And that was terrifying enough. But his mind and his soul and his wit were gone. And she couldn't even grasp what that meant.

Jon. Who was interested in everything. Who was very perceptive and very smart. Who could make her laugh more than anyone else.

Who understood her too, in all her private places. And wanted her to be exactly what she was.

Yet the single most amazing thing about Jon, the thing that made living with him so satisfying and so easy, was that he really did, in the center of his soul, want to do what was right. He didn't always do it. But he wanted to. And he wanted her to tell him what she thought, every time, whatever way she saw it, even when it was critical or when it hurt.

They'd helped each other with that. With seeing themselves as they were. With trying to become more of what they ought to be.

And now she had to learn to live without him.

Ellie had always thought open caskets were barbaric, and she'd never had the least desire to touch a dead body.

But she ran her fingers down Jon's left arm. And she stroked his cheek and his forehead. She traced his lips, which had been so soft and large and resourceful, and kissed them one more time.

Tears were sliding down her face and she was crying with that tearing, gagging, searing kind of sob that contorts your face and constricts your throat and makes your skin hot and your eyes ache.

And then, in a tight strangled desolate voice, she said, "Jonathan, please don't leave me here all alone! I don't think I can stand it without you!"

Because how could she live and not talk to him?

He was the only person she'd ever met she didn't get tired of, eventually. The only one she'd ever talked to who understood precisely what she meant, yet surprised her all the time with the twists and the edges of his own mind.

How could she survive without that?

And what could ever make her want to live again?

To get up in a cold bed. In a cold world.

Day, after day, after day.

There was nothing she could do but pray. And she prayed with her eyes closed and her hands on his arm.

And then she remembered what she'd forgotten.

Only Jon's death would have made her forget.

The door flew open unexpectedly, and a lab technician in a white coat, who was reading something on a pad of paper, shuffled in sideways singing Buddy Holly. He'd gotten to the "Oh Peggy...my Peggy Su-oo-oo" part, when he saw Ellie and looked stricken. He mumbled, "My apologies, madam," quietly, and turned around and left.

Ellie hadn't paid much attention. She was thinking about picking Jon's hand up for a minute and holding it in hers, but she was afraid to try in case rigor mortis had set in and she couldn't stand it.

She laid her cheek on it for a second instead, before she turned and walked to the door. Where she stopped and looked back at Jon one more time.

She stepped into the hall. And Alex and Jane, who'd been talking together with their backs to her, halfway to the elevator, rushed over as soon as the door had slapped shut.

But not before Ellie had put a handkerchief across her mouth and rushed toward the lavatory they'd passed on the way in.

CHAPTER TWO

Wednesday, May 17th

"No, I don't accept this new notion of proper feeding!"

"No?" Ben Reese had been listening to the heavyset, elderly English woman in the flowered dress since Edinburgh while leaning loosely against the seat, following the throb and jostle of the train with his body and half his brain.

"No, they require real meat every day." Agnes White patted the neck of her faded and graying golden retriever, who thumped his tail on the compartment floor and leaned quietly against her legs. "It's what they would eat in the wild, and they simply are not satisfied without it. They tend to scavenge then, and the consequences are quite alarming. Wandering, you know, and worms. And yet one can prevent it so easily." Agnes looked at her sister across the compartment as though she expected corroboration and the sooner it came the better, while Ben folded his arms across his corduroy jacket and tapped a large foot on the metal floor in time to the clatter of the wheels.

"Oh yes, I agree, my dear, meat, absolutely. And if you get to know your butcher, it can be quite reasonable as well." Emma was smaller and thinner and she spoke much more quietly than her sister, while she stroked the head of her portly black lab and scratched his grizzled chin. "It's not a'tall an extravagance, *I* don't think. And I'm quite sure Agnes would agree."

The loudspeaker sputtered, and a deep, pleasant very Scottish voice, which probably would have been impenetrable to the inexperienced, said, "Dunkeld, ladies and gentleman, Dunkeld. Pitlochry, Blair Atholl, and Dalwhinnie to follow."

"Emma and I have so enjoyed talking with you, Mr. Reese, and we do hope you have a lovely visit to Scotland."

"Oh, yes, we do indeed. And if I might make one small suggestion, you really must try to visit Balnagard Castle during your stay in Dunkeld."

"Emma's absolutely right. It's a storybook castle, really. And the present owner, the Earl of Balnagard, has placed his own very amusing comments in every room. We always make a point of visiting whenever we come north."

Ben thanked them and told them he would without mentioning that that's where he was staying, and then helped them gather their suitcases and their parcels. He held the compartment door, and patted the dogs as they labored down the stairs, two feet on each step before moving on to the next. And then he watched the four of them totter off toward the friend they were visiting, all of them managing to look excited and disorganized and dignified at the same time.

Emma and Agnes had discussed their dogs, past and present, from the moment they sat down, which Ben had found highly entertaining on more than one level. And he smiled to himself as he threaded his way back to his compartment to pick up his trench coat and his bags.

He'd meant to work on his notes from the National Record

Office on the train, but he hadn't, not once Emma and Agnes had appeared. For even if he wouldn't want to be locked in an elevator with them for the rest of his life, they were the kind of people who drew him back to Britain.

And maybe he could take them out to dinner. Some place fancy they'd never go on their own.

Anyway, he'd have plenty of time to work at Alex's.

He smiled cryptically and shook his head. Because it's so easy, making assumptions like that about the future, even though you know you can't control the next second.

He'd seen too many days start one way and end another to feel comfortable taking them for granted.

Alex and Jane weren't on the platform. Which was highly unusual. And Ben was about to look in the small Victorian brick station, when a young man in tailored tweeds with black hair and startlingly blue eyes approached him and put out his hand.

"Dr. Reese?"

"Yes."

"I'm Hugh MacLean. Lord Alex Chisholm asked me to fetch you. Things are in a bit of a jumble at Balnagard at the moment, and he and Lady Jane were detained. Please, let me help you with your luggage."

"I'm sorry. I should have taken a cab."

"It's no bother a'tall so you mustn't give it a thought." Hugh MacLean had picked up the overnight bag full of books and was leading Ben around the end of the building to the car park beside the main road. "Did you enjoy your stay in Edinburgh?"

"I always do. It's one of my all-time favorite cities."

Hugh had stopped behind a long gray car with a small door

in the middle of its steeply sloping back, and he pulled the door down carefully, exposing a smallish trunk. "The boot isn't really suited for much luggage I'm afraid. It was intended for a set of golf clubs, and designed so one could drive with a picnic hamper on the opened shelf." Hugh laughed and settled the larger case into the trunk, before lashing the small one on the door with leather straps. "Not very practical, but wonderfully idiosyncratic. Different time then, don't you think?"

"Is it a Bentley?"

"Yes, a 1950 Mark VI." Hugh was on the left side, the passenger side, unlocking the front door. "It was my father's one indulgence before he retired, and I inherited it after he died."

Ben drove a 1947 Plymouth and had very little experience with fancy cars. But the Bentley was comfortable, when he stretched out his legs and leaned back against the gray leather seat, and watched Hugh MacLean adjust the hand brake, and the choke, and twist the dial on the dash that pushed a large lighted arrow out of the pillar by Ben's head, indicating to the world at large that Hugh was about to turn left.

"So you're an archivist, Dr. Reese?"

"Yes. I identify antiquarian objects like coins and documents, and I take care of the artifacts the alumni have donated at a small university in Ohio."

"Alex mentioned that you'll be helping him evaluate the collections he inherited with the estate."

"That's right. Then if he ever decides to sell some of them, he'll have a rough idea of what they're worth." Alex was planning to sell quite a few things right away, but Ben wasn't going to say that. Not to anyone else.

"Did you know Alex and Jane have done up a new tea room for the tourists?"

"Yeah, I think it sounds like a great idea."

"Oh, I agree. Absolutely."

A short silence followed in which Ben told himself to make small talk.

But Hugh spoke first, as though it were an effort for him too. "So you and Alex became acquainted during the war?"

"We met in a hospital in Wales, and then discovered we had a mutual friend."

"You don't look old enough to have been in the war."

Ben didn't do well with compliments in general, and he never saw any reason to talk about how he looked, and all he said was, "I just turned thirty-nine."

"So Alex was in combat, was he? I had absolutely no idea."

"No, Alex was hit by a cab during the Blitz while he was walking down a sidewalk in London. He'd gone into town to do research, and was run over during the blackout."

"Was he at Bletchley then?"

"Yes, he was working as a linguist with the decoders, so they sent him to the military hospital near Swansea that had the tightest security in Britain. It was run by the American First Army and the British Commando Group, and when I came back from France, they put me in the bed next to his."

"Was he badly injured?"

"Broken bones, mostly. An arm and a leg."

"I see." Hugh looked at Ben Reese like he wanted to ask him something else, but was afraid it might be indiscreet, as he downshifted to wait for an oncoming car at the foot of a humpbacked bridge. "I was too young to go, and I still find the war quite fascinating."

Ben didn't say anything.

And it took Hugh almost a minute to change the subject.

"Alex really is a very interesting man. A linguist. A historian. A novelist. The son of a diplomat as well. Did you know Alex was raised all over the world?"

"He can also write better in his sleep than I ever will under any circumstances. Has he learned to drive yet?"

"No. He doesn't seem able to concentrate on mechanical objects. Although he's recently done a bit of practicing with one of those new riding lawn mowers."

Ben laughed and looked out the side window, shading his gray eyes with his left hand.

He had an interesting face, sharp boned and analytical, with a strong jaw and wide cheekbones and a noticeable Adam's apple that made him look younger than he was. He had wide shoulders and big hands and long smooth muscles, and he seemed easy in his body, as though he was used to pushing himself physically and knew what he could count on.

But he was restless. He shoved a hand back through his light brown hair and stretched his shoulders forward and back as though he needed to do something hard and physical and get his blood burning again.

"Now, when we get 'round this lorry, we'll be able to see some really lovely country." Hugh pointed out spots of interest and explained local history in a deep rich voice with a public school sort of accent softened by a lifetime in Scotland.

They passed Birnam Wood on the left, and then went into a wide curve, and suddenly there were high hills on both sides of the road covered with evergreens in military ranks. "It's this bit here where one can clearly see the beginning of the highlands. Look straight north, and you should just be able to glimpse snow-crested mountains in the distance. Assuming, of course, that the clouds aren't too low. Yes, lovely, isn't it?" Hugh laughed briefly and looked sideways at Ben. "I do apologize. I take visitors touring from time to time to augment my income while I finish my doctorate, and I've gotten in the habit of rattling on."

"No, I think it's interesting. What field are you in?"

"Geology. Marine geology is a particular interest. Though history is one of my hobbies, and it paves the way, as it were, with the tourists."

"I see."

Neither of them spoke for a moment.

Ben slid his left hand along the smooth mahogany beside the armrest, his index finger sticking straight out, as it always did, above the scar that disappeared inside his sleeve.

Hugh tapped his signet ring on the steering wheel, while he waited to turn left off the main road. "Actually, I ought to prepare you a bit before we get to Balnagard. Did you ever chance to meet my brother, Jonathan? Alex thought perhaps you had once, when you were visiting a few years ago."

"Is he a minister in the Church of Scotland, and an excellent rider, and does he read a lot of biology and astrophysics?"

"Yes, that's quite an accurate description, actually. But unfortunately, much to my dismay, I have some rather sad news. Jon died very unexpectedly this past week." Hugh didn't volunteer any other information and his face tightened and turned pale, as though he were fighting himself for control.

"I'm sorry." Ben said it quietly and looked away. "Even though that's hardly a consolation."

"Jon suffered from anaphylaxis. Which literally means 'without protection.' It's tragically apt, I'm sorry to say, for it denotes an absolutely lethal allergy to insect stings. Jon was just starting off on his annual walking tour with Alex when he was apparently stung by bees. Though it could have been wasps, of course, or hornets. So as it happens, Alex and Jane just came back from the inquest yesterday, and Jon's wife and I are still with them as well. They're quite a few estate matters to be seen to before the house opens to the public, so I left them to it and offered to meet your train."

"It has to have been an imposition."

"No, not a'tall. It was truthfully a relief to have something to do. At the time, you see, I was absolutely no help. The morning he died, I'd met an American couple in Edinburgh and driven them north, and I wasn't even available to identity Jon's remains."

"So Alex was with him?"

"No, they were to meet a few hours later. Jon was quite alone, I'm afraid, on Holy Island. Of course, it still doesn't seem possible. And it won't do, I imagine, for some time. Jon was only forty-one, and he was wonderfully fit, and one can't quite take it in."

Neither of them said anything else for a moment. Ben looked at the wide green river valley on his right and watched the sheep and the tiny lambs feeding and scattering and staring at the car. He saw the peacefulness of it, the age-old seemliness of the land and its inhabitants. But he also saw the pain and the blood and the mud that comes with birth and only stops with death.

"We're on the estate now, and have been for a mile or more, with something like another mile to go." Hugh braked easily but quickly and backed the Bentley into a "lay by," a spot just wide enough that the oncoming car could sidle past.

They'd been winding on a road that narrow, on the west edge of the Tay River valley, curving through pastures and cornfields, beside wide spots in the river, past sheep and cows and occasional horses, with patches of forest close by on their left, and off in the distance on the right-hand hills.

As they swept around each curve, the view changed. There were patchwork farms, green and brown and yellow, stitched together by stone walls on the hills across the Tay, with stone farmhouses and outbuildings and occasional manor houses the color of porridge and cream, wide spaced, and set like sentinels on the high hills.

Then there was moorland, above the farms on the right, and beginning to be visible in spots on their left, between and up above the evergreen trees and the hardwoods. There were no trees on the moor, just newly leafed green heather and yellow flowering gorse.

And Ben smiled as he looked at all of it. "I never get used to it no matter how many times I come back, the amazing variety on such a small scale. Look at it. Patches of pasture and grain, evergreen forests and moor, wild pink cherry trees and white rowans, all clustered together."

"It is surprising, isn't it? The entire landscape here can change utterly in ten minutes. Here we are. Castle Balnagard."

They angled right off the road and crossed a wide lawn peppered with trees, with the house directly ahead of them. They could see the tall central tower with its corner turrets and the roofs on the highest wings, but they had to pass under the arch in the sweeping stone wall that encircled Balnagard before they could see the ground floor of the castle settled in lawns and woods and gardens.

They slid to a stop in the gravel by the grassy moat, right beside the drawbridge that had been fixed solidly across it for almost two hundred years.

But before Ben could reach for the door handle, half the arched black iron gate clanged open and two dogs rushed across the wooden bridge—a boxer first, a tan and white streak wagging its entire backend, followed by a black lab of more sedate demeanor who looked humbly over his shoulder for approval.

For Alex was right behind him, loping across the drawbridge in an old sweater and corduroy pants, waving at Ben before his door opened. Jane had stopped behind him, and was leaning against the metal railing on the side of the drawbridge, smiling in a pool of sunlight, with her hair glowing like good champagne.

"I still cannot believe that Richard West was murdered. It's an absolute outrage, Ben, it really is." Alex was walking fast, like he always did, as though he'd forget where he was going if he didn't rush. "I've always felt very fortunate to have gotten to know him at Bletchley. And you were much closer to him than I was, of course. Teaching with him all those years. It must seem a very great loss indeed. Was it November that he died?"

"Yes."

"And you've mended, have you, from the murderer's attack?"

"Oh, yeah. I just have to work harder at it than most people because of the old injuries."

"Mind your head, Ben, and we'll pop into the small library."

They were on the second floor in a side wing that was built in the seventeenth century, three hundred years later than the "old" part of the house. They'd passed through the Tapestry Room, which was Jane and Alex's bedroom, and were now crossing Alex's dressing room, a large sunny corner room cluttered with clothes and books.

Alex pushed against a small studded door and led Ben down three shallow stone steps into a rectangular library with tall windows on the long side walls. The white wall at the far end was the only one that wasn't filled with books, and it was half taken up by a dressed stone fireplace with the Chisholm crest above it in raised white plaster.

"You'll have to overlook the mess, I'm afraid."

Ben laughed and walked around the stacks of books and the globes in wooden stands from various ages past that were scattered around a big black oak refectory table with monks heads carved on the trestles. Alex used it as a desk and it was centered near the windows in the left-hand wall, overlooking the front lawn. A large electric typewriter sat in the middle of it in a mass of papers, and drawn up beside it was a leather gondolier's chair Alex's grandfather had brought back from Venice.

"So you do all your writing up here now?"

"I do, yes."

Ben stopped in front of the fireplace and read the motto in the Chisholm crest. "Feros Ferio. I am fierce with the fierce."

"Far less profound than many, but one can't chose one's ancestors. It'll just take me a moment to get the fire going." Alex had picked up the bellows from the hearth and was carefully positioning his thumb over a small tear near the handles. "A peat fire's wonderfully practical because one can bank it so effectively when one leaves the room. We still cut it ourselves, of course, though it's almost a dying art. Where was I, do you remember?"

"Working up here." Ben sat down on the sofa on the left of the fireplace and stretched his arms above his head.

Alex laid the bellows on the hearth and threw himself into the low overstuffed threadbare tan chair on the other side facing Ben. "It's delightfully cut off from the general bustle because it's so out of the way. I couldn't get anything done, with all the summer visitors looking in the windows in the big library. But the circular stairs lead down to it." Alex waved vaguely toward the far corner by the small studded door, where a heavy dark green curtain was stretched across a rod. "And I can easily nip down when needs must. Though why I'm belaboring such a pedestrian subject I don't know, except that I can't recall what we were talking about earlier."

"The funeral."

"Yes, of course. How could I forget?" Alex smiled dismally and laid his hands rather carefully on his angular knees. "Jon's church in Cawdor Village is organizing a memorial service for tomorrow morning, though the burial itself will be down here the following day."

"Here?"

"In Dunkeld, at the Cathedral. Jon's mother's family and their relations have been buried there for centuries. So we're to leave here about two this afternoon, and come home tomorrow straightaway after the service."

"You're sure I won't be in the way? I could stay here and get to work on the collections."

"Certainly not!"

"I'd like to put together kind of a long-term plan that you can turn to, over time, and know what to sell in what order when you need extra money."

"That's very good of you! I only thought you might make a suggestion or two as to what we could sell now, to pay off the debt on the tea room."

"I know you did. But with the upkeep of the estate, and taxes the way they are, and four kids to educate, I thought maybe it would help."

"It would! Oh, yes, and I appreciate it. But it's very important that we have you with us up in Cawdor. For if the truth were known, I hope to enlist your undeniable powers of observation." Alex crossed one stork-like leg over the other and laid his fingertips together beneath his chin. "The long and the short of it is, Benjamin, that there's something a trifle questionable about Jon's death."

"Is there?" Ben had been watching the peat burn, the rolls of it standing on end leaning together like a tepee. But then he looked at Alex, and his mind was there, concentrated in his eyes.

"There's no doubt a'tall that Jonathan's death was caused by bee stings. The pathologist was very good, and he found three distinct bites, even though that's terribly hard to do when one dies from them as quickly as Jon did. For in that case, according to the medical people, there won't be any redness or swelling at the location of the bite. The coroner's inquest subsequently concluded that Jon died of natural causes, and quite properly, I suppose, under the circumstances. As a result, they released the body, along with Jon's personal effects. It was when I went to collect his belongings at the infirmary, and here we come to the crux of it, that I discovered a picnic hamper amongst them.

"Now, I have taken walking tours with Jonathan MacLean since we were children together, and never has he even considered taking a picnic hamper. He always made rather heavy weather of *not* carrying anything he didn't absolutely need, and he often took far less, if the truth were to be told. Yet here was this huge wicker hamper. Cloth lined, complete with dishes and plastic cutlery and a thermos, as well as bread and fruit and biscuits. And it's all wrong. Jon would never have bothered with dishes. He carried one fork and an army knife with a tin opener on it, and either ate out of a tin or brought food he could hold in his hand.

"I asked Ellie straightaway, and she'd never laid eyes upon the hamper. Jon certainly didn't have it when he left home. Ellie drove him to the station in Inverness and watched him get on the train."

"So sometime between leaving home and dying on Holy Island—"

"Right at the foot of Lindisfarne Castle, and one couldn't find a more provocative spot."

"—Jon acquired this basket."

"Exactly. But it's not only that. I picked up the thermos, which was on the top, just puttering, you know, poking about out of curiosity to see what was in the hamper, and I uncovered two dead bees. Which prompted me to stop rummaging about. Though it may mean nothing a'tall, of course. I know that. There may have been bees in the grass, doing whatever it is they do, and perhaps two of them fell into the hamper and couldn't extricate themselves. I know nothing whatever about the behavior of insects and I'm certainly not qualified to draw any conclusions. But I shut the basket and brought it home, and I've locked it in the gun safe, just in case. There won't be time to examine it before we leave today, but when we come back from Cawdor, I'd like you to have a look."

"You're sure you want me to do this? Your legal system's different, and I don't know—"

"Of course I do! You were in intelligence, for heaven's sake! You uncovered Richard's murderer as well as that woman's, whatever her name was. And I should have thought this would be right up your street. Of course, if you find sufficient evidence to indicate that the case should be reopened, we'll contact the police in Northumberland. I've discussed it with Ellie, naturally, and it's very much her wish as well as mine. In fact, we both feel your visit might almost be providential."

"What time did Jon die?"

"The police and the pathologists believe it must have been just about fifteen minutes past six."

"In the morning?"

"Yes. Last Friday. May twelfth, to be precise. His body was discovered around half-six by a young lad named Jimmy Reed. He was home by forty minutes past, and he'd looked at his watch at twenty after, moments before he discovered the body. Jon would've died instantly, within a matter of seconds, and the physical evidence suggests it was a very short time before he was found."

"Did Jon know anyone who lived on Holy Island?" Ben was rubbing the scar on the underside of his wrist with his right thumb, sliding it down toward the center of his palm.

"Yes, I suppose he did, actually. Katherine Burnett." Alex's large squarish head was turned slightly to his left and he seemed to be staring at a row of leather bound books. His hazel eyes were fixed but interested, as he pulled thoughtfully at his right earlobe. "She teaches literature in a public girls' school in Inverness. What you colonials would call a private school. And she's also been a voluntary secretary for Jon at his church in Cawdor, the sort of person who does the typing and writes the parish newsletter." Alex got up and put another roll of peat on the fire.

And Ben watched, waiting for Alex to pick up the thread. When he didn't, Ben cocked his head to one side and said, "What are you leaving out?"

"Out?"

"You're being kind, Alex."

"Am I?"

Ben laughed and stretched his legs toward the fire.

"Well…I'm not altogether sure how to phrase it. They've known each other since Jon was twelve or fourteen, but recently it seems that Katherine's had more of a personal interest in Jon than was acceptable, or than he welcomed, certainly. Ellie could tell you in more detail. But I gather Jon had words with her, and she'd gone off to visit a relative, a cousin perhaps, or an aunt, on Holy Island."

"I see."

"Other than that, I don't believe Jon knew anyone on the island."

Alex's boxer suddenly shot through the dressing room door and rushed down the stairs with his eyes on Alex. He flew across the stone floor and danced around Alex's chair, and then licked the hand that was dangling off the edge of the arm.

"Jake, sit down and behave yourself! That's right, get on your rug." Jake sat on one of Alex's feet instead, and Alex laid a hand on his broad wrinkled head. "Alright, you can stay there if you settle down. No! Leave Ben alone!"

"He's okay." Jake had plopped himself down on Ben's right foot and was leaning against his knee. "I don't mind. In fact," Ben rubbed a soft floppy ear between his thumb and fingers, "he makes me wish I had a dog."

"You're sure?"

"Yes. So how has Ellie reacted to Jon's death?"

"At the moment, I believe she's asking herself why anyone would have wanted him dead. And in some ways I think that's made the grieving easier. They were remarkably close, Ellie and Jon. Really quite unusually so. Both of them were highly intelligent, the sort who are temperamentally self-sufficient because they find their own pursuits so compelling. Yet there was an exceptional intensity of feeling between them. There was something very distinctive about the way they conversed with one another. I think everyone saw it. One found one couldn't keep one's eyes away when they were talking.

"Yet there was nothing sentimental about them." Alex slid his hands back and forth on the faded cotton slipcovers and watched the clouds out the window behind Ben. "They were somehow friends, or allies perhaps, though colleagues might be a better word, in a very objective, impersonal way, at the same time that they were clearly very much in love with each other and physically attracted. Jane and I have both given their relationship quite a bit of thought over the years because it was so striking. I know they had differences of opinion. Not about principles, or the foundational beliefs of life, no. But they were distinct individuals, and they challenged each other's perceptions without giving quarter, the same way they would've done if they hadn't been male and female. Yet they were terribly drawn to each other. I'm not expressing it well, I'm really not. But of all the marriages I've ever known, theirs was probably the one I would've hoped most wouldn't have been severed at such an early stage. Other than my own, of course, that goes without saying."

Ben sat quietly, staring at the fire. Waiting for the awkward pause that he never knew how to avoid.

Alex watched him, before he gazed up at the ceiling. "I never had the opportunity of seeing you and your wife together before she died, but from what Richard said, I suspect you know the sort of thing I've been trying to describe."

"Yes. I think I do." Ben didn't say anything else for a minute. But then he raised his eyebrows somewhat inscrutably and smiled.

He'd been thinking about Jon MacLean's death, instead of Jessie, trying to concentrate on where to start, while he picked at the dog hair on his left knee. "Is Ellie holding up well enough for me to talk to her?"

"I would say so. She'll rise to the occasion if there's something to be done about Jon's death." Alex stared silently at the fire for a minute, with his chin in the palm of his hand. "It's not the first great sadness she's had to bear, you know. Her parents were both killed in a plane crash when she was sixteen. That must have been difficult enough. And then, to make matters more trying, she and Jon weren't able to have children when they both wanted them very much indeed."

"Daddy?" A small thin boy with blond hair, pale skin, and pink cheeks was peeking shyly around the corner of the dressing room door. "I'm sorry. I didn't know you had company."

"It's alright, James. Come in if you'd like."

James didn't come in. He stood by the door and dropped his eyes.

"Is there something in particular I can do for you?"

"Well, I was just wondering, you see, if you'd have time for a quick sword fight before you leave?"

"I don't think I do today, actually. But Friday. The day after tomorrow. Alright? In the morning, very early, before the funeral."

"Mummy wanted you too. She said to tell you that luncheon will be ready at half-twelve, and she wanted me to ask if you've remembered to pack your clothes."

CHAPTER THREE

Thursday, May 18th

CAWDOR VILLAGE CHURCH sits at the center of a small stone village, hidden from Cawdor Castle by a dense woods and a deep banked stream. It's a plain stone cruciform church that probably holds a hundred people ordinarily. But for Jonathan MacLean's memorial service every inch of standing room was taken, and the lawns and the graveyard were also filled with mourners, huddling under the dripping cedars with their umbrellas nearly touching, like a battalion of black-backed turtles tucked in against the rain.

They came from Nairn and Ferness and from Croy and Cawdor. And after Jon's former army chaplain had opened the service, several of them climbed up into the high wooden pulpit to talk about what Jonathan MacLean had meant to them and their families.

An old kilted piper from the congregation piped them out and away with "Amazing Grace" and played them to the Parish Hall, where the women of the church were providing tea and cakes and every sort of scone and biscuit.

Yet they didn't crowd in all at once. They waited in the rain, some of them, holding their umbrellas without talking much, before they filed in in a quiet stream and offered their respects to Elinor MacLean.

Ben Reese had gone in with Alex and the family. And he took his coffee and two small scones over by a window in the long narrow hall and watched. Carefully. From a comfortable distance. Until Alex finished a lengthy conversation with the local taxidermist and arrived beside him with a sherry and a chunk of cheese and his eyes on Ellie, who was standing beside Hugh at the end of the refreshment table accepting condolences as though they might actually help.

Her face was drawn and thin, and the black suit made her seem even paler, but she looked steadily at whoever she was talking to, and she held herself still and straight.

"She seems to be doing remarkably well, don't you think, Ben?"

"Yes, and I know exactly what it's like. Nobody has a clue what to say, so they all fall back on the same two or three phrases and it gets harder to answer as the line goes on. Doesn't Ellie have relatives of her own?"

"Only Rory MacKenzie. He'll be up for the burial tomorrow. It's a very distant blood relationship, and yet he brought her over from America and took her in after her parents died."

"Who's the woman in the navy suit near the fireplace?"

There were fireplaces at both ends of the long whitewashed room, and Alex followed Ben's eyes to a small finely built woman with short shiny brown hair and large brown eyes. She was probably in her late thirties and she had a wide but delicate face that looked like it would dimple when she smiled. She was well groomed and carefully dressed, and she was standing quite still, holding a cup of tea, while she watched Ellie MacLean. "That's Katherine Burnett."

"She seems very interested in Ellie. And yet her face is so closed it caught my attention during the service."

"Really? She is a rather difficult person to get to know."

"So what can you tell me about everybody else?" Ben had finished his second scone and was watching the room analytically (the farmers, shopkeepers, small businessmen and estate workers, in their best dresses and Sunday suits, in their kilts and polished shoes) while Alex waved and nodded, when a friend or acquaintance caught his eye.

"Not much I'm afraid. The rather spotty teenagers standing awkwardly by the coat rack are from the youth club Jon started in Nairn. And of course, the local gentry have put in an appearance, the Earl Cawdor, and Brodie of Brodie, and the Stewarts from Inverness."

"The rest are from the village?"

"Not exclusively. Jon went out into the neighboring villages and preached in long abandoned churches in addition to his own, and they're here as well. Look at them, Ben! The Scots are a wonderful people, aren't they? Sturdy. Stoical. Loyal to a fault, sometimes. I have even more affection for them than I do the land. Hugh is being remarkably considerate of Ellie, don't you think? Keeping the mourners moving and relieving a bit of the pressure."

"Is that Mary Atwood? The lady with white hair crying on Ellie's shoulder?"

"Oh my! Yes. Poor Ellie. Mary must be too distraught to restrain herself, for I know she'd feel terribly upset if she realized she was being a burden."

Mrs. Atwood was very short and somewhat stout, and she was wearing a gray flowered jacket dress with several pieces of costume jewelry. She was holding a lacy white handkerchief pressed to her mouth while she sobbed. And Ellie had her arms around her and was talking to her very quietly with her mouth close to Mary's ear.

"So what can you tell me about Mary Atwood?"

Alex was staring at the ceiling, past the beams above Ben's head, as though he were listening to something no one else could hear.

"Alex?"

"Sorry. Help me remember the phrase 'the caves of Caledonia' when we're back at Balnagard."

"I'll try. Tell me about Mary. I know she's Hugh's housekeeper, but what was her attachment to Jon?"

"Ah, well you see, actually, strictly speaking, she was Jon's housekeeper. Primogeniture isn't so much the norm in Scotland as it is in England, yet neither is it a rare occurrence, and Jon inherited the family home as the eldest son. And also, I think, because Hugh made it known that he preferred the sailboat and the Bentley. Jon's church was too far north for him to live at Kilgarth himself, so Hugh simply stayed on, living there at the weekends, to keep the house open really, and provide a home for Mrs. Atwood. Though that would never have been said in her hearing."

"So what about Mary?"

"She was the boys' nanny when they were young, until she married the gardener and had children of her own. She lived on at Kilgarth all that time, but only became the housekeeper after her husband died. I know for a fact that she was particularly attached to Jon, and she bore the brunt of Mrs. MacLean's last illness with very good grace indeed. Perhaps I ought to pop over there and wean her away from Ellie."

Jane Chisholm got to Mary before Alex did. She leaned her smooth straw-colored head against Mary Atwood's silver one and led her across the room. And then she sat with her beside the fire, after she'd fetched her a cup of tea.

Ben had followed Alex to the refreshment table, where he found an out-of-the-way spot for his empty cup, and stood listening to the conversations eddying around him. The quick Scots voice behind him caught his attention, but he didn't turn around. He listened invisibly, busying himself among the plates and platters, as though he were considering a second selection.

"Aye, I think under the caircumstances, I'll no be giving up my seat on the Kirk Session. There's no real need now, as matters stand. If you ken my meaning."

Ben swiveled sideways, slowly and almost aimlessly, and watched the short flabby-looking man in the gray suit and tan sweater-vest as he talked to a tall weathered gentleman in a red and black kilt. There was something self-satisfied on the small man's large-pored almost sallow face. The look of a trader who's sold a sick cow to a neighbor and is congratulating himself on his wit and nerve.

"I suppose there's no immediate requirement for Mrs. MacLean to vacate the manse, but it won't be long, of course. For we'll be sairching for a new minister to fill the vacancy as soon as may be."

"Hamish MacDonald, how can ye mention such a thing at such a time! What are ye thinking of, man?" It was the tall man in the kilt, speaking in a soft but pointed voice while gripping his sherry glass in a gnarled hand and looking down at the other man with outrage in his eyes.

There was a lull in the conversation then, one of those awkward silent spots that usually happens with reason. And that was when Ellie, who was standing six or eight feet away, said very distinctly in a low clear voice, "I don't think I'd give up the idea of resigning from the Session if I were you, Mr. MacDonald. No, I think you should go right ahead, exactly as you promised Jon in that last conversation."

The little man's face froze before it turned pale. He shoved two pieces of shortbread in his mouth, dropped his plate on the table, and mumbled, "My! I hadna realized the lateness of the hour! I should've taken myself back to the shop a good while before this. Please accept my condolences, Mrs. MacLean, and my vera best wishes as well."

Hamish MacDonald was gone, his hat in one hand and his mackintosh in the other, when the tall man in the red kilt and ancient leather sporran walked over to Ellie and smiled down at her before he spoke. "You did exactly right, and it was grand to see."

"Did I?" Ellie had lowered her eyes and was turning her wide gold wedding band as though she didn't know what to do with her hands. "Jon wouldn't have said it. Not in front of anyone else."

"Perhaps. Perhaps not. There is such a thing as righteous anger. Christ displayed it, as I'm sure ye know. But either way, don't you pay the least bit of attention to Hamish MacDonald. You stay in your wee house as long as ye like. And to my mind, though we'll have another in the job one day, no matter how long or how far we sairch, we won't be finding another man who can take the place of Jonathan MacLean. Not unless it pleases God to perform another of His miracles."

Ellie said thank you, and squeezed his arm, as two tears appeared and started down her cheekbones. She turned and hurried to the other end of the room, and then out through the kitchen door past Katherine Burnett.

Katherine watched her pass with a tight mouth and silent eyes.

And Ben, who'd followed Ellie inconspicuously until he stood beside Katherine, cleared his throat and said, "Excuse me, Miss

Burnett, I'm Ben Reese. I'm a friend of Alex Chisholm's, and he just pointed you out and told me you were one of Jon's oldest friends."

"Yes, I was."

"I only met Jon once, but from what I saw of him, I'm sure his death will be a great loss to a lot of people."

"Thank you. I believe it will."

"Alex also said you were staying on Holy Island when Jon was there."

"Did he?"

"Yeah. It bothers Alex that Jon was alone, and I think he's hoping that he got to see you, or someone else he knew, before he was stung." Ben was doing a semi-bumbling-American-abroad impersonation, talking too loudly and standing too close, while watching Katherine's eyes as though he were hoping for a chance to sympathize.

"You're an American, I take it?"

Ben said, "Yeah, I'm from Ohio," as though he expected her to know where that was.

The fine-boned face with thick black lashes and small remarkably perfect ears studied Ben thoughtfully. Then Katherine spoke again in an educated English voice a lot like Alex's and Jane's. "I did see Jon, once, very briefly."

"Not the morning he died?" Ben looked mildly horrified and blotted his forehead with his handkerchief.

"No, he stopped by the night before. And then only for a moment."

"Well, at least he got to see one last friendly face, that's something. I suppose he must've stayed at the inn. I spent one night there a couple of years ago myself."

"He was camping, as a matter of fact, and he went off to find a suitable spot before it grew dark."

"Boy, I don't know how people do it. I mean it's gotta be exhausting, right? Having to drag around all that equipment? The tent and the backpack and the sleeping bag?" Ben waited. But Katherine Burnett didn't say anything. "I s'ppose Jon did have a tent?"

"No. He carried a rucksack on his back with a blanket rolled beneath it. Though I don't altogether see why you find it so intriguing."

"No reason, really. No, I'm just curious. I thought maybe the British use different kinds of equipment than we do in the States. You use baskets for so many things we don't, I figured Jon might have taken one camping."

Ben saw Katherine Burnett's eyes change at the word *basket*. It was almost imperceptible. Just a quick flicker. Of fear, maybe. Or recognition. Or a physical reflex no more significant than an unconscious blink.

"No, Mr. Reese, he was not carrying a basket of any kind. Now, if you'll excuse me, my aunt appears anxious to leave." Katherine waved to a thin wiry woman who was standing by the far door holding a coat and umbrella.

And then Katherine wove her way through the hot crowded hall, and went out into the rain and the wind that was still blowing inland from the Moray Firth.

Ben Reese watched her, with his eyes squinting inscrutably, and his jaw set off to the left.

"So you don't mind, Ben, staying up at Perach?"

"No, not at all."

"You see, with Hugh and Ellie and Mrs. Atwood staying with us, and with Rory coming tomorrow, in addition to the children

54

and Uncle Robert... Jeremiah, please!" The big black lab had stopped dead, right in front of Alex, and Alex had had to catch himself to keep from falling over him.

It was late afternoon, after the Cawdor reception. And they were climbing a steep dirt path through dripping ferns and tall firs on the north side of Balnagard, having walked the Tay valley for more than an hour, after three hours crumpled in a car.

"Obviously, someone would have to go up to Castle Perach, and we thought—"

"That I'm the logical person. Is it that small white house with the turret you can see up the hill when you're driving from Dunkeld?"

"Yes. And it is terribly small. Only suitable for one, really. The Seventh Thane, who was a bit of a bounder, built it for his mistress sometime before he died in 1720. We don't know when, or what his wife thought, poor woman. But it is a bit of a hike, I'm afraid. A mile or more up a switchback sort of track, so I thought we'd give you the Land Rover."

"No, I'd like the walk."

"Right. Then we'll get your bags sent up straightaway. Of course it does put you out of the stream of things. Makes it harder to observe the rest of us."

"I think I can count on you for enough detail."

"I'm not a'tall sure I like your tone!" Alex and Ben both laughed as they pulled their collars up against the mist that was beginning to turn into drizzle.

"So what about the basket? Is there time to look at it before dinner?"

They'd crossed the drawbridge and walked through the forecourt past the tall original stone tower, and they were just passing through an archway in the south wall under a huge set of antlers.

"Aye, we can pop into the gun room before we wash up. Jake! Stop licking Ben's hand!"

The small, studded, ancient front door was on their left in the second stone courtyard, tucked under a carved coat of arms, and Alex, who was taller than the doorway, had to duck way down as he stepped in. "Now wait a minute! Jake and Jeremiah, sit down and let me wipe your feet."

An elderly man trotted across the far end of that entry hall, heading toward the kitchen door, and Alex shouted, "Uncle Robert! Have you met Benjamin Reese?" while he dug mud out from between Jake's toes.

The gentleman in the three-piece tweeds reappeared and lumbered towards them, as Ben hung his coat on a hook on the left-hand wall above a long row of Wellingtons.

"This is my uncle, Sir Robert Morgan, my late mother's brother."

"Ah." He said, smiling tentatively at Ben and shaking his hand in a ferociously masculine manner. "Good to see you, yes. Brutish weather, what?" He'd dropped Ben's hand already and was staring at Alex rather fixedly. "Couldn't get the children to let me play." He was shortish, stoutish, and entirely gray, with a large mustache, a larger nose, small pale eyes, and a generally red face. And he peered at Ben again with mild interest for a moment, before humming something military in a loud brusque voice.

"What wouldn't they let you play, Uncle Robert?"

"The confounded game, you know! What do you call it? You know! You pretend to be things, and if you're very lucky you get to wear a costume or a hat!"

"Charades, perhaps?"

"Right! That's it. David said I cheat! The cheek! Lizzy defended me."

"As well she might! You just go up and insist that they let you play. Tell them you talked to me, alright?"

"I will, yes." Uncle Robert cleared his throat in a surprisingly shy sort of a way and nodded at Ben as he turned right into the long hall by the kitchen door. "See you at dinner I expect."

"Yes." Alex raised his eyebrows and chuckled quietly to himself before lowering his voice. "Curious fellow, my uncle. Actually has a very retentive memory, in certain specific areas. Remind me to tell you about him later. What were we doing before he appeared?"

"Closing in on the basket I think."

"The gun room, yes. It's just this way, to the left down the long hall, past the stairs—"

"Poppy? Poppy, where are you?" Lizzy was standing on the green tartan carpet on the whitewashed stone steps they called "the square stairs," trying to see around the corner of the white wall they turned around. Only her head was visible, and one long blond pigtail, dangling under her pink freckled face.

"Yes, my dear?" Uncle Robert came out of the kitchen with a large chunk of homemade bread in one hand and a piece of shortbread in the other, and squinted up at her from the bottom of the stairs.

"David was just teasing, Poppy. We all want you to play."

"Do you indeed! Well! Alright, if you insist! I'll be up in a tick. Just let me fetch my tea."

Alex winked at Elizabeth, who blushed and disappeared, and then he stalked off again down the gray stone floor with his usual long running strides, and unlocked one of the heavy pine doors on the right, halfway down the long white hall (which led to the tourist office and the tea room).

It was a well-worn room with sagging chairs and a much used

window seat, and it was chilly without a fire in the grate. There were antique firearms on all the walls, as well as in glass-topped cases, and Ben looked for makers' names and estimated approximate dates, as he inhaled the lingering smells of gun oil, spent shells, and stale tobacco.

Alex unlocked a narrow wooden door in a side wall and stepped into a space like a large walk-in closet. There were racks on either side holding shotguns and rifles, and there was a locked metal cabinet in the end wall. He fished a small key from his waistcoat pocket and used it to unlock the safe.

And then he placed a large wicker picnic hamper on the antique wooden card table in the center of the room.

Ben sat in silence and studied the outside of the basket, concentrating on the brass identification tag that was fastened across the leather strap on top of the lid. "It's looks like a good quality hamper."

"It'tis, yes. It doesn't look new, though, does it?" Yet the brass plate was never engraved."

"When you unfastened the leather strap you weren't wearing gloves, right?"

"No, I wasn't, I'm ashamed to say."

"Why? How could you have known to do anything else?" Ben didn't look at Alex as he spoke. He fingered his jacket pockets for his pencil and his handkerchief and then used them both to slide the stiff leather strap out of its loops and buckle. He opened the lid with the handkerchief and scrutinized the inside, while he hunted for his key ring in the pocket of his corduroy pants. It was a small magnifying glass in a leather cover his father had made him years before for the close work he did as an archivist. And he used it methodically to examine both the outside and the inside of the basket.

It was lined, top and bottom, with navy and white checked gingham. A white pottery plate sat in the center of the bottom, and a heavy matching mug lay on its side in a corner. There were four paper napkins on top of the plate under a plain black thermos, and a single place setting of white plastic cutlery lay scattered around the plate. A moldy bread and butter sandwich, originally wrapped in a paper napkin, was curled and crushed along one side. And a blue and green chunk of what looked like Cheshire cheese, as well as two soft pippin apples and four plain biscuits, were fitted in around the thermos.

"So the only thing you touched was the thermos?"

"Yes, absolutely."

"There's no evidence that the police took fingerprints."

"I don't think they did. They left all of Jon's possessions in the infirmary with his body until after the inquest, and then I went to collect them. We were interviewed by the pathologist the night Jon died, when Ellie came down to identify the body. He asked a whole slate of questions about Jon's general health and physical condition, and of course Ellie told him straightaway that Jon was deathly allergic to insect stings. And then, you see, he found the three bites, and it went on inexorably from there. They'd found the sting kit in Jon's pocket, and it appeared to them that he'd been trying to take it out when he died. There wasn't any reason to look further. They couldn't know Jon wouldn't have had a picnic hamper, and they didn't even think to mention it to us."

"I'd like to fingerprint, but I don't have the equipment. We can improvise, if you could find a—"

"Just a moment. I think I may be able to fix you up."

Alex took a flintlock pistol from an arrangement on the front wall and rushed to the back left corner of the room by the window seat where he struck three sharp raps on the heating pipes with the pistol's engraved silver handle. The acoustic guitar music, which had been quite faint above their heads ceased immediately and Alex said, "John! Can you hear me?"

"Sort of."

"Run down to the schoolroom and ask James to bring me his detecting kit!"

"His what?"

"His *detecting kit!*"

"Alright. Just a sec."

The guitar music began again.

And Alex whacked the pipe once more and shouted, *"Now, John! Please!"*

The guitar stopped and stockinged feet trotted across the high white ceiling.

"Shouldn't take long. Depending on how their charades are progressing."

"Why don't you take the magnifying glass and look at the inside of the basket? See the . . I don't know quite what to call them . . the squiggles? The sticky little trails across the thermos and the cup and the plate? They're all over everything, but they look different depending on the surface. See where the dust and lint seem to stick to them?"

"Yes! What do you think they are?"

Ben carefully touched one of the longest deposits and licked the tip of his finger. "Dried sugar water, probably. Beekeepers spray bees with a dilute solution when they want to subdue them, so they can move them or clean the hive. So if bees, who were sprayed and transported in the basket, crawled across a surface, I think they might leave a trail kind of like that."

"That's very clever of you. Ah! Here's David."

A boy with very dark hair and wide hazel eyes was standing

self-consciously in the door. "James was doing his charade, so I brought it along. You did say his detecting kit?"

"Yes. Thanks, Davie."

"You're welcome. John was poisonous as usual when he asked. Could I speak with you later, Daddy?" David was thirteen and tall and a collection of bones, all knees and elbows and wrist joints. And he had a serious straightforward sort of way about him.

"Of course. Immediately after dinner. Something amiss, is it?"

David sighed and shrugged his shoulders as though there was a great deal wrong with adolescent life in general, before he closed the door.

"Difficult age, I'm afraid. Remember it myself, unfortunately. Do you mind if I watch?"

"No, of course not. Just stand so you're not in the light." Ben dusted the thermos and the apples with white powder, and the white pottery surfaces and the forks and spoons with dark, and brushed the excess away in each case with one of two "Professional Private Detective" soft bristled brushes. He took a complete set of Alex's prints. And then he organized the kit, and put everything but the food back in the basket.

"Well?"

"There were two more dead bees under the rim of the plate. And it's a very good thing we've got the brass tag. It's right where you have to brace your fingers when you're pulling up on the strap, and someone else's prints are there as well as yours. It looks to me like two of them are under yours, but at least one of the unidentified prints seems clear enough to use for comparison." Ben was concentrating on the wall in front of him like a predator with prey, coiled but patient and single-minded, and it made his face look sharper than usual. "The policeman on Holy Island should have worn gloves when he packed up the basket, so the prints under yours may be Jon's. I won't know that, though, until I've seen a set of Jon's prints. Yours are the only ones inside, except for one long smear on the thermos. Which means I need to ask Ellie if she's got something with Jon's prints on it."

"I take it you're assuming that whoever organized the hamper wore gloves?"

"Yes." Ben ran both hands back through his thick straight hair as he gazed down at the River Tay, sliding silver and green in a wide valley under the high hills on the other side. "Who have you told about the basket?"

"Ellie. Hugh. Jane, of course. I don't think I've mentioned it to anyone else."

"Did you tell them all where you've put it?"

"I might have done. I can't really remember. Still, I do think it's quite secure, you know, in the gun safe. There's a combination lock as well as a key. We do paying shooting parties in the fall and winter and we have to keep to quite stringent rules."

"I don't think we should mention the prints or the squiggles to anyone else. Just say we don't know what to think, if anybody asks." Ben was using a pocketknife, scraping flakes from one of the sticky places onto a piece of note paper.

"Right. So what will you do next?"

"Fingerprint something of Jon's." He'd folded the paper and put it in his pocket as he stood in front of the window, with his hands on his hips and his jacket pushed back behind his elbows. "Do you know if Jon had written a will?"

"No. We never discussed it a'tall." Alex had thrown himself on a tartan chair and was beginning to loosen his tie, when his face tightened unexpectedly.

Ben was just turning toward him, and he saw the anxiety and the shadow of some regret.

"Actually, now that I think about it, I'm afraid that's not altogether true. Jon must have written a will, because he told me he was bequeathing me his cavalry saddle. He only mentioned it once, and well over a year ago."

"Did he leave you anything else?"

"No. Other than one or two odds and ends he dug up when we were children. Jon could have been a very fine archaeologist."

"What kind of odds and ends?"

"Nothing valuable I shouldn't think. Some small Roman pieces from Kilgarth, as well as one or two Celtic bits he discovered up here on the moor. I'd found a few trifles at the same time, and Jon thought our 'collections' should be together. For sentimental reasons. In remembrance of our childhood friendship. Not because of their value."

"Did he have his finds appraised?"

"No, and he scoffed when I suggested it. I thought it might keep him from leaving them lying around the way he did. There were always people coming and going, just as you'd expect in a manse, and I was afraid they'd be damaged. But I never thought for a moment that they might really be valuable."

"Exactly what kind of artifacts are we talking about?"

"Part of a Roman fork and spoon, most of a legionnaire's boot, one or two large Roman nails, and a Celtic buckle of plain, rough work. But Jon may have been joking, you know. He frequently did. He may not have left me anything a'tall."

"What would be the usual inheritance plan in Scotland?"

"Well, I suppose Ellie would inherit whatever there is. And I'm sure there isn't much, except Kilgarth. It's been a considerable burden since before his father died, with taxes and upkeep, and

Jon couldn't afford it. Not on a minister's salary. That's why he was planning to sell it."

"I know what I meant to ask you. What's a 'Kirk Session?' I know 'kirk' means church."

"It's one of the two elected governing bodies within the organization of a parish kirk. The Session is responsible for decisions having to do with the worship service itself, as well as spiritual issues which pertain to the service and the church body."

"So there can easily be conflict between the Session and the minister?"

"There can be, certainly. Though Jonathan was able to get along with every sort of personality. Always was, even though he was very firm in his own convictions."

"He didn't get along with everybody, Alex, because somebody murdered him, and whoever it was planned it very carefully. Fate intervened, fortunately. Although God might be a more accurate term. Because the killer obviously didn't intend to leave the basket by the body."

"I'm not altogether sure I see what you mean."

"If the basket were found by the body, Ellie would know it wasn't Jon's. Others probably would too. Including you. Just the fact that there weren't prints raises the issue of foul play. And yet without that basket, nobody would have questioned Jon's death. Since this guy is no dummy, something happened to keep him from retrieving it.

"Yes, but do Jimmy Reed's parents have a phone? That's the next question. And do I have time to find out before dinner?"

CHAPTER FOUR

Friday, May 19th

A WARM BREEZE COMING OFF THE RIVER ruffled Reverend Donaldson's robe and blew his hair in his eyes as he stood with his back to the ruins of Dunkeld Cathedral, looking at one, and then another, of Jon MacLean's family and friends.

He opened his tattered King James Bible as he began to speak in a deep warm voice, with the rolled *r*s and the rising lilt that's bred in the bone in the Highlands. "In John's gospel, Jesus says, 'Let not your heart be troubled; ye believe in God, believe also in me. In my Father's house are many mansions: if it were not so, I would have told you. I go to prepare a place for you. And if I go and prepare a place for you, I will come again, and receive you unto myself; that where I am, there ye may be also.'"

Ellie MacLean was watching Duncan Donaldson with more sorrow on her face than Ben had seen since the war.

But Duncan didn't say anything else for a minute. He stood on the edge of Jon's grave, tall and red haired and barrel-chested, and stared at Ellie like he was waiting for the right words. "Jonathan MacLean took those statements for his own in the midst of a war that was arguably more horrible than any the world has ever known. I was given an opportunity to know Jon at that time, for he and I were with The Black Watch, the 51st Highland Division's Fifth Battalion. We went from El Alamein through Sicily, and in again at Normandy, and on across to Bremerhaven. It was a vera long war, and a horror, and Jon fought well and he fought humanely, as you know from the honors he received.

"I was a chaplain then. Trying to help pick up the pieces that battle makes of men. And I saw with my own eyes the change in Jon that came when he read the Gospel of John and accepted its assertions. So that now, even on the edge of his grave, there is comfort to be found in those words, as well as in Jon's commitment.

"And yet we grieve. Because we miss Jon. How could we not mourn for Jonathan? For there is now an emptiness that only he could fill. Each of our lives will be diminished, in some sense, by his passing. And Ellie MacLean, for one, will face great suffering and loneliness and sorrow. And yet she *will be comforted.* The day *will come* when she will once again be glad to be alive.

"So let us pray now for the living, for the strength and peace and comfort that only Christ can give Ellie and Hugh MacLean in the midst of such sorrow and grief. 'Almighty and Eternal God who amid the chances and changes of this mortal life, remainest the same yesterday, today, and forever…'"

It was a Church of Scotland prayer and Ben didn't know the words. He bowed his head and listened, as he gazed at Jon's coffin. The plain dark wooden box had already been lowered into an opened grave in the last of the Campbell plots beside the ruined nave of the old Cathedral. It lay in the shade of a huge old oak, below the torn tracery of a gothic window, with at least ten generations of Jon's mother's father's family.

"The Lord gave; the Lord hath taken away. Blessed be the name of the Lord."

A handful of dirt scattered across the polished lid. Eyes were wiped. Noses were blown. Backs were patted while Ben watched.

The sound of an organ playing Bach filtered softly from the other end of the ruined church, the part that had been roofed and repaired after it was burned in the Reformation, and was now the parish church.

Ben listened, in that cool thicket of flat upstanding stones, two hundred feet from the River Tay, while he studied the reactions of Jon's mourners. Duncan Donaldson, in his black robe, with his wild red hair and his huge neck and arms, wiped his eyes on the end of his sleeve, as the parish minister carried a cup of water to Jon's two maiden aunts, who were dabbing their eyes and picking at their handkerchiefs on a bench beside the church door. Alex put his arm around Lizzy, without letting go of Jane's hand, while the boys stood by, stiff and awkward, and tried not to let themselves cry. Rory MacKenzie took Ellie's arm. And Hugh handed his handkerchief to Mrs. Atwood.

Ben turned away, toward the sweep of lawn and the clipped shrubs and the sunlight skating on the river, away from his own memory of Jessie's coffin being lowered into hard Ohio ground.

"Ben?... Benjamin?" Jane Chisholm slid her left hand under Ben's right arm, while she held her black straw hat against a gust of wind. "I could do with a bit of adult conversation, and I was wondering if you'd care to drive home with me? I have to start straightaway, to finish organizing the tea."

"I'd like to." Ben smiled down at her and bent his arm to make a corner for her to hold on to. "You remind me of my sister, Alice."

"Do I? I hope I don't dredge up infuriating childhood memories."

"No. She sees what people need."

"Then she's far more perceptive than I. It should just take me a moment to marshal the children. James! Keep your hands to yourself, and Elizabeth stop whining! It wasn't your turn to sit by the window as you very well know. All of you now, come with me. Uncle Hugh will drive Daddy home later."

"What can I do to help with the reception?" They were walking toward the high black iron gate, and Ben looked back to watch the children, straggling across the lawn toward Jane.

"I'm not a'tall sure, at the moment. The boys will help carry from the kitchen to the dining room, and I expect Alex will fill cups and keep conversation afloat. He really is wonderful at that. So we'll see, shall we? There's sure to be something I've overlooked."

The tea and canapés had been well received and the serving had gone smoothly. And most of the guests were leaving. The elders from Cawdor had already gone. The Campbell aunts had said their good-byes and were on their way out the door with Hugh, who was to drive them back to Ballinluig.

Alex and Jane and Rory were talking, quietly, trying to decide how they could help Ellie get through the next few weeks, while Uncle Robert lectured Ned Sutherland (a friend of Jon's father's who was up from London) on what he considered the newly developed shortcomings of the diplomatic service.

Ellie had gone out, once the visitors had begun to leave. Ben had seen her slip away to the wild paths and into the woods that wandered down the hill behind the castle.

Ben had been talking to Duncan Donaldson, and he walked him to his Mini and saw him off to Aberdeen. And then he crunched across the gravel front to the path that started by the library, that led across the side lawn past the chapel on the edge of the woods.

It took ten or fifteen minutes of trotting between rows of tall pine and fir, with his footsteps falling hushed on scented needles, to get to the edge of the hardwood trees and the undergrowth of fern and ivy. The path turned muddy there, without the thick carpet of pine needles, and he could clearly see the prints of Ellie's hard-soled shoes when they turned left into an overgrown track.

She was on a bench in one of Alex's blinds, a small mossy shelter in the middle of the woods, where Alex watched deer and any other animals who wandered by.

She turned toward Ben, without showing much, looking haggard and pale and exhausted, as she said hello.

"I can talk to you later, Ellie, if you'd rather be alone. But I do have to talk to you sometime."

"I don't care. Whatever's good for you." She was stripping moss and lichen off a stick as though it mattered. As though she had to do something with her hands.

"My wife died four years ago, so I do know what it's like."

"Does it ever get any better? Or do you just get better at hiding it?"

"Yes and no." Ben sat down on the long wooden bench and looked out the open place in the elder branch wall at the canopy of trees that blocked the sun. "Do you want a real answer, or something short and simple?"

"I want to know what it's like."

"Your experience may be very different."

"Still." Ellie didn't look at Ben directly. She contemplated him silently from the corners of her dark green eyes, while she stuck a loose hairpin in her chignon.

Ben didn't notice. He was staring straight ahead with his arms crossed across his stomach. "All I can tell you about the first few weeks is that grief felt like fear to me. Like battle anxiety. Physically. The restlessness, and the dry mouth, and the butterflies in the stomach. Even the weight wrapped around my chest when I woke up in the night. *When* I could fall asleep. And I don't think I did much. I was like a rat on a wheel. Going over it, and over it. Like a dog chewing on a sore paw. Picking at the place that hurts. I needed people around me much more than usual, and yet I could hardly stand it when anyone talked to me."

"That's exactly what it's like. And it seems so odd."

"After awhile, I could forget about it in short spurts, usually when I was working. Until there actually came a day when I didn't feel guilty for having forgotten. It still didn't seem real a lot of time, though. I'd catch myself listening for her voice, and waiting for her to walk in the room. But there were also days when I couldn't remember her face. I hated that. Even though I knew memory can't be trusted on a lot of levels. I wanted to remember Jessie the way she was, with the edges and the surprises and the parts of her personality I never saw coming. I didn't want to end up with *my* version of Jessie. Some dead thing I could understand and fit in a convenient box."

"How did you feel about God?"

"Cut off. Abandoned. Shut out in the cold. I was angry too. Sometimes that more than anything."

"It's hard, isn't it? Even when you know better?"

"It was for me. I couldn't accept it in real life the way I could in the abstract. So I ended up thinking all the usual things. That maybe God *is* a figment of man's imagination. Or maybe He's actually worse than that. A sadist who likes watching us squirm. And of course, if God can't be trusted, and Christ isn't who he said he was, I'd never see Jessie again." Ben was sitting with his hands between his knees, rolling an acorn from one to the other. "But that didn't make me want to believe I would if it wasn't true. Even when I was a kid, I hated the thought of deluding myself. Although that's not to say I always know when I am."

"But you got past the anger later."

"Yeah. After while. I'd had too many experiences of God that were too much of a contradiction. One in particular that happened during the war. And one day, I could pray again and have it help."

"That's the way it was when my parents died, and I know intellectually it'll happen again, but emotionally I still can't believe it."

"Maybe it hurts more with Jon."

"Probably."

"Or maybe it's way too soon."

"What was it like after that?"

"There was comfort. Finally. And I knew where it came from. And eventually there was peace. Interspersed with panic, but still peace. Even though I still missed her almost more than I could bear. Do you want me to stop?" Ellie had turned away, and it looked to Ben as though she'd pulled her lips in between her teeth to keep herself from crying.

"No. I want you to tell me as much as you can."

"I don't even know how long it took, but there finally came a day when I could laugh again. And then I could laugh and not notice. Today, I can actually say I'm content. That I'm glad I'm alive, like Donaldson said."

"You're sure?"

"Yeah."

"I guess I can't imagine it at the moment."

"I know it helps me to have work to do that I really love. It would've been a lot harder without my work. Partly because it forces me to forget about myself and do things for other people. I still need to get out in the country, to have trees and animals and sky around me. And it's easier for me if I do physical things too, like riding a horse, or hiking, or even just lifting weights. But a day doesn't go by that I don't wish she was with me. Even though I don't usually talk about it."

"How did Jessie die?"

"She had a baby four months early and died from the anaphylactic shock caused by an amniotic embolism. Which means that debris from the amniotic fluid got into her veins and killed her instantaneously."

"Like Jon died of anaphylactic shock caused by bee stings. Did the baby live?"

"No."

"I'm sorry."

"I'm sorry about Jon."

Ellie was taking the hairpins out of her chignon and putting them in the pocket of her corduroy pants as though having her hair fastened tight against her head was suffocating. When the last one was out, she pulled her dark shiny hair out away from her head and let it fall behind her, almost to her waist. "I really have wanted to talk to you about Jon, ever since Alex told me you'd found your friend's murderer. But it seems like I've had something else to do every single second."

"Has Alex told you we've fingerprinted the basket?"

"No."

"Except for a set on the brass name tag and a long smudge on the thermos, his were the only prints."

"So what does that mean? That whoever packed the picnic basket wore gloves?"

"Yes. And I need to fingerprint something of Jon's to compare with the unidentified ones."

"Would it be okay if we walked? I'm beginning to feel cold in the shade."

"You lead and I'll follow. There were two more dead bees on the bottom too, under the lip of a plate. And there were traces of what I think will turn out to be sugar water. I took a sample to a biochemist in Perth this morning in order to have it tested."

"I'm not sure I see the significance."

"I think there were bees in the basket, and they'd been sprayed with sugar water to subdue them so they could be moved from a hive to the basket."

"So someone deliberately put bees in the hamper and gave it to Jon, knowing he was allergic to insect stings?"

"*I* think so."

"Don't touch the stinging nettles." They were passing through a sunny patch where the path was powdery and covered with dry leaves, and there were wild flowers, bluebells mostly, along the edge, alongside clumps of nettle. "How could the murderer have gotten Jon to take the basket? Jon never carried anything he didn't need."

"I think it was somebody he knew, who met him unexpectedly and suggested a picnic breakfast."

"Yeah, Jon would've gone along with it to be polite. Shall we walk down to the river?"

"Sure."

"It's the path up there on the left."

"Can you think of anyone who would have wanted him dead?"

"Strange, isn't it? You hear that line in movies all the time, and you read it in books, and you can't imagine ever hearing it in real life." Ellie was walking slowly, twirling a piece of cedar in her hand. "I've been asking myself that ever since Alex showed me the basket, but it doesn't seem possible."

"Were you with Alex when he picked up Jon's things?"

"Yes. I waited for him in the cab."

The trees thinned as the path dropped toward the valley, and Ellie started braiding her hair while she walked, to keep it from being blown by the wind. "Were you with us in Cawdor at the memorial service?" Ben nodded, and she said, "Did you hear the conversation I had with Hamish MacDonald about the Kirk Session?"

"I wondered about it then."

"I'll have to give you a lot of background to put it in a context that makes sense."

"Good. Whatever you can tell me will help."

"Well, first of all, Hamish is a pharmacist—that's a chemist in Britain—who owns three shops in Nairn. He was raised on a farm near Cawdor, and grew up to become the son who made 'good,' and then married a woman with money of her own. His family had been active in the Cawdor church for more than a hundred years, and it's almost as though he thinks it belongs to him. I don't know if Hamish holds real beliefs, and I'd never want to say he doesn't, but he seems more interested in form than content. In the letter of the law rather than the spirit."

"So there was conflict between him and Jon?"

"Usually it was laughable. The fact that Hamish's wife, Betty, wasn't chosen to direct the Sale of Work—which is what they call their fund-raising bazaar—or that her knitted scarves weren't priced high enough. But the real conflict came over Carolyn

MacAllister. She's a shy, sheltered farm girl whose brother brought home an English 'friend' from the Navy who seduced her very cold-bloodedly and got her pregnant. She lived with her aunt in Edinburgh until the baby was born, and then she gave it to a young couple from her aunt's kirk. When she came back, she talked to Jon about what she believed, as well as her regrets about what she'd done, and he welcomed her back in the church. Which is exactly what he should have done in my opinion. But Hamish was apoplectic.

"He kept saying 'sinners need to be punished and examples of punishment need to be seen.' And he hounded Jon about it, and threatened to get the church 'declared in an unsatisfactory state.' That's a legal condition that means Jon would've been forced to leave. I don't think Hamish could've pulled it off. Most of the church supported Jon. But Hamish was fit to be tied because Jon wouldn't do what he wanted. He even mentioned in passing, that that's just what he'd expect from someone with Campbell blood!" Ellie smiled.

And Ben nodded. "Glencoe. Three hundred years ago."

"Yes, when Robert Campbell of Glenlyon, under order of the English, had a branch of the MacDonald clan slaughtered in their sleep in the Pass of Glencoe."

"Hadn't the MacDonalds fed and housed him and his men for a week or so too?"

"Right. And there are still MacDonalds today who've never forgiven any of the Campbells, even though there are a lot of branches of the family that had nothing whatever to do with it."

"Human nature. Isn't it wonderful?"

"Anyway, in the middle of the conflict over bringing Carolyn back into the church, one of the kids Jon had had in his youth club, who now works in the Bruntsfield Hotel in Edinburgh, came home on his weekend off and told Jon he'd seen Hamish two nights before at a chemists' convention, very drunk, going into his hotel room with a loose-looking woman who was definitely not his wife.

"Jon asked Hamish to meet him at the church the evening of May ninth, the Tuesday before the Friday when Jon was . . killed . . and told him he knew about the convention, but he wouldn't expose him in front of the kirk *or* the Session if he'd do what was right and resign on his own.

"Hamish was furious, but he agreed. The standards for Session membership are very clear, so what else could he do? He's extremely concerned about what other people think of him, including his wife, and he certainly doesn't want to lose a single customer. But is that a motive for murder? He didn't know who'd told Jon, but there obviously would have been someone else to silence. He now knows I know about it. So will he decide to silence me? It just doesn't seem like a strong enough motive."

"It probably depends on the person. Did Hamish know about Jon's allergy?"

"He made up the sting kit himself."

"If he was raised on a farm, he could easily know about bees." Ben stopped for a minute and stared at the bluebells in a wide clearing, his hands on his hips and his jaw set off to one side. "So who else has come to mind?"

"It seems even more unlikely."

"Just start at the beginning, and give me a lot of detail."

Ellie told Ben that Jon had decided to sell Kilgarth, the family house near Dunblane. Money was short, the house needed a lot of work, and Jon wanted to give Mary Atwood a decent retirement income. He also wanted to establish a small charity fund, so that when people came to him with personal troubles, he could help with a gift or an interest free loan. She and Jon rarely got down to Kilgarth, and Hugh didn't want it. He liked Edinburgh, and sailing the boat he'd inherited from his father, and he didn't want to be tied to a house.

When Harold MacIntyre, the son of one of Jon's parishioners, learned Kilgarth was for sale, he told his boss, Alfred Dixon. Dixon, a partner in an import-export firm, agreed to Jon's condition that Kilgarth be kept a private home instead of being converted into a hotel or a conference center. And at the end of March, they agreed on a price. Dixon then left on a six-week business trip to the Far East, after arranging for a contract to be drawn up.

"Why did Jon want it kept a private home?"

"He felt a responsibility to the neighbors, the Creiths next door especially. They've always been surrounded by pasture and wild land, and Jon wanted to spare them hotel guests tramping across it. I've gone back and figured out the dates, and May eighth, the Monday before he . . died . . Jon got a call from Ned Sutherland. Did you meet him this afternoon? He went to Oxford with Jon's father, and he's Alfred Dixon's senior partner. Ned runs the London office, and Alf oversees the one in Edinburgh. Alf has no idea that there's any connection between Ned and Jon. And Jon hadn't known they were partners either. He'd met Ned Sutherland years ago, but he'd mostly just heard about him from his father.

"Anyway, an architect in Ned's London club happened to mention that he'd been hired to redo a country house near Dunblane, to add a conference wing and turn it into a hotel. Ned asked what house it was, since he'd visited the MacLeans and knew the area. And as soon as he heard it was Kilgarth, and he found out who the buyer was, he called Jon.

"He'd recently discovered that Alf was doing something dishonest with the firm, and he was investigating Alf's affairs, intending to dissolve the partnership. I don't know what he'd discovered. I don't think he gave Jon any detail. But he wanted Jon to know that Alf was not to be trusted.

"So as soon as Jon heard all that, he called Alf's office, I think on the ninth, and asked them to tell Alf that Jon had to speak to him urgently. Alf didn't call often from the Orient, but they did send telexes back and forth.

"So the day before Jon left for Holy Island, which would have been Wednesday, the tenth, Alf got the message and called Jon. Jon told him he'd heard about the London architect, and the deal was off. Alf talked Jon into meeting him that night. Because, you see, the interesting thing is that Alf wasn't in the Orient like he was supposed to be. He wasn't due back until the thirteenth, but he was definitely in Scotland, and his office had no idea."

"Where was he when he called?" Ben was unfastening the chain on an old wooden gate, so they could cut across the pasture where Alex's two horses were watching them in a patch of afternoon sun.

"I have no idea. But he asked Jon to wait at the church for him that night. He told Jon he'd only asked the architect to work on the design in case he had to convert it some time in the distant future, but Jon didn't believe him. And Alf wouldn't let it go. Finally Jon told him that he also knew Alf was involved in other dishonest undertakings, and he didn't want to have any business dealings with him at all. That seemed to panic Alf, and he tried to get Jon to tell him what he knew.

"Jon didn't know anything specific, and Ned Sutherland had to be kept out of it so he could finish whatever investigation he was doing, and Alf just assumed that Harold MacIntyre had talked to Jon when he came to Cawdor to visit his parents. Jon told Alf he hadn't talked to Harold at all, but it didn't look to Jon like Alf believed him. I guess anyone who lies as much as Alf does can't believe that other people don't."

A large chestnut gelding with a white star on his forehead was looking at Ellie, his head high and his eyes wide, and she walked over and stroked his neck. "This one likes his chin rubbed." His eyes were half closed and he'd let go of his lower lip so it flapped when Ellie touched it.

And Ben saw Ellie begin to relax. "I've got one at home who looks a lot like him."

"Where are you from?"

"Ohio. But I was raised on a farm in Michigan."

"I'm from North Carolina. My father was from Scotland, and my mother was American. Dad was a veterinarian, so that was one of the interests Jon and I had in common."

"Did Alf know Jon was leaving for Holy Island?"

"Yes, but Jon left the next morning. That wouldn't have given Alf much time to get a basket and come up with the bees."

"Maybe he keeps bees in his backyard. Could Alf have known Jon was allergic to bee stings?"

"I suppose so. Harold MacIntyre's parents might well have known, and they could have told Harold. Information about the minister does get passed on in small villages."

"What about Katherine Burnett?"

"It's sad, really. Because from what I can tell, she's been in love with Jonathan since she was in grade school."

"That's interesting."

"Yes. Jon was a day boy at a private school in Edinburgh and she went to a girls' school that was a couple of blocks away. When Jon was thirteen and she was a little younger, he rescued a stray puppy from some kids, younger boys who were poking at it with sticks. Katherine had watched the whole thing, and Jon walked up to her and gave her the puppy. He already had a dog, and this one was obviously a stray, and he didn't know what else to do with it.

"*I* think she's been obsessed with him ever since. She started going to the same church he and his parents went to, and she took to hanging around near his house. When Jon went to Oxford, she'd show up ever so often, and she wrote to him constantly when he was in the army. When Jonathan got out in '45, he finished his last year at Oxford, and then went to divinity school at New College at Edinburgh University. And while Jon was getting his B.D., Katherine decided to get a literature degree there as well. She'd invite him to dinner and drop in on him a lot, and yet she never said anything about how she felt about him directly."

"What did Jon think of all this?"

"I think he knew, somewhere inside, that she was out of control, but he didn't want to hurt her and he chose to ignore it as long as she wasn't direct." Ellie gave the big chestnut one more pat and started off across the hayfield toward the river. "After we were married, she went out of her way to be distant toward me, but only when Jon wasn't in the room. Then, after he took the church in Cawdor, she moved up to Inverness, which is ten or twelve miles away, and took a teaching job there. She volunteered to be the church secretary, and she's been driving to Cawdor several times a week just to type his sermons and do the newsletter.

"I was never really worried about her. I knew Jon felt sorry for her, and just liked her as a friend, and I guess I never felt threatened by her. But this winter, we started getting weird phone calls at night. If *I* answered, whoever it was would just breathe in the receiver and hang up. And I eventually noticed that there'd usually be another call later, and if John answered, the caller turned out to be Katherine. The calls started during the day too, when I was teaching or practicing. I'm a pianist and I play with two local orchestras. When she and I were in the same room, her hostility was obviously escalating. And the last week in April, Jon sat her down and told her they would never be more than friends, even if I died the next day. He said she was too wrapped up in his life, and that she should make a life of her own and look for someone else. She went wild, apparently. She admitted that she'd always loved him, and she couldn't understand why he'd married 'that American,' that I only really love my music, and I don't take care of him the way I should, and I couldn't even . . I couldn't even give him a child the way she could."

Ellie raised her eyebrows philosophically and shrugged her shoulders, as Ben opened and closed the wide metal gate by the river.

"Anyway, she let it all out, and Jon could see it, the unhealthy preoccupation and the hatred she felt for me. He told her she couldn't work at the church anymore, and that she'd have to stay away from him altogether."

"So then she went down to Holy Island? To spend her holidays with her aunt?"

"It's not the holidays yet. I think she took medical leave, said she was exhausted or something and took that week off. Jon had called her after the confrontation, to make sure she was okay and suggest that she get away. He called her aunt too, whom he'd known for years, and explained the situation. And Katherine agreed to a visit."

"Do you think Katherine is capable of killing Jon?"

"It seems a lot more likely that she'd try to kill me."

"But that kind of obsession can turn plenty nasty when it's thwarted."

"She did know he was allergic to bee stings."

"And she was right there on Holy Island."

They were walking on the flat rocks on the edge of the Tay, beside close cropped patches of grass and moss, where birds and small ducks fished their territories with single-minded precision.

They sat on a low rock ledge and watched the water slide by for a few minutes in silence, watching birds fish and ducks dive and shielding their eyes from the wind.

"Are most of the guests gone?" Ellie was playing with her braid, twisting the end around her finger.

"Yes."

"I don't know why I had to get away, but I did."

"I think you're handling it very well."

"I don't. But for some strange reason, it's easier for me if Jon was murdered. It gives me something to think about that might be useful. Would it be okay with you if we started back? I'd like to lie down for awhile before dinner."

"Sure. Do you want to take the north path?"

"I was about to ask you the same thing."

"What was Hugh's relationship with Jon like?"

"They got along very well. Considering the fact that Jon was eleven years older. Hugh was too young to be affected much by the depression, or to fight in the war, and so their experiences were very different. Jon was a wild man when he was a teenager, from what he's told me, and Hugh was a very quiet self-contained little kid. So I think when they were young, Jon may have overwhelmed Hugh in a way. But since I've known them, they've seemed to have a very easy-going, well-intentioned relationship without any of the jealousy younger sons sometimes have for an older brother."

"That makes life easier."

"Yes. Their parents did their best to equalize things too. Certainly, in terms of the inheritance, and that's rarer here than at home. Hugh got the Bentley and the sailboat, because he likes mechanical things like his father did. Jon got the house, but then neither of them really wanted it. Jon could have lived in a linen closet and been perfectly happy. And I know Hugh is very aware of the problems with Kilgarth, the taxes and the upkeep, and he's never been the least bit interested. He spent a lot of weekends there, when their mom was dying, but he rents a flat in Edinburgh and he's looking for one to buy. He likes the stimulation of a city, the museums and the theaters. So I can't see Hugh having any sort of covetous feelings about Kilgarth."

"How would you describe Alex's relationship with Jon?"

"It was exactly what it looked like. They were each other's best friend from the time Jon was ten years old."

"Is there anything else? Anyone you haven't told me about? Any details you haven't mentioned?"

Ellie hesitated and Ben thought she looked uncomfortable, or maybe just uncertain. But all she did was shake her head.

"What about the will?"

"Well, there's some family jewelry. Some of it has already been split between Jon and Hugh, that was one thing Jon's mother did before she died. But it doesn't amount to much of anything that—"

"BEN!…WHERE ARE YOU!" Alex was hollering from the top of the hill at the north end of Balnagard, somewhere near the stables at the end of the orchard.

"WE'RE FIFTEEN MINUTES FROM THE HOUSE!"

"GOOD! SOMEONE NEEDS TO SPEAK TO YOU STRAIGHTAWAY!"

CHAPTER FIVE

"AM I INTERRUPTING, ALEX?"

"Ben! Of course not, we've been waiting for you. Though I'm afraid I have a confession to make."

"That sounds ominous."

Jake was running toward Ben across blue Chinese rugs and wide plank floors, wagging his entire body and twisting sideways, and Alex hollered, "Jake, stay down!"

"He will, he'll be good."

"Still, you mustn't feel you have to humor him."

"No, I like old Jake. I like the incorrigible boxer enthusiasm."

"You did meet Ned Sutherland at the reception, I hope?"

"We had quite a conversation." Ben smiled at Ned, at the far end of the long white sitting room, as he rubbed the insides of Jake's ears with his thumbs, which immediately put Jake into an ecstatic trance and forced Ben to hold Jake's head up.

"We discussed the various tests used to date cloth and paper." Ned Sutherland was sitting in a large blue chair on the left of the fireplace, pushing his gold-rimmed glasses up his nose and staring at a Turner landscape. "We also touched upon the chemistry used in preserving ancient documents."

"Ben's a very useful fellow to know." Alex had just stretched his legs out on the sofa that faced the fireplace.

And Ben dropped into the chair on Alex's right, opposite Ned Sutherland. "Okay, Alex, so what have you done?"

"Done? Oh, that! Yes. I'm afraid you may be rather perturbed with me, for on the impulse of the moment, I told Ned of our uneasiness over Jonathan's death. That led him to confide enough details of a related matter that I thought you should hear of it firsthand."

"Good, I need all the information I can get." Ben locked his fingers together on the back of his head and settled a cool gray gaze on Ned, who was very thin and slightly stooped and looked like he could've been sixty until he smiled like a ten-year-old boy.

"I'll just pour us out a sherry, shall I, while Ned begins?"

"I don't care for any right now, Alex, thanks."

"What about you, Ned? Jake, leave Ben alone! Come on boys, both of you! It's time you got on your beds."

Jake mumbled to himself and looked pathetic, but he still flopped on his bed beside Jeremiah under the long refectory table by the door where Alex was pouring very good sherry into two small liqueur glasses.

"Has Ellie told you I rang Jon after I'd learned he was selling Kilgarth to Alfred Dixon?" Ned Sutherland scratched a corner of his mouth where a deep crease cut down from the side of his nose, and then turned from Ben to Alex. "Ah, thank you, Alex. That's lovely."

"She mentioned it this afternoon."

"What I didn't explain to Jonathan, and which I now fear I should have done, was the nature of the other fiddle that has to be laid at Alf's door as well. I shall have to describe the firm and give you a bit of background."

"Fine. I'm sure that'll help."

In a calm, deliberate, very English voice, Ned began by saying, "We're a trading firm that specializes in chemicals and industrial lubricants. I handle trade with Europe and the U.S., while Alfred Dixon conducts business with the Orient and the Middle East. We both have degrees in chemical engineering, but Alf is a junior partner who owns a considerably smaller percentage of stock.

"When Alf was in India in April, the office manager of the Edinburgh office underwent emergency surgery, and I asked my only child, Samantha, who's taken a degree in chemistry and is studying international trade, if she'd take over the clerical work. It was when Samantha was opening the post that she noticed a wire transfer from a Swiss bank, which indicated that a large sum of the firm's money had been deposited into two of their accounts. I knew nothing about it, even though I have sole responsibility for European affairs, and when I contacted the bank, they refused to reveal the identities of the accounts' owners.

"Samantha then began investigating the Edinburgh files, and found shipping documents which indicated that the firm had recently transported a large quantity of a coded chemical, 'A11-A,' from Glasgow to a government facility in Egypt. The firm's chemicals were routinely coded; it was the size of the shipment *and* its destination which drew her attention. For British trade with Egypt has only recently been normalized, after having been banned in 1956 when the Egyptians seized the Suez Canal.

"Samantha eventually discovered that similarly large shipments of 'A11-A' had been sent every six months for the previous three years, though they were shipped indirectly to two traders in neutral countries who forwarded the material to Egypt while Egyptian trade was prohibited in Britain. Although it took considerable effort to uncover the evidence, Samantha now has conclusive proof that the illegal transactions did take place.

"Samantha also found that Alf charged 20 percent more for this coded material when Egypt was its destination than when it was sold elsewhere. And it was then that Samantha approached Harold MacIntyre, the chartered accountant in charge of the Edinburgh accounts department, whose parents attend Jon's church.

"She learned from him that the material coded 'A11-A' was thionyl chloride, which is used to make pesticides and plastics. It's also a precursor of methylphosphonic dichloride, or DC, which is itself an essential precursor in the manufacture of a certain nerve gas. Samantha later found that the payments into the Swiss accounts were always deposited by Alf within days of the Egyptian payments for the thionyl chloride, and the payments were in each case 20 percent of that charge divided between the two accounts, which seemed to indicate that a kickback was being paid to one or more Egyptian officials."

"Did Alf Dixon take a cut himself?" Ben was leaning forward with his elbows on his thighs and his hands hanging between his knees, making notes in a small leather notebook.

"Not as far as we know. Although he may have been given cash, or been paid from those Swiss accounts. We have the books audited routinely by an independent firm, and we've just completed an additional review, which indicated nothing untoward. Still, profits increase with sales, and stock dividends increase when the business does well."

Ned then explained that when Samantha was investigating the thionyl chloride shipments, she had to get several papers from Harold MacIntyre, who asked with some persistence what it was she was looking for. Eventually she told him that even though the thionyl chloride was being shipped to the Egyptian Department of Agriculture and Agrarian Reform, she wasn't convinced that's all they were using it for since they were buying it in such enormous volume. Harold told her it was Alf's opinion that it was not the firm's business what the Egyptians used it for as long as they paid their account.

"It was then Samantha asked Harold what he knew about the Swiss accounts. It was a risk I might not have taken, and Harold did seem to debate the matter with himself, before he told her it was a kickback being paid to the wives of two Egyptian officials. They pay more to us than we normally charge, without their government having a clue, and Alf pays it back to their wives in two protected Swiss accounts.

"It seemed strange to Samantha that Harold should be so forthcoming, and she asked him how he knew that was true, and why was he telling her. He replied that Alfred is in the habit of getting absolutely blind drunk once or twice a year, and in that condition, he confided in Harold a year or more ago. It seems he was so proud of his own ingenuity he felt the need to share the joke. I suspect he had reason by then to think Harold wouldn't object to a bit of larceny. And Harold admitted as much, in the end. In fact, he concluded his remarks by saying that Alf was clearly in a tenuous position, and since I was Samantha's father, loyalty to the Sutherlands made far more sense than helping Alf hide his dirty laundry."

Alex made a thoroughly disgusted noise in his throat and got up to add peat to the fire.

Ben stared at the floor, his gray eyes narrowed and distant and his jaw set off to one side. "So you think that when Alf Dixon went to see Jon, and Jon told him he had reason to believe Alf was dishonest, Alf might have jumped to the conclusion that Jon knew he was selling this nerve gas precursor to the Egyptians?

And that might have led Alf to decide to kill him?"

"I'm in no position to say anything of the sort with any confidence. I'm merely revealing the facts as I know them and enabling you to pose the question. At the very least, Jon certainly could have told him that he had reason to believe that lying about Kilgarth wasn't Alf's only dishonesty, because that is what I told Jon—that Alf was involved in another dishonest enterprise as well. Dixon knew Jon was acquainted with Harold, and he may have feared that Harold had begun to talk."

Ben made another note and asked what Ned could tell them about Dixon's background and personality.

"Alf is rather an emotional person. One might even say he's a violent man, in his own way. He grew up in a very tough part of Glasgow, and he had to fight terribly hard to get an education and better his position. There's a great deal of ambition in his blood, which has enabled him to study and use his talents, and is admirable in that sense. Though it also may be his most grievous fault. He does very much want to be accepted socially. You know the sort of thing I mean. He longs to live in a fine house and be asked to join a proper club. And if he felt as though the parts of his behavior which he's hidden were about to become common knowledge, he might take drastic measures to preserve his way of life."

"Did he know about your connection with Jon?"

"I wouldn't have thought so. I knew Jon when he was a child. His father was the link between us, and he died in '55. Jon might have remembered I was with a trading firm in London, but the name, Rankin's Ltd., wouldn't have been familiar. In fact I know it wasn't. When we spoke on the phone, Jon had no idea of any connection between Alf and myself."

Ben was circling an index finger on his knee and staring out the window behind Ned's chair with a predatory expression that made his eyes look colder and deeper set. "So Alf would have assumed that Jon had probably learned whatever he knew from Harold MacIntyre when he'd visited his parents in Cawdor?"

"I suppose he would've done. Though Harold knew nothing, as far as I know, about Alf's 'architectural' plans for the house, so that might have been a puzzle to Alfred. But if Alf's conscience was bothering him about the precursor business, he might have thought right away that that was the information to which Jon was alluding. Of course, he may be engaged in other nefarious practices I know nothing a'tall about. At the moment, I'd believe Alfred capable of almost anything."

Ben stopped tapping his pen against his teeth and said, "'If he does really think that there is no distinction between virtue and vice, why, sir, when he leaves our houses, let us count our spoons.'"

"Ah, good old Samuel Johnson." Alex smiled as he swiveled sideways on the sofa to face Ben. "A humbling exemplar of both virtue and wit."

"So according to Ellie, as I understand it, Alf was supposed to be in the Orient till the thirteenth, but he was actually in Scotland on the tenth when he saw Jon?" Ben was talking to Ned.

And Ned nodded, as he crossed one well-tailored dark gray leg over another and glanced at his watch.

"So when did Alf finally surface, and how has he treated Harold? It seems logical that Alfred Dixon might go after MacIntyre, if Alf did have something to do with Jon's death."

"Alf appeared at the office as scheduled on Monday the fifteenth, still blithely claiming to have arrived home on the Saturday. Of course, Harold is wonderfully astute where his own skin is concerned as well, and he'd gone on holiday. To an unknown destination, as it turns out, the day after Jon spoke to Alf. Even Harold's wife doesn't know where he's gone, much less when he'll be back. I suspect he's waiting for the storm to blow over. Waiting for me to dissolve the partnership and terminate Alf's employment so everything would be out in the open and Alf would have nothing to gain by attempting to silence him. That's now fully accomplished, by the way. My solicitor delivered the termination papers today while I was here attending the funeral."

Alex snorted quietly and shook his head in disgust. "It's absolutely appalling, isn't it? The greed that would turn its back on the horrific consequences of selling such a compound to an unstable country which would use it to make such a nerve gas, and might well employ it without compunction, possibly against one's own nation!"

"It's unconscionable. It really is." Ned wrinkled his lips as though he had a terrible taste in his mouth, and then looked at his watch again.

"So how did Alf react when you told him you knew what he'd been doing?" Ben was leaning back in his chair, balancing his notebook on his thigh.

"First he lied, as you might imagine, and tried to explain it away. Then he made dubious excuses and promised to be exemplary in the future. But, be that as it may," Ned set his glass on the coffee table, and pushed himself out of his chair, "I'm sorry to say I must dash. If there's anything else I can tell you, don't hesitate to ring. I'll be stopping at the Caledonian Hotel in Edinburgh tonight, but I'll be back in the London office tomorrow afternoon. You've got my home number in West Sussex as well, Alex. And, of course, I shall let you know should anything else develop."

"Has anyone talked to Harold since he 'went on holiday?'"

Ben asked it matter of factly but intently, sitting quietly in his chair, very still and self-contained.

"None of my people."

"Has his wife?"

"Not the last time we spoke, and I, for one, certainly believed her. She's a very unassertive, unprepossessing sort of person who's quite dependent on Harold and very bewildered by his recent departure."

"So we're *assuming* he's still alive and off on vacation, but there's been no real corroboration?" Ben closed his notebook and slipped it in his jacket pocket.

"I suppose it is an assumption. Now that you mention it. And I must say it hadn't occurred to me."

There were conversations running up and down both sides of the long polished table, but Rory MacKenzie wasn't listening. He was staring at the silver candlesticks in front of him, watching the flames flicker and looking torn.

He poured cream in his coffee and reached for his cigarettes. But then he laid them down again and shoved a hand through his thick black hair, pushing it away from his green eyes and his elegant eyebrows and his classically cut bones, as though he hated the feel of it when it was smooth and sleek. He watched Jane at the end of the table, and answered Uncle Robert on his right. And then he turned toward Ellie again, where she sat silently on his left stirring her coffee with a silver spoon. "You would let me know if there was anything I could do?"

"Yes, but there isn't, Rory."

"That's precisely what you said after your parents were killed."

"Is it? I suppose that could be because it's true."

"Didn't you find it helpful having the children around you? Being distracted by the activities of a family?"

"Yes."

"All I'm trying to say is that no one is absolutely self-sufficient. You're far too thin, and you look absolutely done in, and I can't help but worry."

Ellie didn't look at Rory MacKenzie, as he leaned toward her and spoke quietly so no one else could hear. While he watched her as though he could hardly stand not knowing how to help. She smiled a small sad smile and folded her napkin beside her plate. "I'm doing okay, Rory. I haven't been sleeping very well, and I haven't felt much like eating, but I'll be alright. It seems like a normal reaction to me. Don't you think?" She glanced at him quickly and centered her dessert spoon on her plate beside the raspberry trifle she'd hardly touched.

"Perhaps. I don't remember not being able to sleep when my wife died. But of course Veronica's death was anything but sudden, and it was clearly a release for her."

"You didn't love her either."

"Only at the end." Rory didn't flinch, but he looked away. He stared at the wood fire and rubbed his right temple as though it ached. "When she couldn't gossip anymore, or talk about clothes or jewelry. When she'd ceased to recognize any of us. When she had to be fed and turned over and washed like a baby. Then I loved her. The way I would have loved any crippled thing."

"I'm sorry, Rory. I had no right to say that."

"You had every right. And if there's anything I can do, promise me you'll let me know."

"I will. And I appreciate it. But at the moment, all I can

think about is getting into a hot tub and lying there for a very long time."

"Then you should. Jane and Alex will understand."

"Yes, I think I will."

"I shall see you in the morning, shall I?"

Ellie nodded, and thanked Jane for the dinner, for doing so much, and cooking for so many. And then she thanked Rory again for holding her chair.

He watched her till she'd closed the door behind her. And then he sat down and lit a cigarette and twirled his narrow gold lighter in a circle on the table.

Alex spoke to Hugh, and the children asked to be excused, and Mary Atwood told Jane in indisputable terms that *she* was doing the dishes no matter what Lady Jane might have to say on the subject. But Rory didn't listen. Not till Alex offered to give them port in the sitting room.

Hugh and Rory and Uncle Robert accepted, but Ben said he'd be up in a few minutes, that there was something he needed to do first.

Then Alex asked Ben if he could speak to him before he went off on his own.

And Jane, who was standing by her chair in the black suit she'd worn to the funeral, looking like she needed to take her shoes off and lie down and read a book, said, "I'll take everyone up to the sitting room, shall I, and serve the port before you arrive?"

"That's very kind of you, my dear. But, of course, you're the most perceptive of women." Alex had bent down and almost whispered it, before he put his arms around her and kissed the top of her head.

"It's no trouble a'tall. I've been wanting to talk to Rory about the biographies he's begun in the paper. You remember. The 'interviews with authors' series?"

"Of course. Yes. How could I forget?"

As the rest of them walked toward the hall, Alex led Ben to the wall of French doors that looked out on the back lawn where a startling number of baby rabbits were tearing around through the evening mist in the spotlights beneath the trees. "I've been hoping for an opportunity to ask if you've spoken to the young lad on Holy Island?"

"Jimmy Reed. Yeah, I talked to him right before dinner. He says he didn't see anyone the morning Jon died. No one by the bay, or in the fields where he found the body. Not even the milkman in the village."

"That's a disappointment! Oh, well. Something will turn up."

"Why do you remind me of Micawber?"

Alex laughed and said, "Because there are several similarities between us, unfortunately," as he slipped his reading glasses in his coat pocket. "Does that mean Jon was alone, and his death was an accident? No, of course not! The lack of fingerprints is quite conclusive."

"Right. Jon's murderer just made sure he wasn't seen."

Mary Atwood had scraped the plates into the garbage and was standing by the long pine table where the dishes were stacked and ready to be washed, comparing it to her own cutting board table at Kilgarth. Hers was shorter and made of maple.

And Jon used to chase her around it when he was a lad. Not often, for it wouldn't have been good for him. But once in a great while, when she'd let him. In the evening, usually, when he was especially high-spirited and full of fun. Once she'd even let him snap a tea towel in her direction, while she ran around the cutting board and pretended to be frightened. His hair had been blond when he was a lad, and curly, and his face would be so flushed and soft, and he'd looked so pleased with himself, so thrilled that he'd been able to get an adult of any description to treat him like a force to be reckoned with.

Mary sighed and then rolled her sleeves up on her way to the sink, where she would have seen her reflection on the window above it if she hadn't been thinking about Jon's animals. The turtles in the tub and the snakes in his closet. The family of deer he used to wait for in the woods. The stray dogs and the spiders and the wounded baby rabbit who'd been run over in the nest by the push mower. He'd been more frightened than hurt, and Jon had held him in his lap for hours to keep him from dying from shock. All one day, really, and most of the night, squeezing warm milk into his tiny wee mouth with an eyedropper. The rabbit had lived, too, against every adult prediction, and Jon had raised him in the small loo, throwing him grass and clover and keeping him apart religiously for months on end, when it hurt Jon terribly to have to do it, so the rabbit would grow to be wild again and be able to live on his own.

Mary's hands were on the edge of the deep stone sink, and steam was rising from the soapy water, and she was crying quietly, not minding at all, needing to feel the hot tears on her skin and the sobbing in her throat. It was only fitting, really. Jonathan MacLean deserved her tears. Hers and everyone else's.

Aye, but that was not to say that he needed them. He was with his Maker, after all. Satisfied in every way. Safe from sorrow and free from pain. Though Ellie had been left with both, poor wee thing. All alone in the world, really. No parents. No child. No brothers or sisters. No country even to call her own. And what would she do at the end of the day? Would she stay in Scotland, away from her own people? Or would she go back to the land she'd known as a bairn?

Unexpected, really, the way people are. That quiet young Mr. Reese, he wasn't put off by Ellie MacLean's grief. No, he knew how to talk to her when everyone else was at sixes and sevens. The two of them had taken a vera long walk together just that afternoon. Aye, and he was a widower. Perhaps there was comfort there for both of them. A blessing, it might be, in disguise. Ah, and how could she think such a thing, with her own dear boy hardly cold in his grave!

"You shouldn't be doing all these by yourself!"

Mary Atwood pulled a handkerchief out of the pocket of her apron and wiped her eyes before she glared at Ben as though she actually found his interest rather gratifying. "I've done more dishes than these, time out of mind, and never suffered for it! It's soothing, really. It'll take my mind off Jon to have something to do with my hands. And it's my opinion, that with all of us who've come for the funeral, and the castle opening to the public in a few days time, Lady Jane needs all the assistance we can give."

"I agree. Absolutely. So why don't I wash, and you dry and put them away?"

She protested, but gave in. And Ben threw his jacket on the old pine table. Then he rolled up his sleeves, and slid his hands into hot soapy water. He washed a plate in silence while Mary blew her nose. But when she started humming something old and haunting that sounded like a Scottish lament, he said, "Alex tells me you were very close to Jon."

"Aye, he was a fine lad, Jonathan MacLean. I loved him as much as my own children, I can tell you."

"What was he like as a boy?"

"That's difficult to say, isn't it? To describe people so you can see them as they are. Or were, as the case may be."

"Yes, but somehow I think you'll manage."

"I do know he felt things vera deeply. He couldn't bear to see someone being hurt or treated unfairly. He protected the weak one. And he defended the despised. And there was a great deal of blood let and a fair number of bruises because of it."

"That doesn't happen too often, from what I remember about childhood."

"Aye, that's true. It's a rare trait indeed. He was vera observant too. Much more than most children. And he loved animals more than anything else, of every kind and description. He did take risks as a bairn that made the hair stand up on your head. He courted danger, really. For he was headstrong as a wee lad, that I will say. But he liked every sort and condition of folk. Except for those who put on airs. And with that sort, he had no patience whatsoever! He preached wonderful sermons when he grew up. Though I was as surprised as any when he came back from the war and told me he wanted to go into the church. He was vera strong-willed and he'd been a bit of a handful, ye see, as a young man."

"Were you closer to him than you were Hugh?"

"No, not a'tall. Though it's hard to explain the differences in the way you feel for children. I will say that Hugh needed attention more often than Jon. He was put off things easier, and he required more encouragement. Still, they were both independent. They had their own interests. I never had to give either one of them ideas for what to do, like these poor miserable children today. City children are the worst. Though I fear it won't be long till they all have their hands fair glued to the knob on a television.

"Course, whatever Jon thought was stamped there on his face for the world to see, I will say that! Aye, you knew straightaway if he was disgusted with you, but you also knew it wouldn't last. He'd be back in a minute, all over and done with whatever had made him fret. Yet there were hurts he wouldn't talk about. For with all his confidence, Jon took things to heart. Hugh was sensitive too, of course. Vera definitely. Although he didn't show what he felt as much, and you weren't always sure what he needed.

"I think it's Jon being so young that bothers me most." Mary Atwood was up on her toes with her arm stretched above her head trying to hang a copper saucepan on the ceiling rack by the Aga stove. She gave up, finally, and handed it to Ben. "Aye, it seems so much crueler when it's a young person who's taken."

"How old was Jon, exactly?"

"He'd just turned forty-one, but from my point of view, that's quite a young man, and it's harder to bear, somehow. I lost two of my own when they were babes, one to pneumonia and one to scarlet fever, and it's vera hard indeed. When it's your husband . . well . . that's bad enough. Though at least my William had lived his life, and a full one it was, thank God. But it's all a trial, isn't it, when you come to it? And then you think of all the elderly, being pushed off into these homes, just sitting and staring at a telly, hardly knowing what it'tis they're seeing! It's a tragedy, it really is. I hope I die before I lose my faculties, I can tell you. And the way I'm failing, it won't be long!"

"You're sharp as a tack and you know it."

"Not anymore! Oh no!" She smoothed her apron down her stout stiff front and adjusted a wave of fine white hair. "I forget where I put things, and I hardly remember what anyone tells me. The vera day before poor Jon died, I gave myself quite a start. And I began to see then the writing on the wall."

"Why? What happened?"

"I always rise between five and five-thirty, and then I read the

Scriptures and get breakfast on the table at a reasonable hour. Mr. MacLean—Jon's father, the Mr. MacLean that was, and a day doesn't go by that I don't think of him—he and I used to eat together in the kitchen, and I don't think it's too much to say that we both enjoyed it. But—"

"Tell me about him and his family. Alex started to the other day, but somehow we got interrupted."

"I know vera little about the MacLeans before Neil MacLean's generation."

"He was Jon's father's father?"

"Aye. And he was something of an inventor. He bought Kilgarth in the 1870s after making a bit of money in cutting tools, though what exactly they might be, I don't begin to know. It's a lovely house, Kilgarth. Not grand or large or important like Balnagard, but it's vera pleasant indeed, and it was Jon and Hugh's country house when they were children. Of course, the First War and the Great Depression did away with the grandfather's fortune, and Jon's father became a marine engineer. He worked for a large shipbuilding firm near Edinburgh, and they used to say he did quite a bit of the mechanical design on the Queen Mary. When he retired, they sold the house in Edinburgh and moved to Kilgarth. He'd already fitted out a laboratory in the basement, and he was working on a coating to keep ships from rusting, when he died of a bungled appendectomy. It was a terrible tragedy and vera hard on Mrs. MacLean."

"And then she died of cancer?"

"Five years later, nearly to the day. Last January a year ago. She was a vera fine woman, Elizabeth MacLean. A nurse in the First War. And a vera conscientious mother. She did medical charity work when the lads were small, and then directed a hospital in the last war."

"So her death must have been hard on all of you."

"It was indeed."

"What were you saying before, when I interrupted you? Something about not getting up as early as usual?"

"Aye, and how it's always bothered me to miss the morning. My mother was quite strict about it and I've always been the same. But the vera day Jon died, I slept until seven-thirty, which I haven't done in donkeys' years. If my mind weren't beginning to fail, it never would've happened."

"I don't think that means your mind is going. You were probably just more tired than usual."

"Fortunately, Hugh's alarm was set correctly, and that was a blessing, or he would've been late picking up his Americans in Edinburgh."

"What time did he have to pick them up?"

"Half-eight, at the very latest. I heard his car leave at a quarter past six. I opened my eyes, looked at the clock, and promptly went back to sleep, much to my embarrassment, when I woke up later. But you're quite correct, I did feel tired. I was getting over a wee cold. And yet that's precious little comfort, since I also forgot to lock a door in the basement the night before. It's vera important, the locking up, because I'm alone at Kilgarth so often."

"We all forget things like that all the time."

"It's a blunder I never would've made in my younger days. And there's far worse than that I haven't told you. For the eleventh, the vera day before Jon died, was his forty-first birthday, and I forgot all about it! I did! It never even occurred to me, and that's a shame and a scandal. And then to think that right when I got up that Friday, Jon was dying down on Lindisfarne… "

Mary Atwood's chin began to tremble and she pulled her handkerchief out of her apron and turned away from Ben until she'd recovered herself. "And the nerve of some people! To see that madman, that Pilcher person, that lunatic who used to torment Jonathan, standing beside the cathedral as Jon's poor body was being lowered into the ground, it was enough to make me forget I'm a Christian!"

"What madman?"

"Pilcher. Something Pilcher. It'll come to me in a minute. His brother was a soldier under Jon and he died in Africa. And for some reason that no one has ever understood, his younger brother blamed Jonathan for the poor boy's death. He used to follow Jon around, threatening all kinds of disgusting things, and they finally put him in Craig House."

"Craig House?"

"It's a mental hospital down in Edinburgh. They kept him there for years. But there he was, right at the funeral, smiling and smirking, standing off behind a tree. I could see him plain as day, though, laughing as Jon's body was lowered into the grave! It was a horrible thing for him to do! It makes me furious to even think about it!"

"Did anyone else see him?"

"I couldn't say. Gerald! That's his name! Gerald Pilcher."

"Where's he from, do you know?"

"I did, once upon a time. I'll think about it, shall I?"

"Yes. And let me know when it comes to you."

CHAPTER SIX

IT WAS AFTER ELEVEN WHEN BEN CLOSED THE IRON GATE above the moat and stopped to listen to the night. The wind was up and the woods around the castle were wild with noises, the creaking, sighing, scratching, and rustling of trees and small forest animals, punctuated every few seconds by the distant bark of an agitated dog.

A storm was coming. How soon Ben couldn't tell, but he started off toward his house on the hill, angling left across the gravel and the wide front lawn, through the archway in the high stone wall. He was trotting easily, and he'd almost gotten to the line of trees beside the road when he stopped, suddenly. Seconds before a tall black shape slipped from the shadows underneath a cluster of firs.

Ben was already listening, waiting, watching with the night vision that was part of the reason he'd been made a Ranger, as well as a member of "The Nighttime Special" (the Scouting Group from 75th Division, that went out in groups of two to four and took German command posts, night after night, from Normandy Beach past Remagen).

"Dr. Reese?"

"What are you doing out, Rory?"

"I wonder if I might speak with you for a moment?"

"Sure. But I'd feel better if you'd call me Ben."

"I didn't startle you, I hope?"

"No."

"I went for a walk, and then thought I'd catch you on your way to Perach."

"Come up to the house and I'll make us a cup of coffee."

They crossed the road in silence and turned left into the steep lane that led up the side of a high hill to the moor around Loch Skiach. It was difficult footing on a dark night, with the ruts and the sliding stones. And they stopped halfway up to rest for a second, when the moon slid out from under a blanket of clouds. They watched it shatter on the river, in the broad flat valley a mile or more below, while the wind tore at their coats and whipped their hair in their eyes.

After they'd passed the sharpest turn of the switchback track and were almost to Ben's small white turreted house, Rory coughed, by way of introduction, as he pulled a leaf from a sycamore above his head. "I'm a newspaperman, Ben. Equivocation isn't my forte, and if you've no objection, I'll come straight to the point."

"Fine, go ahead."

"Hugh mentioned the hamper that was found by Jon's body, and he's told me a bit about your background, so that by implication, as well as observation, it seems probable to me that you're investigating the circumstances of Jon's death. I'd therefore be interested to know what Alex and Jane have told you about my relationship with Ellie and Jon."

"Nothing. Just that you're distantly related to her. And that she lived with you and your family for awhile, after her parents died. Wait a second and let me get the lights." Ben had just opened the kitchen door, and he walked straight across the old brick floor between the table and chairs on his right and the cutting board counter on his left till he'd found the switches by the French doors. "Why? What would Alex and Jane have told me that you're hoping they haven't mentioned?"

"That's a rather cynical analysis." Rory was squinting against the suddenness of the light, standing tall and dark in the center of the pine-paneled room, taking off his trench coat and smoothing his windblown hair.

Rory MacKenzie might have been fifty, but he was still strikingly handsome, still hard and athletic looking, like a cinema conception of the British upper class, and the sort many women would fall all over. Even so, Ben didn't get the impression that Rory paid much attention to the way he looked. There was nothing studied about him. And though his clothes were good quality and well cut, he chose them to get the job done and wore them unselfconsciously. "Do you take anything in your coffee?"

"No, just black. Thanks." Rory lit a cigarette and put the ash tray in his lap, and then tipped his chair back against the wall.

"Anyway, I'm not investigating Jon's death. Not in any formal sense."

"Informally then? Ellie implied as much too, you know, and I'd like to clarify my position before you feel the need to ferret into my affairs. Would you care for a cigarette?"

Ben had stopped in 1950, except for the Camel or two he still smoked when he woke up from a dream about the war. And he smiled and said, "Thanks anyhow."

"I'm afraid I'll have to give you a bit of family background."

"That's okay. Any kind of background is better than none."

"Then I shall start with the fact that my father died when I was an infant, and my mother subsequently married Ewen Maitland, who was Ellie's grandfather's brother. Ewen was years younger than her grandfather, so he and Ellie's father, Robert Maitland, were almost of an age, and they visited and corresponded frequently, even after Robert emigrated to the States to attend the veterinary college at Cornell University. He married an American woman, who was studying there as an undergraduate, and they settled in North Carolina. Still with me, are you?"

"I think so, yes."

"Ellie was Robert and Anne Maitland's only child, as I expect you've already worked out for yourself. And when she was just sixteen, they were tragically killed in a plane crash on their way to a veterinary convention."

"And that was when you invited Ellie to live with you?"

"Yes. My wife had recently died of a brain tumor, which left me with three young children to raise on my own. And I suppose it was watching what they went through that made me empathize so strongly with Ellie. She was virtually alone in the world, on her mother's side as well. And to make a long story short, although we're not, in fact, blood relations a'tall, I invited her to come to us, and in January of '47, she did. She'd only just turned seventeen. While I was thirty-seven."

Rory crushed out his cigarette and lit another, though he didn't inhale either of them often; he played with them in the ash tray, rolling the ashes off the ends as though his hands had needs of their own. "My wife and I had never really gotten on. You see, my mother was from a branch of the Bowes-Lyon family, which made her a relation of the Queen Mother, and even though my father *and* my stepfather were men of modest means, my wife was taken with the social position she imagined I had, as much as with the money I'd inherited from my mother. Thankfully, I wasn't raised to give much consideration to either. But neither did I notice the modest extent of my wife's intellect and interests. She was a very decorative woman, who was much taken with physical appearance in the male as well. While I, regrettably, was far too young." Rory smiled sardonically and watched a stream of smoke he'd exhaled curl away toward the ceiling.

"After we were married, I could hardly avoid noticing her shallowness and intellectual limitations, and I consequently took refuge in my work. I began as a reporter for a smallish paper—"

"But you're now the editor of *The Daily Scotsman?*"

"Yes. I've long been a student of history and politics, and it gives me an opportunity to indulge my interests. I was a staunch supporter of Churchill before the war, when appeasement was the prevailing view. And I still make my own small attempts at thwarting our cultural, ethical, and political descent.

"So even before my wife died, I was deeply involved in my work, and I lived a monastic sort of life really, fulfilling my obligations to my family while remaining largely untouched. I'd given up hope that I would ever be able to share my commitments and pursuits with any woman, and then—" Rory paused, with his hands locked behind his head and his chair tipped back nearly horizontal, "Elinor Maitland arrived from America."

Rory let his chair down and swallowed his coffee without looking directly at Ben. "It really is most peculiar. I have *never* discussed my relationship with Ellie with anyone except my older son, and only tangentially then, and yet I am now unburdening myself to you, in spite of the fact that we've only just met."

"Sometimes it's easier to talk to a complete stranger. We leave without complicating your life. Though in this case, there is the added impetus of how it relates to Jon's death."

Rory had lit a third Benson and Hedges and was holding the

black and gold box toward Ben.

But even though Ben had been eyeing the pack, he still shook his head and finished the last of his coffee.

"So Ellie arrived, very young, very alive, and very bereft, and I felt tremendously protective of her. She was also extremely attractive, of course. Not beautiful, no, not ornamental the way my wife had been, but absolutely true, absolutely open, absolutely what she was—a highly intelligent, very talented pianist who read voraciously, and had a well-developed interest in history and politics. She was almost the same age as my elder boy, alarmingly, but she wasn't a'tall a typical seventeen-year-old. She was far more mature than any I'd met before, and I enjoyed watching her learn and grow and sharpen her technique as we discussed matters of principle and political policy. She was full of enthusiasm and passion, and I felt very much her mentor. Yet, that next year, after she'd turned eighteen, I suddenly discovered, very much to my surprise, that I loved her with something other than fatherly feeling.

"I was young myself, of course. Relatively speaking. Not quite thirty-eight. About the age you are now, I suspect. Yet even so, I chose not to speak of it. I waited more than another year. And when I did, she told me she cared for me too. And I suppose she did, in her own way. Even though she'd entered the University and begun to mingle with men her own age."

Rory pulled his tie off and stuffed it in the pocket of his black serge suit, and then he rubbed his temples as though they ached. "Naturally, I was aware of the dangers in establishing a relationship with Ellie. She might not know her own mind, or she might meet a younger man later and regret her attachment. Yet I felt it was worth the risk, and I gave myself to another person in ways I'd never thought I could. Though sexually, of course, I felt honor-bound not to take advantage. She was quite religious, you know, even then, and it governed the way she made choices. I wasn't a'tall religious myself, but I saw the value it had had for her when she was recovering from her parents' death, and I would never have wanted to belittle that or interfere in any way.

"So I waited. And then, in the best literary tradition, the middle-aged man and the young girl became secretly engaged the day she turned twenty-one." Rory took one last drag on his cigarette and smiled cryptically to himself as he stubbed it out. "Shortly thereafter, I gave a graduation party for my elder son. To which he invited Jonathan MacLean."

"More coffee?"

"If it's not too much trouble." Rory waited while Ben poured water into powdered coffee and put the kettle back on the stove. "Jon had met my son Richard when Richard was a first year science student and Jon was studying divinity at Edinburgh University, though by the time Richard completed his honors degree, Jon had his own church in Gullane. In any event, the dinner party was in July, and it was a lovely warm day, and we served hors d'oeuvres on the lawn before dinner.

"I'd hoped to announce our engagement that evening, though I hadn't yet had an opportunity to discuss it with Ellie. I'd even purchased two cases of Dom Perignon in celebration. And I remember thinking, rather ironically as it turned out, while I stood and looked on as Ellie and Jon met, that never in my life had I been as truly and perfectly happy as I was at that moment." Rory stared at the small brass ash tray for a minute, and then looked up past Ben. "We aren't allowed everything in life, are we? Or perhaps it's just that fate makes fools of us all."

"We're not given everything we want, no. But then I wouldn't call it fate."

"No? That's interesting. Perhaps that's a conversation we

should have another time. In any event, as Ellie and Jon talked, I stood on the stone veranda by the drawing room, ostensibly listening to an aged relative tell me about his gout, while I watched the life I'd hoped for wither and die before my eyes. You see, they both altered noticeably when they spoke to each other, even later after they'd been married for years. There was an intensity, and a vulnerability, and a businesslike propensity to discuss and debate, coupled with an obvious physical attraction. And I felt a nearly overpowering urge to rush across the garden and snatch Ellie away. Though I forced myself not to interfere, to give her a chance to really choose for herself without any pressure from me a'tall. And so they talked on and on, unable, seemingly, to tear themselves away. Although Ellie came to me dutifully more than once to see how I was, and fulfill her obligations. But I didn't want duty or obligation. And I slipped inside and told Rogers to put the champagne in the cellar.

"Naturally, I did the magnanimous thing." Rory arched his eyebrows over his large green eyes, and then ran a finger down the corner of his soft wide mouth, scraping a fleck of tobacco away and onto the edge of his ashtray. "I couldn't have borne Ellie's pity. And I released her.

"And not too surprisingly, they decided to marry quite soon. She asked me to give her away. But I couldn't. Though I did have the presence of mind to try to act as though I was over her and that it had just been a brief infatuation of the sort many older men feel for a younger woman. I helped her make the arrangements for the wedding and for the reception she wanted to have at home. And then I invented a business trip and left for Mikonos two days before they wed. Do you know Mikonos? It's a very small, very beautiful island off the coast of Greece that was utterly undeveloped at the time. And there I rented a crumbling villa and drank for a solid week, though I'd never drunk like that before or since. Still, I pulled myself together, finally. And I came back and took up my work. I saw Jon and Ellie seven or eight times a year. I was very correct. I refused to make myself any more ridiculous than I already felt, and only once did I act in a regrettable manner.

"And I did like Jon, you know. Very much, as a matter of fact. That was the worst of it in a way. I respected him tremendously, and I had to forego the pleasure of hating him for what he had. But of course I couldn't look at him without wishing. And so you see, on the surface, I have an excellent motive for wanting Jonathan MacLean dead. More concrete, at least, than any other I'm aware of."

"What was the act?"

"Sorry?"

"The one you regret."

"It's a personal matter I'd prefer not to discuss."

"I can understand that. But so is Jon's death."

"True." Rory paused and wound his watch before he crossed his arms across his stomach. "They came to stay last New Year's Eve, and I walked Ellie to their room while Jon was playing billiards with Richard, and I kissed her the way I used to. I apologized, of course. And I don't think she's held it against me. But she kept me from entertaining any sort of hope in that direction."

They were both quiet for a moment. The wind was battering the house, sweeping around it where the hill grew up to the moor, and the old house shook and sighed, while something metal clattered mechanically in the top of one of the chimneys.

Ben listened to the rain begin, pelting at the slates on the roof and pecking at the glass in the windows, while he absently rubbed the cleft in his chin.

Rory watched him, almost as though he expected Ben to

speak, and was slightly disappointed that he didn't. "Jane told me about your wife's death."

"Ah. So it almost amounts to the same thing. Either way, we've been left alone."

"Yes, we have indeed."

"Do you mind if I ask where you were when Jon died?"

"I was on my way to the office."

"Alone?"

"Yes. I'm often driven into town so I can work on the way, but that particular day I drove myself." Rory sat quietly, watching his thin gold lighter slide through his fingers, before he exhaled noticeably and looked at Ben. "I've been writing a series of articles on historical and contemporary authors, and I was down in Jedburgh to interview Jamison Tree. I spent the eleventh with him, and drove back to Edinburgh early the next morning."

"What time did you leave Jedburgh?"

"Between five and six, I should think. I'd awakened before four and decided to make an early start."

"Isn't Jedburgh fairly close to—"

"Holy Island? Yes, actually, it'tis. Two hours perhaps. Maybe a trifle more."

"Did you stay in a hotel in Jedburgh?"

Rory gazed at Ben impassively and then he looked away. "No. In a very small inn called the Bishop's Arms."

Saturday, May 20th

The old Bentley rolled north, purring like a large cat, swaying peacefully around curves, as Ben slept. It was probably a three and a half hour drive, much of it through the mountains, and they'd started at six, since Hamish MacDonald had agreed (with obvious irritation) to see Ben in Nairn at ten. Hugh was making steady time, humming Scottish ballads and bits from the Brandenburg Concertos.

And Ben woke up as they turned due east, having just left Inverness behind. "Where are we?" His thick wheat-colored hair had fallen in his eyes, and he felt cold and cramped, and he thumped his desert boots on the floor to get his blood moving.

"Fifteen minutes from Nairn, depending on the lorries."

"We haven't passed Cawdor?"

"No."

"I told Ellie I'd bring her some things from the house."

"That's alright. Cawdor's the next turning but one."

Ben stretched his arms over his head and rubbed his hands together, then licked his lips and shuffled through his pockets looking for a stick of gum. "I must have been out for quite awhile."

"It did look like you could do with a nap."

"Yeah, I stayed up too late."

"The sky looks more promising, doesn't it? We left the rain behind at Dalwhinnie. You know what they say, 'If you don't like the weather in Scotland, wait a quarter of an hour.'" Hugh glanced sideways at Ben and smiled.

And Ben thought how much Hugh had the look of the black Celts (as he imagined them, at least); the thick black hair and indigo eyes, the fair skin and pink cheeks and heavy dark beard of the fighting men and the poets who'd driven away the Romans and defended the forests for hundreds of years. "I really do appreciate your driving me up, you know."

"No, please, I enjoy a good run, and it's a relief to be able to be of help. I've felt terribly useless ever since Jon's death."

"Why?"

"Well, Alex and Jane provided the funeral tea—"

"Because the burial was in Dunkeld."

"Right, but even the day Jon died, Ellie had all the trouble of trying to find me, and when she did, I was obligated and couldn't get away."

"You were driving an American couple?"

"Yes, Mr. and Mrs. Harvey Miller from Winnetka, Illinois. I took them up the east coast toward Dunnottar, and on into Deeside the following day. Odd, really. That day Jon died. From the moment I arose, everything seemed to go wrong. And then when I heard about Jon, I—"

"Why? What went wrong?"

"Well, first of all, I was still up at Kilgarth. There were several small jobs Mary needed doing, and I'd been putting them off a bit, as one does. I had an easy week of it with my own work in town, so I decided to dash up to Kilgarth on the Wednesday and drive back into Edinburgh Thursday evening, to avoid the rush on Friday morning when I was to meet the Millers by half-eight."

"But you didn't drive back on Thursday?"

"No. Every task took longer than I expected. They always do, and I should've known. So, as it turned out, I had no choice but to stay the second night. Though I did leave early Friday, about six-fifteen I should think, to allow a bit of leeway for rush hour, which turned 'round to be a very good thing, because the traffic into Edinburgh was absolutely horrific."

"At least it's not as bad as London."

"For which I shall be eternally grateful. I honestly don't think I could cope with that sort of traffic every day."

"Did the Millers stay at the Caledonian? There seem to be more Americans there than anywhere else."

"No, they didn't actually. I collected them at the North British Hotel with several minutes to spare, only to discover that they'd brought an inordinate amount of luggage. Most of it wouldn't fit in the boot, so it had to be arranged in the back around Mr. Miller, which was not a circumstance to which he was accustomed. And then, much to my dismay, not one, but two tires blew on the way to St. Andrews."

"That must have been embarrassing."

"Yes. I had to arrange a taxi to take the Millers to the nearest pub after the spare went, while I procured the right sort of tire. Mr. Miller was obviously none too pleased. And then, when we finally arrived at our hotel, there was no record of our reservations. The matter was put to rights, thank God. But when one is escorting a party of visitors, one feels these little difficulties more deeply than when one is alone. There's really quite a heavy sense of personal responsibility."

"It must've been a long drive to Dunnottar."

"It would've been, yes, but we only went as far as St. Andrews. Mr. Miller could hardly contain his passion to play golf at the famous course, so we stayed at Rufflets, which is a lovely country house hotel nearby. I showed Mrs. Miller St. Andrews University and the ruins of the cathedral, while he spent the day on the course. He *is* an enthusiast. One of those really incorrigible golfers. For even though I arrived in Edinburgh fifteen minutes early at least, he was already waiting by the curb with the golf clubs he'd brought at considerable expense all the way from America, and he seemed impatient to be off even then. I really do think the punctures were almost more than he could bear."

"If that's the worst thing he ever has to put up with, he'll be a very lucky man."

"I am relieved that you've undertaken this, you know."

"What?"

"The investigation of Jon's death." Hugh looked sideways at

Ben with a serious, subdued expression as he wiped the damp off the inside of the windshield with a cloth he kept in the door. "The Northumberland police were clearly at a disadvantage because of the debacle with the picnic hamper. You know. Them not mentioning it, and us not knowing about it, till after the inquest. His death must have looked quite straightforward to them, and it seems a bit awkward trying to revive an investigation at such a distance. But if you can uncover something more substantive, or more concrete, then it will be far easier for us to officially reopen the case. As soon as I heard about the hamper, I told Alex there was something fishy afoot."

"I don't think we should talk to anyone else about it, though."

Hugh glanced at Ben before he flipped the turn signal dial on the dashboard and swept into a road on his right. "Have I already been indiscreet?"

"Not anymore than anyone else."

"You're referring to Rory, are you?"

"Others have heard about it too. And though there will be people who have to be told, we need to keep it as quiet as we can."

"Yes, I see."

"What's happening with the will?"

"Our solicitor has been on holiday in the Channel Islands, but he'll be back in the office the day after tomorrow. He'll come up to Kilgarth the following day, Tuesday, and we'll read the will there. Ellie and Alex and I thought we'd all drive down Monday and get settled in. Balnagard opens to the public the first of June, you know, and Jane has a great deal to sort out. I shall need to get back to the University quite soon myself."

"Kilgarth is near Dunblane?"

"Right."

"So it's fairly close to Linlithgow and Stirling?"

"Yes."

"What can you tell me about Jon's will?"

"Very little, I'm afraid. Jon was the least materialistic of men, and we never discussed that sort of thing a'tall. Of course, Ellie will inherit Kilgarth, thank God. It is wonderful in its way, but it's far too costly to keep up."

"Do you think she'll sell?"

"I imagine so. Though I don't really know. It's much too large for a single person. Or at least I would think so, if it were me. Here we are. Jon and Ellie's manse." He'd stopped in front of a two-story stone house with high white windows and a plain white door. "I do hope the kirk won't expect her to move before she's had time to decide what to do."

"Thanks. I'll be back in a second."

"Do you need me to come in?"

"I don't think so. Ellie gave me the keys and told me what she wanted."

She'd also told him where to find a good set of Jon's prints. And he knew he'd have to hurry to get to Nairn before ten.

Ben held the door for a woman with packages, and then paused by the pipe tobacco in Hamish MacDonald's small chemist shop. It was crowded with cardboard displays and shelves full of odds and ends, and it reminded Ben of the small town drugstores he'd grown up with in rural Michigan (except that this one didn't have a soda fountain with a marble top and a row of stools that swiveled).

Three middle-aged women were catching up on family news

by the diet aids, the nail polish, and the perfume, while a small boy studied the candy display and slowly counted his coins. A heavyset girl in her early twenties, who had a fondness for turquoise eye shadow, was working behind the back counter, where a large sixtyish gentleman in three-piece tweeds had just picked up a parcel with huge work-worn hands (having paid for it out of a very old leather coin purse with silver hinges). He had a kind shy face, and he was smiling broadly, as he said, "That's grand! Thank you. Just the job! Aye, just the job indeed!" as though he found himself deeply in her debt.

It wasn't the usual offhand "I suppose I might as well say thank you just to be polite" approach. It was part of the reason Alex and Jane had sold the house in London to raise their kids in Scotland.

"May I help you, sir?" The girl behind the counter was watching Ben shyly, having already stared at his desert boots and his obviously American Levis.

"Yes. I'm Ben Reese and I have an appointment with Mr. MacDonald."

"Oh, aye. I'll just nip back and tell him you've come." She smiled and ducked through the doorway to the left of the pass-through that opened into the room where prescriptions were made up and handed into the shop.

Ben could hear voices, but he couldn't understand the words.

And then she was back, adjusting the ribbon that held her plain brown hair away from her face. "If you'll step this way, I'll take you through to him."

"Thanks."

"Thair's no need to lead the man back, Janet! We've paying customers who require sairvice, and I'll not have them neglected!"

"I'm sorry, Mr. MacDonald, I only thought—"

"I know what you thought, and as usual we're of two minds." Hamish MacDonald was standing in an old white coat at the end of the narrow room that had floor to ceiling shelves on the left wall, filled with bottles and boxes of medicine, and a cluttered counter on the right beneath the pass-through to the shop. Small black reading glasses were hanging on the end of Hamish's nose, and he held a ledger in his left hand and a cup of tea in his right. "You can come in here if you've a mind to, though I hope this will no take more than a wee minute."

Hamish led Ben into a small dark room that seemed to be a depository for folding chairs and cleaning supplies, but also had a hot plate on a dirty wooden counter. He sat in one of the metal chairs beside a folding card table that was speckled with sticky spots and tea rings, and folded his arms across his softish stomach.

Ben ignored him, as he pulled a chair up to the other side of the table, and sat before he spoke. "I know you're busy, and I'll try not to take up too much of your time, but there are certain irregularities about Jon MacLean's death that have led the family to ask me to investigate it informally with an eye to reopening the case—"

"And why would you wish to contact me?"

"You're a very direct person, Mr. MacDonald. So I don't suppose you'll mind if I'm direct too. As I understand it, you and Jon MacLean didn't see eye to eye on several matters involving the church."

"Aye, there's much that could be said on that subject, but I don't intend to waste my breath, since you've come from the grieving widow and you're bound to have haird her side of it and be conformed to that in your own mind."

Ben pulled the sleeves of his shirt out past the cuffs of his brown corduroy jacket as he gazed imperturbably at short sallow Hamish MacDonald, with his muddy-colored hair and his grease spots scattered across his coat. "Mr. MacDonald, I don't want to prolong this interview any more than you do. I know that you were seen by an acquaintance of Jon's entering your room at the Bruntsfield Hotel in Edinburgh, quite inebriated and in the company of a woman of questionable character—" Hamish started to interrupt, but Ben raised his voice and talked over him. "A woman who, at the very least, was certainly not your wife. When Jon confronted you with this information, you agreed to resign from the Kirk Session, since behavior of that sort can't be overlooked in a position of spiritual authority. It's possible that someone in your situation might have felt that he would profit from Jon MacLean's death. You might not have wanted your wife to learn of that event. You might have felt that having such information in the hands of someone you considered an enemy was dangerous, that Jon might have been tempted to use it unscrupulously. I'm not in any way implying that you did in fact have anything to do with his death, but—"

"I should bloody well hope not!"

"But in order to eliminate you from any further investigation, I wonder if you'd be willing to tell me where you were on the morning of May twelfth?"

"And why should I tell you the first thing?! You're not a policeman! This is not a proper investigation, and you have no right whatever to intrude upon my privacy!"

"That's absolutely true. But there will be an official investigation, and cooperating with me now might make it possible for you to avoid the publicity of being involved in one later. Depending, of course, on what you were doing at the time."

Hamish MacDonald rose from his chair. Only to sit down

again and pull a handkerchief out of his back pocket. He wiped his forehead and folded it without comment. And then he drank the rest of his tea. "If you must know, I was visiting my spinster sister near Peebles."

"Which is how far from Holy Island? Two hours maybe, or two and a half?"

"And what if it'tis? That means nothing a'tall and you know it well!"

"Was there a particular reason that you went down to visit her at that time?"

"Aye, as a matter of fact, there was. My mother, who's over ninety, lives with my sister, and she'd gone down with pneumonia, so my sister rang me and asked me to make a visit. It was an inconvenient time, for I was endeavoring to complete an inventory, but I gave over my shop to my assistant, and drove down to Peebles on the Thursday, the eleventh. I arrived about six in the evening."

"And what did you do on the twelfth?"

"I got up about eight. I ate breakfast with my sister—"

"What time would that have been would you say?"

"Around a quarter to nine I suppose. And I left in the forenoon, by half-ten perhaps, and maybe a bit sooner. And I was home as you'd expect by evening. Eight or nine, as I recall, having stopped for lunch and dinner."

"I see. How's your mother now?"

"She's had a miraculous recovery."

Hamish had glared at Ben more or less from the beginning, and his tone of voice had been condescending at best. But when he'd made that reference to his mother, there'd seemed to Ben to be an added edge of irritation. "I will need your sister's name and address, if that's alright with you."

"Will you indeed! So you can corroborate my alibi!"

"Yes. Exactly." Ben was looking at Hamish without any sort of rancor or emotion. Which seemed to make Hamish even more irate.

"You've got a bloody nerve!" He spluttered first and then hesitated. He turned a pen over repeatedly, tapping the bottom of it and then the top on the table. But eventually he pulled a pad from the pocket of his pharmacist's jacket and wrote furiously, while Ben gazed at him across the table.

"Thank you. It was good of you to cooperate."

"I'll not be required to put up with your sarcasm as well, young man!"

"You're right and I apologize." Ben stood and put the paper in the inside pocket of his jacket.

"And why are you smiling may I ask?"

"No reason."

"Then I expect you can find your way out on your own!"

"I think I can manage. Thank you, Mr. MacDonald. I appreciate your help."

Ben smiled again on his way down the hall. Because Hamish, the married man, who'd had his fling in Edinburgh, had tried to hound a teenage girl out of the church for doing what he'd done without the treachery.

But then we all do it, Ben was telling himself, as he waved to the girl behind the counter. It's the usual beam-and-mote. The blind spots we've all got in some part of our lives or another.

The dark red door in the small gray stone cottage opened as soon as the brass knocker fell, and Katherine Burnett's cool brown eyes stayed fixed on Ben's face from the second she opened the door.

"Miss Burnett."

"Won't you come in, Mr. Reese? It's fortunate you were able to drive up today since you wish to speak to my aunt, for she'll be taking the train down to Holy Island first thing tomorrow morning. Please, sit down."

It was a small sitting room full of dark wooden furniture and overstuffed chairs, with deeply set windows and wide moldings painted in bright shades of yellow. The walls were papered with yellow flowers, and there were patterns on every cushion. And Ben, whose house was all white walls and empty spaces, was surprised, in a way. He would've expected something less fussy and more refined. And he was asking himself why, when Katherine motioned him toward her camelback sofa.

"So how may I help you, Mr. Reese?" She'd sat in an upholstered Victorian rocker, and was crossing her legs and adjusting her wool skirt, as she gazed at Ben like a teacher with a difficult parent.

"There are circumstances surrounding Jon MacLean's death that don't seem altogether straightforward, and Ellie and Hugh have asked me to look into it in order to determine whether or not there's reason to alert the police in Northumberland."

"I find that very surprising. Are you sure?"

"Yes."

"Why didn't the police investigate at the time?"

"They weren't aware of the significance of a particular piece of evidence."

"What piece of evidence?" Katherine Burnett spoke very calmly and with obvious control.

But Ben could see her hands tighten around each other, as she swallowed delicately and licked her lips. "I'm not able to discuss the evidence in any detail at the moment, but I wonder if you'd be willing to answer a few questions."

"I'm anxious to help in any way I can, of course. If Jon was murdered, which is what I assume you're implying, I would certainly want to see his killer brought to justice."

"Good. So would I."

"Though, with all due respect, may I ask why you, in particular, are considered qualified to undertake such a task?"

"Experiences I've had, both during and after the war, have led Ellie and Hugh to think I'm reasonably well suited."

"Then I shall assume they know better than I. You do seem far more businesslike than you did at the reception in Cawdor."

"Thank you. Maybe you could start by describing Jon's visit on Holy Island."

"There's not much to tell, really." She was turning a gold bracelet on her right wrist, while looking out the window beside her, a small casement window that was almost half-covered with ivy. "As I believe I told you in Cawdor, he stopped to see me the night before he died. About six, I should think. He told me he'd come by train to Berwick upon Tweed, where he was met by a friend of his, who then drove him on to Holy Island. We chatted for a few minutes about nothing in particular, and my aunt gave him tea before he left. Not later, I wouldn't have thought, than a quarter of seven. We offered him the spare room, but he was intent on camping where he'd camped as a boy, and he took himself off toward the dunes on the north of the island." Katherine shook her short smooth hair and then tucked one side of it behind her ear. She was wearing a pink sweater set and single pearl earrings, and both emphasized the delicacy of her bones and skin against the darkness of her hair and eyes.

"Do you remember the name of the friend who picked him up?"

"I don't, actually. I seem to remember it was a friend of his from Oxford, but I'm not absolutely certain. It could've been someone he knew at the University of Edinburgh."

"I assume Ellie would know."

Katherine didn't say anything. And her face was as unreadable as ever.

"You were at school with Jon when he was taking his divinity degree?"

"I wouldn't say we were actually at school together. We both attended the University of Edinburgh, but it's divided, as I'm sure you know, into very distinct and separate faculties, and we had only a moderate degree of contact."

"You'd known him since you were children, though?"

"Oh, yes. We lived near one another in Edinburgh."

"And you moved up here and became his parish secretary?"

"I was offered a position at an excellent girls' school in Inverness, yes." Katherine's eyes still held Ben's, but there was irritation in them now, dampened and suppressed, perhaps, but there nevertheless.

"Let's get back to the night he visited you on Holy Island. Can you tell me what he was wearing?"

Katherine looked away again, at the flower and fruit still life on the wall behind Ben. "As I recall, he was wearing a brown tweed suit and waistcoat with an informal shirt. I think it was a cream and brown tattersall plaid. He wore a solid brown wool tie and thick leather walking shoes with heavy dark socks."

"What kind of camping equipment did he have?"

"He was carrying an olive green rucksack on his back, with an army-issue blanket rolled and strapped beneath it." Katherine looked straight at Ben again and waited.

And Ben thought he saw a shadow of self-satisfaction, or

maybe a hint of slyness, in the small thin mouth and the half-closed eyes. And yet it was an accurate description that matched Ellie's account and Alex's memories of the inquest. "You're very observant. At least when it comes to Jon MacLean. Did he have a basket or a picnic hamper with him?"

"No. I told you that at Cawdor."

"Yes, you did tell me that, didn't you? So how would you describe your relationship with Jon?"

"We were childhood friends. We stayed in touch over the years. There's very little else that can be said on the subject. Though I can assure you that our friendship has nothing whatever to do with his death."

"Murder usually has a great deal to do with relationships though, don't you think?"

"Perhaps. I haven't made a study of it. All I can tell you is that I grew up in Edinburgh near Jon, and we subsequently wrote, or spoke, sporadically over the years. I attended his church in Cawdor, naturally, when I took a teaching job in Inverness. And I chose, as an act of charity, to become the parish secretary, to improve the quality of the various texts that are typed and produced for the parish."

"Really? As I understand it, your relationship with Jon was more complicated than one might expect between a minister and his secretary."

"I have no notion a'tall what you could possibly be referring to. Although it does sound like the type of gossip one might expect from a small provincial mind of the sort one finds in—" A tiny gray haired woman, very short but wiry, had appeared in the doorway from the dining room. "Ah, Aunt Dorothy. Come in. Miss Dorothy Burnett, Mr. Benjamin Reese. Mr. Reese is a friend of Lord Alex Chisholm's, and he's asking questions about Jon

MacLean. It seems that there's some question about his death, and they may be calling in the police."

"Surely not! Jon was such a wonderful man. Surely there couldn't possibly be anyone who would've wished him ill."

"Perhaps not. But there's enough that's suspicious about his death that we've begun trying to piece together any information we can about his actions Thursday night and Friday morning."

"We saw him Thursday night. Didn't we, Katherine?"

"Yes, Aunt Dorothy, I've just been telling Mr. Reese."

"He stopped by early in the evening, and we gave him a good tea. He didn't eat much though, as I recall. Just one cup and a wee biscuit. And then he rushed off to camp in the dunes."

"Is there anything else we can help you with?" Katherine was smiling politely from the edge of her chair.

"So the only time you saw him was for that few minutes on Thursday night?"

"Yes."

"Then I think that's everything. For the moment. Though I may have more questions later. Will you be here or on Holy Island?" Ben had turned toward Katherine.

"I shall be here, yes. Term doesn't finish until the end of June."

"And you Miss Burnett?"

Dorothy Burnett smiled at Ben as though she were pleased to be asked. "I? I'm setting off for home tomorrow. I live on Holy Island, you see. Katherine was just visiting me for the one week. I only came back with her so I could attend poor Reverend MacLean's funeral."

"Would you be willing to give me your address and phone number? I may need to contact you again."

"Yes, of course. I'll just pop out and get my bag. I should

have one of my visiting cards. The phone service isn't terribly dependable, but the number's there on the card."

She opened the front closet, and found her purse, and then handed Ben a small white card of the sort genteel ladies once carried, as he waited by the open door.

"Thank you." Ben smiled his most open innocent smile, and his eyes crinkled at the corners, as he slid the card in his wallet. "I really do appreciate your help." He nodded at Dorothy Burnett and stepped out onto the porch before he turned and smiled at Katherine. "It was especially significant that there wasn't any sort of basket in his possession, and no one else could have told us that."

"I'm glad I could help. Good-bye."

The door closed like a shot.

But not before Ben had seen the look of consternation that Dorothy Burnett had given Katherine.

CHAPTER SEVEN

Sunday, May 21st

"NOW, ONE WHOLE-GRAIN FOR JAMIE, one whole-grain and one white loaf for David, one—"

"But I don't want the whole-grain!" James's thin face was flushed, and his eyes were anxious, but he still spoke in a quiet, polite voice. "I'd rather have a sticky bun, Uncle Robert."

"Nonsense! You've had one already, and whole-grain is good for you. Look at all the crunchy parts! Makes you grow up to be a man! You know you'll get a cinnamon bun when they're done. Now, where was I?" Uncle Robert was sitting in Alex's chair at the end of the long oval table with two children on either side, both baskets of hot toasted homemade bread pressed close to his chest, and a look of serious concentration fixed on his warm red face. "I'll take a whole-grain, a second croissant, and a sticky bun as well, then that means Lizzy may have the white loaf and one sticky bun, leaving three croissants, one for John, one for David... Oh! It's you." Uncle Robert stared at Ben as though his arrival had been unimagined and might be a complication.

"Good morning, Sir Robert."

"Good morning. I suppose you'd like some toast, would you?" Uncle Robert sighed audibly. And then suddenly looked more hopeful. "There'll be more in a moment, I shouldn't wonder. Though perhaps you'd rather start with the fruit and cereal? It's over there, you see, on the sideboard."

Ben asked for a piece of whole-wheat toast and smiled.

"Ah, that's alright then! And I can recommend the honey without fear of contradiction. No, not that! The other side of the table, in the white pot. Lizzy, pass the honey to Dr. Reese. Cameron brought a new gallon jar over from the farm this morning. Lovely wild honey. Last year's crop, of course, but extremely fine. Now, where were we?"

"Do the Camerons live on the farm where the family will move when Balnagard opens?"

"No, no. No, that's BalMacNeil where we'll go, just up the road to the north. Balmuir, the Cameron's farm, is south. Two fields over, on the other side of that bit of fir forest."

"He's the gamekeeper?"

"Head keeper. Right."

"And he raises bees?"

"Always has done. There've been bees kept on at least one of the farms as long as anyone can remember. The butter comes from the estate too, of course. I expect you'll have noticed the flavor. Most people today don't realize how much they're missing with all the new centralization and regulation."

"Yes, I know what you mean. So this is wild flower honey?"

"It'tis, yes."

"It's good. It's thicker than what we usually have in the States too."

"Bit thin, is it?" Sir Robert looked sympathetic and flicked a finger at the crumbs that had caught in the center of his mustache.

"Alright on a croissant I suppose, but one wants something substantial to stand up and hold its own on a thick piece of wholegrain! Ah, here they come! Mrs. Cameron's cinnamon buns!"

Ruth Cameron had just laid a basket of them on the table and all four children said, "May I have one, please!" while Uncle Robert bellowed, "Hold on, hold on, don't grab!" Even though none of them had.

"Aye, so it's as I feared!" Mrs. Cameron planted her hands on her hips and watched with a slightly amused but still appalled expression on her face. She was a monumental woman, very tall and straight backed and heavy. And she had a large determined face; not stern, exactly, but serious. "I see you're teaching the children to be as greedy as some others I could mention, but won't, since I, for one, was brought up to have civilized manners!" She laughed, even though she still looked uneasy.

And Sir Robert smiled back, with ragged teeth and gentle eyes and no indication that he'd taken offense. "I simply cannot tell you how good it'tis to have you back!" His mouth was full of cinnamon bun and his enunciation was somewhat muffled. "Jane's a wonderful woman, of course, and a very fine cook, but she hardly bakes a'tall anymore. She seems to think the smallest dose of sugar will kill every one of us in our beds! Your baking, on the other hand, as I'm sure you know, is incomparable! Both rich and subtle as well."

"Flattery's terrible for the soul, Sir Robert, as you vera well know."

"That was not flattery, I was—"

"And I've not come back for good, you know."

"No?"

"I'm merely helping out a wee bit, with all the company in the house."

"I thought you were to cook for the tea room!"

"I'll train the cooks in the beginning, and I'll bake a bit when it's convenient, but it's time I had a rest. Aye, and look at the time! You children should be dressed by now! We'll be leaving for the kirk in a quarter of an hour. Your mother waited for you at table as long as she could, and then she asked me to send you up in time to get ready."

"I had my bath last night, so it won't take me long a'tall. I thought I'd wear my white cotton." Lizzy always spoke like a much older child (she'd started with complete sentences before she was a year), but she was still only six, with sticky fingers and a milk mustache and an old flannel nightgown turned wrong side out.

"I should've thought it would take ye a year to get the tangles out of your hair!" Mrs. Cameron chuckled, while patting Lizzy on the head. And Lizzy laughed.

"*I* think she looks like the Wreck of the Hesperous." John was still at the petulant and pimply stage, and he looked at Lizzy with elaborate disdain.

Which made Mrs. Cameron turn a cold gray eye upon him. "You needn't take that tone, young man. None of us have reason to be smug, and as the oldest you're expected to set an example in proper manners. I'm sure Elizabeth will look vera fine when the time comes to leave."

"Mrs. Cameron?"

"Yes, Dr. Reese?" She was tucking a stray wisp of salt-and-pepper hair into the small neat bun at the nape of her neck, when she turned and smiled at Ben.

"Would it be convenient for me to stop by your house and talk to your husband sometime today?" Ben had just poured a small amount of coffee in Jamie's milk, and Jamie was smiling, and stirring in a teaspoon of castor sugar.

"Of course. Though we will have to fix the time. Michael's already at the kirk, and this afternoon we're driving to our daughter's near Glamis, but we'll cairtainly be home by supper. Shall I send him up to you at Perach?"

"Whatever's easier for you."

"I'll send him up, shall I? About half-seven?"

"Fine. I appreciate it."

Mrs. Cameron nodded and went off into the kitchen, carrying plates and untying her apron, as a pair of high heels came clicking down the hall from the stairs.

"Ben?"

"I'm in the dining room."

"Could I speak to you for a moment?" Jane was standing in the door in a pale lemon suit pulling on her white kid gloves.

"Sure."

"The rest of you please take your dishes into the kitchen and run upstairs and dress! You too, Robert, or we'll be late, and we simply *cannot* embarrass Michael by straggling in at the last moment when he's reading the First Lesson."

The children went, with Uncle Robert rumbling behind them. And Jane waited to speak to Ben until they'd gone. "Alex just got a call from Ned Sutherland. It seems that Harold, the chartered accountant who'd gone off no-one-knows-where, reappeared at his home last night, and Alfred Dixon, who must have been watching the house, accosted him by the door and beat him senseless in the front garden before Harold knew what had happened to him."

"Did Harold call the police?"

"No. He won't, he says, for reasons of his own."

"I was going to try to talk to Alf this afternoon, so the timing might be interesting."

"Yes, it certainly might."

"Would it be convenient for me to borrow a car? He lives this side of Stirling."

"Of course you may, that goes without saying. But you might want to have Hugh drive you. It is simpler."

"We can decide after church."

"Did you see Ellie this morning?"

"No."

"She was out walking at first light, and when she came in, she couldn't even finish a piece of dry toast. I don't think she's slept since Jon died, and I know she's barely eating."

"That's probably normal, don't you think?"

"I don't know. Perhaps it'tis. But she doesn't look a'tall well. And I do wish there were some way we could help."

Ben found Alfred Dixon's tall stone house on a large plot on an old street on the outskirts of Stirling, set back from the road behind a row of trees and a wide circular drive.

He left Jane's gray Rover Saloon in the street, and walked toward the house, studying the windows. If anyone had been watching him they would have seen him searching his pockets and consulting a small piece of paper, or looking for numbers by the door.

But no one was. And Ben faded into the left side of the garden, snaking his way behind bushes and trees, until he'd examined the back lawn and the painted toolshed, as well as the gardens on both sides of the house.

Alfred Dixon didn't have a beehive.

At least not at his home in Stirling.

And Ben wove his way back to the Rover, and drove straight to the front door.

It was just before three, overcast and almost raw, when he climbed the shallow stone steps and pushed the brass button by the black door.

He could hear voices and footsteps long before it was opened by a medium-sized, middle-aged woman in taupe wool.

"Mrs. Dixon?"

"Yes?" She looked distractedly over her shoulder and said, "Don't disturb yourself, Alice, I've answered it already," as another woman of about the same age, who was wearing an apron and carrying a dust cloth, stuck her head out of the dining room a few feet down the hall and eyed Ben speculatively, before pulling her head in and turning on the sweeper.

"My name is Ben Reese, and I wonder if I could speak to Mr. Dixon. I'm a friend of Lord Alex Chisholm's, and I think Ned Sutherland told Mr. Dixon I'd be in touch."

"Oh. Well, I don't know. Alfred is in his office, and he doesn't usually wish to be disturbed when he's working." Her voice trailed off uncertainly and she patted her permanent out of habit, in the silence that had settled once the vacuum cleaner had been turned off.

"I'll go and see, shall I?" Alice had stepped into the hall without waiting for an answer and was already heading toward the back of the house.

"I suppose there are those who would be offended by the way Alice takes matters into her own hands, but I don't mind, myself. Of course, she didn't come to work two days this week, so she's here on a Sunday as a result. I'm giving a luncheon party tomorrow, and I simply must have help with the house."

Ben wasn't sure how to respond to any of that, so he smiled and said, "Yes, I can understand that."

"It's blowing again I see. Come in and let me close the door.

I've lived in Scotland twenty years, but I never shall become accustomed to this climate. Of course, there are quite a number of scientists who say it's the beginning of another ice age, and I shouldn't be surprised a'tall." She glanced at Ben, and then looked away and waited awkwardly for a moment, as though she were working her way toward a difficult decision. "I'm sure Alice will be back presently, and I don't wish to be rude, but do you think you'd be alright on your own? I was watching a program on the nuclear arms buildup and I hate to miss the finish. It's a terribly alarming situation that really does make one wonder how long the world will survive. Of course, it is awfully provocative, don't you think? The way the United States is putting its bases all over Europe?"

"*I* don't, no. I don't think it's nearly that simple."

"Really? Yes. I expect that's just the way an American *would* see it. Nationalism being what it is. That's the crux of the trouble, isn't it?" She almost smiled, almost sadly, while she played with a cameo ring. "Well… if you'll excuse me…"

"Of course. Go right ahead."

"Thank you. Perhaps we'll meet again." She nodded vaguely and turned back down the hall, pulling her cashmere sweater down over her knit slacks as she disappeared through an archway on the left side of the foyer.

It was probably less than a minute later that Alice and Alfred Dixon walked around that same corner.

"Reese?" It was clipped and cool, but not hostile, as the small brown eyes in the wide tanned face studied Ben analytically.

"I apologize for not phoning. I did try several times, but your line was busy. I wonder if I could speak to you for a few minutes?"

Alfred Dixon evaluated Ben silently, while he slid his hands in the pockets of his navy blazer. "I expect I can spare a few moments. Sutherland suggested, in a not very subtle manner, that he'd appreciate it if I did so, and I suppose I should accommodate him, at least while we're still negotiating. We can talk in my office, if you'll come this way."

They turned left into the side hall that led past the open door of the sitting room where Mrs. Dixon sat watching TV in semi-darkness, surrounded by what appeared to be stacks of old newspapers and magazines.

"It's DDT and nuclear war at the moment." Alf closed the door and walked on with short quick strides. "It's always been one thing, followed rapidly by another. The destruction of the world by this, and then that. It makes her rather depressed, as you might imagine, but it does give her an interest in life, and I suppose that's something."

The next door opened into Alf's office, which was filled with new mahogany and old leather and a row of gray metal file cases (looking incongruous against Georgian paneling) where Alf had been sorting and discarding. Two file drawers were open, and stacks of manila folders had been thrown on the tops of the cabinets, as well as on the floor and in the wastepaper basket.

Alf closed the drawers on his way past, and then sat back at his polished desk, with his hands still buried in his pockets.

"Is that Prince Philip?" Ben was in the guest chair closest to the door, looking at a wall of photographs of Alfred with various dignitaries, pointing to one of the largest.

"Yes. It was taken at a trade dinner in Hong Kong a year or two ago. So what can I do for you, Reese? You didn't drive down from Dunkeld to discuss my memorabilia."

"True. There's some reason to think that Jon MacLean's death may not have been accidental, and his family has asked me to gather whatever information I can to help them decide if they should ask the police to reopen the case. You were one of the last people who actually saw Jon alive, and we were hoping you might be able to help."

"I can assure you that if I could, I would. But the truth of the matter is I know nothing whatever about it. I saw Jon briefly in Cawdor—"

"On the tenth?"

"Yes, and yet according to the obituary in *The Scotsman*, that was two days before he died."

"Thirty-six hours is probably more accurate."

"Though even that's hardly a suspicious circumstance."

"Right. I didn't mean to imply that it was." Ben had been absently picking Balnagard dog hair off the knees of his corduroy pants, but he stopped then and looked impassively at Alf. "Your meeting with Jon must have been something of a disappointment." Ben waited. But Alf didn't react. "For one thing, Jon told you he'd decided not to sell you Kilgarth."

"It was a business reversal. Hardly the first. Obviously not the last." Alf took off the tortoise-shell reading glasses he'd been looking over and leaned back casually in his chair. He was quite short and slight and probably over fifty, with well-matched features and expensively groomed brown hair. His clothes were carefully put together. His wristwatch and his cufflinks were intended to be seen. And there was something premeditated in the way he moved and spoke and watched with silent eyes.

"Losing Kilgarth may only have been an inconvenience, but Jon also told you he knew you hadn't been honest with him. That you were working with an architect to turn the house into a hotel when you'd already agreed not to. Information like that, if it gets out, can damage anybody's reputation."

Alf didn't say anything. He stared at Ben and shrugged his shoulders before taking a cigarette from an inlaid box and tapping one end of it on his desk.

Ben had seen the swelling and the bruises on Alf's hands when they'd first met in the foyer. He saw the cuts as Alf lit his cigarette, even though he slipped one hand in his coat pocket again and dropped the other with the cigarette down beside his chair. "Jon also told you that he knew you were involved in another undertaking that was even more dishonest."

"That sounds like hearsay to me."

"We both know it's true. And if it were known, it would ruin your reputation. And reputation's important if you want to be accepted in 'society' and do business with 'all the right people.' And you obviously do. You've applied to several private clubs in Edinburgh and in London—"

"Our Ned has been quite talkative, hasn't he?"

"Not very. I had to call him up and ask pointed questions. I suppose reputation makes a difference too, if you want to be invited to elegant events. Like last year. When you were asked to the Royal Garden Party at Holyrood Palace, 'in appreciation of your contributions to international trade.' You consequently had very good reason to want to suppress the kind of information Jon referred to."

"That's rather naive of you. Honesty is a relative term. And those who draw up invitation lists know that as well as I. There are innumerable decisions made every day, in every sort of field, which may appear, at first glance, to be 'right or wrong' to an outsider. When those who actually grapple daily with the real complexities of those situations will see several defensible positions. Life isn't simple. And business decisions aren't easy."

"Selling to Egypt, even indirectly, during the Suez trade ban was a cut-and-dried violation of national law, even if the material involved had had no military application."

"I've given you more than enough of my time, Reese. I had nothing to do with Jon MacLean's death, and there's no reason I should submit to further angling for information or your insulting insinuations. I'm embroiled in a disagreement with my partner as you know, though you've only heard his side of the issues involved. There are, as a result, far more pressing matters that require my attention."

Ben gazed imperturbably at Alfred Dixon, while he pulled Jane's car key out of his coat pocket. "Where were you when Jon died?"

"I don't think that's any of your business!"

"Perhaps not. But you will have to tell the police. And assuming you have nothing to hide, telling me now might keep you from being questioned by them in a far more public manner. There appears to be . . what shall we call it? . . 'questionable behavior' in several areas of your life, and I think if I were you, I'd want to avoid a police investigation. I also imagine your wife might be interested in the fact that you were in Scotland on the tenth instead of the Orient, as you'd told her."

"Stooping to blackmail, are we! You're a right bloody meddler, and no mistake!" Alf's accent had been changing subtly. It was no longer the measured pronunciation of an educated Englishman. There were traces of the cockney he'd learned from his father, as well as the rhythms of the Glasgow docks, as he bristled at Ben across his desk.

"You also attacked Harold MacIntyre last night, which is certainly a police matter. And I'd be willing to bet your motives for beating him to a pulp are much the same as your motives might have been for wanting Jon MacLean silenced."

"What happened between MacIntyre and myself has nothing to do with Jon MacLean. I can also prove I was elsewhere when Jon died, should the police require that information."

"Good. I'm glad to hear it. But if you decide you'd rather talk to me than the police, I'm staying with Alex Chisholm at Balnagard." Ben laid Alex's card on Alf's desk, and then stood up and turned toward the door. "I'm up the hill on the left in the white house, before you get to the main gate. Don't bother to show me out. I'm sure I can find my way."

"On the contrary, I intend to see you do leave without threatening anyone else!"

Ben had eaten dinner on his own—bread and cheese and a can of tomato soup. And he was sitting in his thimble-sized living room in front of a wood fire, listening to the wind and the rain beat against the house.

He'd been considering how he should evaluate Alex's things, when the investigation of Jon's death was done. And he'd decided to start with the statuary, the porcelain, and the tapestries, because Alex would rather part with those than the books or the coins or the paintings. He'd need to burrow into the big library, and the muniment room too, and see what there was there. Though, of course, the gun collections were valuable as well. So there were a lot of options—in which the Eighth Earl of Balnagard had very little interest.

Alex had never been very practical. And he was lost in this century, in general. He hated big cities, and he couldn't manage machines, and his eyes glazed over during the shortest financial discussion. He was much more at home with forestry and crop management. With farm animals and pheasant and grouse. With cutting peat, or making butter and cheese.

And that led Ben to honey.

And the piece of notepaper he held in his hand. He'd found it in a sealed envelope under his kitchen door when he drove in from Stirling:

Dear Benjamin,

I saw Dr. Cooper (a friend of Alex's and a biochemist from Perth) at tea at the manse in Dunkeld this afternoon. He took me aside, and asked me to "tell Dr. Reese that the sample is what he thought it was, and he'll receive written confirmation shortly."

Does that make sense?

Jane

Yes. But did it make any sense that Alex hadn't known that sugar water's used to transport bees, when they'd been making honey at Balnagard since before he was born? Alex had acted as though he'd never heard of such a thing. And he hadn't made the connection with the sticky places in the basket.

He was also a mile from Holy Island the day Jon died. Closer than anyone except Katherine Burnett.

But why would Alex have wanted Jon dead?

He'd said a lot of complimentary things about Ellie. No, it couldn't be that. Alex and Jane were exactly what they seemed to be. Real. Though nothing could be discounted completely. Not yet. Even though Alex had been the one who'd set the investigation in motion. Because that can be a smoke screen too.

There were too many motives. Too many opportunities. Too many people with both. Hamish had reason, if twisted. He'd been raised on a farm and could easily know about bees. He'd also been in striking distance. Alibi still unconfirmed, since his sister seemed to be away from home, or at least wasn't answering her phone. Katherine had been right there on Holy Island. And she seemed oddly uncomfortable whenever baskets were mentioned. There was the man from the mental institution too, whatever his name was, who'd hated Jon and threatened him, who'd also been at the funeral. Nothing about opportunity or abilities known. Rory was still in the running. Love and jealousy and only a stone's throw away. And Alf, of course. With motive. Maybe. But no data on opportunity or knowledge of beekeeping with which to work.

Ben put his feet up on the coffee table and his hands behind his head, before he muttered the word *motive*. Were any of them strong enough to actually make somebody murder Jon MacLean? Obviously they had been in other cases. Jealousy, fear, frustrated desire and the rest of them. But were they this time in this case?

Of course, the will might change the look of it. Wills have a way of bringing more than motives into focus. Alex was the executor of Jon's will, and Jon had apparently bequeathed him his Roman artifacts. Maybe there was more there than met the eye. Even though it seemed unlikely. Presumably Ellie would be the major beneficiary of whatever there was. But there could be surprises. Or some sort of twist he couldn't see now.

And what about Ellie? Could he absolutely eliminate her as a possibility? Maybe she'd been jealous of Jon's relationship with Katherine for years, and had finally gone over the edge.

Ben had just popped a large crumb of Cheshire cheese in his mouth and added half a cracker, when he stopped chewing and listened. He thought he'd heard something. Somewhere in the house. And he strained to listen past the rain and the wind and the crackle of the fire. It was too early for Michael Cameron.

Unless one of them had gotten the time wrong.

But he'd better go see if there was someone at the kitchen door. No one ever came to the front where he was. They went to the back where the turnaround ended by the kitchen.

Alfred Dixon was standing in a trench coat with his collar up, huddling against the rain on the other side of the glass door.

"It looks pretty nasty out there." Ben said it to make conversation, while Alf took off his coat.

"I couldn't see the road in places, on the last stretch coming from Dunkeld." Alf wiped the rain off his face with a handkerchief, and then tucked it in his inside coat pocket. "The point is, I've come to convey a piece of personal information."

"Shall we go in the living room?"

"It won't take a moment."

"How 'bout coffee or tea? The water's hot."

"Alright. Coffee, if it's not too much trouble."

Neither of them spoke while Ben made two cups of instant. Alf just sat at the kitchen table, with windows all around him, while the last of the light faded behind his back. "Thanks. May I have an ashtray?"

Ben dug it out of a cupboard and set it on the old pine table.

"I've decided to tell you where I was when Jon was killed, but I shall only do so if I have your word that you won't reveal what I'm prepared to say *except* to the police. And then only if it's absolutely necessary."

Ben considered it, and then agreed.

"I have your word?"

"Yes, you have my word."

"You can count on me holding you to it." Alf lit a cigarette, and exhaled slowly and deliberately, while staring at the clutter on the table. "I'm involved with another woman and have been for many years. I came back to Scotland on the eighth and stayed in her apartment through the thirteenth. I spoke to her today after you left and told her about the conversation we'd had, and she's quite determined that I explain the situation. So if you—"

There was a knock on the door, and when Ben turned and looked, Michael Cameron was squinting through the streaming glass.

"I've got an appointment, Alf, but it won't take long. Would you mind sitting in the living room until I'm through?"

"Alright."

"Thanks."

Alf picked up his mug and his ashtray and walked through the only other door there was. He was just shutting it behind him as Ben opened the outside door for Michael Cameron.

"Ruth told me you wished a word, Mr. Reese, but if it's not a convenient time, I'd be happy to come back later."

"No, this is fine. And I appreciate your coming here."

"Not a'tall." Michael Cameron had pushed the dark green hood away from his face, and he was standing carefully on the doormat, as though he'd rather slit his throat than get water on the old brick floor.

"Come on in and sit down."

"If you're sure?"

"Of course. Would you care for some coffee or tea?"

"No, thanks. I've just finished a pot of tea. So how can I help you, Mr. Reese?" He'd hung his mackintosh on a peg by the door and left his boots on the mat, and he was just sitting down at the end of the table.

"I understand you keep bees."

"Always have done."

"Then am I right in assuming that if you wanted to transport a small number of bees, you'd spray them first with a solution of sugar and water, the same way we would in the States?"

"Oh, aye. Small number or large, either one. It quiets them like. Makes them docile. They're feeding, you see, on the sugar, licking it off themselves and each other. And they won't become agitated or disturbed a'tall when they're feeding."

"I see. And are there magazines about beekeeping in Britain?"

"Aye, though I've never read one. I learned from my father, and he from his, and I've never seen the need. Nor had the time, really." Michael spoke in a deep gentle voice, and when he stopped he seemed to see no awkwardness in silence. He ran his hands down his thick black beard and smoothed the sides of his mustache with fingers half-covered by brown wool gloves.

"Has his lordship ever been involved in the honey making or the beekeeping, like he's been with the horses and the other estate animals?"

"As a lad, he was a wee bit. And sometimes now when we're separating the honey, the bairns and his lordship will come and watch. But he's not had the interest in bees. He knows the managing of the moor, the grouse population and the pheasant, and how to control tick, but…" Michael shook his graying black-haired head slowly and settled into a comfortable silence.

"Who helps you with the bees?"

"My eldest son, William. It's not been long since we finished cleaning the hives and readying them for the season. Bees are dormant and in the hives, you see, over the winter, so there's cleaning to be done in the spring."

"Is there anyone else on the estate who's shown a particular interest in bees?"

"No. Not that comes to mind."

"Have you given away bees or sold any in the last few months?"

"No. Not to anyone." He looked at Ben calmly and said nothing more.

"Well. Thank you. That helps me a lot."

"Then I suppose, if there's nothing else?"

"No. I think that's everything."

Michael had pulled his Mac on and was just stepping into his boots.

"You're a lucky man to be married to a cook like Mrs. Cameron."

"Aye, and for thirty-five years and more. Good night, Mr. Reese."

"Good night and thanks again."

Michael Cameron smiled and turned to go. But then he looked back and hesitated. "May I ask you a question, Mr. Reese?"

"Sure."

"Are you asking about bees because of young Jon MacLean? Are you thinking that maybe he didn't die natural after all?"

"The family just wants to make sure."

"Aye. I can well understand that. So I take it you must be wondering if someone could've arranged about the bees somehow, and brought about Jon MacLean's death?"

"Yeah, more or less."

"You've asked about his lordship too. And I'd like to say a word on his behalf."

"Go ahead."

"I've known him since the day he was born. I've seen him with gentry, and I've worked with him with the lads on the estate, and I know him to be a vera kind man indeed."

"Yes, I'm sure you're right."

"When my daughter's first child lay ill, and dying, as it turned out, there was a wait getting the poor wee thing into a National Health Hospital. Lord Chisholm put her in a private hospital straightaway, at his own expense, at a time when I happen to know he was vera strapped himself. He paid for the operation. A ruptured appendix, as it turned out. And he's never let us pay him back. He wouldn't hurt anyone, Mr. Reese, least of all Jonathan MacLean."

"I know what you mean. I feel the same way."

"Well. I'll leave you to it then."

"Thank you, Mr. Cameron."

"You're vera welcome."

"I would appreciate it if you wouldn't mention that there's any question about Jon's death."

"I understand. And ye have my word."

"Alf?" Ben opened the door to the living room at the same instant Alf dropped into a chair by the fire.

"I was glancing through the issues of *Country Life* over on the other table. It's quite a valuable collection. They go back almost thirty years."

Ben said, "Do they? I hadn't noticed," while wondering if Alf had a particular reason for explaining what he'd been doing. "You'd just finished telling me that you were staying with your mistress the week Jon died."

"Yes. In Glasgow. We're clearly taking a very great risk in trusting you, and I, for one, am not a'tall sure it's wise. Still, Marjorie is absolutely bound and determined to keep my name out of any police investigation, and she's insisted that I give you

her name and telephone number so you can speak to her as well."
Alf stood and handed Ben a folded piece of paper, and then buttoned his navy blue blazer. "So there you have it. And it's time I got back."

"So you were with her in Glasgow from the eighth to the thirteenth?"

"Right."

"Thanks. I won't mention it to anyone except the police. And not to them, if I can avoid it."

"There's one other point I wish to emphasize. If you don't treat Margaret with respect, you'll have to answer to me."

"I'd treat her with respect, regardless."

Neither of them said anything else until Alf was standing on the gravel. The rain had stopped for a moment, and he stood in the glow of the outside light, pulling his driving gloves out of his pockets.

Ben said, "Thanks for your help," from the doorway.

But Alf didn't answer. He nodded noncommittally and then opened his car door.

He'd just backed around the side of the house and begun to turn down into the lane, when Ben picked up the piece of paper that had fallen out of Alf's left pocket as he pulled out his leather glove.

It was a parking lot ticket, dated the day Jon MacLean died, from a parking garage in Newcastle upon Tyne.

Newcastle is probably fifty miles south of Holy Island.

And the time on the ticket was 11:15 A.M.

Ben shook his head in amazement, and then whistled the beginning of Beethoven's Fifth as he took the ticket into the kitchen, wondering what the chances were that Alf would drop it without noticing, right in front of him.

Almost too good to be true?

And yet Alf wouldn't deliberately plant a piece of incriminating evidence. Would he?

Not unless Jon's murder was a lot more complicated than Ben thought.

Ben was sweating by the time he'd finished his calisthenics. And he stood in the new tile shower and let hot water run over him for a long time, savoring the feeling as his muscles relaxed, while he breathed in the heat and the steam.

His scars looked whiter than the rest of his flesh (the long jagged gash across his left ribs, the slick-looking bullet holes on his arms and his legs and his torso, the broad incision that cut through the muscles the length of his left arm and up around his shoulder toward his back). But Ben didn't pay any attention. He just dried himself off with a towel he'd taken from the cupboard, while he planned what to pack for Kilgarth.

He was standing naked in front of the sink, just beginning to brush his teeth, when he noticed that the rug under his feet felt cold and wet. He wondered sort of absent-mindedly why that was. And then, as he was turning off the faucet with his left hand, he reached for the hand towel on the electric towel rack on his right.

His right hand touched the metal bar.

And two hundred and twenty volts shot through him.

His whole body clenched and shuddered, and he couldn't pull away from the rack. His hand was frozen in a death grip around the top horizontal bar. And a searing, relentless, white hot jolt burned into him.

All his muscles were clamped and contracted. His entire body was shaking and jerking.

And he couldn't survive much more of it.

PULL THE PLUG!

PULL THE PLUG NOW!

He had to swivel around so his left hand—the injured hand, the hand with the index finger that didn't bend—could slip behind the tall rectangular rack and yank the cord from the socket near the floor. And he had to let go of the hot water knob first. He hadn't even realized he was holding it.

DON'T TOUCH THE RACK!

YOU'RE DEAD IF YOU TOUCH IT AGAIN!

Ben leaned down, and around, and slid his hand behind the rack and felt for the cord. Blindly, mindlessly, unable almost to think, he found the plug and yanked it out.

The metal bar released him. And he dropped to the floor, and lay panting and shaking and quivering on his left side, on the cold wet rug and the icy tile.

He was twitching, pulled in on himself like a small child, curled in a fetal position. And then he was up on his hands and knees. Swaying. And about to buckle.

Get up! Now! Get yourself up off the floor!

When he could push himself all the way up, he sat on the edge of the tub with his head in his hands. He was freezing. Naked and wet and sitting on cold enamel, shivering uncontrollably. He made himself stand up, after a few minutes. Though he had no idea how long it took. And then he forced himself to walk into the bedroom.

He found sweat pants and a sweater and thick socks, and sat down again, this time on his bed, and talked to his stomach for a minute. It was rolling around unpleasantly, and he swallowed against it, and thought about everything else.

He pulled the sweater on first, slowly and painfully. Every

muscle in his body ached. Especially his right arm.

He shuffled down the turret stairs in his socks and made himself tea in the kitchen. He added castor sugar to help with shock and drank it by the fire in the living room. His whole body was in rebellion. He was still weak and a little disoriented. Almost like he was fighting a concussion.

He sat in the flickering light for quite awhile, ticking off names. Watching Alf drop into a chair as the door opened. Asking himself who else had opportunity and the necessary knowledge to do what he thought had been done.

Then he got a screwdriver and a pair of pliers from a drawer in the kitchen and took them upstairs to the bathroom.

The rug in front of the sink had definitely been wetted down. Thereby making it more likely that Ben Reese would be burned to a crisp.

Likely. Not certain. Not like bee stings and Jon MacLean.

But having his hand on the metal knob had helped too. Having a hand in water would have worked even better, and could have happened just as easily.

So was it meant as a warning? Or was it a serious attempt that failed?

Ben thought about the implications while he took the towel rack apart at the bottom left-hand corner, where the cord came out of the plastic housing.

The ground wire had been cut and the hot wire had been stripped and shorted to the metal in the tubular frame.

Exactly as Ben had expected.

He sat on his heels and stared at the wall and smiled at the wonders of cause and effect.

Of course, if the British had used different voltage, 110 instead of 220, it wouldn't have been such a close thing.

But they didn't.

And precautions had now become necessary.

CHAPTER EIGHT

Monday, May 22nd

"HOW LONG AGO DID HUGH LEAVE with Ellie and Mrs. Atwood?"

"I would say forty-five minutes before we did at most. I watched them pack the car from my dressing room window. Yes, and it wasn't long after they left, that I saw a very curious sight from that same window. I don't wish to pry, Benjamin, and yet I wonder if I might ask what were you doing under the car this morning?"

"Trying to make sure it hadn't been sabotaged."

"I see! Yes. I never would've thought of that." Alex's face was tight and distracted as he watched Ben nurse the Rover through a hairpin turn. "It was a miracle you weren't killed."

"Last night? Yeah, it was." Ben was driving south toward Kilgarth on a one lane, winding road, and he'd just snaked around a sharp bend down into a narrow glen with pale green bracken on the hills and a shallow stream in the valley, close to the left side of the road. "So basically you're saying that anyone at Balnagard could've gotten a key to Perach?"

"Yes. All the keys, including the ones to the outbuildings, are clearly labeled, and they hang on hooks in a cupboard in the estate office, straight down the long hall past the gun room. We lock the office quite conscientiously once the castle opens to the public, but there's never seemed to be a need before the first visitors arrive."

"So whoever sabotaged the towel rack knew Perach had one. Knew that I was staying there. Had access to the Castle. Knew where to find the keys. And was able to do the wiring. That's got to limit the possibilities."

"Even so, there must be several, right on the estate. We have builders who repair and restore and can turn their hand to anything. Any farmer today, as well as the groundsmen, the gillies and the keepers, all have to be terribly mechanical. Though it leaves me out, I'm ashamed to say, since I'm hardly capable of managing a can opener." Alex smiled half-apologetically and ran a finger along the inside of his shirt collar. "I've involved you in a very dangerous situation and I feel terribly responsible."

"Don't. It's not your fault, and it won't do any good. I just hope I can help."

"You will. Without doubt."

"I can't see what motive there'd be for one of the estate workers. Unless the towel rack attempt had nothing to do with Jon's murder. And that's possible. Even if it's unlikely. I helped train a group of British commandos in Wales during the war. Maybe I made an enemy I haven't recognized. Yet that's not to say there isn't a connection between Jon and one of your estate workers that we don't know anything about. But Alf Dixon was right there, conveniently alone in my living room." They'd come to a Y, in the middle of green peaks and sharp descents, and Ben studied the options with the gearshift in neutral and his foot on the brake. "Which way do we turn? Right? Which I assume is south?"

"Oh dear! Toward Crieff? I think. Is that right? No no! Yes, Crieff!"

Ben smiled and said, "Just as I thought!" as he reached for his ordnance survey map. "Alf could've run upstairs while I was talking to Cameron, but he would've had to have known there was an electric towel rack, and where to find it, and brought the tools along with him too. Even then, he couldn't have counted on being left alone."

"He could have asked to be shown the loo."

"That's true. Why didn't I think of that? Although I'm not sure he would've had time to take it apart and put it back together. But we can test that, of course, later. We do have to turn right toward Crieff."

"You must also remember that a very large number of houses in Britain, certainly of our sort, could be absolutely counted on to have an electric towel rack. The dampness, you see, and the expense of central heating. Many of our homes are still without it, and the owners of the rest rarely allow themselves to turn it on."

"Then maybe the real question is who else knew I was up at Perach? We should ask Jane if anyone called for me and was told I was staying there. Everyone at Balnagard knew. Including Rory."

"Speaking of Rory, John and David were riding on the moor up above Perach yesterday afternoon while you were off to Stirling, and they said Rory had come back from Gullane."

"Why would he drive all the way back up to Balnagard?"

"We don't know for certain that it was Rory, really. They saw an MG like his, same color and model apparently, which they seem to think is rather rare, running back toward Dunkeld from up by the house, and they simply assumed that it must be he. I can't think why he would've come back all that way on the

Sunday, having just left for home the morning before."

"Time will tell, I suppose." Ben hummed something quietly improvisational as he eased the Rover down the steep narrow street through the center of Crieff, threading his way around mid-morning traffic. "So who else at Balnagard would have known how to rewire a towel rack?"

"Uncle Robert. Before he came to us, he lived in a ramshackle old vicarage down in Yorkshire, and I know he did most of the repairs himself."

"I assume we can eliminate Jane and Ellie?"

"Yes."

"And Mary Atwood and the children?"

"Right. None of them has any knowledge of electrical repair. Whether or not Hugh might be able to manage it, I couldn't say. His father could have. But Hugh's a trained geologist, not an engineer. And of course, he could never have killed Jon."

"Ellie says it takes almost five hours to get from Kilgarth down to Holy Island. And then another two hours north from Holy Island up to Edinburgh."

"I would say so, yes. We know when Hugh left home, and when he fetched the Americans in Edinburgh, so he's obviously well in the clear. I can't imagine him ever wanting to kill anyone, that goes without saying. But I'm absolutely certain he would *never* have killed Jon. No, I've known Hugh all his life, and he's a very civilized chap. Very reasonable and accommodating. He and Jon always got along extremely well."

"Yeah, I'm sure you're right."

"Hamish, on the other hand . . no, he wouldn't have known you were up in Perach. Katherine, either, for that matter. Unless, of course, they'd called."

"Exactly."

"When do you think the towel rack was tampered with? When you were down in Stirling in the afternoon?"

"Maybe. Who was doing what while I was gone?"

"I know Hugh took Mrs. Atwood to see Blair Castle, and they didn't return until shortly before dinner. Mary hadn't seen it, and we all thought an outing might do her good. The rest of us were home. Except for Jane, who was off taking tea at the manse. Alfred clearly made a point of coming to see you."

"And I did threaten him mildly, in the afternoon. I made him think I might talk to his wife, and I let him know that I know about the nerve gas precursor."

"So if he did kill Jon to keep him from revealing that ignominious affair, he'd want to silence you too because of your investigation. Even if he does say he has an alibi for Jon's death. What was it, by the way, this alibi of his? You haven't said."

"I told him I wouldn't discuss it with anyone but the police."

"I see. Yes. And no gentleman would betray a confidence."

"Which reminds me. Please don't mention the towel rack episode to *anybody* else, even Ellie. Alright?"

"Of course. Whatever you say."

"There were other times the towel rack could have been sabotaged too. I ran before breakfast, and that took awhile. Although the rack was still alright when I showered. Either that, or I never touched the metal. I went to church too—"

"We all went together, every one of us staying in the house. So that must mean it was tampered with in the afternoon."

"It could've been. I was gone for three or four hours."

"Have you a theory now as to who Jon's murderer might be?"

"Not really. But I couldn't talk about it at this stage even if I did. I might slander an innocent person. And it might be hard for you to treat everyone the way you would normally."

"Yes, I do see that. And I would want that same sort of consideration, if it were I in danger of being blackened."

"I thought you would." Ben glanced at Lord Alexander Chisholm, the Thirteenth Thane and the Eighth Earl of Balnagard, and laughed.

Alex smiled back, looking slightly disconcerted, while he tried to find a better way to fold his storklike legs.

Forty-five minutes later, they'd passed a high wrought-iron gate beside a small stone gatehouse and were weaving back between pastures and soft green hayfields on a drive lined by old trees. They'd gone a little over half a mile when they curved around an ancient cedar of Lebanon and saw Kilgarth for the first time, sheltered by beeches and evergreens, on the top of a gentle rise.

It was a long, gray stone, Georgian farmhouse with a wide flagged porch above shallow curved steps. Which was where Hugh had left his Bentley, right below the teal blue door.

It was an arched double door, and the right half was standing open. And as the Rover's tires hissed through the gravel, Mary Atwood flew onto the porch. She was standing like a wren with its feathers fluffed, almost hopping from foot to foot. As soon as Ben opened his door, she shouted, "She's gotten a poison-pen letter! And with all she's had to bear, it's too dreadful, it really is!"

Ben took the stairs two at a time (which wasn't actually too unusual) and found Ellie in a chair by the front staircase holding a piece of typing paper loosely in her lap.

Hugh was next to her, in the middle of a snarl of suitcases, looking like he wanted to do something useful, but had no idea what that might be.

"Anonymous, I suppose?"

"Of course." Ellie handed it to Ben, her green eyes burning in her thin face.

Hugh had moved a suitcase and stepped close enough to Ben to read the letter, and he said, "Good heavens! It's absolutely pornographic! Why would anyone do such a thing?" As Alex approached from the other side.

The envelope had been typed, and mailed in Aberdeen, but the letter itself was pasted together out of black-and-white cut-outs from a standard newspaper.

how does it feel _____?
no man no baby no job
nothing but just desserts
you won't like living alone
not after I get through with you
and maybe you won't
who knows
you witch you _____
you American ____ _____

"That's monstrous! Don't pay any attention to it, Ellie." Alex knelt on one knee beside Ellie's chair and took her right hand in both of his. "I have no doubt that Ben will get to the bottom of it in short order!"

Ben was studying the paper and the envelope with the magnifying glass on his key ring, and he shook his head and said, "We *hope* Ben gets to the bottom of it, even though he hasn't dazzled us so far with his performance. Is this the only letter you've gotten?"

"Yes. Too bad it won't be the last." Ellie smiled thinly and touched the bone above her left eye as though her head ached behind her eyes.

"I'll take your things up so you can get settled in whenever you'd like. I thought perhaps the back bedroom rather than—"

"Jon's and mine? Thank you, Hugh. I appreciate it."

Hugh started up the stairs, moving purposefully and slowly, as though thought and order could dispel the malicious and the unexpected.

Before he'd gotten to the landing, Ben asked Mary Atwood if she had any of Jon's parish newsletters.

"Yes, of course." She'd been hovering beside him, not quite wringing her hands, but looking like she wanted to while making soothing noises in Ellie's direction. "I asked Jonathan to send them to me as soon as he was given his first kirk in Gullane."

"Could you find one for me? A recent one?"

"I'll try. They're monthly, and I discard the old when the new arrives, but I can cairtainly look."

"There's something else I wanted to ask you too." Ben put his arm around her shoulders and led her down the hall away from Alex and Ellie, her white curly hair barely reaching his shoulder, as she tilted her face up toward his.

"Mother isn't here."

"I didn't come to see your mother." Ben looked at the tall emaciated man who was holding the door halfway open and peering around the edge as though he'd rather be somewhere else. He was probably in his late twenties, but he looked older around the eyes. Deadened somehow, or injured, or prepared to avoid a blow of some sort; physical or emotional or imaginary maybe.

Ben told himself not to make judgments out of his own preconceptions, and then smiled before he spoke, slowly and softly and more carefully than normal. "Actually, it's you I wanted to see, Gerald. I'm Benjamin Reese."

Gerald looked at him without much interest. Like he was in his line of vision, but that was all.

"I called yesterday. Remember? You said you'd see me this morning around eleven."

"Did I?" He tugged at a tuft of light brown hair and then scratched the side of his face. He seemed to be considering what he ought to do as though decisions weren't something he made.

"Is it alright if I come in? It won't take long, and you might be able to help someone whose husband just died."

Gerald Pilcher backed away from the door, then turned his back on Ben and shuffled away in his carpet slippers. Ben shut the door and followed him slowly through the narrow center hall.

He smelled of cigarettes even at a distance, and the sitting room was choked with cigarette smoke, ancient, apparently, as well as current. The curtains were drawn and it was hazy and dark. The only light, except for the TV, was an ineffectual floor lamp between a rocking chair and a side table that was covered with ash trays and cigarettes. It was a bare room, colorless and nearly empty. No plants, no books, nothing on the walls. Just one chair, one footstool, two tables, and a television on a wire stand. There was no program being televised, but it was turned on, and the salt and pepper screen flickered and buzzed inescapably.

Gerald sat down in the upholstered rocking chair next to a burning cigarette he'd left in one of the ash trays, and Ben sat on the ottoman, after moving it toward the end table.

It was the only expression of anything personal in the room, Gerald's end table. For there was a picture in the middle of it of a breathtakingly young man in the khaki shorts, knee socks, and tam-o-shanter that the Black Watch had worn in North Africa. There was a slingshot in front of the picture and a model airplane behind it, along with other pictures of that soldier as a boy. There was one of him in the Boy Scouts, and another at the beach, and a third with him holding a horse in a paddock with some part of the highlands in the distance. The smallest picture was in front, and it showed the same boy, maybe thirteen or fourteen, straddling the limb of a tree, with a toddler on the ground looking up at him.

"Is this your brother?"

"Yes."

"I bet he was a good soldier."

"He was a war hero."

"What was he like?"

"He was tall. He won races."

"Running track?" Gerald nodded. "In school?"

A calico cat with a white chest and a white stripe on its nose sauntered nonchalantly into the room and stopped in front of the television. It stretched and feathered its fur and then stalked over to Ben, where it sat rather abruptly and gazed condescendingly at his face.

"What's her name?"

"Daisy." Gerald Pilcher lit a new cigarette from the butt of the old and began rocking back and forth, pushing the chair farther and farther till it was almost back as far as it would go.

Daisy jumped in Gerald's lap, and he slowed his rocking. She curled up and licked her paws and then lay still as he stroked her back, her eyes damped down into yellow slits.

"It must be nice to have a cat around. I don't know why, but I've never had one." Ben waited. But Gerald didn't say anything. "So was your brother a lot older than you?"

He nodded, a slow deliberate nod.

"How much?"

"Eleven years."

"What was his name?"

"Dennis."

"I bet you really looked up to him when you were a kid."

"He was my friend. He was murdered in the war." Gerald was so thin. His face was so pale, stretched like rice paper across his bones and faintly yellowed, almost as though the cigarette smoke had stained his skin.

"It looks like your brother did a lot of things outside. Scouting, and riding, and climbing trees. Do you do things outside?"

"Not since he died."

"You did go to Jon MacLean's funeral. That was outside. I thought it was beautiful there by the river."

Gerald didn't say anything. But he pushed his chair back farther than before.

"Why did you go to his funeral?"

"I wanted to see him put in the ground. I wanted to see them throw dirt on his coffin. My brother's buried in the desert. I don't even know where. He was a bad man and he murdered my brother and I'm glad he's dead! He should have been buried alive!"

"Do you know what Jon died of?"

"A bee stung him." Gerald was rocking faster and he lit another cigarette from the other, even though it wasn't half gone. He laughed, high and hard. And then it sounded like it died in his throat. "Bees don't sting unless you're afraid. He was a coward. And he murdered my brother."

"Why do you think he killed your brother?"

"Because he was a coward."

"I mean what reason do you have for believing that he killed him?"

"Dennis told me."

"Your brother?"

"Yes."

"I see."

"He wouldn't help Dennis and Dennis died."

"Did you want to kill Jon MacLean?"

"Yes. I'm not supposed to talk about it." Gerald had started tapping his nails against the artificial leather on the arm of his chair. But then Daisy stood up and rubbed her head against his chest. And he stopped rocking and put his cigarette in the ash tray and wrapped his arms around her.

"You did try to kill him once, didn't you?"

"I tried to run over him with the car. I waited for him. I waited till he stepped in the street."

"Where was this?"

"In town."

"Linlithgow?"

"You don't know anything." The skeletal face was cold and detached.

"Edinburgh?"

Gerald looked disappointed and let the cat go. She leapt off his lap and shook herself and leaned against one of his legs.

"Did you try to kill him any other time?"

"I might have." Gerald smiled with tobacco-stained teeth, and then lit another cigarette.

"When was that?"

"Long ago."

"What did you do?"

"I put ground glass on his beef stew. But he didn't eat it."

"Did he know you did that?"

"Oh yes. He knew. He looked at me and threw his lunch in the rubbish."

"Where was that?"

"In town."

"Where in town?"

"At the University."

"When?"

"Before I went into hospital."

"How did you know where to find him?"

"I followed him. I followed him everywhere. I knew everything he did. I used to kill animals and throw them by his door. I told him that's what I would do to him, and I would have."

"You talked to him, face to face?"

"Oh no. I couldn't talk to him. No. That would have been too... No. I wrote him. I wrote him and told him what I would do. I put notes in the bags with the animals. I wanted him to be afraid. Like Dennis was. I wanted him to worry. I killed a squirrel and cut it up. And I killed a rat too. I'm not supposed to talk about it." Gerald wrapped one long thin leg all the way around his other shin and tucked his foot around that ankle. He was taking very deep drags on his cigarette, and french inhaling, and he was rocking back and forth at the same time. "I don't want to talk about it any more."

"I'm sorry if I upset you."

"I'm not supposed to talk about him. I'm not supposed to. I start thinking. I lived there. Long ago."

"Where?"

"In the country where he was buried. Long ago. Denny had a horse. Uncle gave it to Denny. They wouldn't let me ride it. They said I was too young. But Denny did."

"You used to live in Dunkeld?"

"In the country."

"Near Dunkeld?"

Gerald didn't answer. He left the cigarette dangling in his mouth and reached for Daisy, but she slipped away from him and tore across the room to the door, where she sat and washed her chest.

"Have you ever been to Holy Island?"

The television spoke unexpectedly, a deep bass voice from the BBC, and Gerald stared silently at the screen.

Ben watched him for quite awhile. And then he stood up to leave. He said good-bye. And thank you.

But Gerald didn't look at him. He lit another cigarette and then dumped the butts from the ash tray he'd been using into another, and carefully wiped the first one with a Kleenex.

Ben put a note for Gerald's parents on the table in the hall, and he was letting himself out the front door, looking at the perfectly kept perennial beds in the low walled garden, when he heard a car behind the house. It was a row house, so he couldn't get to the back on the outside, and he walked through the hall into the kitchen, to see if Gerald's parents had come home.

There was a large back garden, and a small garage beside the alley, but there wasn't a car. The one he'd heard had turned into the house next door. But there was a beehive. Sitting in the back corner by the gooseberry bushes.

"What did Gerald have to say for himself?" Hugh slipped the Bentley into gear and looked over his shoulder as he pulled away from the curb. "By the way, would you care to see a bit of Linlithgow while we're here?"

"No, I need to get back."

"You're feeling alright, are you?"

"Yeah, but it's a good thing I don't do this for a living." Ben loosened his tie and unbuttoned the top button of his shirt, and then locked his hands together on the top of his head. "Badgering someone who's ill does not make one feel fulfilled."

"But if Pilcher did murder Jon, it's a noble act."

"It's necessary, that's for sure. But doing it doesn't feel noble. What do you remember about Gerald?"

"Very little I'm afraid."

"Are those the ruins of Linlithgow Palace?"

"Yes. Mary Queen of Scots was born there, and it's really rather an interesting spot. Children are particularly fascinated by the vomitorium. Which are a bit thin on the ground today, as you might imagine."

"You must have heard about Gerald's attempts to murder Jon?"

"Yes, of course. But, you see, after Jon came back from the war, he only lived with us in Edinburgh for a very few weeks, aside from the odd weekend at Kilgarth, so I observed very little firsthand. I do remember that a bag with a mutilated rabbit was once deposited at the door of Kilgarth. And I also remember thinking that Jon seemed to feel rather sympathetic toward Gerald. Even though, objectively speaking, one mightn't have thought Gerald deserved it."

"You don't think there could have been anything in Gerald's accusation?"

"Absolutely not! Jon's commanding officer came to dinner several times after the war, and *he* certainly didn't think so, even though he was there when the incident occurred. And yet I always thought Jon went out of his way to shield Gerald Pilcher. He never told the police about the hounding he suffered, or the vicious letters."

"What kind of letters?"

"The usual poison-pen."

"How were they done?"

"I can't swear to it, of course, but I seem to remember that they were made of cut-up newsprint."

"Like Ellie's."

"Yes!"

"So how did Gerald try to kill Jon?"

"There was some sort of attempt at the University right after Jon came home from the front. Mary will remember more than I. But I know it wasn't until Gerald tried to run him down with a car that Jon had a word with our family physician. It was Graham who spoke to someone else as a result. I can't recall the details, but ultimately Pilcher was packed off to Craig House."

"Is Dr. Graham still around?"

"Oh, yes. He has a practice in Dunblane."

"What happened at El Alamein that makes Gerald think Jon killed his brother?"

"As I understand it, Pilcher was shot by a sniper while his section was out between the lines. That's the essence of it, certainly. Though I can't even remember the brother's name."

"Dennis." Ben didn't say anything else for a moment. He watched the countryside. The countless shades of green. The old buildings made of stone and wood that belonged to the earth in ways most buildings of this century don't. "There was one interesting thing I noticed."

"Oh?" Hugh was watching him, when he could, with his quick, careful, indigo eyes.

"The Pilchers have a beehive in the back yard."

"Do they, by Jove! Well, it's a good job you've looked into Gerald's affairs after all! That may explain a great deal."

"It's not conclusive in any way."

"I never have understood why they let him out. If you put a homicidal killer back in society, you give him the opportunity to kill again."

"I agree. In general. But are you saying Gerald killed somebody I don't know about?"

"No. Simply that he made those attempts on Jon. Oddly enough, I don't think Jon was a'tall convinced that Gerald was trying to harm him. Of course, Jon did have a tendency to give people the benefit of the doubt. Which can certainly be an admirable trait, if one isn't unduly naive."

"What kind of things did Jon say about him?"

"Oh, my. I won't be able to quote him precisely, but as I recall, Jon seemed to think Gerald went about it in such an obvious way that he didn't really wish to succeed."

"Jon MacLean was an interesting person."

"Yes, he was. Quite out of the ordinary."

"What was he like as a brother?"

"Formidable, when we were young. He was eleven years older, so I was very much in awe of him and wanted desperately to be like him."

"Gerald's brother was eleven years older too."

"Really? That's quite a coincidence, isn't it? Of course, from my point of view, at least, Jon was rather different before the war. Very physical and impetuous and quite strong headed. Once . . it wasn't long after he'd begun to drive . . he must have been seventeen and I must have been six, because we'd just gotten a 1937 Morris. It was a 25 Coupe Saloon, which was a small, ordinary runabout. He was driving rather fast, and we came around a curve and completely overturned. I was absolutely terrified, but Jon didn't seem to be a'tall concerned. Of course, there was the age difference. Still, it was almost as though he felt immortal. As though no risk was too great to give him pause. He was different after the war. He was no more frightened or cowardly. Certainly not. Somehow even less. But there wasn't the bravado and the recklessness. He was quieter and not as impulsive. Though I, for one, could hardly believe he'd decide to become a minister. It seemed absolutely out of character."

"Why?"

"Jon was something of a rebel. Before the war. When he was an undergraduate. He drank a bit, and his relationships with women weren't always circumspect, if you know what I mean. And he had rather an irreverent point of view. He had no use a'tall for tradition and the usual social observances. And he never seemed to me to be remotely interested in religious matters. I really would've expected something a bit more dashing in the way of a career."

"Sometimes people like that have a real hunger."

"For what?"

"Meaning. God. 'The permanent things.' I'm quoting from T. S. Eliot."

"Yes, I do see that, of course."

"Was Jon popular as a boy? With adults and with kids his own age?"

"Oh, yes. He was quite charming, and he had a wonderful sense of humor. My mother and Mrs. Atwood both thought he could do no wrong, and the lads at school admired him a great deal as well. Here we are. Kilgarth. If you'll excuse me for just a moment, I must make a quick stop."

Hugh set the hand brake and got out by the small stone gatehouse. He unlocked the door and stepped inside for a second. And then explained, as he drove up the long drive, that a young couple had recently rented it and were moving in later that afternoon.

As he turned off the engine in front of the house, Hugh twisted in his seat to face Ben. "Do let me just say once again how glad I am that you're looking into Jon's death. I really do appreciate it, and I know Ellie does as well." He pulled on the brake and pocketed the key and then reached for his raincoat on the back seat. "To think that Gerald Pilcher would have a beehive in the back yard!"

As Ben Reese walked into the small sitting room by Kilgarth's front hall, the phone rang and he picked it up.

It was for him. Mrs. Cecilia Pilcher. Who wished to say, in no uncertain terms, that she failed to understand how a grown man could viciously attack a defenseless invalid such as her son and continue to live with himself. She'd intended to protect Gerald from any such interrogation, but she'd been unavoidably detained at the dentist's office. Gerald was now in such a state that he might have to be taken back to Craig House, and Mr. Pilcher was consequently on his way to Kilgarth, where he would have a great deal more to say to Mr. Benjamin Reese.

Ben didn't defend himself. She'd made up her mind and it wouldn't have done any good. He just listened and let her hang up when she was ready.

Then he called Katherine Burnett's Aunt Dorothy on Holy Island and asked if Jon had had a basket with him when she'd seen him the night of the eleventh.

She hesitated, briefly, and asked how Katherine had answered when Ben had asked her.

"She said Jon hadn't had a basket of any kind."

"Then I wonder if you'd be willing to call me tomorrow, after I've had an opportunity to speak to Katherine? I know it must seem a strange request, but I do have a very good reason."

Ben agreed, and hung up, while he tapped his pen on the edge of the desk and considered the possibilities.

Then he called Alfred Dixon's mistress.

Marjorie Wilson told him she'd been with Alf at her flat in Glasgow every single moment of the eleventh and twelfth.

"Really? That's odd. Because he dropped a parking lot ticket from Newcastle upon Tyne by my kitchen door that's dated and timed at a little before noon on the twelfth. That means Alf was fifty miles south of Holy Island the morning Jon died."

There was a sharp intake of breath. And a long uneasy silence. Before Marjorie asked Ben if he'd meet her the next day at a small quiet pub in Dunblane.

A car Ben didn't recognize was scattering stones by the front door as he hung up. And he walked down the front steps half-preparing himself for another flaying.

Instead, Ian Pilcher climbed out of his immaculate Mini Minor and shook Ben's hand quite calmly. He was small, graying, and pleasant looking. And he asked if they could walk along the drive while they talked. "It's a lovely day, and the rhododendrons along the lane are at their full effect."

"I'm sorry Gerald was upset by my visit. I tried to be careful and not panic him, but—"

"My wife has rung, has she?"

"Yes."

"Then I wish to apologize, Mr. Reese, for anything condemnatory she may have said. I'm sure Gerald will be quite all right. Relatively speaking, you understand, bearing his infirmity in mind. Mrs. Pilcher's a bit upset herself, for as I'm sure you can imagine, Gerald's condition is a constant worry for a mother, and I'm afraid she isn't always as objective as one might wish. So you mustn't blame yourself in any way." Mr. Pilcher was walking briskly, switching his gaze from the vista in front to those on either side. "The landscaping was designed with a vera fine eye."

"Your wife said he might have to go back to Craig House."

"I don't think so, no. One of his favorite programs will be starting shortly, and by the time it's over, I'd be willing to wager he'll have settled down quite nicely. You mentioned when we spoke on the telephone yesterday that you're looking into the caircumstances of Jon MacLean's death."

"Yes. The evidence suggests that he might not have died of natural causes."

"And you thought perhaps Gerald might be involved?"

"Well, I—"

"Please don't feel you have to dissemble for my sake. If I were you, I'd be asking myself the vera same question. The truth sets us free, Mr. Reese. It's fantasy and wishful thinking that weaken and destroy."

"Yeah, I know what you mean."

"Gerald made two attempts on Jon MacLean's life, even if they were a bit muddled and halfhearted. And he turned up at the funeral as well, able to get himself about, and still concerned with Jon's affairs. You have every reason to wonder, and if there are any questions I can answer which will make your efforts any easier, I, for one, am more than willing to do so." Mr. Pilcher took a handkerchief out of his coat pocket and blew his nose quite matter-of-factly, before folding it neatly and putting it away. "First of all, because I would like to see justice served, and secondly, because I would be very much surprised if Gerald had anything to do with it, and I believe that laying the facts before you will serve both ends."

"But also because you want to be objective?"

Ian Pilcher chuckled as he slid his black-framed glasses higher up on his nose. "Aye. We all like to think we're objective, don't we? Even when one recognizes that no one on earth is. Isn't it grand! Look at the bluebells, like a blue velvet carpet beneath the flowering shrubs!"

"It's beautiful, but I don't appreciate it the same way you do. Do you think Gerald's right that Jon MacLean was responsible for your son Dennis's death?"

"Not a'tall! Quite the contrary, in fact. And I can say that with some assurance, because I investigated it vera thoroughly after the war. Dennis was assigned to the Fifth County of Angus Battalion of the Black Watch. Or The Royal Highland Regiment, to give it its proper title. I talked to men in Dennis's Section, and I met with the C.O. and the Intelligence Officer. I studied the reports and the papers at Regimental Headquarters, as well as at Balhousie Castle, the Regimental Museum in Perth. If there had been any dereliction of duty, I cairtainly wanted to know of it. Yet, I saw instead a vera real need to wean my wife and son away from what I'd come to believe was a wrongheaded and destructive path. It did no good, I'm sorry to say. Gerald is unable, as well as unwilling, to accept the truth of the matter, and so, I fear, is his mother, though cairtainly to a lesser degree. I had the advantage of having been in the First War. I was in the trenches for quite a long while before I was wounded and sent home, and I know what battlefield conditions are from experience."

Ben nodded, as he watched a small black sheep in the pasture on their left, behind the shrubberies and the high row of trees. "The ones who go, and the ones who stay can't help but see things differently. What exactly did happen to Dennis? If you don't mind talking about it."

"He died at El Alamein, as I assume you already know. At that time, Lieutenant MacLean—who was promoted more than once, of course, later—was instructed to take a patrol out to inspect an abandoned German gun. An 88mm, as it happened, on the right flank of the Battalion position. The C.O. wanted a protective screen placed around it in case the Germans tried to retrieve it during the night, and the section Lieutenant MacLean took out was led by my son, who was then a corporal. MacLean oversaw their digging in, and during that time, he located snipers on the ridge in front of them. He warned the men, gave them their instructions, and departed to fulfill other duties he'd been assigned.

"All was quiet, until four of our First Armoured tanks arrived and started a shooting battle with the enemy. The entire section was at risk, and in his attempt to get out of the tank battle, my son was shot by a sniper. All the others in the section were wounded, although they survived because MacLean sent out a carrier to bring them in."

"So it was one of those screw ups that happen all the time?"

"Aye. War is a very untidy business. One's artillery sometimes shells one's own men. That happened at Alamein too, you know. Which is why I suspect that those who haven't experienced warfare often find it much easier to place blame than those who've been fortunate enough to survive its terrors." Ian Pilcher smiled ironically.

And Ben said, "That's exactly right."

"But in the largest sense, of course, it happens as it must. We haven't been abandoned, Mr. Reese. Our hairs have been numbered, if you take my meaning. And I've found comfort in that over the years, in more than one caircumstance. Lieutenant MacLean had no control over the situation. In fact, he was a particular favorite of Dennis's, and I know he felt Dennis's death vera deeply. From all accounts, he was an excellent leader. He was much decorated for his bravery, though such commendations don't mean as much in every case as one might wish. What particularly struck me was how highly his men thought of him.

"And yet, you see, my wife and son both seem to feel a need to blame someone for Dennis's death. It's sad, really, and wrong as well, but they want there to be someone they can hate with impunity. In fact, I would have to say that though they were delighted by Jon MacLean's death, they've both been a bit depressed ever since, as though they've been deprived of their raison d'être. Though, of course, Gerald still talks from time to time as though he's forgotten Jon's dead. Perhaps the anger and the hatred have been a part of him for so long, he finds it difficult to live without a target for it. You do realize, I presume, that Gerald is highly intelligent? Oh yes, unusually so. But incapacitated, you see, by his illness and his propensities."

"It can't be easy to watch."

"No, it'tisn't." Ian Pilcher spoke unemotionally and politely. And then he took a notebook from the inside pocket of his pin-striped suit. "Would you mind if I pause a moment to make a note? This is quite a rare variety of azalea and I've not seen it before in this part of Scotland. And yet in all honesty, I would have to say that the shrubs and trees aren't particularly well looked after. Shows a recent lack of interest, don't you think? Or a lack of funds. That might be more realistic."

Ben was trying to imagine what Ian Pilcher's life was like, with his particular wife and son. And then, unexpectedly, he heard himself say, "You're a very interesting man."

"I? Oh no! No. I'm a simple man, Mr. Reese. I've established a modest insurance firm which supports us in a small way. I try to help my family find some measure of contentment. And I console myself with my garden. There I find solace in something deeper, and older, and more profound than any aspect of my own pedestrian existence."

"I'm not sure I understand what you mean by that."

"There I see the 'wheels within wheels.' The Omniscient Mind, if you will, and the order of the universe, Mr. Reese, writ large for those who care to see it. Linnaeus and Mendel, they understood, and they spent their lives describing that order and organization. In my own small way, I do a bit of hybridizing and grafting, simply for my own amusement, of course. I've managed a tree rose I'm rather fond of. And I'm hoping that once I retire, we shall be able to purchase a small cottage in the country where I can expand my horticultural horizons."

"I noticed you have a beehive in your back yard."

"Aye, it's a related interest, observing the pollen gathering and the honey making. I try to effect the flavors of the honey by growing particular plants to attract the bees. It's quite fascinating, observing their behavior. And I find that the more one understands the workings of the natural world, the more one is able to accept what one isn't able to change." He smiled softly.

And for awhile they walked in silence beside a pasture sown with sheep.

"Did I understand Gerald to tell me that you once lived in the country?"

"Near Dunkeld. Aye, we did indeed. We had a small farm close to Amulree, though we never actually farmed. I was a clerk in an insurance firm then in Dunkeld."

"And he has an uncle who lives there still?"

"You may have met him. My wife's brother, Callam Douglas. He's the head gardener at Balnagard. So we've heard all about the comings, and goings, and the funeral party from Callam. He's a very different kettle of fish than his sister. Imperturbable, Callam is. He's a grand gentleman and a very knowledgeable horticulturist."

Ben said something noncommittal while he considered their connection with Balnagard. Gerald could have known Ben was at Perach, that he was investigating Jon's death, that there was an electric towel rack in the bath. He could have known where Jon was going on his walking tour with Alex, and when as well. And he certainly had access to bees. "Does Gerald drive?"

"He used to. He hasn't in a considerable time, though he'll take the wheel in the country, occasionally, when we're off on a jaunt. My wife drove him to Mr. MacLean's burial without my knowledge." Ian Pilcher was gazing fondly at a cerise rhododendron, his head off to one side and his eyes half closed with concentration.

"Is he mechanical?"

"Aye, he is. From a child, he could take anything apart and put it together in no time a'tall. It's one of the few things now that seems to pull him out of his torpor, a mechanical piece that needs repair. That, and perhaps the odd trip to Dunkeld to see Callam."

"And bees, he's learned about them from you?"

"A bit. It's not one of his great interests, but he knows something of it. That's one of the reasons I consider it a blessing he had such a terrible turn earlier in the month. Once I'd read that Jon MacLean died of bee stings, you see, and Callam had told us that his death seemed a bit dodgey."

"Callam told you that?"

"Aye. There's not much that goes on at Balnagard, or any work place, really, when one thinks of it, that isn't noticed and passed on amongst the workmen. What day was it Mr. MacLean died?"

"Friday, the twelfth."

"That's what I remembered from the paper. And that's the blessing of it. For Gerald was in Craig House that whole week, the eighth through the sixteenth. You see, the tenth was Dennis's birthday, and it's always a difficult time for Gerald, and this year we had to readmit him. He was losing touch again. Though that's not a very helpful term. He's schizophrenic, basically, and they let him out because he's considered to be in remission, and he is better, there's no doubt, with his medications and his treatment. But this year Dennis's birthday was quite a struggle."

"I see."

"Do you think the MacLeans would object if I cut one small blossom? I may have just the spot for this variety of rhododendron, but I'm not absolutely sure the color suits in that part of the garden, and I'd like to take it home and see how it works into the overall effect."

"I'm sure they'd be delighted."

"Excellent! Then I'll dampen my handkerchief at the house, if I may, and use it to moisten the stem."

Ben slammed the door of the Rover and studied the collection of gray stone buildings that lay loosely strung together behind the old stone farmhouse, making a kind of courtyard between the house and the stable. There were chickens wandering around, and pigs in a side pen, and six or eight Jersey cows standing beside them in a field by a gate, hoping it was time to come in. Several cats scattered across the cobbles at the sound of a strange car and two Shetland sheepdogs came from the stable to examine whoever had arrived.

Ben was talking to both of them, and had just squatted down

to pet them, when the back door of the house opened and a low gentle voice said, "May I help you a'tall?"

"Mrs. Creith?" Ben had stood already and was turning toward a woman who was probably in her early sixties.

"Yes?" She was shading her eyes with one hand, while holding a basket of clothespins in her other, her long white hair wrapped on the back of her head, her long checked apron covering a worn wool skirt.

"I'm Ben Reese. I'm staying down the road with Hugh MacLean, and I wonder if I could talk to Mr. Creith for a minute? If this is a convenient time."

"Aye, he's with the horses. If you can wait just a moment, I'll show you the way."

"Please don't bother. Not if that's the stable over there."

"Aye. If you're sure." She smiled and turned toward the side yard, as Ben walked away from her across the cobbles.

It was a long stone building, beautifully built like all the rest, simple and old and mossy, with a slate roof and huge wooden doors and stalls set out by stone partitions.

There were six horses in their stalls, standing under the carved stone names of horses who'd been dead a hundred years—four percheron draft horses with feet the size of platters, and two well-made riding horses who looked like they had thoroughbred in their bones.

"Mr. Creith?"

He was pouring water from one bucket into another by the head of a calm looking percheron, and he patted the neck of the huge old gelding, before saying, "Aye, you've found him. And what can he do for ye, lad?" His bright blue eyes looked younger than his weathered face, and he smiled widely and wiped his right hand on his corduroy trousers before offering it to Ben.

"I'm Ben Reese, Mr. Creith. I'm staying at Kilgarth with Hugh MacLean."

"I knew a party had arrived. Mary Atwood phoned this morning. It's a bad business, Jon's death. I knew him from the day he was born, and he was a grand chap. Never came home to Kilgarth without coming to us here, or fetching us for dinner. We never had a son of our own, you see, and Jon . . well . . and Hugh... "

"You know he died from bee stings?"

"Aye. And it was here he was first stung. Used to follow me about while I worked with the beasts. Had a way with animals, on his own. Wanted to be a vet'nary in those days, as I suppose many young lads do."

"What happened when he was stung?"

"Well, I was setting up a new hive, moving a portion of an old colony, as ye do, and Jon was standing back behind me, when he was stung. Only once, mind, but he nearly died as it was. It was terrible, watching him gasp and struggle for breath. Dr. Graham was here at Glengarth, thank God, seeing to one of our daughters at the time, so he gave Jon an injection and rushed him into hospital, and together they saved his life. Gave me a turn, I can tell ye. Gave us all a turn, Jon's family and ours." Mr. Creith was working as he talked, watering the horses, pitching hay into the wrought-iron racks by their heads, pouring grain into buckets that hung on bailing twine from carved Georgian posts.

"Was Hugh interested in the animals too?"

"Well . . ye ken he was years younger?" Mr. Creith wiped his forehead and smoothed his long curling white hair before he replaced his cloth cap and turned the full force of his wild white eyebrows on Ben. "He'd appear once in a while, 'specially in the spring when there were new young beasts about, but there seemed to be a sort of fear in him, a distrust of horses, and a dis-like of cows. I don't think he cared much for the smell and the roughness of the place. But he was always most polite and well behaved, and we were glad to have him when he came."

"I wonder if I could ask your help, in a confidential matter that has to do with Jon's death?"

"I learned to keep my own counsel, young man, long before ye were born, so if ye've something to say ye don't wish repeated, ye can count on me to do my part."

"There's some question about whether or not Jon died of natural causes, even though he was stung, and—"

"Are ye saying Jonathan MacLean was murdered!"

"I'm saying he might have been, and Ellie and Hugh have asked me to look into it, to see if the police ought to be brought back in. I need to talk to someone who knows about bees, and Mrs. Atwood suggested I talk to you."

"If there's the least way I can help a'tall, I'm your man." Mr. Creith was unrolling his shirt sleeves on his forearms, which appeared to be the size of most people's thighs, but he was concentrating completely on Ben.

"First of all, could bees be transported in a healthy condition in a cloth-lined wicker picnic basket?"

"Aye. I would say so. If the openings in the wicker were small enough to keep them in, of course, and there was proper ventilation as well. If the cloth lining was rubberized, or if it covered every wee bit of the wicker surface there might be a problem, but otherwise, yes they could."

"And you'd spray them with sugar water to subdue them when they're moved?"

"Oh, aye. Ye couldn't do it any other way. Ye'd have to spray them to get them into the basket to begin with. They feed on it, ye see, they lick the sugar off each other, and pay vera little atten-tion to anything else. But ye also must remember that bees will not survive a temperature lower than forty-one degrees Fahren-heit. And they'd be pretty well comatose under forty-five to fifty degrees, so the temperature would have to be suitable."

"Ah. I didn't know that."

"Aye. It's also been my experience that bees that are handled in that way . . now, I'm talking about bees that are moved more than two miles from their home hive, that's an important point. If they're subdued and then transported, they're quite intimidated by the experience."

"Would they fly out and sting the person who opened the basket?"

"I would think that they'd have become quite docile. That they'd only be worrying about their situation. I wouldn't think they'd fly right out and attack someone, no. Once the basket was open, they'd begin to move about and eventually they'd leave, yes."

"But they wouldn't just rush out and sting whoever opened the basket?"

"I wouldn't have thought so."

"That's rather a fly in the ointment. Pardon the pun." Ben moved his jaw off to the side and silently tapped his eyeteeth together. He was looking past Edward Creith, as Creith coiled his hose and hung it beside the faucet. "What would happen if some-one opened the basket and reached in for something, without see-ing the bees? Maybe he touched one or more of them without realizing?"

"Now, in that case, in my experience, they'd sting. Yes, if they were touched, or they felt threatened or endangered, they'd pro-tect themselves, cairtainly. If the temperature was warm enough,

and all the rest of it. But wouldn't Jon . . I presume you're referring to Jon? . . wouldn't he have heard them, or even seen them,
upon opening the hamper?"

"I don't know. Maybe. He was in a field on an island off the
coast of Northumberland, and apparently it was very windy that
morning, so maybe he didn't hear them. He might have been
thinking about something else. Or looking at something I suppose. He certainly wouldn't have expected to find bees in a basket.
Unless he'd heard them. But that is an important point. Especially
for someone who knew he had reason to be afraid of bees."

"Aye, he cairtainly did that."

"As I understand it, there are beekeeping journals published
in Britain."

"Oh, aye. I have a wall filled with *Scottish Beekeeper*. It's a
monthly magazine and quite helpful."

"Could I borrow all your issues from the last two years?"

"Of course! With the greatest of pleasure! Let me first bring
the herd in and then I'll fetch them for ye."

"I can help you milk if you'd like."

"Oh, no, I couldn't possibly impose."

"No, I'd like to."

"Would you? That'd be lovely. Thanks."

"My grandfather had dairy cows when I was a kid. Do you
ride?" Ben was scratching the withers of a dark bay hunter.

"Not often anymore. I keep the big fellows about, even
though I'm mechanized, because I wouldn't know what to do
with myself without them. Mrs. Creith says I've grown soft and
sentimental, and doubtless she's right. The other two belong to
the grandchildren. They all ride and go to the gymkhanas. That's
how I got to know Jon, ye see, as well as I did. He kept his horse
here too, even during term when he was in Edinburgh. A great,

gentle, workman-like bay. I think I fancied Bert as much as Jon. We went to Jon's burial, ye know. But we couldn't stay on for the tea."

"It's the first time I've heard her play since Jon died." Mary Atwood was standing next to Ben in the hall at Kilgarth outside the drawing room, staring at Ellie's back. "Course whether that's a good thing, I couldn't say. It's a terrible bit of music. Makes my blood turn cold."

"It's one of Mahler's Symphonies. The Sixth, I think. He had a presentiment that something tragic was about to happen, and right after he finished it, his daughter died."

"Look at her! Poor wee thing, you can see her shoulder blades as plain as may be, even through a heavy sweater, and her dungarees are hanging on her as though there's no meat left anywhere a'tall! I don't like the look of it, I don't indeed." Mary ran her hand down her corseted front, smoothing the fabric belt of her pale purple heathery wool dress, taking comfort apparently in the solidity of her own frame in view of so many bones. "I think we should have Dr. Graham in. Course it isn't my affair, is it? Still... " She looked at Ben meaningfully, as though she hoped he'd say something. Even though he didn't. "Well. I'll set the porridge on the stove before I go up, and I'll see you in the morning."

"There is one thing I meant to ask you, Mary. I'd appreciate it if nobody cleaned my room."

"Alright. I'll do my best to remember."

"Thanks, Mary. I'm also going to be keeping my door shut."

"I'm sure you have a very good reason."

"Yes, I do."

"Well. I'll wish you a good night then." Mary shook her head as she looked at Ellie, and trudged down the hall as though her feet hurt.

Ben listened to the last of the Mahler, which was as unnerving and despairing as a piano version of the Sixth could be, for Ellie was an exceptional pianist.

She was sitting on the padded bench by the grand piano with her hands in her lap staring at the music rack as though she didn't see it. Her face was flushed and sweaty, and her hair hung on either side of it, till she pulled it impatiently behind her back.

Ben waited. But she didn't move. And then he walked into the big cedar-paneled room and sat in one of the comfortable chairs settled in a bay of high wide windows. "That was beautifully done."

"Thanks. It's kind of a hack transcription, but the Mahler's an amazing piece of work."

"Can I talk to you for a second?"

"To tell you the truth, I was just on my way to bed."

She had the same delicate sort of bones that Jessie had had. But even though they were both tall, and Ellie's hair was more or less the same dark brown, she didn't remind Ben of Jessie, exactly. Only that there had been a Jessie, and now there wasn't. "I thought I might summarize what I've found out so far."

"I want you to, I really do. But could we talk in the morning? I didn't sleep well last night, and my stomach's a little weird for some reason."

"We can talk sometime tomorrow. But could I ask you one quick question?"

"Sure. Go ahead."

"What do you know about Jon's will?"

"He wrote it last fall, and it's pretty much what you'd expect. I do know he never talked about it with anyone else. Except Alex.

He told him about the saddle and the Roman stuff when Alex was asking him how he took care of the metal pieces. I'm sorry, Ben. I have to go." She put her hand across her mouth and rushed out of the room and into the lavatory that was just their side of the stairs.

Ben could hear her retching. She hadn't even had time to close the door.

Alex was looking up at the stairs, wondering what he could do to help. He hated to see Ellie so obviously unwell, and yet he felt absolutely powerless. For what can anyone do in the aftermath of death? Except pray. And pay attention. And try to keep the widow occupied without her noticing.

He did have a very old friend in the Edinburgh Symphony. Perhaps it might be rather a good thing, in a few weeks' time, to put Victor in touch with Ellie?

Alex threw himself on the bench by the umbrella stand and leaned against the wall, while he waited for Ben to come down again. Ben had told him he needed to talk to him, before he went upstairs with Ellie, and it had looked to Alex as though Ben thought the matter was of some importance.

Yet he felt himself at such a loose end. There was no real work he could do without his typewriter. Other than contemplating the new book and jotting down notes as usual. Of course, he wanted very much to be able to help with the investigation, and yet he didn't wish to put Ben in an awkward position by raising the issue himself.

How anyone could murder another, cold-bloodedly and deliberately, defied generalization, while peaking the imagination. Take Burke and Hare, for example. Suffocating all those unsuspecting

Edinburgh lodgers and selling their bodies to the anatomy school. And for what? A trifle over £7 per body! What is it that makes a human being capable of disregarding the right of another to live out the full number of his days? Arrogance? Self-centeredness? A failure of imagination? Excluding, for the sake of discussion, self-defense, warfare, and legal execution. For interestingly enough, the accurate translation is "murder," in the Ten Commandments, and not "kill" as it's often rendered.

Perhaps he should read about Burke and Hare again before he drew the villain in the new book. Though he still had to create that other character as well. The observer who sees the real significance of what's done, in the midst of the hurly-burly. It could be a hermit in the Caledonian forest. Or a traveling wool merchant, who knows the Continent and the Middle East. Even a titled lady would work as well, one who's been left to oversee the castle and its village and lands, when her lord goes off to war. Many were, of course, and their positions afforded a great sweep of social, economic, and religious influence.

Yet, so few today know the medieval period. Having lost sight of daily life in every age but our own. Like lost souls, abandoned on a desert island, without the least idea of how we got here. We're little more than the followers of fads. The worshippers of celebrities. Believing every picture we see on the telly. Blinded by the provinciality of time. Like "the insects of the moment," as Edmund Burke wrote when he first—

"Alex?" Ben was smiling at him, looking down on his high wide forehead and his rumpled hair, where he sat against the wall with a tattered black umbrella in his lap, his long legs spread out in front of him, and his wide hazel eyes fixed somewhere above the staircase on the other side of the hall. "This is the twentieth century."

"Ben! I'm sorry. Did you say something?" His eyes had begun

to focus, and he was looking at the umbrella as though he'd never seen it before.

"Could I talk you into taking a walk?"

"Oh, yes! It's a lovely evening, and I'd like the exercise. There's actually quite an interesting path that leads back toward the home farm."

The night was very warm and soft, and the stars were out. And as the two of them walked around the west side of the wide stone house, they could hear the two horses, who belonged to Mary's granddaughters, cropping grass in the dark in the paddock behind the big cedar.

"Do you know who drove Jon down to Holy Island?"

"Yes, a friend of his from divinity school. From when Jon was in divinity school, not the friend. What was his name? Ellie would know, of course. He's a physician now in Berwick upon Tweed. What *is his name!* This is quite frustrating, it really is."

"It doesn't matter. You can tell me later. But I wonder if you'd do something for me when you remember?"

"Of course!"

"Would you call him and find out whatever he can tell you about meeting Jon and driving him to Holy Island?"

"Absolutely! I'd like very much to be of use."

"One other thing too. I don't suppose you know anyone who works at Craig House?"

"I do, as a matter of fact. It has a very good staff, from what I've been told, and one of the physicians is rather a friend of mine. Why? What can I do to help?"

"According to Mr. Pilcher, Gerald was in Craig House from the eighth through the sixteenth, and if that's true, he couldn't have been involved in Jon's death. Would you call and find out if he was there the whole time? Make absolutely sure he didn't leave the hospital, even for an hour."

"I'll ring him straightaway tomorrow, shall I? Before I become embroiled in the reading of the will."

"Good. That would help me a lot."

"It occurred to me that perhaps we ought to invite Jon and Hugh's family physician, whatever his name is, over to dinner tomorrow. Get him to take a look at Ellie without making too much of an issue of it. How does that strike you?"

"I think that's a good idea. Have you asked—"

"Roger Evans! Roger Evans was the friend of Jon's who drove him down from Berwick! I'll ring him first thing as well."

"Have you asked Hugh about inviting the doctor for dinner?"

"No. It would be for Hugh to decide, certainly. I'll approach him in the morning. Did you believe Mr. Pilcher?"

"Yes, I did. But we've still got to verify it. How warm was it on the twelfth, on Holy Island?"

"It was very warm by the time I arrived at Beal. Unseasonably so. Though it had been terribly breezy earlier in the day."

"Could you find out exactly what the temperature was at say six o'clock in the morning?"

"Certainly. I'll put a call through to the weather people. It's a wonderful sound, isn't it?"

They were out on the farm track, by the back pastures, standing still in the darkness, listening to the bleating of newborn lambs.

Ben was in the dark, lying in icy water, sand scratching his skin and his lips. Something was dripping in his eyes, and a stiff, heavy unrecognizable object lay across his mouth. He knew he couldn't move, even though he didn't know why. And every breath was a fight against the weight that pinned his ribs down in the cold and wet.

He didn't know where he was, or why he couldn't move, or why there was the smell of death all around him.

He told himself to get up. To get out from under the weight and the stench. To push himself free so he could breathe out from under the darkness that held him down. He was buried in a pit. That's what it was. A pit or a shell hole. Where claustrophobia, and his own horror of the weight and the dark, was making him crazy. He wanted to wipe the sticky stuff off his face, the sweet salty taste of it that was in his mouth and his nostrils, more than he'd ever wanted anything.

His hands were pinned behind him, so he lunged with his chest and rammed against the weight with his head. And then, as he shoved and scratched, once his hands were free (and why they were suddenly free he didn't know), a leg, lying on his mouth, twitched and rolled across his eyes. He screamed and tore away from it, away from all the other arms and legs, that were holding him like a giant squid and slithering across his naked skin.

Then the dream changed, suddenly, melting away into a village street. A cobblestone street in France, probably, windy and deserted and cluttered with rubble from the bombing. It was still dark, but he knew it was nearly dawn. And he was alone, sliding his shoulder along a bullet-chipped wall, trying to get back to the American lines. He knew he'd been up for days, but something else was wrong too. And he didn't know what. Except that adrenaline was all that was left of him.

He'd just taken a command post, he remembered that. That's what he did for a living. Three Germans. Killed silently. Papers and maps photographed. Radio messages copied. Papers put back and order preserved. No sign left of what he'd done. Except for the three dead men.

Where was Schmidtty? Nobody went out on recon alone. Maybe the new guy was with him and not Schmidtty. Yeah, but what was his name? He had no idea. He must've stopped listening to names. So he wouldn't miss the men they belonged to when their faces were gone or their guts were on the ground.

Why couldn't he pick up his feet? He was carrying the earth on his back, dragging something cold and heavy. But he wasn't allowed to turn around and look.

Then he was standing in a doorway, staring at the door, his face six inches from the peeling paint, and he couldn't make himself move. What was wrong with him? Why was he standing there, when somebody was running toward the door?

A middle-aged woman opened it and screamed. And he tried to tell her to be quiet, but couldn't get the words out.

He turned back into the street and tried to run. There were boots coming after him, clattering on the cobblestones. More boots. Pounding. Running faster all the time. More shouts. Then a spattering of shots. And yet he couldn't make himself run. Something kept slapping against his legs, pulling him back somehow, and dragging him down. He reached around to the small of his back, where his canteen should have been, and felt fingers wrapped around his belt. This time, when he tried, he could look over his shoulder—into the sunken eyes of a dead German officer, hanging by a hand from his belt, his head bobbling against Ben's knees.

And then he was in an evergreen forest, south of the Ardennes again, east of Luxembourg and across the German border, in the Saarbrucken Forest near Trier.

This part was real. Everything that would happen now had

happened in real life. And the dream was almost over.

He'd been attacked by two Tiger tanks, and he had fifteen thirty-caliber bullets buried in his body (7.62mm to be exact) and even though nobody thought he'd live, they were flying him into France in an old artillery spotter, under the anti-aircraft guns, to a railhead that could take him to a hospital in Paris.

Snow was spitting in his face. And they were strapping him on a stretcher. And lashing him to the undercarriage of a Piper Cub.

He was hanging under the Piper Cub. So cold it made him cry. Flying through treetops, screaming.

He woke up covered with sweat, the way he always did, and shoved the pillow off his face. He kicked the comforter on the floor and sat up, fighting for air like a runner after an uphill race.

He didn't know where he was, but Jessie wasn't there. And he told himself not to look for her.

There was a window behind him on his right. And another at the far right end of the room. It was dark out. There was almost no moon. And he had to turn a light on fast.

You're in Scotland. You're at Kilgarth. There's a table on your right with a lamp on it.

He sat with his bare back against the four-poster frame, his chest still heaving and his skin sliding with sweat, and stared straight ahead at a cold hearth.

He turned the light off after a minute. Once he knew where he was. And then he got up to find his towel. It was hanging on a wooden rack by the door to the hall, and he wiped the sweat off his face and chest.

He opened the drawer in the desk and took out a plastic bag. His Camels were in it so they wouldn't dry out between dreams. And he lit one as he walked—window to door, door to window, window to door, in the dark.

He thought he heard someone in the hall and he stopped to listen. He wondered if he'd screamed out loud and waked somebody up. But then it was quiet again. And he started walking.

It wasn't that he regretted going.

Or doing what he'd had to do.

It was a just war. And it was over.

This was just one of his dreams. Thank God.

And by the time he smoked a second cigarette and read for awhile, he might even try to go back to sleep.

But why did it always end with him dangling under the Piper Cub?

Why wouldn't it?

Nothing else had gotten that much of his attention.

Except the cliffs above Omaha Beach.

And he'd been fortunate then too. Just shrapnel.

In safe places. In the middle of a bloodbath.

He'd been assigned to a Canadian Group (Canadian Strike Force D2) that landed in Normandy on June fifth, the night before the Invasion. A sub dropped them off, and they went in in inflatable rafts to try to take out the big guns on the cliffs above Omaha Beach. Seventy-seven out of a hundred and ten had been killed. All but five had been wounded. And Ben had never talked about it in any detail. Even with Alex, in the hospital in Wales, before he went back as a Scout.

He'd had to push it all back, so he could live again.

Why wouldn't it wake him up in the night?

Parts of men, lying in hospitals. Thousands of them still there. Patient eyes. Waiting for a letter. Silent eyes. Waiting for a way out. Outraged mouths. Twisted by bitter tongues.

He'd seen all kinds, in a year and a half in hospitals. Especially that year after he'd married Jessie. And he didn't want to forget them. *Or* the men who didn't make it. Who made him wonder why he did. He didn't want to turn his back and just take what he'd been given.

And it *was* a gift.

He'd been ambushed by two Tiger tanks and lived to dream about it.

And it was his fault too, as much as anybody's. He'd asked a ninety-day kid lieutenant, who hadn't been there long enough to know anything, how it looked in front, when he should've asked what G-2 said was out there. The kid didn't understand. And Ben walked out in three feet of snow in a khaki uniform and got pinned down by machine gun fire. Gene was killed before Ben silenced the machine gun. And then two Tiger tanks came out of nowhere, rolling straight at him. He used Gene's bazooka to stop one of the tanks, but the other took him out with those fifteen 7.62mm slugs.

He lay there for three hours, between the lines during a fire-fight, bleeding to death and packing snow in his wounds. Someone said later that the snow's what saved him.

But he'd looked down on his own dead body that morning, crumpled on a white drift. He'd seen the future, happening in front of him. And yet the next instant he'd known—with the same certainty that he knew his own face—that it wouldn't happen. He knew he was being saved. In order to do something. For somebody. At the right time.

Ben shivered by the window and watched a smoke ring hit the glass, the gray glass, in a gray night.

Somebody was sitting on the bottom step.

Ellie. In a raincoat. With her head in her hands.

Tuesday, May 23rd

MARTHA MACDONALD HAD DRESSED FOR WORK and dropped
the last breakfast plate in the dish drainer, when she looked to see
if her mother had finished her tea.

She hadn't yet. She was staring out the window at the back
garden with her hands in her lap in front of a cold cup.

"Watching the robins, are you, Mum?" Martha didn't expect
an answer. Her mother heard very little and generally said even
less. But she looked content that morning, and there was reason
to be thankful for that.

The phone rang in the hall, and Martha ran to answer it. It
wasn't often that anyone called them, and then it was usually in
the evening. "Good morning, MacDonald residence... Yes, of
course I'll wait."

Martha looked back at her mother, and glanced at the hall
clock, before she said, "So Hamish is helping you, is he?... No, I
can well believe he wouldn't remember. Hamish has never paid vera
much attention to time, or place, or the ordinary details of life...

"Oh aye, he was here, Mr. Reese, yes, but we didn't have our
breakfast together. Hamish had an appointment in Edinburgh,

and he left the house before I was up... Really? I expect it must've slipped his mind. Though I do recall thinking at the time that he seemed a bit preoccupied... I don't, no. I rose later than usual. About nine o'clock, I should think, for I'd been up with Mother in the night. I wasn't going in to work, you see, because she was so unwell, and I didn't see him a'tall that morning. He did tell me the evening before that he'd be leaving no later than seven...

"No, we've not spoken a'tall. I took Mother to our sister in Galashiels for a few days, once her health improved, just for a bit of a change, and we only returned yesterday evening... Aye, you're right about that, Hamish has phoned. He left two messages with our next door neighbor. I haven't yet rung him back, though." Martha laughed softly, and then shook back her thick red hair. "I was hoping he'd ring us, and I'd not have to shoulder the expense. It sounds shameful, I know, but Hamish is a bit better fixed than we... No, that's quite alright. I was glad to help... Aye, and thank you."

Her mother hadn't moved since Martha had left the kitchen, but when she walked back in, her mother looked at her and smiled. Martha patted her arm, and then bent down and kissed her forehead. "You'll never guess who that was, Mum. It seems Hamish is helping an American gentleman with a murder investigation! I said, "HAMISH IS HELPING WITH A MURDER INVESTIGATION! Oh well. Never you mind. IT'S TIME WE GOT YOU SPRUCED UP A BIT. MRS. INGERSOLL WILL BE STOPPING DIRECTLY, SO LET ME HELP YOU WITH YOUR CHAIR."

Dorothy Burnett was sitting in her dining room on Holy Island at a drop-leaf table beside a small bay window, drinking India tea and reading *The Daily Scotsman*. She'd turned to an article on Holyrood House and the preparations for the Royal Garden Party, partly because she knew someone who'd been invited, when her phone rang in the parlor.

She took one more sip of her jasmine tea, and then walked briskly through to the next room, fluffing one side of her wiry gray hair and adjusting her cardigan on her shoulders. "Good morning, Elsbeth... I shall be happy to wait, of course."

Dorothy Burnett wiped a finger across her mahogany desk, and wondered if there was time to dust before she left for the vicarage. "Yes, good morning, Mr. Reese. I thought it might be you... Aye, I have spoken to Katherine, and I wonder if I might suggest that you ring her again yourself. I think she's prepared to be a bit more forthcoming, since she and I spoke. And it should come from her, you see, for her sake as well as yours. Of course, if you have any further questions after you've spoken to her, please don't hesitate to ring me back, for I'd be only too pleased to help... I will, yes... Good-bye for now."

Dorothy Burnett looked out the window at Lindisfarne Castle, half a mile or more away, and sighed as she tied back the curtain. She'd seen it coming years ago. Not this, in every particular, but some sort of tragic end to a stubborn, willful, silly pursuit of Jon MacLean that had started when Katherine was just thirteen.

It had been a wretched business from the beginning. And even then, her poor, dear, addlepated parents had been no help a'tall. But pursuing him to Cawdor was terribly wrong as well. Jon was a married man by then, and Katherine hadn't cared tuppence. She was clever, though, subtle and hard to pin down, and the rationalizations she used made one *almost* wonder if one had it wrong.

And yet, why had she lied about the hamper when it seemed such a trivial detail? Perhaps she couldn't see the difference anymore, between absolute truth and falsehood, having lied so deliberately for so long.

Dorothy had tried to talk some sense into the girl herself, on more than one occasion. Yet all one could really do was force Katherine to tell the truth whenever an opportunity arose. Even though it did not make one feel very helpful in the greater scheme.

Still, it was time to set off toward the vicarage. To pack up the jumble, and take it to the orphanage, and find the Harris boy again. There'd been a hunger there the last time. Poor wee soul. He needed someone to listen and take an interest. And perhaps she ought to take him that illustrated book, the one about Merlin and Arthur that Robert had loved when he was little.

It was probably in the bookcase in the back bedroom, and as she walked, she wondered if she'd remembered to tell Mr. Reese when they'd spoken the day before, that Katherine had gone for a walk the morning that Jon MacLean died. And very early it was too, for she was back by seven, or a few minutes after, to bring in the milk and the hamper.

Dorothy would've been very much surprised if it had any bearing on Jon's death. But she'd meant to mention it to Mr. Reese, for Katherine's sake as much as his. And she wasn't a'tall sure she had.

Katherine Burnett was just beginning her free hour when Jennifer Odell crashed through the door the way she always did and told her there was a call for her in the staff lounge. Katherine thanked her politely and said she'd be right down.

She'd been expecting it, since Dorothy had called. Witch that she'd always been. Smug and sanctimonious. And meddling again as well.

Katherine had been bracing herself against the humiliation, against the shame of having to take back what she'd told Reese, and she'd come to the conclusion that elevated dignity would still be the best approach. A sort of untouchable cool resignation. Something like Ingrid Bergman in her new film. No, not Bergman. Garbo would be better. The distanced restraint she'd shown in that very early movie, when she'd worn the little hat.

There was no one else in the staff room, which was a considerable relief. But she opened the other door to the back passage anyway, to make sure no one was listening in, before she walked to the desk and picked up the receiver lying beside the cradle.

"This is Katherine Burnett... Yes, of course, Mr. Reese, I understand... Let me just begin by saying that I was not entirely frank with you when we spoke before. Certain events, which I've had to endure in the past, have made me, I fear, painfully aware that justice is not always done. One's own motivations and actions will be misconstrued in the most alarming ways, so one must remain upon one's guard when—

"No, I don't feel able to discuss the particulars of my earlier experiences at the moment. But for precisely those reasons, I was reticent when speaking with you, and I chose not to reveal all the circumstances surrounding Jon MacLean's visit to us on Holy Island. The whole truth is that my aunt prepared a small hamper of food for Jon to take with him when he camped that Thursday evening. I suppose we both did, for I helped too, though it was her idea initially... We gave him potted shrimp sandwiches and oatcakes, in addition to a thermos of tea. He took the hamper with him when he went off to the dunes, and Friday morning, when we went out to bring in the milk, the hamper had been left on the stoop... It was seven, or perhaps a few minutes before, when I discovered it... Yes, the food was gone, the thermos had been rinsed, and there was a note thanking us for our thoughtfulness...

"I've told you why! I felt as though my own motivations and involvement would be misconstrued! I don't wish to speak unkindly of the bereaved, but Elinor MacLean sometimes behaves like a jealous, insecure woman, and my fear was that her perspective of my relationship with Jon would inaccurately color your perceptions... No, that's the only piece of information I didn't share, and I can see now that it was an unnecessary attempt at self-protection...

"No, I had no idea that there was any significance to the hamper per se, I simply... Well, I may have done, but... No!... How can you suggest that I was 'watching him'? I was simply taking a walk! I know I didn't mention it, but... I don't *know* if the hamper was on the stoop when I left the house, I went out by the back door. I woke early and decided to take a turn along the marsh... Of course I knew his campsite was nearby, but he'd left the dunes before I got there, and I... No! It wasn't like that a'tall!... I was coming around the east end, up by the old lime kilns, and I saw the police removing a body. It was a terrible shock, obviously. And then when I learned later that it was Jon, it was even more of a blow, as you can imagine... Yes, I saw them taking away the hamper. And it seemed very odd that Jon would have one. Once I knew it was Jon, but... No, I had no wish to become involved, and I didn't mention the hamper so as not to—

"No, of course not! Why would I write her a vitriolic letter?... Oh, I see!... And do you have any material proof that I sent this epistle, or is this entirely conjecture on your part?... Indeed! No, *let* them examine my typewriter, yes, and the one here as well!… Absolutely not! *If* the type on the envelope matches that of the church typewriter, that still does not mean that I—

"*Do* you! I think you're grasping at straws!… Oh?… If Ellie MacLean does receive another such letter, I will *not* allow myself to be hounded by… Let me assure you that my position at this school is beyond any power of yours to—"

Katherine Burnett stared at the dead receiver and then set it quietly in its holder. She looked around the room again, to be sure no one had slipped in unnoticed, and then she sat down behind the desk. Tears were gathering in her eyes, and she took an embroidered handkerchief out of her bag and carefully dabbed at her lower lids so as not to smear her mascara. She swallowed several times and worked to keep her hand from shaking as she took out a compact and powdered her face. She adjusted her earrings and pulled a section of bangs farther to one side, and then she began searching through her purse. Her chin was trembling as she removed a metal nail file from its leather sheath and began working at shortening a nail. Then she paused. And drove the point into the palm of her hand.

"Of course this is Hamish MacDonald. Who would you expect it to be in my own home?… Alright, Fiona, I'll wait." He was standing in a dark hall beside the small rickety table that held the phone, tightening a worn brown cord around the middle of his gray robe. He was unshaven and his hair hadn't been combed, and his eyes looked red rimmed and bloodshot.

He reached through an archway into the living room beyond and pulled a small desk chair into the hall. He sat as though he were too tired to stand, and said, "So it's you, is it?" in a colorless voice. "Well?… What if I did intend to tell Martha what to tell you? And that's not to say she would've agreed… Perhaps I resented having a total stranger prying into my personal affairs… No! All I want is to be left in peace! Of course, *you're* so bloody persistent… Oh?… You promise, do you? I have your word that I won't be bothered again?… Right then. For it's bound to be public information soon enough… Not *that* early, no. I didn't leave my sister's in Peebles until a few minutes before seven, when I drove into Edinburgh to a medical appointment that was fixed for nine o'clock. It was a second opinion, as a matter of fact. With a vera well-known and expensive specialist… Aye. But I only heard the final results yesterday. I suppose I should've expected it. For the tests confirmed the diagnosis of the Edinburgh man, and the quack up here as well… It seems I have terminal cancer. And they don't think I'll live to see the winter."

Hamish was staring at the wall in front of him, sitting still and spent and speaking in a flat dry voice. "Up here? I consulted him a week or more before MacLean died… Oh, aye! Condolences and all!… Well, I'm touched I'm sure… You do have a bloody nerve, don't you!… Alright! Fine!… Dr. Robert Jones on Princes Street… So can you see at last that I had nothing whatever to do with MacLean's death, even if I couldn't stomach the man?… Aye. You may now go and hound someone else who has nothing whatever to hide."

Ben was standing in the small yellow and white sitting room, staring out the windows toward the drive. He'd had the operator place calls to Winnetka, Illinois, as well as Jedburgh, Edinburgh, and Gullane, Scotland. And he was waiting for her to call him back with whatever call went through first, when Alex knocked on the door.

"Ben?"

"Come on in."

"Have you finished your calls?"

"I'm waiting for the operator to call me back."

"Ah. Well, whenever you're done, I shall begin those other inquiries."

Ben told Alex what Hamish had told him.

And Alex shook his large square head, before he said, "Poor Hamish. That must be a *terrible* blow."

"I know."

"One can't even imagine it."

"No."

"So. You're off to meet this mysterious witness of yours, are you?"

"After I finish here. Have you seen Ellie? She wasn't in her room."

"She went off to the butcher's and the green grocer's with Mary Atwood. They're expecting the solicitor to stay to dinner, and hoping to invite Dr. Graham as well. He rang to say he'd be stopping on his rounds to offer his condolences, and Mary asked if he'd take a look at Ellie."

"Good. I'd like to talk to him too."

The phone rang, and Ben grabbed it, with his eyes on Alex, who turned then and started toward the door.

The Feathers was a small stone pub six miles from Kilgarth on the edge of the old part of Dunblane. It was at least two hundred years old and it had sloping floors and huge black beams and smelled pleasantly of wood smoke.

Ben was early, but Marjorie Wilson was there already, sitting at a table in a far corner away from the bar and the door. They decided on the bar lunch, ordered tea, and helped themselves to the buffet.

But before either of them had picked up a fork, Marjorie Wilson (who was probably in her forties, and maybe twenty pounds heavier than was fashionable), looked up from her plate of cold meat salad, smoothed her napkin across her red paisley dress, and glanced self-consciously at Ben. "Thank you for giving me time to collect myself."

"I don't want to make this hard on you."

"Yet ye do want to know where Alf was when Reverend MacLean died."

"Yeah, but I'm only interested in Jon's death. I won't drag anybody into it who shouldn't be there."

Marjorie Wilson didn't say anything while she studied Ben with one raised eyebrow and a penetrating look in her small dark eyes. "I hope that's true, Mr. Reese, I really do, for I'm risking a great deal more than you realize. Alf is not a'tall pleased that I'm speaking to ye, and yet I feel I must, for he has enough to cope with at the moment without being questioned in a murder investigation. Especially if the police are brought in and the papers get hold of the information."

Ben nodded neutrally and wiped his mouth with his napkin.

"I don't know where to begin, really, but I'd like you to understand Alf a bit better than ye do." Her hair was brown and shoulder length, but it still curled in wisps around her forehead, and she pushed one away from her left eye as though it were an irritation.

"How'd you get to know him?"

"We met in Glasgow when he was fourteen and I was nine. He was vera much an older brother to me then. Though he needed friendship and attention too, for his mother had left him and his dad when Alf was just eight. His dad moved them away up to Glasgow from London not quite a year later, and there he became a welder for one of the big shipbuilders.

"Alf was left on his own a great deal, in a city where he knew almost no one. So whenever he had a bit extra, he'd take himself off to the pictures. He'd see all those lovely people on the screen in their big fancy houses, and he'd compare that to life on the docks. He wanted big cars, and other people looking up to him. And he could see that getting an education was the only way for him. He worked terrifically hard at school, and he was an errand boy for the firm where his dad worked too, and a Mr. Ferguson there, he took an interest in Alf, and when the time came, he helped him get through technical college in Glasgow. Alf studied chemistry and did well at it, for he's a very intelligent person."

"Yes, I'm sure he is."

"Anyway, there was nothing between us a'tall but friendship until my final year at school, even though I was vera much in love with him long before that. I think he was with me as well. And yet he married an English woman from a well-to-do family instead. They'd met in London when he'd first taken a position as a chemical engineer. I know he longed for the social connections and the money she had by rights. And I was hurt, of course, as you might imagine. I wasn't over him, though. And after he found precious little satisfaction there, he came to me, and I took him in. I was young and miserable, and I was willing to have him at any price. Foolish of me, wasn't it? To go straight on with it, when I knew better?"

"All these years?"

"Aye. All these years." Marjorie Wilson sipped her tea and stared at the old wooden dart board hanging beside the bar.

"What I have to tell you now, we've kept completely dark for ten years and more. And I cannot *begin* to say how important it'tis that ye tell no one a'tall."

"If it isn't connected with Jon MacLean's death, I promise you I won't repeat it."

"Ye mustn't. There are many more lives at stake than mine and Alf's. For as it happened, Mr. Reese, we had a daughter born to us ten years ago. My elder sister, Helen, and her husband couldn't have children of their own, and they adopted Sarah right from hospital. They've lived in Cambridge ever since, and they've been very good to Sarah and me as well. I visit her several times a year, and I write her and send her little gifts, and I think she likes her Aunt Marjorie as much as one could hope.

"At least once every year, Alf comes with me to see Sarah too. So she thinks he's my husband, and her Uncle Alf, and this year, on Sarah's birthday, we met her and my sister in York. It was to be a special treat, and Helen took her out of school for the two days. We stayed in a fancy hotel at Alf's expense, and it was a wonderful time, *I* thought, even though there was just the one day. Helen and Sarah stayed on longer, but Alf could only get away the eleventh and twelfth. So we started *vera* early on the eleventh, long before dawn, and drove down to York, down the East coast, along the ocean. On the twelfth, we stopped for lunch in Newcastle Upon Tyne, on our way back north to Glasgow, and that's when we stopped in the parking garage."

"I see."

"I've told no one about Sarah except one friend I have good reason to trust, and Alf's never mentioned her to anyone a'tall. So you can see, Mr. Reese, how important it'tis that you take vera good care as well."

"If what you say is true, and Alf had nothing to do with Jon's death, I won't mention it to anyone. I will need to contact your sister, though, and I'd like the name of the hotel in York."

"Will you fix it up so Helen doesn't know that Alf's in trouble?"

"Yes. If you want me to."

"Aye, I do. We were registered under the name of Wilson, Alf and me. Sarah thinks I married a man with the same last name as me. It does happen in life, and it saves a bit of confusion."

Marjorie wrote her sister's name and address, and the name of the hotel in York, while Ben paid the check. And then she looked at him as though she were debating what to say next. "Do you think your friend Mr. Sutherland will prosecute Alf for this other business?"

"He hasn't told me one way or the other, but I had the impression when we talked earlier that his primary concern was getting Alf out of the business as cleanly as possible. Do you know what Alf has done?"

"I don't suppose he's told me everything. And I haven't questioned him in any detail."

Ben didn't say anything. He just stared at the scar underneath his left wrist where it slid down across his palm.

"I've hurt him already, and I don't want to make it worse. I do love Alf, and I understand why he does many of the things he does, but I have come to the point in my life that I can't continue the way I have done in the past. It's not right, Mr. Reese. I didn't want to admit that, even to myself, for a vera long time. But I've come to it, finally, and I've only just told him this week. I don't want him to have too many blows all at once, but there has to be a clean break."

"I see."

"Do ye?" Marjorie Wilson smiled, as she picked her pocket-

215

book up off the floor. "I've given up a great deal for Alfred Dixon, and I don't think now it was vera wise. I should have had a husband to love, and a child who was mine to raise. I should have made a life of my own, Mr. Reese. And sometimes I still tell myself it might not be too late."

"I don't imagine Mrs. Dixon has had much of a life either."

"No. I expect you're right." Marjorie looked directly at Ben and then turned away toward the door. "Well. I must run. I have to get back to the office."

"What kind of work do you do?"

"I manage the customer service department for a perfume manufacturer in Glasgow. Thank you for lunch, Mr. Reese. I do hope ye find the person who murdered Mr. MacLean. I can't begin to fathom what his wife is going through."

Rory MacKenzie was driving north from Dunblane toward Kinbuck, following the narrow, shallow river called the Allan Water. He had the top down on his black two seater MG, and he was taking the curves and the corners fast. He liked the feel of the wind in his face, and he liked the countryside, the small farms and the gentle hills and the clusters of grazing sheep.

But his heart kept battering against his ribs like it had when he was young, and he told himself not to be ridiculous. Yes, he'd be seeing Ellie, but that meant nothing more than it had since she'd first met Jon. She was in mourning, real, deep, debilitating mourning. And Ellie, being the sort she was, might never get over it. Not enough to marry again, certainly.

Yet here he was, fantasizing already, imagining a life with her when there was no reason a'tall to hope. He was being unrealistic *and* self-centered. And any normal man would be ashamed of himself, with Jon hardly cold in his grave.

And yet he wasn't. He was wondering if he could manage to see Ellie alone without attracting too much attention. He needed to talk to her when she wasn't distracted.

Even though he'd been nothing *but* distracted since Jon died. Why couldn't he simply feign indifference and stop acting like a lovesick school boy?

It was ironic, really. For there were actually quite a few people who wished they had lives like his. Young ambitious newspapermen who longed to edit the paper. Plus the usual sort who covet one's home and one's bank account, as well as the women who buzz around all "successful" men. Of course, they're the kind of women who relish the aristocratic connections, who adore the social events that ought to bore them to tears, who hang on one's arm and smile up into one's face, and absolutely reek of shallowness and death. When Rory MacKenzie would give up all that, all those trappings and those "advantages," if Ellie MacLean would look at him once the way she'd looked at Jon.

No. Not everything. He did truly care about the paper. There was a deep steady satisfaction in being able to do work he felt was worth doing. And Ellie understood that. Ellie actually admired him for that, if nothing else.

Yes, and it was time he took charge of himself and thought about the interview he was set to do with Daphne du Maurier, while he looked for the turnoff to Kilgarth.

Even so, he drove past the gatehouse, down the drive, around the old Cedar of Lebanon and up to the front door, with his insides in a snarl.

And then when he watched Ben, waiting for him on the front steps, the expression on Ben's face made Rory feel even more ridiculous. Ben would see it. Ben would know he was beginning to hope, and it wouldn't do.

For more than one reason, when he stopped to think of it. For it made his proximity to Holy Island on the morning of May twelfth even more suspect still.

"Of course, Ellie wasn't surprised." Alex was standing with his back to the sitting room fireplace, glancing from Ben to Rory. "She knew. She and Jon had worked it out. And one does see the wisdom of giving Hugh the house. Even though one could also see it was a bit of a blow for poor Hugh. Ellie did try to prepare him, before we read the will. She missed him at breakfast, and then searched for him again right before McGuire arrived, when Hugh was off with a tenant."

"Isn't it unusual not to leave the house to your wife?"

"It'tis, Ben, yes, and yet he did leave it to her, in a manner of speaking. You see, the will states that if they had children, or she was pregnant at the time of his death, she was to have the house so she could raise the children in Scotland and then let them decide what was to be done with Kilgarth. If that was not the case, and Jon explained this very carefully in the will, he and Ellie had long been agreed that Hugh should have the family home because of its personal associations.

"Ellie is to have the paintings, the books, the jewelry and all the furnishings to do with as she wishes, for the feeling was that without children, she'd probably go back to America. She owns a house in North Carolina she's leasing, apparently, and that *is* home to her, after all. Ellie did explain, after the will had been read, that she and Jon had decided not to tell Hugh in advance so he'd be free to plan his own life as he wished, without feeling tied down to Kilgarth. They hadn't expected Jon to die so soon, and they'd intended to change the will later, if it looked as though Kilgarth would be an encumbrance for Hugh."

"Did Jon have an insurance policy?" Ben was watching Alex from an old wing back chair, making notes on his small leather pad.

"Yes, of twenty thousand pounds. Ellie's to have that too, so she will have funds for awhile." Alex paused and stretched his arms above his head and then threw himself on the old camelback sofa, where he sorted through his pockets for a peppermint lozenge. "Of course, now that they aren't tied to a parish, Ellie will be free to live wherever she'd like, and begin to really concentrate on her career."

"What other provisions are there?"

"Well, Jon has asked Ellie to give Mrs. Atwood two thousand pounds from the insurance money outright, in addition to a few pieces of family memorabilia, and he's asked Hugh to provide an income for Mary as well. Still, Ellie intends to give Hugh some of the paintings and the furniture too, so he'll be able to sell a few things if he needs to, to help with Mrs. Atwood's maintenance."

"How did Hugh react?" Ben had stood up by then and was looking out toward the front drive with his hands in his pockets and his jacket shoved behind his elbows.

"He hasn't said much, of course, but one could see he doesn't want the house. He looked quite appalled when the blow fell. There is another stipulation too, that if he does sell, he's to give a third of the proceeds to Ellie."

"So Ellie agreed to all this beforehand, but neither of them told Hugh?"

"Yes. He's a very accommodating chap, and they didn't want him to feel obligated to take it on. They also assumed they had plenty of time to alter the will. Which ought to be a lesson to us all."

"What did Jon leave you?"

"Exactly what he told me he would. His wonderful old cavalry saddle and his Roman and Celtic artifacts. The ones we dug up as children."

"Are they valuable?" Ben had turned toward Alex and was watching him steadily with his cool gray eyes.

"I haven't the foggiest. You're much better placed than I to have an opinion. He's also made me the executor of his will, because he didn't want Ellie to be bothered with all the details."

"Where *are* Ellie and Hugh? I haven't seen either of them since I arrived." Rory had lit a cigarette and was sliding his lighter back and forth from one hand to the other.

"Ellie asked to have a quiet word with McGuire, the family solicitor, and Hugh's gone down to the gatehouse. Apparently, there's very little hot water, and no electricity a'tall in the sitting room, so he's arranging to call someone in. Now, who can that be?"

A car was scattering gravel across the drive, and Alex got up and looked out the window. "Dr. Graham! I forgot all about him. I shall just dash out and let him in."

Ellie was in the hall already, having just said good-bye to Mr. McGuire, holding a stiff-sided leather case he'd brought her from the car.

"Isn't McGuire staying to dinner?" Alex was watching him shut his car door, while Graham was opening his.

"No, he says he's coming down with a cold, and he wants to get to bed early. He's staying at the pub in Kinbuck, and he'll come back in the morning and retrieve the family jewels. Dr. Graham!"

"Hello, my dear." Dr. William Graham's large pink face was fixed on Ellie as he set his medical bag down and wrapped his arms around her. "I can't tell you how sorry I am. I wish I could've come to the funeral, but I simply couldn't get away."

They stood silently for a minute, holding on to each other, rocking gently from side to side. And then with her face buried against his chest, Ellie very quietly said, "Thank you for coming now."

"Alice sends her love, of course. And she asked me to tell you that she wants to have you to the house for dinner the first moment you feel up to it."

Alex introduced Ben and Rory, and Dr. Graham shook hands with all three, before he looked back at Alex. "Where's our Hugh, then?"

"He should be home shortly. He especially asked us to invite you to dinner."

"Ah, that would be lovely, thank you. I never refuse an offer to enjoy Mary Atwood's cooking. So let me look at you, my dear." Dr. Graham slid his hands in the pockets of his navy blue trousers and rolled back and forth on the balls of his feet as he observed Ellie critically from under a patch of thick gray hair. Then he turned to Alex and Rory and nodded his head toward Ellie. "How's she doing in your opinion?"

"Well—" Alex started to answer.

But Ellie interrupted him. "Do you always talk about people as though they aren't there, or do you just assume most of us are incapable of speaking for ourselves?" Ellie was trying to smile at Dr. Graham.

And he laughed and said, "It generally depends on the person. Are you eating and sleeping yet?"

"Not the way I normally do."

"Can't say I'm surprised. But you are looking a bit frail, you know. And that's a condition I find particularly suspect, never having suffered from it myself!" Dr. Graham chuckled quietly as he straightened his protruding vest.

"I think I'm doing alright."

"Well—" Alex tried again.

But Dr. Graham held up his hand before Alex got any farther. "Perhaps you are, my dear, but I shall be absolutely forthright and tell you straightaway that I've spoken to Mary Atwood *and* Hugh, and it seems everyone here is concerned about your health, and they've asked me to look you over. You might as well give in gracefully, you know, because I shan't take no for an answer."

"I see!" Ellie looked sharply at Alex. But then stopped and considered before she spoke. "I don't suppose I mind, really. I know you mean well. Even if you did go behind my back."

"Good! Then why don't we go straight upstairs and get it over with without further ado?"

"Now?"

Dr. Graham nodded.

"Alright. I suppose it's as good a time as any."

"Good girl! It takes brains to know when you're licked! Course you and Jon always had brains, anyone could see that." Dr. Graham raised his eyebrows conspiratorially toward Alex, as he picked up his bag and followed Ellie up the U-shaped stairs.

It had been an elaborate meal, consommé and salmon and roast lamb. But with Rory MacKenzie and William Graham bringing news from the outside world, it wasn't until the dessert plates had been cleared and the coffee and the fruit brought in that the table talk died in fits and spurts.

Mary Atwood left to tackle the dishes. And then Ellie folded her napkin and pushed her chair back away from the table. "I think I better go on up. I still have to sort through the jewelry Mr. McGuire brought us from the bank, and I'd like to get to bed early."

"Could I speak to you for a moment first?" Rory was standing too, holding his napkin in front of him, looking inordinately handsome, but tentative at the same time. "It won't take more than a moment."

"Sure. Why don't we go in the library?"

Ellie was starting toward the door when Dr. Graham pointed his finger at her across the table. "Now, my dear, you remember what you promised. When you're ready for bed, you take two of the sleeping tablets I've given you."

"I will tonight. But I can't promise that I will tomorrow."

"Tomorrow night too!"

"I don't like taking anything."

"I understand that, and you're quite right, in the normal course of events, but for these two nights, I want you to take the tablets. Your body needs rest, and something to break the sleepless cycle."

"Okay. But nothing after that."

"Good! I'll stop again tomorrow with the results of the blood tests."

"I appreciate it. And please thank Alice for the dinner invitation. Hugh, could you come up and see me after I've talked to Rory? I'd like you to look at the jewelry too."

"Of course! What time shall we say?"

"Nine maybe? Does that give us enough time?" Ellie looked at Rory and he nodded. "Thanks, Hugh. Good night everyone."

Ellie and Rory left together, looking more alike, with their black hair and their green eyes and their fine pale skin, than a lot of people who are closely related.

"It's been a long day." Alex had loosened his tie and was turning his water glass in front of a candle, watching the flame shatter through the cut glass.

"It's certainly been a day of unexpected events. I *never* would have thought for a moment that Jon would bequeath me Kilgarth, and I'm afraid it's been a bit of a jolt."

"Why?" Ben was gazing at Hugh over his own coffee cup, as Dr. Graham passed him the plate of chocolates.

"It's hard to explain, really." Hugh had poured himself a second cup of coffee and was reaching for the small silver cream pitcher. "I do appreciate Jon's thoughtfulness in wanting me to decide the fate of the family home. It was very kind of him, and extremely well intended. But Kilgarth is something of a financial drain, and I suppose I'm feeling a bit stunned." Hugh had been staring at the peonies in the center of the table, but then he looked at Ben with a half-bewildered expression in his intensely blue eyes.

"So what do you think you'll do?"

"I don't have a clue. And I suppose I shall have to guard against making a hasty decision. I've been asked to teach another course in the autumn, after I've got my doctorate, and I have hopes of finding consulting work with a rather large petroleum company that's looking for offshore oil. I shall have to live in town, as a result, and I've just found a lovely flat, so I don't know. Kilgarth needs someone who will really take an interest. And if I sold it, I could provide for Mary a bit more easily. Though I don't know the full tax implications of inheriting *or* selling. Still, it's been in the family for a hundred years. One can't simply sell it without a backward glance."

"Yes, it's a very difficult decision. Though I was fortunate, because I could write very happily at Balnagard."

"Before I decide anything, I know I shall have to carefully examine the business end of things here. But it's not as though Kilgarth is a national treasure, with historic or architectural importance, like Balnagard. Though whether one will find willing buyers is another question entirely."

"Every house sells. It's just a question of when." The room was lit entirely by candles and Ben had been watching the reflection of the flames on the tall dark windows by the back garden. But then he turned to Dr. Graham, who was sitting on his right, with his chin on his chest and his eyes half closed. "So how do you think Ellie's doing, Dr. Graham? If that's not an indiscreet question."

William Graham's eyes flew open and he sat up and reached for the coffeepot. "Well . . in general terms, she's a bit run down, just as one might expect. I did phone her doctor in Inverness, and we decided it might be as well to run a few blood tests. Anemia, and the usual things, nothing out of the way. So I drew blood this afternoon and shall run it into the lab in Dunblane as soon as I leave here. But all things considered, I don't think she's doing too badly."

"We've actually been rather worried about her, haven't we Alex?" Hugh looked at Alex, who was staring at one of the Campbell portraits and didn't seem to hear.

Dr. Graham consulted a large gold pocket watch, and then drank the last of his coffee. "I really must be going. I still have another call to make after I stop at the laboratory. Thank you, Hugh, it was a lovely dinner, and I shall dash into the kitchen and thank Mary as well. I shall also ask if she sampled the trifle. She still fights against her diabetes, and she's not always trustworthy when it comes to sweets."

"I'll walk out with you." Ben was up from the table before Graham pushed back his chair. "I've still got some calls to make before it gets too late."

"I thought you finished this afternoon." Alex was smiling at Ben with a piece of Cheshire cheese halfway to his lips.

"No. And I've got to learn about bees too. Remind me to tell you tomorrow."

CHAPTER ELEVEN

Wednesday, May 24th

"WHAT'S THE MATTER, MARY?"

"Oh . . it's distressing when you realize your faculties are beginning to fail." Her soft round face looked flushed and uneasy as she handed Ben his bowl of porridge and lowered herself into the chair across from him at the kitchen table. "I'm losing my memory, and it's hard to bear."

"Why, what's happened?"

"I've been giving myself insulin injections morning and night for thirteen years, so you'd think I'd know what I'm about, and yet when I came down this morning to open a new package from the icebox and start on a new bottle, I discovered that I'd already opened the box and used two bottles as well."

"I don't understand what that means, because I don't know how it's packaged when it comes from the chemist."

"Well, it's done up in paper, and when you open that, there's a cardboard box with six little bottles separated by bits of cardboard."

"How long does it take you to finish a bottle?"

227

"Five days."

"So you would've had to take two bottles of insulin to Balnagard?"

"Aye, I took a half-bottle and a new bottle as well. I finished the full one last night. How could I open a brand new package and use two bottles and not remember!"

"You went up to Balnagard on the sixteenth, right? And came back here on the twenty-second? You could've opened the new package before you heard about Jon's death. Or even after, when you were waiting for news from the inquest, or when you were packing to go to Balnagard for the funeral. It'd be easy to forget something like that, because of the shock and the confusion."

"But I was in and out of the icebox all day yesterday, and if you'd put a Bible in my hand, I would have sworn that box hadn't been opened!"

"I still don't think you need to worry about it. We all make mistakes like that."

"I've been ordering food in too, and then I find I've got whatever it'tis in the larder."

"I do that all the time." Ben had taken his toast out of the toaster and was reaching across for the butter.

"You know, that's the very toaster Lord Alex fixed for me last winter. I've never understood why he says he's unmechanical. I don't think he is a'tall. Though he's always been very quick to point out his own shortcomings."

"Have you had a chance to find the photograph?"

"Aye, I have it here." Mary reached into the pocket of her apron and handed Ben a plain white envelope. "Though why you'd look through all my photographs and ask for one of old Mr. and Mrs. MacLean picnicking by the road on a drive to Port Appin, I can't begin to imagine."

He took out the three-by-five black-and-white print, and said, "Thanks, Mary. It's exactly what I wanted. I don't suppose Rory's up yet is he?"

"He left an hour and a half ago. He had to be at his office by half-seven, so he left about five-fifteen. We ate our breakfast together, and he asked me to say good-bye."

"Nuts. I needed to talk to him."

"More coffee?" Ben nodded, and Mary handed him the white china coffeepot with the tea cozy still in place. "I haven't told you everything about my loss of memory. I've twice forgotten to lock the doors in the basement. The one door the night before Jon died, and the other the night before last."

"That doesn't mean—"

"I'm very particular about the doors because I'm here alone so much. I always make a point of seeing to them myself, and yet I still forgot, and I find it quite alarming."

"Mary—"

"My mother went terribly wrong, mentally, before she died, and I've dreaded it all my life. A great deal more than death itself." She was stirring her tea, staring at the spoon with soft blue eyes that looked strained as well as embarrassed.

"That doesn't mean it's happening to you. Everybody overlooks something in the refrigerator, or forgets to lock a door. You're expecting the worst because of your mother."

"It's always in the back of my mind, I will say that. But how could I forget Jon's birthday! Jon, of all people?"

"Why don't you tell me everything that happened the night before he died, so we can see if it's actually worth worrying about?"

"Well . . to start, I put the dustbins out front to be collected by the dustman the next day, and then I locked the doors the same way I do every night. Or so I *thought*. I went to bed a little before ten. And I dropped right off, the way I do, but I was awakened later by a noise outside my front windows. It sounded like an animal, a cat or a dog I imagine, had gotten in amongst the dustbins and knocked them about. It happens quite frequently, for there're quite a few small animals on the land.

"Hugh was still up, so he heard it too, and when he heard me rustling around, he came and looked in on me. I remember we talked about how we used to drink hot chocolate together years ago at bedtime, when he was a wee lad. Though now I'm not allowed to have it, because of the diabetes… Why did I mention that? See? I can't even remember what I'm talking about from one moment to the next!" Mary's smile looked forced and uneasy, as she brushed a crumb off the collar of her dress.

"So what time did the noise wake you up?"

"A wee bit before twelve. Then Hugh made himself a cup of hot chocolate and brought me a cup of hot milk with vanilla and a wee drop of coffee in it. We chatted for a few minutes, and then I went back to sleep. Hugh does that. Makes the occasional hot drink before we go to bed."

"That's nice of him."

"Aye, it cairtainly is. I told you the rest at Balnagard, I believe. How I overslept for the first time in years and rose at seven-thirty, and then remembered that the day before had been Jon's forty-first birthday. It was a terrible shock, to find I'd forgotten. I always baked him a tin of shortbread and posted it to him with a wee gift."

"So what happened when you got up?"

"Well, Hugh had set his own alarm, as he always does. And he'd left me a note here on the kitchen table, saying he'd first planned to leave at half-six, but had then decided to start at a quarter past, with the traffic the way it'tis in the morning and him having to meet the Americans at a set time. I heard his car when he left, for I woke and looked at the clock, and saw it was six-fifteen. Yet I still went back to sleep and didn't wake until half-seven, much to my own shame. He'd packed himself a wee bite to eat on the road, and he left me the note to tell me he'd used the last of the ham."

"So—" The door from the hall opened, and Ben turned to see Alex shuffle in in his slippers and robe, with his eyes almost closed and his face half-shuttered. "You're up awfully early."

"Awoke at three, unfortunately. Eventually gave in and took up a book." Alex had already wandered over to the stove and was picking up the lid on the oatmeal. "Reading was a bit of a strain. I misplaced my glasses after dinner. May I help myself, or isn't there enough porridge?"

"There's more than enough. Would you care for toast?" Mary was pushing herself out of her chair, when Alex laid his hand on her shoulder and said, "You sit down and finish your tea while I fend for myself." He dished up his oatmeal and sat at the end of the table, after depositing his bread in the toaster.

"I didn't tell you before I went to bed, did I, that Hugh's car broke down in town?" Mary looked at Alex first and then turned toward Ben. "He drove into Dunblane after he talked to Ellie, for he couldn't reach the electrician at home and was told he could find him at the Thistle and Crown. When Hugh was ready to drive home, his car was leaking oil . . or it wouldn't start, I don't remember which . . and he had to take a room at the pub. He's to get it into a garage first thing, and then stop at the gatehouse to make sure the work's underway."

"What time did he call?" Ben popped the last of his toast in his mouth, while Alex buttered his.

"Eleven or so. From what I remember. Assuming I remember anything a'tall." Mary had already taken a bottle of insulin out of the icebox, and was opening the hall door. "Don't bother with the dishes. I'll freshen up a bit, and straighten my room, and then do the washing up."

"Thanks for the help, Mary." Ben set his dishes on the counter, as the door slapped shut behind him, then turned on the water and squirted soap in the sink. "How did your phone calls turn out yesterday?"

Alex looked blank to begin with, but then the mists cleared, while he licked orange marmalade off his thumb. "Well, first of all, Gerald Pilcher was definitely in Craig House every moment from the eighth to the sixteenth."

"Then that eliminates Gerald."

"I would've thought so, yes."

"Hamish was in Edinburgh too, for his doctor's appointment. He was waiting on the steps when the office staff appeared at eight-forty, so it looks like that leaves him out. Except that we only have his word for when he left Peebles. And I think I may call his sister again and find out if any of her neighbors actually saw him leave. So what about the friend of Jon's who drove him to Holy Island?"

"Ah, Roger Evans. He told me Jon made a point of mentioning how much he was looking forward to our walking tour." Alex brightened visibly and coughed as though he were trying not to look too pleased.

"Was he carrying a basket?"

"No. No, he did not have a hamper of any kind when Roger dropped him off on Holy Island. What else was I supposed to ferret out?"

"The temperature on Holy Island the morning Jon died."

"Yes, of course! The low for the day was fifty-three degrees and the high was seventy-four degrees, so it was warmer than one might expect the middle of May, just as I remembered. Does that help?"

"Very much." Ben smiled out the window at the kitchen garden, and then propped his bowl in the dish drainer.

"I also spoke to Jane, and she says no one at Balnagard remembers taking a call for you. So apparently there's a very limited number of people who knew you were staying at Perach."

"That helps. Even if it isn't conclusive."

"Have you found out when Rory left the inn in Jedburgh?"

"I spoke to the night clerk, and he says he left a few minutes before five."

"What time did he arrive at the paper in Edinburgh?"

"Seven-forty. His secretary comes in early on Fridays, and he dictated letters until his staff meeting started at eight-fifteen. Then this Sunday, when your boys saw the MG by Balnagard, he was sitting in the front row in Gullane at his youngest daughter's piano recital."

"He'd have quite a little drive up to Edinburgh from Jedburgh. Farther than Peebles, surely." Alex slipped his own dishes into the sink and then took the dish rag from Ben. "The road from Jedburgh to Holy Island would be terribly slow for quite a bit of it too."

"So all of that would eliminate Rory. *If* the night clerk remembers correctly, or wasn't bought off before I talked to him."

"You have a frightfully suspicious mind!"

"Don't I have to, to do this?"

"Yes. I suppose you do. It's quite complicated, isn't it, all the research and the checking one has to do? When I wrote the mystery novel, I talked to experts in chemistry, pathology, hydraulic engineering, and medieval herbs, and that was all there was to it."

"Yeah. Reality's not so simple."

"Please don't answer if I'm prying, but what is it you've been doing this last day or two? You've been closeted in the sitting room for hours on end, and the few calls I know about can't account for it." Alex was sitting at the table again, with his legs crossed beside it, swinging a foot up and down like it wouldn't have been easy for him to stop.

"I'll tell you about it later when I've found out what I need to know. Alright?"

"Of course. It's just that I have a niggling feeling I'm not being trusted completely."

"Mary told me you repaired the toaster."

"Did she? The controls hadn't been properly set. No, I'm absolutely hopeless with gadgets, and I'm quite inept with my hands. I grew too quickly when I was sixteen, and the nerves didn't develop properly. I can't work with nuts and bolts, or unravel knots, or manage bits of wire."

"I didn't know that."

"It's not a serious condition, I'm happy to say, but that's why my handwriting is so appalling. I do type reasonably well, having learned as a child. And oddly enough, I am able to inoculate horses, which saves quite a bit on the vet bills. I can't bring myself to inject a dog, though. They seem so small and delicate, don't they? In comparison?"

"Why would Mary have trouble with the controls on a toaster she's used for years?"

"I have no idea. I wondered that at the time."

"Anyway," Ben was opening the hall door, holding a large mug of coffee and watching Alex, "if you need me, I'll be in the sitting room all morning."

There was an open copy of *Scottish Beekeeper* in his lap, but Ben wasn't reading it. He sat slouched in a tall chair, his shoes on the edge of the coffee table, his hands locked on top of his head and his mind on Jon MacLean's murder.

Hugh *did* meet the Harvey Millers in Edinburgh at ten after eight, and he did take them up to St. Andrews, exactly as he said he did.

And Hamish is out of the running, since Margaret's neighbor saw him leave right at six forty-five while she was frying the family eggs.

Dorothy Burnett says she's remembered that Katherine woke her at six by running the water in the bathroom, even though she can't say for sure when Katherine left for her walk. She thinks it must've been about six-fifteen. But either way, the timing's iffy. Jon was already dead by a quarter after, and Katherine would've had to meet him well before six to give him the basket and disappear before Jimmy Reed was out and about.

Not necessarily, though. Jimmy didn't notice anyone that morning, even Jon. But Katherine didn't bring a basket to Holy Island. She had no car. She went nowhere on her own to buy bees *or* a basket. She's had no experience with bees in the past. And it would've been very hard to keep them in a cottage that small without Dorothy suspecting. And Dorothy, to her undying credit, never covers up for Katherine. Or if she does, she's better at smoke screens than almost anybody I know.

Marjorie's alibi for Alf checks out with both the hotel *and* the sister.

And if the night clerk's right, there's no way Rory could've made it to Holy Island and back up to Edinburgh by seven-forty. Not unless he paid off his secretary *and* the clerk too. And there's no real reason to think he did. Not if you accept Ockham's Razor. The old "take the theory that covers all the data with the fewest number of assumptions" approach. Which I do. Since it's still a basic tenet of the scientific method, even after seven hundred years.

So keep the clerk and the secretary in mind, and pay attention.

Rory could have driven up to Perach and sabotaged the towel rack while I ran before breakfast, or ate with the kids, or went to church. But why would he kill Jon? Jealousy and hatred, and "maybe Ellie will love me if Jon is dead"? Yeah, but is Rory really naive enough to make that kind of assumption? It doesn't make a lot of sense.

The strange thing about Jon's death is that so many of the alibis are based on timing, with very long stretches between witnesses. You end up asking what's probable and what isn't, because there's almost no hard data. No concrete, measurable, observable physical stuff. Other than the basket. At least, not yet.

Even Alex's alibi comes down to timing, with long periods unaccounted for. We know he took the train to Edinburgh on the afternoon of the eleventh so he could meet his agent and publisher for breakfast the morning of the twelfth. He was there, eating crumpets and eggs at nine. But he could've checked into his club the afternoon of the eleventh, then snuck out and picked up the bees, having already arranged for them ahead of time. He could've taken a train down to Berwich upon Tweed, camped somewhere for the night, and given Jon the hamper at five-thirty, before he caught a train back north for his breakfast at nine.

Which is not to say that Alex is guilty. He's got no motive at all that I can see. Because it's hard to imagine him coveting Ellie, much less the Roman artifacts. If he's not happy with Jane, he's the best actor I've ever seen. And he's not a mad collector type. He hardly pays any attention to the artifacts at Balnagard.

Although motive isn't everything.

And when I know how, I'll know who.

But it's not going to be easy to prove my own favorite theory. Because even if I am right, I've got to come up with a direct connection to the bees. How can I make the phone calls fast enough? When there are other journals besides this. And other sources besides them. That's why it's the kind of inquiry the police do best.

Just dial and pray, boy. That's all you can do now.

Mary Atwood opened the door, stuck her head around the corner, and said, "Mr. McGuire has arrived," seconds after Ben had dropped into the desk chair and picked up the phone. "Hugh hasn't come home yet, Alex is in the library in his bathrobe, and Ellie is still sleeping. It's the tablets Dr. Graham gave her, I expect, and I do hate to wake her."

Mr. McGuire was waiting in the hall by the stairs, and as soon as he saw Ben, he apologized for calling so early. He'd told Mrs. MacLean he'd arrive at nine, but when he'd checked his appointment calendar that morning, he found that a very important appointment in Edinburgh was earlier than he'd thought, and he needed to talk to Mrs. MacLean as soon as may be and retrieve whatever jewelry she didn't wish to keep herself or give away in the near future.

He was tall, thin, graying, and probably in his sixties, and he was wearing an overcoat and scarf even though it was almost seventy. Ben asked if his cold was better, while trying not to stare at his briefcase, which appeared to be nothing but torn rust-colored strips of ancient leather hanging from a handle and frame.

"I'm very much better, thank you. I am sorry to disturb Mrs. MacLean, but I'm afraid I have very little choice."

"Oh, aye." Mary looked at him pointedly, and then started up the stairs as though her legs hurt.

"Mr. McGuire! I thought I heard your voice!" Alex was flapping down the hall from the cedar room with his bathrobe and pajamas fluttering around his legs. "How do you do? Better I hope? Could I offer you a cup of tea? I've taken a pot into the library and I can easily fetch another cup."

"Well, now that you mention it," Mr. McGuire glanced at Alex's pajamas and then gazed tactfully at the front door, "a nice cup of tea wouldn't come amiss."

"Good! Make yourself comfortable in the library, and I'll be back in a flash. You know where it'tis—straight into the cedar room, then through the door on your right." Alex smiled at Ben and lowered his voice after David McGuire had started down the west hall. "I'll amuse him until Ellie appears, and you can get back to whatever it is you're so intent upon."

"Thanks, Alex. I appreciate it."

Alex charged off down the east hall toward the kitchen.

And Ben crossed from the stairs to the sitting room. But before he could open the door, Mary Atwood leaned over the banister and called his name in a chilling voice, weak and pleading and panicked at the same time.

She was standing in Ellie's doorway, in the west wing on Ben's right, as he ran up the last leg of the U-shaped stairs. Her right hand was clamped against her mouth, and her left clutched the door frame as though she needed some support to keep from falling. Her skin was too pale and she was trembling. And Ben helped her into the bedroom and made her sit on the sofa inside the door on the left.

He saw what it was that had made her knees buckle. But he rubbed her hands and helped her get her head down between her knees, before he took time to make sense of it. "That's better. Just try to breathe normally. I'm sorry it was you and not me."

Ben kept his left hand on her shoulder, while he kicked the door shut behind him and stared at the four-poster bed. At Ellie. Lying dead. Half covered by the corner of a comforter. Her heavy black hair streaming across a clean white sheet.

Mary sat up then and started to sob, and Ben grabbed her shoulders and squatted down beside her so their faces were almost touching. "Mary, listen to me. You've got to get yourself under control and be absolutely quiet. I'm going to try to find out what happened to her, and you're the only person who can help me. I don't want Alex and McGuire up here. Do you understand? Mary, listen to me!" He shook her firmly, and then took her face in his hands, before he handed her the handkerchief from his back pocket.

"It was terrible finding her like that!"

"I know."

"I don't understand what could have happened!"

"I don't either, but I've got to have time to look around before anyone else comes in here, or the police seal off the room."

Mary nodded and shivered and put her head down again. And then she worked at controlling her breathing, while she held the handkerchief against her mouth.

Ben stood next to her, concentrated and self-contained, as he silently studied the room.

The body would wait. A child could see that. Ellie was past all pain, as well as any help from him. And he wanted a photograph of that room in his brain. An immediate overall impression. So he waited and gave himself time to take it in, with his hands on his hips and his jaw set off to the left.

It was a large room, the same size as the library below, with a bay window in the long wall on his right, where the four-poster bed stood centered, opposite the sofa where Mary sat. There was another bay window straight in front of him, across from the door he'd come in, with a desk placed to face the view. The fireplace was on his right too, but on the short wall behind him, past the door to the hall and the one that opened into the bath. A reading chair sat in the corner beyond it, between the fireplace and the round bedside table next to Ellie. There was a chest of drawers against the far side of the bed, with a chaise lounge between it and the desk.

A moss-green carpet covered most of the oak floor. The paneled walls were a paler green. Family pictures crowded the table tops and needlepoint cushions cluttered the sofa and chairs.

It was a prewar room. Another generation's. Only the suitcase lying closed on the floor, and the high heels and stockings by the closet door, the hairpins too on the chest of drawers, had anything to do with Ellie.

Ellie didn't fit there. Anymore than she'd felt like she fit anywhere since Jon died.

And it was that that bothered Ben most. The sense of isolation, of being lost and alone and a stranger in a strange land, that Ellie hadn't had time to get over.

Ben was already on his stomach, with the side of his face on the carpet, looking at the surface between the door and the bed. He worked his way forward, from one side of the room to the other, until he was maybe two and a half feet from the end post on the right side of the bed by Ellie. And there he took out his magnifying glass and examined a small gray splotch. "When was this room vacuumed last?"

"Yesterday. I did it myself before the solicitor arrived. Why? What is it you've found?"

"I don't know. Nothing maybe. A spot of cigarette ash. Does McGuire smoke?"

"Aye, but he wouldn't have been in Ellie's room."

"Ellie did ask to talk to him, after the reading of the will. Maybe they came up here."

"It couldn't have been Mr. Rory, I know that. He never would've hurt Ellie." Mary's voice broke and she stuffed Ben's handkerchief against her mouth.

"We don't know that anyone did, yet. And it's too early to have an opinion." Ben was standing by Ellie's side, his mouth tight and his eyes unreadable as he leaned down to examine what was left of her.

She was lying on her back, with her left arm hanging off the bed. Her palm turned up, her fingers curved above it, the hollow of her elbow looking vulnerable, too thin and too fragile. Her left leg was out from under the covers and bent beneath her, with the foot under her right knee, so that it looked as though she'd drifted off to sleep quite comfortably on her back. Her right arm was on top of the comforter with her hand curled at her throat, and her head was turned to the left toward Ben and the door behind him. She looked pleased, almost. And peaceful.

And it didn't make any sense. She was thirty-two years old. A doctor had pronounced her healthy the day before, even with the stress of Jon's death. There were no signs of suffering or any sort of thrashing around. And there was no indication that there'd been a struggle.

The liver mortis had been obvious (the band of dark blue discoloration on the underside of her body), even from across the room. So she must have been dead at least eight or ten hours, or it wouldn't have been as pronounced.

Ben measured it with his thumb. And then used his magnifying glass to examine the exposed parts of Ellie's body: her right arm, her face and part of her neck, her left leg, her right knee and lower leg, and part of her right thigh. He looked at the whole length of her left arm. And he examined, more carefully than anything else, the place on the vein where Dr. Graham had drawn blood.

He studied the covers, and the arrangement of the pillows, and then got down on his hands and knees and picked up the cream-colored dust ruffle.

Alex had left his glasses under the bed.

Directly under Ellie's body.

And Ben glanced at Mary to see if she'd noticed.

She hadn't. Which made things easier. She was gazing at the desk with tears streaming down her face.

"You okay, Mary?"

"Aye. You needn't worry about me." She was sitting very still, clutching his handkerchief in both her hands.

Ben considered the bedside table, the glass of water in particular, between Ellie's watch and a picture of Jon. He sniffed it and studied the surface, before he started on the porcelain lamp. He examined the bed frame next, the undraped posts and the headboard. Then the curtains, the window frames, the locks, the one half-opened window, and the view of the back garden.

He pulled tissues out of the box by the lamp and used them to open the drawers in the desk and the chest of drawers. He sat back on his heels while he opened the leather boxes in the bottom drawer, and said, "Tell me about this jewelry."

"It's good quality. Most of it from the Campbells. The pearls are fine. And there're a few gemstones, the way you'd expect with an old family, but there's nothing like what Lord Alex will have inherited, or Mr. Rory, either one."

"So it's nothing to scoff at, but there's not a fortune involved either."

"Aye, exactly right."

Ben studied the contents of Ellie's suitcase, then looked at the window frames and opened the closet door. He inspected Ellie's clothes and shoes, while Mary sat with her hands in her lap and rocked backwards and forwards on the sofa.

Tears came and went, but she didn't sob or moan or do any of the other physical things she might have felt like doing, except shiver once in awhile against the cold inside.

Ben patted her knee as he walked past on his way to the fireplace—where he found ashes under the grate, cold and maybe three inches deep, with a cellophane wrapper from a cigarette pack lying on top toward the front. "Does this other door open into the bathroom?"

"Yes. You look like a hound hunting a hare, you know. You're nose is fair quivering and you're too thin. Your bones are that sharp in your face."

"Thank you, Mary. I'll keep it in mind. This was Jon's mother's room?"

"She moved in here from the front bedroom after her husband died. That's the very same bed Elizabeth MacLean died in. And I was the one who found her too." Mary sighed and twisted her wedding band, while she chewed on her lower lip.

"And this was her bathroom?"

"Aye. I still think of it as hers."

Ben used Kleenexes to open the bathroom door into a long narrow room, tiled entirely in white, with a window at the end on his left, above the tub. He checked it all out carefully and quickly, and then opened the medicine cabinet above the sink.

There were dried toothpaste streaks on one of the glass shelves, as well as an empty bottle of mouthwash and several bottles of medicine that had been prescribed for Jon's mom. Ben used his magnifying glass on all of it, and then looked at the medication Dr. Graham had given Ellie. The bottle was on the sink, and Ben examined it carefully without picking it up, trying to count the pills without touching any prints that were on it.

He stared at the inside of the cabinet again, and then stuck his head back in the bedroom and asked Mary if she'd come in.

She pushed herself off the sofa and pulled her old navy blue cardigan across the front of her flowered dress, hugging it against herself with both her arms as though it helped to have something to hold on to.

"Has this bathroom been used on a regular basis since Jon's mother died?" Ben's voice was deep and businesslike like normal, but it was clipped and quick, and colder than usual, too.

"It hasn't been used much a'tall. It's quite a distance from Hugh's room and mine in the east wing, and the other lavatory's larger. We're accustomed to sharing, when he's here, and I haven't wanted to use hers. She was so ill for so long, I don't like to be reminded."

"So no one got around to throwing out the medicine bottles or the mouthwash that belonged to Mrs. MacLean?"

"Aye, I expect that's true. We've scrubbed the floors and cleaned the fixtures many times, of course. But I haven't had very much help, and there's a great deal to do in a house like this. Of course, Hugh never throws anything out. He's absolutely notorious in the family."

"Would you say that everything's here that was here when she died? Does it look like anything's missing?"

"I can't say absolutely, but it seems very much the same."

"What about this space here on the second shelf? Everything's been rearranged. There's no dust in that one spot. And there're rings there on the glass like a liquid dribbled down from a bottle."

"Is that important?"

"I don't know. But it looks like there was a bottle there until recently."

"What does that have to do with Ellie's death?"

"It's too early to tell. Was there something else she took that isn't here?"

"There could've been, I suppose."

Ben didn't say anything while she stared at the inside of the medicine cabinet. But when she shook her head and turned away, he closed the door with the tissue.

"Tell me if you think of anything else—a stomach medicine she used to take, a bottle of cough syrup, anything. No matter when it is, alright?"

"I will. Vera definitely."

"I want to run through all the rooms on this floor, and any part of the first floor I haven't seen yet, and then check out the basement."

"Why?"

"It's too complicated to explain right now."

"If you won't say more, you won't, I suppose."

"It's nothing personal, Mary."

"I should hope not!" Her eyes flared at Ben and her mouth snapped shut on her irritation.

"I am trying to help, you know."

"I know you are. Don't mind me. I'm not myself. I don't seem able to take it in. Not Ellie's death as well. But be that as it may, I suppose the mudroom downstairs is the only room you wouldn't have seen. Except, of course, for the basement."

"We ought to call Dr. Graham before we tell Alex and McGuire. But first we've got to lock Ellie's room. You have the key I hope?"

"Aye. Yours and Alex's are the only bedrooms that don't lock." Mary pulled a bunch of keys out of the pocket of her sweater. Most of them were old-fashioned skeleton keys, tied together with a black grosgrain ribbon, and she handed them to Ben and blew her nose.

He locked Ellie's door and the hall door to the bathroom, and then he dropped the keys in the pocket of his corduroy pants. "Let me keep them till I've had a chance to go over the house, okay?"

"Fine. Would you like me to call Dr. Graham, since Hugh isn't here to take charge?"

"Why don't you call on the hall phone up here, while I run through the bedrooms? Rory used the same bathroom Ellie was using?"

"Yes. I laid his towels out for him in his room, but it would've been much closer than the one in our wing."

"Where do you keep your syringe?"

"In my lavatory, in the medicine cabinet."

"I'd like to look at it with you when you finish on the phone. I'll get started, and then you meet me there when you're done. Are you doing alright?"

Mary nodded, even though she looked beaten and bewildered and a little tottery on her feet, as she walked slowly toward the telephone table farther along the hall.

Ben went the other way, to the front west bedroom above the cedar room, where Rory had slept the night before.

Both windows were open, the covers were folded back, his

used towels were hung on the wooden rack, the ashtray had been emptied into the ashes in the fireplace and wiped with a Kleenex he'd thrown in the wastepaper basket. And yet the most obvious sign of Rory was the lingering smell of his Benson and Hedges.

Ben examined the hall, before and after he passed Mary at the telephone table, but nothing seemed out of the ordinary. His own room was just past her on the right, but before he opened his door, he checked to see if the thread he'd stuck between it and the frame was still in place. It was. And everything else seemed untouched. So he grabbed another handkerchief, replaced the thread, and walked across the hall into Alex's room.

There was nothing particular that caught Ben's attention. Nothing in his dop kit, or his suitcase in the closet.

And Ben moved next door into Hugh's room, at the back east corner of the house. It was clean and ordered, but unlived in, like the rest. Though there were pictures of his parents in front of the Bentley, and what looked like grandparents as well, two sets together behind Kilgarth, beside a color shot of a sailboat with Hugh and his dad at the rail. They were on a small desk between a wardrobe, that was half-full of well-worn clothes, and four shelves of books from his childhood and adolescence.

Ben read a few of the titles, and then looked under the bed, before he walked into the bathroom that separated Hugh's room from Mrs. Atwood's.

It was down the short hall that ran from the back of the house to the front. And he'd been in there long enough to look at everything but the linen closet and the medicine cabinet, when Mary Atwood knocked softly and peered around the door.

"I got through to Dr. Graham, finally. He felt terrible of course. Says he can't fathom it a'tall, but he'll be out directly, as soon as may be."

"Will you show me your syringe? Don't touch it with your hands, though. Use your handkerchief or a tissue. Have you given yourself an injection this morning?"

"No, but I should've done. I'm later with it than usual, because of..." Mary's chin started to quiver, but she managed to get control of herself, before she took a narrow pan from the medicine cabinet and set it on the sink.

"How do you sterilize your syringe?"

"I boil it once a week in its stainless steel pan, and then keep it in the pan in alcohol." Mary had taken off the lid and was staring at her syringe with a puzzled expression. "It doesn't look right somehow."

"Why? What's different?"

"I don't know exactly... Yes, I do! When *I* put it in, the needle is on the left. I'm right-handed, so when I clean it and set it in the dish, the needle's always pointing the other way."

"Could you have turned the pan around?"

"Why would I? I pick it up and put it in the cabinet straight-away."

"Do you have another hypodermic you could use?"

"I keep a new one put away, yes."

"Then it'll help if you use that. Does anything in the medicine cabinet seem unusual in any way?"

She considered the contents, hers and Hugh's, and said, "I don't see anything, no."

"I'd like to lock this bathroom too. We can use the ones downstairs."

"I suppose." Mary looked dubious, and then shook her head. "Poor Ellie!" Her voice was shaky, and she sighed loudly and blew her nose again, and Ben turned toward her from the linen closet.

"You can't think about Ellie right now, Mary. You've done

very well, and I know this is hard for you. But if I'm right, and Jon and Ellie have both been murdered, you've got to help me find out who did it."

"Have you found something then, since you first saw the body that makes you think it was murder?"

"I'm at least working on an idea. Is it okay if we look at your room?"

They stepped next door to the front bedroom, which was bigger than Hugh's and Alex's, with a fireplace, like all the rest, and a small TV in a corner.

"Does it look like anybody's been going through your things? Check the closet and all the drawers."

It didn't take her long, and she seemed relieved when she said, "No. Nothing's been shifted a'tall."

"Then where's the mudroom?"

"Right below my room. Let me just fetch the new syringe and give myself my injection."

Ben looked out her front windows, after she'd gone, analyzing their position in relation to the front drive. He glanced out the east windows too, where there was a farm track past the shrubberies up by the house.

And then he followed Mary down the paneled stairs across the hall from her door.

"Now, this staircase was the servants' in the early part of this century, though this east end of the house, the squarish section with Hugh's room and mine, and the ones you and Alex are in, was the original Georgian structure. The rest was added later. Though why I should mention it with Ellie lying dead, I couldn't begin to say."

They were on the first floor by that time, in the front by a fanlight door. "Then this was the original front door?"

"Aye."

"And the mudroom's the first room on the right if you're looking toward the back?"

"Yes."

It was lined with cedar, and there was a long hanging area full of outdoor clothes, as well as a wall of shelves for storage and boots, plus drying racks beside the fireplace.

"We keep the guns locked in that cabinet. And there's very little else to see."

"Is that a dog basket in the corner?"

"Mrs. MacLean's old spaniel died just after she did. I doubt very much that we'll ever have another dog, but Hugh can't stand to throw anything away, so the leash and the rest of it are still in that box beside the bed."

Ben looked at all of it, the guns and the dog paraphernalia and the outdoor gear, before he turned and walked into the hall. "Why don't you go ahead and tell Alex about Ellie. Don't say *anything* about me thinking the death might be suspicious. Just say we've locked the doors and called Dr. Graham, and I'll be there in a minute. Is there anything I need to know about the basement?"

"Just that the door to old Mr. MacLean's laboratory is always kept locked. It's the long black key with a bit of carving on the handle."

"He was trying to develop a coating that would keep ships from rusting?"

"Yes, he was indeed."

"Did Rory or Alex know about the laboratory?"

"Oh, aye. They've both been in and out of the house for years. But you're not thinking that—"

"How many sets of keys are there?"

"There's my set, and Hugh's, and there's an extra one in a drawer in the pantry."

"So anyone who's a friend of the family would know where you keep that set?"

"Aye. I suppose they would."

"What door did you leave unlocked?"

"I beg your pardon?"

"Night before last."

"The door beneath us, where we take the dustbins out. Though the night before Jon died, it was the storage door in the west wing. The ground slopes, you see, and it's the only door you can drive up to and deliver the coal and wood without having to bother with stairs."

"Thanks, Mary. Your mind's just fine, believe me."

He glanced at the stone-floored storage room below the mud-room, where the coal and wood and garbage cans were kept. And then opened the outside hall door and took the short U-shaped outside stairs up to the fanlight door.

He stood on the gravel, on the far right side of the front turn-around, and looked up at Mary's windows.

Then he went back into the basement, followed the short side hall to the rear of the house, and stopped by a locked door. He could feel the damp rising off the cold stone floor as he worked the lock, and he could smell the scent of earth and age as he pushed hard to open it, where it dragged on the flagstone floor.

It was a big laboratory, organized around a center workbench, and Ben looked at the floors on his hands and knees, the three sides he could see from the end near the door. He walked to the far side by the windows and worked counterclockwise around the island, opening bottom cabinets (full of glassware, mixers, metal strips, common chemicals, and cleaning supplies, usually in gallon jars) to the big stone sink on the short back wall.

He moved to the cabinets on the long inside wall, and put his head down near the black stone counter so he could study it from several angles. He opened the base cabinets with his handkerchief and found acids, alkalis, solvents, fatty acids, and organics arranged alphabetically in separate sections.

The inorganic reagents were up above, in pint bottles and wide-mouthed jars, in two glass-fronted upper cabinets between boxes of test tubes and pipettes. He used his magnifying glass again, concentrating on one shelf, of one cabinet where calcium carbonate, silver nitrate, sodium chloride, sodium dichromate, and zinc chloride were organized alphabetically. He smiled at the ceiling for a minute, with his head cocked to one side. And then looked at the shelf again, and the counter, and the floor on that side of the lab.

He gazed at the whole room from the doorway, with his hands in his back pockets. And then he locked the door.

He ran through the front rooms—the laundry, the drying room, the larder, and Jon and Hugh's old playroom (where there were boxes marked "models," "trains," and "miscellaneous" in Hugh's meticulous handwriting). He looked at the empty room across the corridor, then examined the storage door at the end of that hall, the double door with the dead bolt, that Mary had forgotten to lock.

Then he heard her, calling his name from the front stairs, and he answered her as he locked the door.

"Dr. Graham's arrived and he wonders if you'll come let him in to Ellie's room."

"Tell him I'll be right there."

ア ア ア

Ben followed William Graham out of Ellie's bedroom and locked the door again, while Graham walked to the windows across from the front stairs. He set his bag down on the hall runner and clasped his hands behind his broad blue back, and then stood motionless with his face to the glass.

Ben watched two male pheasants swagger and scoot across the front lawn, then shoot under the Cedar of Lebanon, before he said, "I do think I should tell you that there's reason to believe that Jon MacLean's death wasn't the result of natural causes."

"Are you implying that Jon MacLean was murdered!" His heavy square face turned on Ben, as his stiff gray eyebrows shot up in disbelief.

"Yes. Ellie asked me, for reasons that aren't important at the moment, if I'd investigate Jon's death, so that she could contact the Northumberland Police if there was enough evidence to support such action."

"Is there?"

"*I* think so. And I *hope* to have, and I'm deliberately emphasizing the word hope, two more pieces of concrete evidence in the next twenty-four hours. I also think Ellie's death is probably suspicious too."

"I can't say what caused it, that's certain. And I shall have to get on to the Procurator Fiscal in Dunblane. In a case of unexplained death, he'll come here to 'the locus' himself. He, or his depute. And he'll send a pathologist as well, and order a postmortem and dissection. If that looks suspicious, he'll get the C.I.D. from Perth down here directly."

"When you drew blood yesterday, did you have to put the needle in more than once?"

"Certainly not! It went in clean as a whistle. Why?"

"It looked to me like there was a scratch, or another very slight puncture, off to the side of the actual site in the vein where the blood was drawn."

"I didn't notice that."

"You didn't use a magnifying glass. I also think you should know that when Mary Atwood came down this morning, expecting to open a new package of insulin, she found it was already open and two of the bottles were missing."

"You do know insulin can't be detected in the body? Yes, there's supposed to be an assay that's being perfected in some posh laboratory, and there's even talk of a Nobel Prize, but it's certainly not ready for general use, not by a long chalk. They can check the blood sugar level in the aqueous humor of the eye, and if that's unduly low, it's at least an indication of insulin. But it would take a very large dose to cause death. Two bottles would be enough, I think. Though a pathologist would know better."

"Mary might have opened the box before she left for Jon's funeral and forgotten, but, all things considered, I'd be surprised. How many Soneryl tablets did you give Ellie?"

"Fourteen. I wanted her to have a week's supply, hoping that once she got a good night's sleep or two, she'd see the wisdom in taking them for another few days."

"There're twelve left, so it wasn't that."

"No, it wouldn't have been. Not normally. Let me get on to the Procurator Fiscal, and then you and I should have another chat. How's Hugh taking it? He's always been very fond of Ellie." Dr. Graham picked up the heavy black receiver and dialed from memory, gazing intently at Ben while he waited.

"He doesn't know yet. Alex is walking to the gatehouse to tell him now."

CHAPTER TWELVE

BEN CALLED RORY AND TOLD HIM it was very important that he get back to Kilgarth as soon as possible, and even though Rory didn't sound pleased that Ben wouldn't give him an explanation, he still said he'd be there about eleven. Ben thanked him and hung up, just as Hugh opened the door.

He'd come from the gatehouse, after Alex went to get him, looking numb with grief and shock. And when he walked into the sitting room, half an hour later, his mouth was still strained, and his eyes seemed slightly disoriented. "I can't understand it a'tall. Why would Ellie die? She didn't seem that ill, did she? Not sick unto death, surely?"

"It didn't look like it to me. But we'll have to wait for the autopsy to make sense of it."

"That's precious little comfort."

"I know. How's Mary holding up?"

"Fairly well, I think, although she weeps rather frequently." All Hugh's movement were quicker than usual, and his arms looked restless, even before he dropped into a chair and rolled his shirtsleeves up his arms like he couldn't stand the feel of them against his skin. "She asked me to tell you she's baked a batch of scones. She seems to think sugar will counteract shock."

"Maybe it helps her to have something to do, too."

"It's quite an unusual gathering in the kitchen. Alex is pacing from one end of the room to the other, expounding one of several theories, only to follow it rapidly by another, while Graham spreads jam on a series of scones, and McGuire voices his oft repeated hope that the Procurator Fiscal will arrive soon." Hugh's dark blue eyes were fixed and staring, as he looked past Ben to the front lawn and rubbed a patch of stubble on his chin. "I know I'm being much too critical, and babbling as well, but it simply doesn't seem fair. She was young and gifted, and her whole life lay before her!"

"I know. And yet I guess I can accept it if she died of natural causes. But then I wasn't as close to her as you were."

"Is there reason to think she didn't die of natural causes?"

"No. I'm just talking hypothetically. There's not enough data to have an opinion. So the Bentley broke down in Dunblane last night?"

"Yes. Hence, the unshaven state. I couldn't get it put right until the garage opened early this morning."

"What was wrong with it?"

"A bad battery cable, apparently. As soon as they replaced it, the old engine fired right up. What shall I tell Mary about the scones?"

"I'll be there in a minute, but all I want is a cup of coffee."

Robert Kerr was the Procurator Fiscal for Perthshire and he arrived at nine-thirty and left by half past ten, right after Dr. Allan, the police pathologist he summoned to all "unexplained deaths," finished examining Ellie's body. Kerr arranged to have it "conveyed under escort" to the police mortuary at Dunblane, where Allan would do the postmortem and dissection. And then Kerr locked Ellie's room and took the keys away with him.

McGuire departed moments later, having given Kerr his phone number and explained his pressing appointments.

Graham left shortly thereafter, telling Ben on the side that he'd have a word with Allan, who was quite a close friend, after the PM had been finished, and he'd try to stop back in the afternoon.

Ben went up to his bedroom, took the thread out of the door frame, got the *Scottish Beekeeper* he needed from the suitcase under his bed, replaced the threads between the top two issues, and stuck another one back in the door. He slipped the journal under his belt, under the back of his jacket, then trotted down the stairs toward the sitting room.

As he passed the window seat by the front door, he saw Rory's MG slide around the last curve. He had to talk to Rory alone. And he stepped out onto the gravel at the foot of the stone stairs, just as Rory cut the engine and said, "What's all this about?"

"Why don't we walk while we talk?"

"Alright. If you wish." Rory was wearing black-framed sunglasses and a black blazer, and he pulled off his tie and stuffed it in his jacket pocket as they started down the drive.

"It's bad news, Rory. And there's no good way to prepare you."

"Go on then."

"Ellie died in her sleep last night—"

"No!"

"—and Mary found her this morning. I'm sorry, Rory."

"How can that be!... You're sure there's no possibility that—"

"No."

"No, there wouldn't be, would there? Why would I think there'd be room for doubt? Somehow I hoped that... Still... I need to be on my own for a moment." Rory wheeled to the right, wandering off toward the Cedar of Lebanon, tall and striking and shuffling like an old man.

Ben waited on the edge of the grass, holding the envelop Mary had given him that morning, watching Rory out the corner of his eye, where he stood stooped in the shade under huge spreading wings of cedar, with his hands hanging dead by his sides.

Dr. Graham was in his surgery, reading case notes at a cluttered desk, with his thick gray eyebrows raised high above his reading glasses, and a telephone receiver pressed against his ear. "Reese?... Yes, Graham here. I've only a moment or two till my one-fifteen appointment, but I thought you'd want to know that it's become a two person postmortem. That means that 'suspicious circumstances' have been found, and a second pathologist's been called in. The body has also been taken from the police mortuary in Dunblane to the University Mortuary at Glasgow, where there are much more sophisticated facilities. You can expect someone from the Criminal Investigation Division in Perth to arrive at Kilgarth fairly soon...

"No, I'm afraid I'm not at liberty to reveal the preliminary findings... Ah yes, that's true... Yes, I understand... There is that, because of this situation with Jon... But even so, you *must* keep it absolutely confidential... You see, Allan has concluded, by a process of elimination more than anything else, that death was caused by cardiac arrest. What makes it suspicious is that there aren't any signs of the normal pathology one would expect. There are no blockages, no congenital defects, nothing that points to the actual cause... Right. If Allan weren't an exceptional pathologist, it might easily have gone undetected. A great many country practitioners would never have drawn the appropriate conclusions...

"I did mention the insulin, yes, just as a possibility, and Allan will test the sugar level in the vitreous humor, that's the gelatinous substance inside the eye, and compare that to the level of sugar in the blood. Blood sugar rises immediately after death, but sugar levels remain more stable in the eye, so a great discrepancy, a very low level of sugar in the vitreous humor, could indicate that insulin had lowered the sugar level. It wouldn't be conclusive, but it would certainly be an indication...

"I shall be speaking to Allan again, when he has more to report, and I'll ring you back as well. *If* I can trust you to keep it completely confidential. For any sort of slip would compromise my position... Just a moment, Ben, my nurse wishes to speak to me... I must run. An emergency case has just come in, and I'll have to ring you later, either tonight or tomorrow."

Ben mumbled "Blast!" under his breath as he dropped the receiver into it's cradle. There were three questions he needed to ask Graham fast. Because life got more dangerous without the answers. And one more death became more likely.

Detective Inspector Grey, head of C.I.D. in Perth, had already examined Ellie's room and spoken to Mary about finding the body, and he was standing with his hands clasped behind him, at the back of the foyer under the landing of the front stairs, gazing out the french doors. Police Superintendent Mills, from

Dunblane, and Hugh MacLean (now shaved and changed) stood near the foot of the stairs discussing where to do the interviewing.

Ben had been introduced a moment earlier, and he was watching Grey and listening to Mills from the doorway of the small sitting room, when Grey turned unexpectedly and looked directly at him, like he'd felt Ben's eyes on his back.

Kenneth Grey couldn't have been much more than five feet six and probably not younger than sixty, and Ben could see he'd been in the military, even without the army tie. He carried himself like an officer, trim and straight backed and still. And his carefully brushed mustache and impeccable white hair were so right for the stereotype, Ben caught himself picturing him in a dress uniform. His clothes were plain and polished—good shoes, dark blue suit, the regimental tie in green, navy, red, and yellow stripes Ben knew he'd seen somewhere. And he asked, "Cameron Highlanders?" with his head cocked to one side.

Grey, who'd been studying Ben too, with his penetrating brown eyes, answered, "First Argyll and Sutherland Highlanders." Then shifted his attention to Hugh. "I want to make it very clear from the beginning, Mr. MacLean, that there is no conclusive evidence of *any* sort to suggest this unfortunate death was the result of anything but natural causes. Yet, as a matter of procedural routine, we've instructed two Detective Constables to photograph and fingerprint the deceased's room. We shall need to make a few general inquires as well, and if it's quite convenient, I'd like to begin with you. Excuse me just a moment. Detective Sergeant Briggs?"

"Yes, sir?" A large uniformed policeman froze halfway to the landing of the U-shaped stairs.

"I'd appreciate it if you'd ask my men to pay close attention to the adjoining lavat'ry. I'd like particularly painstaking photos of the medicine chest, inside and out."

"I will, sir, right away."

"So," Grey turned and smiled at Hugh, "is it the library you've decided upon?"

"It'tis comfortable, and very discreetly situated."

"Then lead the way, by all means."

It was a paneled room with two big bay windows in walls stuffed with books, where old black-and-white photographs of fishermen and hunters hung above the bookcases, and three sets of antlers were arranged above the doorway around a large stuffed trout from the Allan Water.

Grey seemed to consider the sitting area at the fireplace end of the room, but chose instead the sofa and chairs in the window in front of him, opposite the door to the cedar room. He sat on the worn Chesterfield sofa with his back to the light, and gazed politely at Hugh MacLean, who'd taken the wingback chair at his end of the sofa. "We shall try not to take too much of your time, for I know you've had a very difficult fortnight. Losing your brother, and his wife as well, must have come as a frightful shock."

"It has indeed." Hugh leaned his head against the back of his chair and watched Mills arrange a large, muscular, well-padded body in the smaller chair opposite his.

"Superintendent Mills will assist me by taking notes, but before I ask any questions a'tall, I think I should tell you that it appears as though Elinor MacLean's death was caused by cardiac arrest. Even so, as a sudden and unexplained death, we're required to make routine inquiries until the final results of the postmortem have been submitted. I shan't ask you, as a layman, to comment, except in passing, on her recent physical condition, but there are issues surrounding the death that you may be the best placed to answer." Grey adjusted his army tie and then paused to clear his throat. "I understand your brother's will was read only yesterday?"

Hugh described all the terms and bequests, along with his own surprise and uneasiness at deciding the fate of Kilgarth.

Grey then asked him if Ellie had made a will of her own.

"She had, yes. She mentioned it last night, as a matter of fact. She owned quite a large house in America, which had been leased since her parents' death, and she left it, quite naturally, to Jon."

"Did she explain the terms that apply to her husband's property, if he were to predecease her?" Grey had asked the question.

But it was Mills who was writing deliberately with a large freckled hand on the notebook spread across his enormous thighs. He looked up at Hugh then, with his broad meaty face, brushed a palm across the bristles of his thick sandy hair, and waited for him to reply.

"She said she'd left most of the furniture and jewelry to me, though a few pieces were to be passed on to Jon's two surviving aunts, as well as Mary Atwood. Mary was to have five thousand pounds outright, and a yearly stipend as well, with three thousand each to be given to both Jon's aunts, and myself. Whatever other funds there might be at her death were to go to two Christian charities, including the proceeds from the sale of her house in America."

"Was McGuire her solicitor?"

"No, she used a man in Inverness, though she didn't say which one."

Grey pulled at the right side of his mustache and stared at the coffered ceiling. "Why were you discussing the will last evening?"

"It cropped up on its own, really. McGuire had brought the family jewels, such as they are, and we were looking them over and deciding what to give the aunts, and Mrs. Atwood, and what

Ellie should keep for herself."

"That's the jewelry in her bureau cabinet?"

"Yes."

"I wonder if you'd look at it when we finish here to be sure that all is in order?"

"Of course, I want very much to be of help."

"Then the jewelry led her to discuss her will?"

"In a way. We were talking about Jon's will, and my mother's, and Ellie's parents' as well, and hers came up quite naturally."

"Had she been unwell in any way?"

"She hadn't been sleeping *or* eating the way she normally did, but we all assumed it was simply the strain of Jon's death. Dr. Graham examined her yesterday, and he seemed to think she was doing reasonably well, considering the circumstances. Though he did say she needed rest, and he prescribed some sort of sedative."

"Did she seem emotionally stable, or was she in such a state of despair over her husband's death that she might have wanted to take her own life?"

"One can't say with any certitude I suppose, but *I* thought she seemed quite stable. I can't imagine Ellie even entertaining the idea of doing away with herself. Though, certainly, when one's husband has died, one is bound to be a bit depressed."

Detective Inspector Grey settled his reading glasses on the end of his nose and wrote a short note in a notebook he'd pulled from an inside pocket. "Did anything unusual occur last night? Anything that might seem relevant to your sister-in-law's death?"

"I don't think so. Nothing I'm aware of." Hugh set his elbows on the arms of his chair and tapped his fingertips together in midair. "We were all at dinner. Dr. Graham was with us, and Rory MacKenzie as well. He stayed the night and left early this morning for Edinburgh—"

"Roderick MacKenzie, the editor of *The Daily Scotsman?*"

"Yes, he's in the sitting room. He drove up again, as soon as he'd heard the news. After dinner, I remember Ellie got up from the table, intending to retire early, but Rory asked to speak to her first. He's a distant sort of relation on her father's side, and she'd lived with his family before she married. As they were leaving the dining room, Ellie asked me to look at the jewelry, after they were finished, so Mr. McGuire could take the bulk of it back to the bank when he left this morning."

"Where was it you spoke with Mrs. MacLean?"

"In her room. She asked me to stop in about nine. We chatted a bit, and sorted the jewelry, but I thought she looked absolutely done in. Nervous too, the way she'd been since Jon died. So I nipped down and made us a cup of hot chocolate, hoping it would have a soothing effect."

"What time was that would you say?" It was Mills who asked, in broad Scots, with his pen poised above his pad.

"I don't think it was quite half-nine, though it could've been a few minutes either way. We talked about Jon then, when I came back. What he was like as a child, and what he'd gone through in the war. She mentioned that she'd taken the sleeping tablets Dr. Graham had given her. And I thought she did seem to be relaxing a bit by the time I left."

"What time was that would you say?"

"A few minutes before ten. Perhaps as early as a quarter till."

"What was done with the jewelry?"

"Ellie placed it in her bureau in the bottom drawer, with bits of paper inside each box indicating who it was to go to, now, or in the future. She arranged the boxes in two stacks, those to keep or give away now, and those to send back to the bank. She didn't keep anything out for herself, now that I think of it. But there were pieces she wanted to give away."

"And that was the last time you saw her alive?"

Hugh's face flushed while he bit his lower lip, as though he had to do something painful to keep himself from breaking down. "Yes. She was a wonderful woman, Inspector, and I shall miss her very much indeed. I have no relations a'tall now, in my own generation. The war took it's toll, as you might expect."

"Yes, it did indeed. What did you do after you left Mrs. MacLean?"

"I drove into Dunblane. We're having electrical problems at the gatehouse, where a young couple has just taken up residence, and I couldn't reach the electrician at home. His wife told me he'd gone to a pub in Dunblane, and I went along there to discuss the situation with him and try to persuade him to get on to the wiring today. Then, when I got ready to leave, my car simply wouldn't start. I did everything I knew to do, but it's an old model Bentley, and a bit temperamental, and of course the garage that can do the work had long been closed for the night."

"Did one of the household fetch you home?"

"No, it's on the far side of Dunblane, and everyone was tired, and if they had come to fetch me they would've had to bring me back early this morning as well, so I booked a room at the Thistle and Crown, called home to let Mary know, and went to bed. The garage fetched the car first thing this morning, and put it to rights quite promptly. I was able to drive back and meet the electrician at the gatehouse right at eight. Lord Chisholm walked down and told me about Ellie sometime before nine."

"What was the trouble with your car?"

"A bad connection in the battery cable. Once they replaced that, it started straightaway."

"Is there anything else a'tall that strikes you as pertinent?

Anything, no matter how small, that seemed a bit odd or unsettling?"

"Only that Ellie had received a really vile anonymous note. Oh yes! It was waiting for her here when we arrived home from the funeral. We suspect it was from a rather unbalanced woman who'd become far too interested in Jon, much to *his* dismay, I assure you. It's a very long story, but Jon and I have known Katherine Burnett since childhood and she'd developed a bit of an obsession with him. I don't know that it has any great significance, this letter, but Dr. Reese has it if you'd like to have a look. He was in Army Intelligence during the war, and was also an Army Ranger. American, of course, but I believe he taught some part of a course for British Rangers as well. In any event, he was looking into it for us."

"Then I shall certainly look forward to speaking to him. I shall also need Miss Burnett's address and phone number."

"I know she lives away up in Nairn, and I shall be happy to ferret out the particulars, once we've finished here."

"Is Dr. Reese a medical doctor?"

"No, he's an archivist. An expert on ancient documents, and objet d'art, you know the sort of thing."

"What position does he hold in the household?"

"He's a friend of Lord Chisholm's, actually, and he's quite a useful fellow. It's a rather involved situation, and the explanation should come from him." Hugh smoothed his navy and green MacLean tie, and then glanced at Grey almost tentatively.

"Is there anything else you'd care to add?"

"Well . ." Hugh took his handkerchief out of his coat pocket and wiped the outside corner of his right eye, before he said, "I suppose there is something, yes, although I don't for a moment think it means a thing. Still, in all good conscience, I feel I should mention it and let the two of you be the judge."

"You should do, Mr. MacLean, without doubt." Mills laid his huge sandy-haired hand on his broad knee, while he solemnly stared at Hugh.

"You see, I was coming out of the dining room last night, when Ellie was starting up the stairs, having just had her chat with Rory MacKenzie in the cedar room. I heard Rory say something that struck me as being a bit odd. I'm sure there's a very reasonable explanation, but I did hear him say, 'If *I* can't have you, then no one can.' I might not have heard it correctly, and I'm sure it doesn't mean anything improper a'tall, but Mrs. Atwood was there too, in the hall, so she must have heard it as well."

"I see, yes. I appreciate your frankness." Grey nodded at Hugh and adjusted a cuff, but the expression on his face didn't change. "There's one other question, while I'm thinking of it. Who would have known that the jewelry was in the house?"

"All of us, really. Alex, Rory, Ben, Mary Atwood, Dr. Graham, Janet Price, she's the daily who was in to clean yesterday. And Tom Atwood too, of course. He's Mary's son, and our part-time gardener, and he was here in the kitchen after dinner talking to Mary, so he could've known, certainly. Assuming she thought to mention it."

"Is there anything else you'd like to ask?" Grey was asking Mills.

Who was unbuttoning the bottom button of his gray flannel vest. "Was the family jewelry worth a great deal?"

"There're a few pieces of value. A pearl necklace, brooch, and bracelet. There's a rather fine sapphire pin. And an opal ring that's quite lovely."

Mills made a note on a clean page, before he said, "We may

need to speak with you again shortly, so please hold yourself available, if you will."

"Thank you, Mr. MacLean. I appreciate your willingness to help, at what I know is a difficult time. Still, if you wouldn't mind going over the jewelry with our men upstairs, Superintendent Mills and I would both be very grateful. Yes, and would you ask Mrs. Atwood if she'd step in again for just a moment?"

"Sorry to bother you once again, but there's one other question I feel I ought to ask."

Mary was standing behind the tan leather wing chair, gripping the top of the back.

"Please sit down and make yourself comfortable."

Mary sat, but she didn't look comfortable. Her eyes were puffy and red rimmed and she was turning her wedding band like she couldn't stop.

"First of all, as you've already heard me say, this appears to be a simple case of death by natural causes. Even so, Hugh MacLean has told us that as his sister-in-law was on her way upstairs last night, he heard Mr. MacKenzie say something to her which struck him as unexpected. He doesn't believe there was any ill will on Mr. MacKenzie's part. And yet we do want to be sure Mr. MacLean heard Mr. MacKenzie correctly. I'd also be interested in your own impression of Mr. MacKenzie's intention."

"I didn't think it was anything out of the ordinary. You could see how much he sympathized with her, in her grief. And I'm sure Hugh understands that vera well."

"He does, yes. And yet I must ask you to tell us precisely what it was you heard."

Mary had been staring at the partner desk in the other bay

window on her left. But then she sighed and settled her chin against the hanging folds of her neck. "Rory had come out of the cedar room with Ellie, and I haird him say, 'If *I* can't have you, then no one can.' Or nobody else can, or words to that effect. But he never would've meant anything wrong. He's a vera fine gentleman, and he loved Ellie like his own daughter!"

"Yes, I'm sure you're right. Thank you, Mrs. Atwood. You've been a very great help indeed. Oh, one other thing. Who in the household smokes cigarettes?"

"Mr. Rory. And Mr. McGuire, the solicitor from Edinburgh who talked to the Procurator Fiscal. He was here yesterday afternoon, and then again this morning."

"There was something else I wanted to ask too. Yes. Who owns a pair of gold reading glasses?"

"Lord Alex. He misplaced them last night. Though that's hardly surprising, for he loses them from one moment to the next."

"Ah, Mr. MacKenzie." Detective Inspector Grey stood and held out his hand.

"Inspector." Rory shook it, sat in the leather wing chair, and took out his cigarettes and lighter.

"May I introduce Superintendent Mills from Dunblane?"

Mills and MacKenzie both nodded, as Mills turned over a new page in his notebook.

"You're a journalist, Mr. MacKenzie, so you know we're legally bound to investigate all suspicious deaths, even though most result from natural causes."

"I'd be very surprised if Ellie's death turns 'round to be so straightforward."

"Would you? May I ask why?"

"Dr. Graham thought she was doing well, when he examined her last evening. And it seems highly unlikely that a thirty-two-year-old woman who was very fit, in the ordinary way of things, should suddenly die in the night, not quite a fortnight after her husband."

"Are you suggesting suicide?"

"No. Certainly not. I have no opinion as to what could have brought about her death, but the statistical odds don't favor natural causes." Rory exhaled and rolled the burning end of his cigarette in the silver ashtray he'd taken from the desk. He was pale and drawn and there was a slight twitch in his right eyelid, as well as two deep vertical lines between his eyebrows that weren't normally so noticeable.

"I'd like you to tell me, if you will, what transpired last evening between you and Mrs. MacLean."

"We all dined together, as I'm sure you know. And I then asked Ellie if I could speak to her before she retired. We were distantly related, and she'd lived with my family for several years, and I—"

There was a knock on the door and Grey said, "Come in," while he slid his reading glasses back in their leather case. "Yes, Briggs?"

"I thought you might wish to know, sir, that Mr. MacLean has discovered that several pieces of jewelry are missing from Mrs. MacLean's room. The majority are there, in the bureau cabinet, but an opal ring and a pearl necklace are missing, along with a pair of diamond clips."

"Are they indeed!" Superintendent Mills leaned forward in his chair, put his elbows on his knees and stared at Kenneth Grey. "Shall we whistle up the extras from Dunblane so we can make a thorough sairch of the premises? They're in Kinbuck, two miles away, mopping up after a motor accident." Grey nodded and Mills turned to Briggs. "Call in Fitzwilliams and Grant, and begin a sairch of the house and outbuildings."

Briggs nodded and closed the door behind him as Mills reached in his shirt pocket and drew out his pack of Benson and Hedges. "A sairch will take time. This is no wee cottage, after all."

Grey didn't answer Mills immediately. He stroked his mustache, and then pulled at his right ear, while he gazed at the trout above the door. "I very much doubt we'll find a thief has left the jewels on the premises. Though it may be that Mrs. MacLean, for reasons of her own, moved the pieces somewhere else herself, after she spoke to Mr. MacLean. Still, we shall have to search the house, as you say, Superintendent, and hope that evidence of one sort or another turns up in the shuffle. I do apologize, Mr. MacKenzie, for the interruption. You were telling us that—"

"That I'd asked to speak to Mrs. MacLean. I'd been trying to think of a way the family could help her during her time of mourning, and it had occurred to me that Amanda, my youngest daughter, could travel to Cawdor with Ellie when she returned, and stay with her there for two or three weeks during her school vacation. She could help Ellie pack, when the time came, and make the adjustment a bit easier."

"How did Mrs. MacLean respond?"

"She mentioned how fond she was of Amanda, and thanked me for thinking of it, and said she'd consider it and let us know. Yet I still had the impression that she thought she'd do better on her own."

"There was nothing else conveyed of any importance?" Grey slid his large black fountain pen from one hand to the other, while watching Rory MacKenzie with a cool appraising eye.

271

"Not that comes to mind. Of course, I did offer to let her stay with us after she moved from the manse. Living in church housing meant that she would have to make some very significant decisions quite soon, and I thought it might help her to be able to postpone the decision of where to go, and what to do, of whether to rent a home of her own or return to America, and the rest of it. My children are all very fond of Ellie, and since our home in Gullane is not too far south of Edinburgh, she could've pursued her musical career there without the longer drive and the painful associations of staying here at Kilgarth."

Detective Inspector Grey leaned back against the cracked leather cushions of the old sofa and crossed his arms across his stomach. "And that was the last you saw Mrs. MacLean?"

"Yes."

"Then when was it you left the cigarette wrapper in her fire-grate and dropped ash upon her carpet?"

"Last night. I'm sorry, it slipped my mind. She called to me from her room, after she'd talked to Hugh, to ask about Amanda's piano recital. She told me she'd meant to inquire earlier, but hadn't remembered. I opened a new pack and lit a cigarette, right before I left the room."

"What time would that have been?"

"I don't know exactly. Nine-thirty or so. Hugh had gone to make hot chocolate and hadn't yet returned."

"I think it's only fair to tell you that we've received reports of your conversation on the stairs with Mrs. MacLean which cast rather a different light upon your relationship with her."

"Oh?" Rory's green eyes settled on Grey's face with a cold bloodless look that had made more than one prime minister nervous.

"Was your interest in Mrs. MacLean purely that of a distant

and older relation? Or was there more between you than your previous remarks would lead us to believe?"

"My relationship with Mrs. MacLean was circumspect in every way, and I find your implication offensive!"

"Do you?"

"Ellie MacLean was very much in love with her husband, and the thought of any sort of impropriety is absolutely preposterous, as well as insulting!"

"I'm not imputing any sort of impropriety to Mrs. MacLean. Quite the contrary, in fact. Still, the fact remains that *you* were overheard to say, 'If *I* can't have you, no one can.' Or words to that effect."

"I can assure you, Inspector, that there's a very different explanation than the one you seem to be suggesting. It's laughable really." Rory ground his cigarette out and pushed the ashtray across the end table, before he made an obvious effort to look at Inspector Grey. "I said it in jest, really. I suppose it was a rather lame attempt at lightheartedness. I said 'if I can't have you'—to stay with us, you see, my family and I—'then no one can have you'—again meaning to stay with them at their home. Hugh and Mary, or Alex and Jane. Do you see? It wasn't any sort of threat or sexual innuendo a'tall. It was a teasing sort of remark. Ellie knew exactly what I meant. That I was awkwardly trying to offer her a refuge without pressuring her in any way."

"Isn't that exactly what you were doing, pressuring her subtly? Telling her she was expected to stay with you, if she didn't wish to incur your displeasure?"

"No! It was just one of those things people say to one another. There was no deeper significance a'tall."

Grey glanced at Mills, then slid a hand along the arm of the sofa, before he looked over at Rory. "I find it interesting, Mr.

MacKenzie, that you avoided answering my earlier question. I asked, if you'll recall, whether your interest in Mrs. MacLean was only that of a distant and older relation."

"I fail to see that my personal feelings have any bearing on her death."

"In my experience, as well as yours I'm sure, it's the relationships between people, the emotions themselves, in fact, that most often lead to murder. Take unrequited or rejected love. That's certainly led to murder on a considerable number of occasions."

Rory drew a cigarette out of the pack and held it in the palm of his left hand, while he lit his lighter with his right. His eyes were still fixed on the flame, five seconds later, when he relaxed the muscles of his jaw.

"You're a powerful man, Mr. MacKenzie." Grey tapped the large volume of *Debater's Peerage* he'd already consulted and left open on the sofa beside him. "The editor of Scotland's second largest newspaper. An aristocrat who's a relation of the Queen herself—"

"It's a *very* distant connection, I can assure you."

"You're a wealthy man too, I'll warrant. With an estate in Gullane, and an MG sports car waiting by the door. You're also a much sought after bachelor whose photograph appears with some regularity in all our glossiest periodicals."

"Always without my consent."

"It's not often, I expect, that Roderick MacKenzie doesn't get precisely what he wants, one way or another. Perhaps you couldn't abide not having Ellie MacLean?"

Rory's head snapped up and he glared at Grey with real hostility and irritation. But then he looked out the window behind Grey's back, lit his cigarette, and slowly exhaled at the ceiling. "I don't blame you for trying it on, Inspector. Nor do I intend to take it personally. You'd be remiss if you didn't pursue every possible line of inquiry. But please do me the courtesy of listening with an open mind when I tell you, as clearly as I know how, that *if* Ellie MacLean was killed, and we still don't know that she was, it was *not* I who killed her. My feelings for her were such that I am probably the least likely person in all the world to take such a step. I was in the house last night, and I shall therefore, necessarily, be involved in your inquiry. I understand that perfectly, and I applaud your thoroughness. But her death has been a terrible shock, and a severe personal loss, and there's nothing else I wish to say at the moment."

Grey was watching Rory, while turning his fountain pen end over end. "I'd like you to stay at Kilgarth until I've had an opportunity to speak with you again."

"Of course."

"Would you also ask Lord Chisholm if he could spare a moment?"

"Certainly."

"And if it's not too much trouble, tell Dr. Reese I shall also be with him shortly."

"You wished to see me, Detective Inspector?" Alex was standing in the doorway with his large square head a hand's breadth away from the top molding.

"Ah, Lord Chisholm. Please, sit wherever you'd like. I understand you were quite a friend of Reverend MacLean's."

"We were each other's closest friend from the time he was ten. Our wives were very fond of each other too, and we got on wonderfully well as couples. Which is all too rare, as we all know."

"How well was Mrs. MacLean managing, would you say, after her husband's death?"

"She was terribly crushed, of course. Anyone could see that. But she was a very strong woman. I know she hadn't been eating and sleeping particularly well, and she had a bit of an upset stomach from time to time. But she was very self-sufficient, and a deeply religious person, and I feel sure she would've recovered well. *If* she'd been given enough time."

"When did you see her last?"

"After dinner. She'd already gone over the jewelry with Hugh, and as I was coming up the stairs, she asked me to stop in and look at a ring she intended to give my daughter. Jon had been especially close to Elizabeth, and Ellie wanted her to have the ring to remember him by, if I thought it was something she'd like. It was a child's ring, gold, with a very small garnet, that had come down through Jon's mother's family."

"She gave it to you last night?"

"She did."

"When was that exactly?"

"It should think about nine-thirty. Twenty to ten. Something like that."

"How did she seem?"

"She said she'd taken a sleeping draught, and one could see she was beginning to relax. She'd been strung up very tightly, and it seemed to be doing her good. Though I'm generally quite uneasy about the use of sleeping drugs. Much better, I always think, to let nature take its course."

"Was anyone else with her when you spoke to her?"

"No. I did wonder if Rory might have been in the room previously, for I thought I caught a whiff of cigarette smoke. Though it might have come from down the hall."

"Yes, perhaps it could have done. How did your glasses come to be under her bed?"

"Were they!"

"Directly underneath Elinor MacLean's remains."

"I had no idea! None. And it is a bit unsettling, isn't it? Dear, kind Ellie. I still can't believe she's gone."

"What can you tell us about your glasses?"

"Well, I first missed them when I went to bed, for I always read before I settle in for the night. Of course, I found myself at a complete loss as to where I could have left them. So I looked through my pockets, but to no avail. Which side of the bed were they nearest?"

"The long side closest the door."

"Yes. You see, the trouble is, I lay them down in all sorts of places without noticing. Though last night, I do know I took the garnet ring over to the bedside table to look at it under the light. Perhaps I put my glasses on the table then. They could've fallen off, I expect."

"Perhaps."

"And then I might have kicked them without noticing." Alex stretched his legs out in front of the sofa and laced his fingers together across his vest, as he smiled a small embarrassed smile.

"That seems a bit far-fetched."

"Does it?"

"How could you not have noticed?"

"Ah, well. That's a question I often ask myself, even though I rarely produce a satisfactory response."

"Will you join us in a cup of tea, Dr. Reese? Mrs. Atwood was kind enough to bring a tray."

"I've had one, thanks." Ben leaned back in the wingback chair and watched Grey hand Mills a cup. "I'm glad to get a chance to talk with you though."

"I understand you viewed the body before the doctor arrived on the scene?"

"Yes, I did." Ben described what he'd noticed in the bedroom, including what seemed to him to be some indication of a second needle in Ellie's vein. He mentioned the cigarette wrapper and Alex's glasses in passing, and told them about the insulin and the rearranged syringe. He was moving on to the medicine cabinet, when the door opened hard and fast, and Detective Sergeant Briggs rushed in.

"Excuse me, sir, but I thought you'd want to know that we've found the missing jewelry hidden away in the garden shed."

"Have you, Detective Sergeant!"

"If we hadn't been extremely thorough, we would never have found it a'tall. It was in a small brown paper parcel tucked in a stack of clay pots."

"That's rather surprising."

"It was a rare bit of good fortune," Briggs stood at attention, with his helmet in the crook of his arm. "For it was only the second outbuilding we'd begun to sairch."

"Yes, I find that very surprising indeed. And I think, if you'll excuse us, Dr. Reese, Superintendent Mills and I had better take a look at the situation ourselves. I shall bear in mind what you've said, and I shall look forward to talking with you later in the day."

"There're other matters involved too that I think I ought to explain."

"I know I shall want to discuss the poison-pen letter Mrs. MacLean received as well." Grey put his glasses, pen, and notebook in his pockets as he stood up and stepped toward the door.

"You don't know anything about this jewelry, do you?"

"No. Nothing except that McGuire brought it for her to sort through, and she and Hugh said they were going to look at it last night."

"Right. Well, thank you very much for your help, Dr. Reese. We shall talk again later at some length."

CHAPTER THIRTEEN

BEN WAS TRYING TO TRACK the person who'd sold the bees to Jon's murderer (if such a person, in fact, existed), and he was either getting closer to running him down or discovering instead that he'd wasted a lot of time he couldn't spare.

He sat in the small sitting room, making one phone call after another, working his way through the offers of "Bees For Sale" in Scotland and England in the want ads in *Scottish Beekeeper*.

He'd waded through two years of journals in not quite forty-eight hours, even though many of the beekeepers didn't have phones. All he could do with them was leave messages with their local exchange operators asking the beekeepers to call him. Every one of the operators delivered the messages personally, which amazed Ben, because all the collect calls he'd hoped for had actually come in.

But *Scottish Beekeeper* was only one journal. Eleven smaller local ones advertised in it too, and he'd tracked them through the library in Perth, where a very helpful librarian gave him phone numbers over the phone for many of the beekeepers who'd advertised in those. Ben spoke to all the ones he had names for, and then contacted two commercial catalogues, Steele & Brodie as well as Thorne's, and called the leads they gave him.

But there were names they hadn't given him, and lots of bee-keepers never advertise, and he knew he couldn't cover enough ground. Even the police wouldn't be able to investigate all the possibilities.

Jon's murderer could also have raised the bees himself or gotten them from a friend. Although it didn't look like the likeliest suspects had. Using an alias and a false address and picking them up from a stranger would be a lot safer for the killer than exposing his own identity.

He could've had them shipped to a post office box too. But then how would he have paid? By mailing a check or a bank draft? No. Cash in person and a phony name.

Even so, the odds of Ben placing a call and finding the right beekeeper on the other end were so slim as to be almost non-existent. But he still wasn't ready to give up. And he dialed the next name on the list, and hung up a few seconds later. Mr. Lyon had been "out of beekeeping for nearly a year at least."

There were only two names left in *Scottish Beekeeper*, and Ben sighed as he tapped his pen against his teeth and reached for the warm metal receiver.

Reginald Morse-White's wife answered in Kirkcudbright and promised to have Reginald call as soon as he came home from the office.

That brought Ben back to Jamie MacIntosh, the man he'd been calling for two days, in Kinnesswood, wherever that was.

He told himself he should've looked it up before, location being as important as it was. Because the bees were probably bought on the eleventh and taken down to Holy Island fast, since it was a lot more likely they'd survive if they'd been bought at the last minute. They wouldn't have been sitting around then either for somebody else to see.

So is Kinnesswood close enough to Holy Island? And where did I put the map?

Yes. Kinnesswood. North of Edinburgh. East of Kilgarth. In the county of Kinross.

Nuts. Why couldn't MacIntosh answer and simplify my life? Yeah, and what if he's away for a week? There's no more time. Not if Ellie was murdered the way I think she was.

The beekeeper who supplied the bees that killed Jon is the only direct connection to the murderer, which means he's got no future of any kind, and either I have to track him down fast or get the police to do it. So I've got to talk to Grey before he leaves.

Motive took awhile. Partly because of the travel-time-distance issue. Until I saw how he got around it.

But I still think we may be able to prove he was on Holy Island, and hopefully we'll know that by tomorrow. But without a connection to the bees, it won't be enough. Not in a court of law.

The motive for Ellie's death is supposition too, of course. I won't know for sure till Graham gets here. And now wouldn't be too soon for him to do that, if *I* had anything to do with it.

The door handle rattled and was followed by a loud knock, and Ben dropped the pen he'd been playing with and stuffed his notes in a desk drawer on his way to unlock the door. "I was just thinking about you."

Rory didn't say anything. But his eyes looked irritated and the muscles in his jaw were knotted as he walked to the front windows with his hands in his trouser pockets.

Ben didn't say any more either. He just glanced up and down the hall, before he closed the door.

"Let's make sure we get this bloody murderer, shall we?" Rory kept his back toward Ben while he slammed his fist into the wall, and then he sucked his knuckles like he felt ridiculous but wouldn't have admitted it to anyone.

"*I* think we stand a very good chance."

"Do we! Did you know they're interviewing Mary Atwood again at this very moment, and they've sent someone to fetch her son from work and take him to Dunblane for questioning?"

"Grey did that?"

"He did indeed. The logic seems to be that because the jewelry was found in pots in the potting shed, Tom Atwood the gardener is the most logical suspect."

"Rather than the least logical person, which is probably a lot more likely. Of course, Grey may just want to question Tom about the shed as much as anything, and get his fingerprints right away to help them process the scene. How's Mary taking it?"

"Not a'tall well."

"I think Grey's an intelligent person. It won't take him long to eliminate Tom."

"No? I can't say I'm as optimistic."

"Where does Tom work?"

"A garage in Auchterarder."

"So how soon can you leave for Edinburgh?"

"Straightaway. Grey has given his approval, as long as I report any 'subsequent movements.'"

"He is at a definite disadvantage. He doesn't know about Jon's murder, so he doesn't have a context for Ellie's death."

"You will be explaining it to him, I presume?"

"Any minute, I hope. I've left messages with two of the constables. Will you have time to get the photograph copied tonight?"

"Yes, and I shall have three reporters on Holy Island first thing in the morning. We'll be working around the tides, of course—"

"What about sending them to the grammar school first, before they go door-to-door? Assuming the school will let you."

"That's very clever of you!"

"I know what I was like at that age."

"Yes, very clever indeed."

"Have you heard what they've done to Tom!" Mary was in the doorway, looking flushed and indignant, her eyes and her mouth working against each other as though she were trying not to scream or cry.

"I know the police want to interview him."

"I'm sorry about Tom, Mary." Rory was walking toward the door as Mary was coming into the sitting room, and he patted her elbow as they passed. "But even so, newspapers wait for no man, and it's time I got back to work. I shall be in touch again the moment I have something to report."

"Thanks, Rory. Don't drive too fast."

"Right!" Rory arched an eyebrow at Ben and then closed the door behind him.

"So tell me what happened." Ben slipped an arm around Mary's shoulders and walked with her toward the sofa.

"The police think Tom killed Ellie for the jewelry! Can you imagine? My Tommy! Who's known Ellie since she and Jon wed!"

"It's probably just routine procedure. They have to talk to everyone who was here yesterday."

"You think that's all it'tis, do you!" Mary's eyes were fierce and half-frantic as she blotted one with a crumpled Kleenex. "They asked me about the insulin and the syringe, and whether Tommy knew where they were kept, and if he'd know how to use them, and whether or not I'd told him the jewels were in the house." Mary's chest was pumping up and down, and wisps of damp white hair were sticking to her cheeks, as Ben handed her his last clean handkerchief. "I did tell Tom about the jewelry, I was making conversation the way one does, when we were chatting in the kitchen before dinner. But I know my son, and he'd never have hurt Ellie. Never! Not if his own life depended on it."

"Then Grey will figure that out."

"Neither would he take anything that wasn't his! Not now, not as a grown man. Though he did borrow a car that didn't belong to him once when he was a lad and drove it about for an hour. And it's that coming back to haunt him now. Can you imagine the embarrassment? Being dragged away by the police in front of your own employer! Tommy must have suffered terribly."

"They'll find out he's innocent, but they have to investigate all the possibilities."

"They did question me about Rory too, I will say that. They made it sound as though he might've had personal reasons to kill Ellie as well, though I put-paid to that, I can tell you, in short order. They had the nerve to ask how his wife died, and whether he'd given her her injections!"

"They have to question us about Rory. There's more reason to think he could've killed Ellie than there is to think your son did."

"You don't believe it was Rory, do you!"

Ben could hear wheels spitting gravel across the drive, and it sounded like more than one car. He shot across to the front window, hoping it wasn't Grey. Just as Hugh opened the door and walked in.

He looked tentative and ill-at-ease as he gazed at Mary like he wanted to say something comforting, but didn't know where to begin. "I'm terribly sorry about Tom. I'm sure they'll come to their senses as soon as they probe a bit deeper."

"It's a frightful miscarriage of justice! It makes me furious, it really does!"

"It must be horrific for him." Hugh sat next to her on the sofa and spoke in a calm, quiet voice, as though he hoped that was the best approach. "It will all come right in the end, and his employer will be made to understand. Before I forget, Detective Inspector Grey has asked me to tell everyone that they've sealed Ellie's room and finished with the preliminary investigation they needed to do here, and they've gone into Dunblane to talk to Tom. They'll turn up here again quite early in the morning, *if* the next round of results from the P.M. indicates that there's reason to. Though they seem to think that's far from certain. They do want all of us to call in to the station in Dunblane, though, if we're planning on traveling anywhere a'tall, simply to let them know where we can be reached."

"Great!" Ben shook his head in disbelief and then set his hands on his hips.

"I beg your pardon?" Hugh sounded disconcerted.

And Ben turned toward him and smiled. "I wanted to talk to Grey about Jon's death and didn't get a chance before he left. I suppose I'll have to call him in Dunblane."

Mary sighed while she folded Ben's handkerchief.

And Hugh said, "Yes, I'm sure you should." He was yawning at the same time and stretching his arms up above his head. "I don't know about the two of you, but I'm absolutely done in. It must be the emotional strain. Though I did help at the gatehouse this afternoon too, carrying in the new hot-water heater and doing a bit of hammering, so it may be exertion as well. Is there time to have a soak before dinner, Mary, or should I simply change and dash down?"

"I haven't given dinner any thought a'tall. What time is it now, do you know?"

Ben looked at his watch and said, "Five after six."

"Well, it won't be an elaborate meal. Of course, who would want it to be? With Ellie dead and gone, and Tommy being treated as though he's a cold-blooded murderer and a thief as well." She was fighting to keep her chin steady as she pushed herself up off the couch.

"We can fend for ourselves, can't we, Ben? Mary shouldn't be expected to cook at a time like this. I'll have a quick bathe, and then dash down and do whatever needs to be done."

"Oh, aye! I can just picture the three of you muddling about in my kitchen! No, I'll be much better doing something useful than sitting and brooding." She was walking away from them down the hall, her steps slightly irregular and her head hanging off to one side.

The phone rang while Ben was helping Alex set the dining room table, and he sprinted down the hall to the sitting room.

It was Reginald Morse-White, but he hadn't sold bees to anyone so far this spring. "Of course, no one would have sold bees in the winter months, when they hibernate, but there is generally quite a brisk trade starting in early May. I'm simply behind times, due to the demands of work."

Ben thanked him, and then placed yet another call to Jamie MacIntosh. He waited, listening to the phone ring, sliding his fingers along the smooth wooden arm of his chair, until he'd resigned himself to the fact that no one was going to answer.

He was back in the dining room, putting soup bowls on dinner plates while Mary and Alex set glasses on the table, when Tom Atwood thundered through the kitchen door.

Mary threw herself against him and burst into tears, and Tom rubbed her back and made soothing noises, as he glared over her head at Ben and Alex. He was shortish, muscular, and thick necked, and looked at that moment like an irate bull, except that his thin blond hair (which had been carefully combed sideways across the top of his head) had slipped forward in a stiff sprayed sheet, exposing a pale pink tender-looking scalp, that made him seem vulnerable too.

"It's over and done with, Mother. They've checked my alibi and let me go without any sort of blot upon my name."

"You're sure? They've not just released you to pursue you again later?"

"No, I can't see how they could. I was at The Black Bear playing darts with Joan in plain view of most of Kinbuck till nearly nine last night, when Sam Applegate came in to fetch me. Joan went home to the children, and I went off and helped Sam repair his truck. It took us till nearly three in the morning. He had a delivery to make in Edinburgh by seven, so we couldn't wait to do the work. His wife was with us as well, fetching tea and sandwiches, so there was vera little the police could say."

"Then it's a blessing you were with Sam and no mistake!"

"Aye, but that's not the end of it, is it? What infuriates me is that someone put that jewelry where I'd be blackened by it." Tom glared at Alex over his mother's head. "And when I get my hands on the lad who did that, it'll be some little time before I let go of his cowardly neck!"

"No one would try to incriminate you on purpose!" Mary was pulling up the collar of Tom's tattersall shirt and smoothing it across his sweater.

"That's just what *was* done! We're only the hired help, and at the first sign of trouble, the police will always look to us, just like the family did in years past. You know it's unfair, yet you'll never admit it!"

"And is it fair that Mrs. Jon lay dead in a cold bed this morning at the age of thirty-two? No, it'tis not! And as you very well know, the MacLeans have treated us better than we ever had a right to expect, in spite of what was done to their car years ago. Jonathan MacLean loved *you* like a brother, and he was selling this house to give me a good pension, while he helped others in Cawdor as well."

"Aye, well, we'll never know that for cairtain now, will we?"

"Jon was cut off too, in his prime. Is that fair? No! It's infernal wickedness is what it'tis. But will it come right in the end? Yes! In the next life it will, if not in this."

"Well, it won't happen here as it should, I know that. Where's Hugh?"

"He's been working up at the gatehouse, and he's having a bathe and a quick lie down. It's been vera hard on him, I can tell ye, losing both Jon and Ellie within a fortnight. But will ye come in the kitchen, Tommy, please, and tell me what the police finally said to you?"

Mary had almost gotten to the kitchen door, when Ben heard his own name being called from the front hall.

Dr. Graham had thrown his mackintosh on a chair by the library desk and was just adjusting his coat sleeves as Ben closed the door to the cedar room and said, "Boy, am I glad to see you. I thought maybe you weren't coming."

"Allan didn't phone until a very few moments ago." Graham settled himself on the sofa where Grey had sat that afternoon, and considered Ben with a serious, detached expression. "You're still prepared to keep everything I tell you completely confidential?"

"Of course. And it is important that I know what Allan's

found, because if I'm right, there's another life in danger too, and the police don't know anything about it."

"You haven't explained the situation to Grey, then?"

Ben told him about the jewelry and the interrupted conversation. "I think the jewelry's just being used to mislead the police. But either way, Grey left here before I could talk to him, so he doesn't have all the facts. I called him in Dunblane, but he'd already left for Perth. I phoned there too and left a message asking them to have him call me. But if I can't get to Grey soon, it'll be me trying to protect the other person. *If* I'm lucky enough to track him down."

"And you need Allan's findings to help put the pieces together?"

"Exactly."

"Well, he still doesn't know what caused the cardiac arrest. They found no pathology a'tall. No physical reason for her heart to fail. But neither do they think she was dosed with insulin, for the sugar levels in the vitreous humor were similar enough to that found in the blood, that insulin, in any sort of sizeable dose, couldn't have been present."

Ben nodded, while he rolled his shoulders up and back.

"You don't seem very surprised, laddie."

"I'm not. I think the insulin was a red herring."

"Do you? I had no idea. They did find Soneryl, the sleeping draught I'd given her, but in a very small quantity, one which would've been totally harmless and in line with the dose I'd prescribed. The unexpected discovery was that chloral hydrate was present as well, though not nearly enough to be lethal. The sort of dose that would've made her unconscious for a few hours and perhaps given her a headache in the morning."

"I thought they might find another sedative."

"Did you?"

"Because of the empty space in the medicine cabinet. It seemed likely to me that Jon's mother might've taken chloral hydrate, or some other strong sedative, orally, in liquid form, during her last illness. But I didn't know for sure."

"Aye, Elizabeth did take chloral hydrate. The cancer specialist in Edinburgh prescribed it."

"And there *was* a second injection site?"

"There was indeed. The track was very clear inside the vein upon dissection."

"Could the combination of the Soneryl and the chloral hydrate have caused cardiac arrest?"

"Allan certainly doesn't think so."

"But she *was* pregnant, I take it?"

"You knew, did you!"

"No, but I suspected."

William Graham's thick gray eyebrows shot halfway to his hairline, while he studied Ben's face. "She told me yesterday when I examined her, but she said she hadn't mentioned it to anyone else. That's why she'd been having so much tummy trouble, and why I ordered all the blood work."

"Why didn't she tell anyone?"

"She said Jon was the only person who knew, other than her physician, and it made her feel a special sort of bond with Jon. She didn't want to sever that tie by discussing it with anyone else."

"It might've been an awkward announcement to make right then too, with everything else she was going through."

"Aye, and she wasn't very far along either—eleven weeks, or perhaps twelve—and she feared a miscarriage as well. It had taken her years to conceive, you know, and she seemed to feel it was too good to be true. Perhaps she couldn't face the thought of having to cope with everyone's sympathy, if she were to lose the baby early on."

"There weren't any signs of an amniotic embolism?"

"No. Nor any other complication from the pregnancy."

"What about an injection of potassium chloride?"

"Now that's a possibility, isn't it? Potassium chloride. Yes, it would certainly cause cardiac arrest."

"But it wouldn't be detectable in the body. Right?"

"Virtually impossible, I should think. A great deal of potassium is naturally present in the body, and one wouldn't be able to distinguish that from whatever had been injected. One could compare the blood level of potassium to that found in the vitreous humor, but the results would be inconclusive. Aye, if a sizeable dose were administered, and it were injected into a vein speedily enough, it would stop the heart without doubt. But it would have to be injected into a vein."

"And death would occur quickly. Correct?"

"Yes. I'll have to talk to Allan to get his ideas on the subject, but I would've thought death would result in ten or fifteen minutes, *if* enough were administered. Yet why would such a thing occur to you?"

"There was the mark in the opening into the vein that suggested a second injection, so that set me on the right track. Pardon the pun. But the idea really came from a friend of mine years ago, when he was in medical school. I remember one time when he was joking around, he said that's how he'd kill someone if he ever wanted to—one quick shot of potassium chloride."

"But—"

"Then I examined Robert MacLean's laboratory. The reagents were all carefully organized and arranged alphabetically, but there wasn't any potassium chloride, and that made no sense at all. Any lab would have it, and the shelf it should've been on looked like it had been recently rearranged, because of the dust patterns and the old stains. There were actually three chemicals missing from that cabinet that should have been there. One of them was potassium chloride."

"So you think the murderer removed it to reduce the likelihood of anyone thinking it had been taken from the lab and used to kill Ellie?"

"Right. Work had been done on the bench too, and the center of the surface had been wiped afterwards. But that still doesn't point to a particular person."

"You must have your own ideas on the subject."

"Yeah, but I don't have proof."

"May I ask whom you suspect?"

"I can't talk about it yet, but I hope to be able to tomorrow." Ben picked up a small fragment of paper from between the cushion and the arm of the sofa and rolled it between his fingers. "Anyone who knew the family could have known that old Mrs. MacLean took chloral hydrate, that the bottle was in the medicine cabinet by Ellie's room, and that Mr. MacLean had had a chemistry lab. The same way they would've known that Mrs. Atwood used insulin and kept a syringe in her bathroom. Although *I* think her syringe was rearranged just to shift suspicion, and another one was used on Ellie. One with a larger needle."

"Yes, it was a larger needle."

"The murderer didn't want any traces of potassium chloride to be found in Mary's syringe. He wanted Ellie's death to look as though she'd died of cardiac arrest, unexpectedly, certainly, but without any reason to suspect foul play. If Allan hadn't been exceptionally sharp, that's what would've happened. The insulin was only a false trail the murderer thought he had to prepare in case somebody got suspicious. And of course I was here to get suspicious. But except for the distraction of the jewelry—"

"I don't see the significance of the chloral hydrate."

"I think it was used to sedate Ellie so it would be easier to inject the potassium chloride. He didn't know how strong the Soneryl was, but he knew chloral hydrate would knock her out cold. She'd be lying there helpless in a complete stupor, and all the murderer had to do was tie on a tourniquet and get the needle into her vein in the hole where you'd drawn blood. He probably didn't know how hard that is to do without making a second mark on the inside of the vein."

"And yet there are many pathologists who wouldn't have seen a need to dissect the vein."

"Yeah, I'm sure that's true."

"I can hardly bear the thought of Ellie lying there defenseless. Falling prey to a cold-blooded predator. What sort of person would do such a thing?"

"Someone who wants what he wants when he wants it. But then isn't murder in any form the ultimate act of arrogance?"

"It's even more horrible to contemplate when you've known the person to have been a gentle soul who wouldn't have harmed her worst enemy. I can't even imagine her having one."

"I think he was improvising with her death. He complicated matters a lot more than he should have, but then I don't think he decided to kill her until last night."

"Well, I, for one, will do anything I can to bring the cad to justice!" Dr. Graham had been fiddling with one of the crested buttons on his blazer, but he let it go then and pushed himself to the edge of the sofa. "Still, I must dash. We've company coming for dinner and I'm late already."

"I really appreciate your help, Dr. Graham."

"Not a'tall. It's the least I could do. I do hope Grey gets back to you soon. I've had dealings with him in the past, and he strikes me as a person who would welcome another point of view."

Ben laughed and said, "I hope so. Would you mind if I don't see you out? There's a phone call I ought to make."

"No, go right ahead. But do let me know how matters develop. I'll get back in touch myself when Allan has more to report."

Ben sat at the partner desk in the west bay and stared out at the dripping trees while the exchange operator worked at connecting him. It had rained for at least three hours, peppering the stone walls and spattering against the glass, but now a fine mist hovered between the firs and the ash trees, their pale green-gray moss-covered branches furred with delicate new leaves. The waist high ferns were bent with the weight of the rain, and the wet rhododendrons looked darker and slicker than normal. There wasn't much wind, and it was growing dark. For the night comes down suddenly in Scotland, even in the spring, and the mist made it grayer still.

It was a quarter of eight, and Ben's stomach was growling viciously, while the phone rang time after time in Kinnesswood, the same way it had since Monday.

Yet this time, as Ben was about to give up, the receiver clunked hard against the holder on the other end and he heard a breathless voice say, "Good evening to you! Jamie MacIntosh here."

He'd been visiting his daughter on the Isle of Skye, but he was home, finally. Thank God. For Jamie MacIntosh had indeed sold bees on the afternoon of May eleventh to an elderly woman who's name he couldn't recall. She'd written to place her order.

But her son had picked them up. And MacIntosh's description of him wasn't a surprise to Ben. "What color were his eyes, do you remember?... Blue. I see. A very bright blue... I can't explain on the phone, but it's extremely important that I talk to you as soon as I can get to Kinnesswood... Thank you. I appreciate it. Will I need directions? I'll be coming from near Kinbuck... So after I go around the curve toward Kinnesswood with Loch Leven on my right, I turn left, which is north, onto Kinrossie Road, and you're the first house on the right?... Great. Thank you, Mr. MacIntosh. I'll leave right away and see you as soon as I can get there... Oh, by the way, if that same young man were to call or visit... "

Jamie MacIntosh had rung off.

And when Ben had the operator place the call again, the party line was engaged and he couldn't get through.

He hummed Beethoven's Ninth anyway as he ran up the front stairs and turned left into the east hall. His bedroom was the first door on the right, and he almost opened it without thinking, but then he remembered the thread at the last second.

It wasn't there. Not in the door frame.

It was lying on the paper-bag colored carpet a foot or two inside the room.

Ben closed the door behind him and turned on the lamp by the fireplace. Nothing looked like it had been disturbed. At least not superficially.

Although what mattered was under the bed, and he dragged out his overnight case. The lock hadn't worked in years, and he undid the clasps and examined the stack of journals. All the *Scottish Beekeepers* were stacked the way he'd left them. But the threads he'd laid between the top two were gone or moved into different positions. Which meant Jamie MacIntosh was in more danger than he'd been at six-fifteen, when Ben had last checked his room.

He pulled off his desert boots and hurried into hard-soled shoes. He got his flashlight out of his big suitcase, and grabbed a towel from the wooden rack so he could wipe the Rover's windows if the defroster worked like it usually did.

He looked to see if Hugh was still upstairs.

But he wasn't.

And Ben charged down the stairway at a dangerous pace and ran down the hall to the kitchen, where Tom Atwood was talking with Mary and drinking a glass of bitter, while she dished up potato soup and Alex put bread in a basket.

"I've got to borrow your car again, Alex, and I need ordnance survey maps of Perthshire and Kinross."

"You still have the keys, I expect? Good. Maps, on the other hand . . Mary—"

"I should think they're in the sitting room in the bottom drawer in the desk."

"How long will it take to get to Kinnesswood?"

Tom Atwood answered, looking considerably calmer than he had before. "An hour or more, most likely. Take the route through Bridge of Allan, Dollar, and Carnbo, and then on to the north side of the loch. It's not far, actually, but the roads are slow going and poorly marked. They haven't put the signs back since the end of the last war."

"Great!"

"Why are you dashing off?" Alex was holding a large bread knife, while staring intently at Ben.

"Bees. It's a long story. Where's Hugh?"

"I haven't the foggiest . . No, I remember, he walked down to the gatehouse to make sure the water's been properly laid on."

"You're sure he walked?

"I would've thought so. It stopped raining, didn't it, half an hour or more ago?"

Hugh's Bentley wasn't in front *or* in the garage. And Ben muttered an army expression under his breath he hadn't used in years as he lay down on the cold stone floor and slid under the Rover Saloon's matronly fender and bulbous hood. He swept his flashlight across the underbelly out of respect for the towel rack at Balnagard.

And then he opened the hood so he could examine the engine for nasty surprises. The beam from his flashlight lit the distributor and six cut spark plug wires—just as he heard Tom Atwood drive out the back drive.

Ben flew back into the house and hollered at Alex to call the people at the gatehouse. "Tell them it's a matter of life and death, and I've got to borrow their car!" He waited, pacing the hall, till Alex had someone on the line.

And then he shot through the front door and took the steps three at a time.

It was only half a mile to the gatehouse. And Ben set his pace and settled into it. And then tried to figure out how long Hugh had been gone.

CHAPTER FOURTEEN

THE EWINGS' CAR WAS A NEWER ROVER than Alex's, but the defroster didn't work any better, and Ben had to wipe the windshield every few minutes to see at all.

Driving on the left took concentration, on tight twisting roads in the mist and the dark, when there were almost no road signs and very few houses where he could stop and ask when he came to a confusing crossroads.

There were patches of fog too, spreading along the low ground and swirling in front of him, lying in wait when he'd tuck into a turn and sweep down into the fold of a hill. He came around one sharp bend into a wall of fog and had to fight to keep from sliding off on the driver's side where a sharp graveled edge hung above a deep ravine. Then as he shifted up through the gears again, a white shape materialized out of the mist and jumped in front of him. He slammed on the brakes and slid to avoid it. A ewe, with a lamb behind her, two feet away, white and black and matted with dirt, four eyes ringed with fear, hard cloven hooves clattering across concrete.

He told himself to hurry, to shift fast and get to MacIntosh. Because Hugh knew those roads like his own face, and he had too much at stake to care whether he killed again.

The Rover was a ponderous car to drive under the best conditions, "heavy in the hand" as the British would've said. And Ben couldn't get it up to more than thirty-five, with too many stretches of considerably less where he lumbered around the curves and corners, while he picked at his own decisions.

I couldn't have gotten to MacIntosh any sooner. But I could've protected Ellie. That's the worst part. I should've worried less about how she felt and made her talk about the will that first time I asked. Then I would've seen the motive a lot sooner and been able to keep her alive.

So will second-guessing yourself help now?

No. But that doesn't make it any easier.

I wonder why Grey didn't talk to me before he left? They might not have given him the message. Which probably means I should've pushed them harder. I didn't, because I thought it made more sense to track the connection to the bees fast, before Hugh had time to do away with it. But maybe I could've done both.

Rats! Why didn't I have Alex call MacIntosh and warn him about Hugh! Dumb. Very dumb. Very shortsighted.

It was drizzling in places, and the wipers slapped ineffectually across the steamy glass, until the rhythm of them beating out the time he was losing and the mistakes he'd made, made it more galling, as he lost his way twice and had to backtrack.

Then finally he came around a wide turn to the left that swept north around the end of Loch Leven, where the road climbed briefly before it dipped into Kinnesswood, a tiny gray village of high stone walls and small stone cottages, set close to narrow streets.

Almost before Ben could blink, he was through it. And he still hadn't seen a sign for Kinrossie Road. He went on, with the loch lower down on his right and rising fields on his left, leading to what seemed to be the high spine of a hill.

No, this isn't right. Kinrossie Road should've been on the other side of Kinnesswood. Yeah, but how could I have missed it? He said there's a sign, and I checked every intersection.

He turned around in a farm track and whipped back through the village on its narrow main street, saying, "Don't let me be too late, let him be alive when I get there!" while he forced another car to pull halfway up on the sidewalk to let him pass, when he usually would've pulled off himself.

He was almost back to the big curve, when he saw "rossi" on a broken white board nailed to his side of a tree at the entrance to a road on his right. It made more sense than any of the other possibilities, and he shot into that side road, running northwest away from the loch.

It was a quiet country lane. No houses at all for almost half a mile. Then faint lights finally on the right, on the other side of a low stone wall.

Ben stopped and backed the Rover onto the edge of the grass, fifty feet before the driveway of what turned out to be a small two-story stone cottage with a slate roof.

There was still no wind, and fortunately it wasn't raining, but a fine mist settled on his skin and began beading on his woolen jacket as he followed the gravel and mud drive inside the low stone wall. He threaded his way to the front door through overgrown borders that spilled and dangled dripping leaves and loose petals against his legs as well as the moss-covered walk.

He hadn't seen a name or a house number on the wall by the road. And he couldn't find either by the front door. But he dropped the heavy brass knocker two or three times and waited, staring at the hall stairs through the sidelights by the front door.

There was no sound and no movement, but he knocked again and then stepped to the dining-room window on his left. There was a light on in the back of the house, so he could see there was no one there. And he started back the way he'd come and looked in the living-room window between the door and the driveway, at an empty sofa and three chairs and a fire dying in the grate.

He stood still and listened. Breathing in the cool damp air, the wet grass, the new plants, the moss on the stones, the heaviness of freshly turned soil, the trees dripping rain through the scent of new leaves, while he listened for sounds of life.

There was a dog down the road, and sheep closer by. There were scurryings in the stone walls, and large wings flapping in the woods, as he walked along the driveway to the back. Not risking a flashlight. Stepping softly, slowly, stumbling once on the uneven ground, on a clump of grass in cobblestone in a once paved courtyard, while he asked himself where MacIntosh was, if this was Kinrossie Road, and whether Hugh had had time to finish what he'd come to do.

Hugh couldn't have had much time to spare, because when Ben had met Graham by the front door, he'd heard Hugh talking on the upstairs phone.

Of course, the Bentley was nowhere to be seen, but that was no surprise. Hugh wouldn't have left it in plain view.

A low stone stable sat in front of Ben, parallel to the house behind him, but set back quite a distance across the courtyard on the edge of a field or pasture. There was a small orchard on his right, running straight back from the road on the other side of the driveway. And when the clouds parted suddenly and the moon broke through, he could see eight white beehives between the trees in two neatly spaced rows (which Ben thought was encouraging, even if it wasn't conclusive).

He started toward the light at the back of the house, picking his way silently to the kitchen window on the right, where a hanging light lit both the kitchen and the living room enough to show him there was no one there.

The upstairs windows were dark, so he couldn't tell whether or not the rooms behind them were empty. The back door was locked, like the front. And he decided not to break in then, but to try the stables first.

All three doors were shut, and there was no light seeping around the frames. And yet he opened the smallest door, quietly. Slowly. Waiting and listening before he stepped in.

Hugh's Bentley wasn't there. And no one was hiding in the corners around the rusty tractor, or the bailing machine that hadn't been used in years, or the old Mini-Austin that was registered to James Fitzwilliam MacIntosh.

Ben slipped back into the night, closed the door quietly, and leaned against it.

There was a very faint light, now, on his right, that hadn't been there before and seemed to be coming from a rickety greenhouse attached to a low stone shed.

One of his hard-soled shoes scratched across a cobblestone as he tried to put that foot down silently, watching the corners of the house and stable, searching the shadows in the orchard behind him, weaving his way through the mist and the moonlight, and the jet black patches where a cloud blew across, while he listened to a hundred sounds.

He was sniffing the air like a predatory cat, skin pulled tight against his bones, eyes black and sunken in the night, in the smoke-gray haze floating around him, glowing silvery and alive in the light from the greenhouse that made the night unearthly.

And yet the light wasn't coming from the greenhouse. It was

spilling over into it from the shed on the left. And it wasn't as strong and steady as electric light. It was thinner. Fainter. It could've been candlelight. Or maybe a kerosene lamp.

Ben edged his way to the far side of the shed, looking for doors and windows, while he listened to the bad news.

Bees. Thousands of them in the greenhouse. A huge deafening mass of them. Panicked. Frantic. Scattering across the glass like buckshot.

Ben's right shoulder hugged the cold stone wall of the small shed, adrenaline up and running, his cheek wet with grit and sand, as he tried the padlock on the shed's only door. Quietly. Very quietly. Listening. Holding his breath. Waiting for a reaction inside.

It was locked. And both sides of the hasp were securely fastened.

He could break it with tools from the stable. But not without noise. Not without alerting whoever had lit the light in the shed.

The only way in was through the door to the greenhouse. The greenhouse filled with bees. Millions of them, crawling on the walls, blackening the glass, buzzing and whirring and slapping against the wood-framed panes of the walls, the door, and the ceiling.

Ben's back was to the orchard now, and his face was pressed against that door with his hands cupped around his eyes. The bees were so thick, crawling across the glass, that he could hardly see the inside of the room even in the light from the shed.

There was no human movement. Or human sound. Though if there had been he probably wouldn't have heard.

Wait.

Something's on the floor in the far right corner. Light at one end. Dark at the other. The shape and size of a man.

Ben pulled his shirt collar up against his neck, and the collar of his jacket over that and then tugged his cuffs down over his wrists as far as they would go.

Not that he thought that would help much. It was all he had time to do before he opened the door and stepped into that swarming hive.

Bees hit him from all directions, and he was stung too, twice. Three times. At random. Not in a deliberate attack. Probably. More like he was in their way.

He told himself not to swat at them. To keep his hands still and check out the shed before he tried to help the man on the floor.

He plastered his chest against the short wall on his left (perpendicular to the door he'd come through), while bees flew into him and crawled across his back, without paying him much attention. He stood on the left side of the doorway to the shed. Listening, but not hearing anything but bees. Smelling smoke, either charcoal or wood, plus a kerosene lamp and a candle maybe, that's just been lit and blown out, mingled with mold, damp soil, and new plants.

The constant high-pitched buzzing of the bees made it almost impossible to hear danger coming toward him. But he held his breath, his chest still flattened against the wall, and looked around the doorway.

The light was coming from a glass kerosene lamp sitting on a workbench on the long wall on the right, in a room that wasn't more than twelve feet by fifteen, with shelves on most of the walls. An unlit candle, a ball of twine, a carving knife, and what looked like a long white shoelace were on the workbench too, scattered around a bee smoker with a thin trail of smoke curling from its funnel end.

There were a few carpentry tools on the shelves, but they

were mostly filled with clay pots and gardening supplies, though the hoes and shovels and large tools were hanging on the left wall on either side of the padlocked door. There was a wooden trunk on the far side of that door near the corner, and two garbage cans on Ben's side next to a stack of newspapers and an open bag of leaf mold.

He couldn't see the corners closest to him, even though there was no door in the door frame. And he stuck his head all the way into the room and looked to the left and right.

No one. Which came as a surprise. Because Hugh MacLean had to be somewhere.

Unless he'd already killed MacIntosh and left before Ben had gotten there.

Ben was considering the trunk at the other end of the room and was about to decide it didn't look large enough to conceal a person, inside or out, when four bees landed on his face.

They were crawling across his skin—one below his right eye, one on his forehead moving toward his nose, another on his right earlobe, and the last in the cleft of his chin.

They were angry and agitated and they moved constantly, twisting, switching their tails, making his skin prickle and his scalp crawl.

The one on his forehead slithered between his eyebrows, then over and above his right eye just below his eyebrow. It twirled in a circle, pushing its tail down against Ben's lid, buzzing and vibrating almost as though it were humming.

The one that had been under his eye had crawled down his cheek to the middle of his upper lip, right below the groove between his lip and his nose. The buzzing and the beating wings made his nose itch, and he could hardly force himself not to slap it away.

If he swatted they'd sting. And he told himself to hold perfectly still, to stand there like part of the wall, to breathe slowly and think about something else, while sweat slid down his forehead, and collected on his upper lip too.

The bee under his eyebrow had stepped down onto his eyelid and was crawling across his cornea. Turning. Quivering. Making the eyelid itch almost uncontrollably.

The bee from his earlobe had crawled inside his ear, and he tried not to think about that at all, while the one on his chin joined the other on his upper lip. One of them was walking sideways, buzzing, tramping, right below Ben's nose, scratching through a day's growth of stubble.

He had to sneeze. He didn't know how to stop it, even after one of them stepped down on his bottom lip.

Then they were gone. As suddenly as they'd landed.

And Ben slapped an index finger across the base of his nose, just managing to stop a sneeze that would've sounded like an explosion.

He had to get to the man on the floor. And he covered his ears with his hands and then stooped and ran to the other end of the greenhouse, where the two walls with workbenches met. He squatted down on his heels and pressed two fingers on the jugular vein of an elderly man, sprawled on his stomach on damp bricks, with his left arm under him and his right lying limply above his head.

The old man was off somewhere on his own, and Ben couldn't bring him back. His pulse was slow too. But probably not slow enough to be dangerous. He was cold and clammy and could've been drugged (Hugh's past history being what it was). Though Ben thought his pupils looked reasonably normal, once he'd turned him over on his back.

MacIntosh had been stung six or seven times on the face and hands, but it didn't look like his reaction had been extreme or unusual. There was whiskey on his breath, but he didn't reek of it. Certainly not the way he would've if he'd drunk enough to pass out.

There was a flat of tomato plants and a cardboard box beside him, and two wooden frames from a beehive three or four feet away, half under one of the benches. He would've had to use the frames to carry the bees from the hive. Which meant they were probably trying to get back there now, crawling across the glass, looking for a way out. And Ben told himself to prop the door open, as soon as he finished with MacIntosh.

There was a cocktail glass on the bench with a fraction of an inch of whiskey in the bottom that didn't smell right. At least Ben asked himself whether it did or not, without being certain either way.

There was nothing Ben could do for MacIntosh, except get him a doctor later. But if he *was* drugged (if he hadn't passed out because of some other physical condition), someone else had been there and not very long ago. Yes, someone who'd lit the lamp.

Ben could feel it coming back again. The psychology of the sitting duck. The nighttime tightness he'd felt with The Nighttime Special. Adrenaline taking over in enemy occupied territory.

But the bees were disorienting. The nerve-wracking noise of them, buzzing like a battalion of chain saws, drilling themselves against everything they touched, kept him from hearing what he needed to hear.

The constant pelting too of their tiny brittle bodies, and the unpredictability of a random sting, even more in a way than the pain itself, worked against the night vision and the hearing and the sense of smell he had to have to keep himself alive.

The smell of smoke was getting stronger. And Ben started to stand up, even before the light from the shed was cut off behind him.

It wasn't snuffed out or extinguished. It was blocked. Suddenly. So that as Ben turned toward the shed, an ax handle smashed across the back of his head.

He told himself to get up.

He said it again louder, somewhere inside his head. But he didn't seem to be listening. It wasn't pain getting in the way. He didn't feel any then. It was just that nothing was working. A fog had settled in on him. The brain, the eyes, the ears, the legs. None of it could be counted on. The control was gone. Completely. He had to wait for someone else to take charge. If he wouldn't. And keep him from getting killed.

Why wasn't he coming out of the mist? He was talking somewhere inside. He could hear himself say, *Come on! Get up! Get on your feet fast!* MOVE NOW!

Because someone was moving him.

His arm had already been pinned down, hard. And something was wrapped around it. The one over here. The one that was hurt. Is that the left? Where there's something heavy and sharp...a knee, that's it, a knee pinning down my left shin.

He's trying to stick something in my arm!

Ben Reese's hands shot up and grabbed Hugh's upper arms just below the shoulder joints so that the thumbs bit against the bones, freezing Hugh's arms and yanking him savagely over and above Ben. Ben's right leg thrashed up, the knee bent and the foot in Hugh's gut, and catapulted Hugh over his head.

The net-covered beekeeper's helmet Hugh had been wearing

fell off as he landed half on a bag of potting soil and half on a stack of clay pots. The syringe skidded across the brick floor, seconds before Ben ripped the tourniquet off his left arm.

He was thinking, Why bees? Crawling all over me. And why do I smell smoke and feel like I'm about to choke? Yet he still grabbed a clay pot as he stood up and threw it through a section of glass near the outside door.

The bees rushed toward the hole, toward the outside, near where Hugh had picked up the bee smoker—the small metal can with bellows attached that's made to be worked with one hand.

He was trying to pump smoke in Ben's face, while he grabbed the ax handle and rushed toward Ben again, swinging it at his head.

Ben swerved and ducked and took the next hit as a glancing blow across the top of his left shoulder. It bounced and grazed his ear. And he staggered for a second, as he leapt back and sideways, almost on top of MacIntosh.

Something warm and sticky was sliding into his ear and the ear was ringing, muffling the noise of the bees, as well as Hugh circling around him. Ben shook his head twice, as he swept his right arm back to the left across his chest, setting the fingers and turning the outside edge into a weapon he'd been trained to use back when he was young and crazy.

It was army-issue instinct, even with a half-blurred brain, that hit the arm that held the ax handle. It connected on some sweet spot, like a lobbed ball in the center of a well-strung racket, and the ax handle dropped and skittered across the bricks.

There were bees swarming around Ben, still peppering him on their way out the broken pane, while he kicked the ax handle across the room. Hugh was backing toward the outside wall, trying to reach the door, pumping smoke into Ben's face.

Ben choked and gagged and tears streamed down his cheeks, but he still came straight at Hugh.

Hugh had grabbed something from the floor near the stairs before he started toward the door. And he was circling again, warily, holding the smoker in his left hand, aiming the funnel at Ben. He was coughing too, coughing and circling, carrying a syringe of potassium chloride.

Ben lunged in Hugh's direction to see how he'd react. And Hugh jumped back and pumped another shot of smoke at Ben.

Ben avoided most of it, ducking his head and crouching sideways away from it, just before he smashed his right shoe with its hard-edged heel on Hugh's left arch.

Hugh groaned and almost doubled over, even before the edge of Ben's left hand sliced into his left wrist, knocking the smoker out of his hand. Ben couldn't see where it landed, but he heard it rolling across the bricks away from the outside door.

He slashed his right hand into Hugh's left trapezius muscle, and then he whipped that hand into Hugh's right forearm so that the syringe shattered on the bricks.

Ben scraped his shoe down Hugh's shin from knee to ankle before Hugh could recover from the blow to the arm, and then he started tearing at Hugh's raincoat. It was a stiff waxed cotton, fastened together with heavy snaps, and Ben tore at it from both sides, ripping it open across Hugh's chest.

Hugh kicked at Ben's legs and flailed at him with his fists. But only until Ben got his coat open.

He was telling himself not to kill Hugh. Not to shove the small bony projection so hard against Hugh's heart that it ruptured his aorta.

No, Hugh MacLean is going to stand trial. Everybody's got to see him for what he is.

Ben drove his hand, palm up, thumb out to the side, fingers together, ends facing forward, straight into Hugh's solar plexus right below the sternum.

Hugh's heart stopped instantly. And he dropped on the floor like he'd been shot.

A trickle of bees was still streaming past Ben toward the hole in the shattered glass as he stood over Hugh, looking at his empty face, and untying his own tie.

CHAPTER FIFTEEN

BEN BOUND HUGH'S ANKLES to the front legs of a large upholstered chair, then took his tie off Hugh's wrists and fastened
Hugh's hands straight down on either side of the chair arms with
a triple thickness of garden twine pulled tight under the seat,
between the front and back legs.

He got MacIntosh from the greenhouse and laid him on the
sofa. And then went to find the phone.

When he came back into the living room, he dropped his
mud-smeared jacket on the floor and sat in the other upholstered
chair facing Hugh across the fireplace. "C.I.D. should be here
from Perth in about an hour, and MacIntosh's doctor is on his
way from Wester Balgedie. You seem to be doing okay." Ben had
pulled out a crumpled handkerchief and was wiping blood off his
right ear.

"I'm conscious, if that's what you mean. And I'd like a drink
of water." Hugh's face was gray and strained, but his voice sounded
condescending, as well as slightly self-righteous.

It was the look on Hugh's face that Ben found fascinating—
the arrogance and the defiance and the contempt. "I'll get you
some water later, after you and I have had a talk."

"I wouldn't have imagined that we'd have much to say to one another."

"No? I thought you'd enjoy explaining how you've manipulated everybody you know."

Hugh started to smile, but then stopped and set his face toward the fire on his right.

"I assume you killed them for Kilgarth."

Hugh still didn't say anything. He just looked at Ben like a well-bred public schoolboy who's pretending to be polite, but can't quite camouflage his own sense of superiority.

"Why do you want Kilgarth? What you said about it is true, the inheritance taxes will be horrendous and the upkeep must cost plenty. It's not a national treasure like Balnagard that you can open to the public and charge money to see. So there's got to be some other appeal. Family pride? A hunger for possession and prestige maybe?"

"It's rather more complicated than that." Hugh made a point of not looking at Ben, of only gazing past him toward the windows in the back.

"I've got time."

"The question is, have I?" Hugh laid his head against the orange and brown upholstery and looked at MacIntosh for a moment, as though he were weighing the alternatives. Then he glanced at Ben again, before he turned away. "I found it reprehensible that Jon was prepared to sell Kilgarth with very little soul-searching and absolutely no perceptible regret. That, and the fact that he'd decided to do so in order that he might give the money away to whoever struck his fancy from one moment to the next, when *none* of us, not one of the MacLeans or the Campbells of close connection, was financially secure. I found that absolutely infuriating."

"Most people would understand why you felt that. It's a predictable human reaction."

"It's a great deal more than that, in this case. For our family has owned Kilgarth for over a hundred years. We enlarged the estate to its present boundaries. We introduced modern agricultural techniques to the county. We employed Lutyens and Jekkyl, whose landscape designs were the finest in Britain in the early part of this century, and they made the estate a showplace, even though one can hardly imagine the effects they achieved when one sees the grounds as they are today. We rightfully took a leading role in the political and social life of the county, as anyone would've expected.

"And yet today, all of us are in straightened circumstances because of economic reversals after the First War, which none of us could've controlled since they affected every facet of British life. Jon lived on practically nothing, and I've had a very difficult time supporting myself while taking my degrees. Hence the necessity of lowering my sights to the humble estate of tour guide and transporting obese Americans from one posh dining table to another. Even our two sequestered aunts in Balinluig are hard pressed to maintain any sort of gentility a'tall. And it hardly seems reasonable that the proceeds of the family estate should be squandered elsewhere without a thought to the family's necessities."

"Wasn't Jon trying to give Mary an income too?"

"He was, yes. And certainly I would want to do the same, up to a point. Though there are government programs, as you know, and she does have children who are self-supporting, who might be expected to take some responsibility upon themselves."

"That's not all, though, is it? There's still something else."

"It's a bit more ephemeral, and therefore more difficult to explain. It was clearly not a concept Jon was able to comprehend,

I can assure you. For Jonathan was doing quite deliberately what one of our maternal ancestors did out of wantonness hundreds of years ago. Jon exhibited exactly the same lack of concern for family honor, position, and property, even though his motivation differed superficially." Hugh stared at the fire for a moment.

And Ben sat and watched without interrupting.

"My mother's maternal ancestors were Fosters, and they were a powerful border clan for many hundreds of years. They were very farsighted and quite clever politically, and the clan chiefs were given the grand title of 'Lord Warden of the Middle Marches,' for they were employed by the kings of England to keep the unruly Scots north of the English border."

"That must have made them popular with the rest of the Scots."

"With some, yes, but not with others as you might expect. You see, Mother's branch of the Fosters took the long view. They realized that the economic realities of geography and climate were such that England was destined to conquer in the end, and they quite wisely chose to align themselves with the winning side. As a result, they were given Bamburgh Castle on the coast of Northumberland, just a bit south of Holy Island, which they owned for many, many years. It's a majestic castle, much larger and more imposing than Balnagard, and a very efficient bastion for repelling invaders from the continent."

"I remember. It shoots up out of the cliffs like it's defying the north sea."

"Yes, it's spectacular really, in setting and design. And yet one of the clan chiefs, General Thomas Foster, as it happened, was a bit of a reprobate. He ran through the family fortune at quite an appalling rate, until at the end of the day, he actually lost Bamburgh Castle in a card game."

"That's pathetic."

"He had no son to inherit, and he claimed he was trying to recoup the fortune he'd squandered. But he had no sense of lineage. No concern for the honor of the family. No feelings of responsibility to those who might come after. He showed no respect a'tall for the men who had built the family fortunes and placed him in what was clearly a position of considerable power."

"And you thought Jon was doing the same thing."

"Jon's motivations were different on the surface. He wasn't acting out of profligacy or selfishness in the usual sense, but it amounted to the same thing. He was clearly only too happy to sell Kilgarth. A lovely Georgian estate in a beautiful setting, which is very well placed to take advantage of the development of Scotland, when it comes. The MacLean family had lost everything it had except Kilgarth. And yet it meant *nothing* to Jon. He took no pride in the family accomplishments a'tall, and I found it impossible to overlook."

"So you killed Jon almost in plain view of Bamburgh Castle. That must have given you quite a feeling of accomplishment."

"I'd like you to loosen the restraints on my wrists."

"Why? You can swing your arms back and forth."

"A few inches only. And I still need a drink of water."

Ben brought him a glass and held it to his lips. And then sat back by the fire.

"There has been one consolation in driving tourists—"

"Aside from putting food on the table and getting you through school?"

"I've been able to visit the great houses and historical sites and be paid rather well for the pleasure. You see, I want to preserve our architectural treasures, which have existed, some of them, for more than a thousand years, and have made Britain absolutely unique in all the world. Yet today, because of our unconscionable death duties and obscene taxes, they're being torn down, or turned into insane asylums, or given to the state, or made over into hotels with 'swimming pools and conference centers attached.' And I, for one, was not about to stand by and see that sort of desecration done to Kilgarth!"

"But it wasn't up to you was it? It was left to Jon."

"Wasn't it, just! Yes, the inalienable rights of primogeniture."

"It's not as much a custom in Scotland as it is in England, so your parents must've made a very deliberate decision."

"It's not as frequent an occurrence, no. And of course, in our particular case, Jon always got the best of everything."

"I thought your father gave you the sailboat and the Bentley and a share of the paintings to make up for Jon getting Kilgarth?"

"He went through the motions, but it hardly amounts to the same thing. Oh yes, everyone loved open, straightforward Jon! Mother and Mary both made fools of themselves over him. All the boys at school admired him, even Creith the farmer, who was quite the local hero when we were young. Of course, the Eighth Earl of Balnagard, who was a loathsome beast when he was a boy, was beside himself too. And Katherine. She was absolutely pathetic. Even Rory, who practically drooled on his own shirt-front whenever he saw Ellie, thought Jon was a wonderful fellow. Of course, Jon was the returned prodigal, and he'd become *so* religious Father was hopelessly besotted. Even though there's nothing more repellent than an adult convert."

"No?"

"They're so enthusiastic, and they take their enthusiasms to such extremes. I don't mind the nominal churchgoer, one who appreciates the atmosphere and the architecture and feels a pleasant kinship with the traditional observances, but Jon tried to apply his beliefs to matters he should've had sense enough to leave well alone."

"Duncan Donaldson might disagree. Along with quite a few others."

"Oh yes, how could I have forgotten? Jon was a war hero too, of course, *and* a superb horseman. Ask anyone who ever met him. While *my* accomplishments, which were quite considerable I can assure you, even as a child, went nearly unnoticed. Except for the occasional, 'Yes dear, that's nice,' from my mother. Is it entirely surprising then that I should bridle at both his usurpation of the family inheritance *and* his decision to sell it away from me and fritter the money on his causes?"

"He did will Kilgarth to you instead of his wife, which was interesting."

"But only if he died before he sold it."

"I wonder if he knew how you felt."

"I never said."

"You wouldn't. But I bet Jon understood you better than anyone else."

Hugh shrugged and rubbed his chin on his shoulder.

"So once you'd gotten Kilgarth for yourself, how would you have managed to keep it, with all the expenses involved?"

"I've studied the estate finances quite closely, and I think that if there were conscientious, daily, expert attention paid to the agricultural workings of the estate, it could be made to be quite a bit more profitable than it is today. Farming is always uncertain, however, so if necessary—and only if necessary—it could be converted, fairly inexpensively, into a small, rather elegant inn, or perhaps even a bed-and-breakfast. I wouldn't manage it myself, of course. I'd live there and commute, while supplementing my income with my geological work. If worse came to worse, I could also take guests 'round the house and describe the history of the building and the family. For that is the sort of personal attention tourists seem to enjoy."

"Somehow I don't think you'd mind at all." Ben smiled to himself and shook his head and then set his fingertips together under his chin. "It must've been quite a blow to find out Ellie was pregnant. I assume that is what she wanted to tell you last night? And of course, that meant she had to be murdered or Kilgarth would go to the child. So you put your mother's chloral in Ellie's hot chocolate to make it easy to inject her with potassium chloride. That was lucky for you, wasn't it, the chloral and the lab right there, waiting to be used on the spur of the moment? Where'd you get the syringe? It wasn't Mary's. Yours was larger."

"I used it to give Mother's dog his injections. He had spondylosis his last few months and had to be dosed twice a week. Mother couldn't do it, so that left me, as usual. Jon was too 'busy with his congregation,' just as he always was when the family needed attention. Do you know what it's like to fetch and carry, and watch someone die rather messily of cancer? Jon didn't. He made sure he was too far away."

"So last night you drove to the pub, booked a room, called Mary to say your car wouldn't start, took the back roads to Kilgarth, and back to Dunblane, and then loosened the battery cable."

"Yes. Very carefully, though. It wouldn't do to have it look as though the cable had been tampered with in any way."

"Then tonight it was Jamie MacIntosh's turn, and you added chloral hydrate to his whiskey in the greenhouse."

"He fancies himself a connoisseur. A laughable delusion, but useful. We talked of it when I bought the bees, and tonight I brought him a present of Bunnahabhain. It's a twelve-year-old single malt from Islay that no whiskey aficionado could possibly resist. I told him my mother had decided on a further supply of bees, so he took the frames into the glass house to spray the bees and put them in a box for transport. I hoped to inject him under the hairline, if I were able to isolate a vein. Although bee stings would camouflage the mark either way, if all went well and the bees bit their keeper."

"Much like the insulin and the turned syringe and the jewelry were intended to divert attention and incriminate Tom Atwood. That wasn't very convincing, was it?"

"I had no time to organize the thing a'tall. Ellie told me she was pregnant at nine o'clock. Which I found rather ironic. For who would've thought our Jon's one regret in life would be removed at the eleventh hour? Why does that happen? Years of 'trying,' which always manages to sound terribly grim, and then once the barren couple gives up hope, so to speak, they conceive a child overnight?"

"So what about Ellie?"

"She said she'd tried to talk to me before McGuire arrived to tell me about the pregnancy, but once the will was read in public, she felt she should talk to me alone first before announcing it in company. She thought it would be more considerate, to speak to me in private, even though she didn't think for a moment that I'd mind losing Kilgarth. In certain ways Ellie was ridiculously trusting and unobservant, though remarkably astute in others."

"You said you didn't want it so often she believed you. She wasn't the cynic that I am." Ben poked at the fire and threw on another log. "I presume you intended to retrieve the picnic basket from beside Jon's body, but Jimmy Reed interfered."

"I was to whisk the hamper away the moment Jon had died, but despite the absurdly early hour, there was that one grubby little boy on the path and I couldn't approach Lindisfarne without being seen. Such a possibility had occurred to me, needless to say, which is why I made sure there were no prints in the basket. I knew, of course, that that in itself might arouse suspicion, and I did try the last time I saw Jon to get him to use the utensils I'd bought for the occasion. Unfortunately, food was never of much importance to Jonathan, and I couldn't persuade him to eat *or* drink. Still, if all went well after his death, no one would think to bother with the contents of the hamper. Was I right that Ellie didn't know Jon had told me about the will?"

"Yes, and I believed her. It was you not knowing about it that kept me from seeing the motive for far too long."

"It appears to have been one of the few bits of personal information old Jon did keep from Elinor in all the years they were married. It probably seemed so inconsequential to Jon it didn't occur to him to mention it. He told me at Christmas that he'd left me Kilgarth. And then, at the end of January, when he'd come down to Edinburgh for a meeting, he rang me up and told me he was considering selling. Never thinking, apparently, that I might be disappointed, or have feelings, or desires, or a point of view that was in any way different from his own. If he'd planned to hold on to it himself, I never would've interfered, you know. It wasn't that I wanted it for me as much as I wanted it in the family."

"Right!"

"It is rather touching, don't you think? That if Ellie had known he'd talked to me, she would have made more of an effort to tell me she was pregnant before the will was to be read. Being as considerate as Ellie always was." Hugh added the last phrase in a contemptuous voice, as though her kindness had been ridiculous, if not insincere. "And then I would've had much more time to plan her death in detail."

"That was your biggest mistake. Deciding to kill Ellie so

soon. It would've made more sense to wait a few more months."

"Perhaps. I clearly couldn't wait till she'd had the child, and there were several suspects right there in the house—Rory, Tom Atwood, perhaps even Alex—who helped keep you busy as well."

Ben didn't say anything. He just watched Hugh, concentrating on the expression of disappointed hopes and frustrated hostility. "Why? If all you wanted was for the house to stay in the family, why kill Ellie and the child?"

"You don't understand a'tall."

"No, I understand only too well. You liked the idea of owning it yourself. You'd been planning what to do with it and thinking about how good it would feel to be in charge, and you couldn't give it up. Maybe it didn't start out that way, but you ended up being seduced by the idea of becoming the local squire. And you'd already killed once, so what difference would it make if you killed again?"

"It wasn't like that a'tall! I couldn't be sure what Ellie and the child would do with it."

"Who was more intelligent—you or Jon?"

"No gentleman would answer such a question honestly without appearing immodest." Hugh was smiling, leaning back against his chair and smiling at Ben.

"So from your point of view, it must have been a constant irritation that other people didn't recognize your own intellectual superiority."

"You're approaching the situation rather simplistically, wouldn't you say? Assuming that it was jealousy, as well as pride that motivated my dislike."

"Wasn't it?"

"No! And neither was it greed that led me to want Kilgarth! I've done what I've done for the good of the family—past, present, and future. As well as the historical contributions that can be made for Scotland today *and* tomorrow by family estates such as ours."

Ben sympathized on one level. He hated what the twentieth century was doing to the great houses and historical sites. But would he murder for stone walls and perennial beds? Not under any circumstances he could imagine at the moment. And he said, "That sounds like rationalization to me."

"Does it, indeed? So Benjamin Reese is omniscient?"

"No. But I think it's very likely that we'll have evidence tomorrow that you were on Holy Island when Jon was killed. Rory's reporters are taking a photograph of the Bentley to the elementary school there, and then door-to-door if they have to, and I think they'll find somebody who noticed it. *Or* the license plates. The S36. The thirty-sixth plate issued in Scotland, which is almost as distinctive as the car. We don't take plates from one car to the next in the States like you do, so we don't think of them as collectors' items. But it's somehow fitting, don't you think? That the car and license you took such pride in may turn out to have been your undoing?"

"It was the crack of dawn, you'll remember, and there are so few inhabitants on Holy Island, one shouldn't count upon success."

"So why, after the attempt on me at Perach, didn't you try again?"

"I saw the towel rack episode, in hindsight, as something of an ill-considered act. I had intended, of course, to rewire the rack before your body was found. But still, it drew attention to those of us who were staying at Balnagard, and it made you even more convinced that Jon's death had been caused by foul play. It was quite disconcerting, you know, to hear of your background, and then discover that you were investigating the whole business because of the lack of prints. I could cheerfully have strangled old Alex. He's usually so wonderfully oblivious. If I hadn't had such rotten luck—"

"You believe in luck then?"

"Of course. Chance. Odds. The law of averages. If that idiot boy hadn't been on the path, I'd have been able to retrieve the hamper, and Jon's death would have forever remained a matter of 'natural causes.'"

"That's why he was on the path."

"I beg your pardon?

"I see purpose where you don't."

"Ah. Well, to each his own, I suppose. I shan't argue. I shall save my breath to cool my porridge."

"That can't be all that kept you from trying to kill me."

"I didn't like to draw attention to myself on home ground. Jon had so many unexpected enemies too, I thought it wouldn't be wise to barge in and muddy the waters any more than I already had. That was a bit of a laugh, you know. Good, kind, godly Jonathan MacLean having all those lovely enemies who absolutely hated him for an interfering old toad! It added an unexpected piquancy to the entire affair. Of course, I wasn't expecting to have to put Ellie out of the way, and I thought 'better to leave Reese alone.' I also saw you examining your car before driving off anywhere, so I assumed you were taking other precautions as well."

"Then tonight you found the *Scottish Beekeeper*s."

"Precisely. The circle of suspicion was drawing closer with Ellie's death, and your constant telephoning was worrying. Then when I found the journals, I knew it was only a matter of time till you uncovered the venerable Mr. MacIntosh, and that meant he had to be got rid of. I had intended to wait some months. But he would've had to go eventually."

"Would he?" Ben looked at Hugh in disgust, while he carefully felt the lump on his head, the stiff bloody hair with the cut in the center. "So the afternoon before you killed Jon, you drove up from Edinburgh and bought the bees."

"After I'd taken a long nap in the office so I'd be fresh enough to drive through the night."

"You used a phony name, and told MacIntosh the bees were for your fictitious mother, having already written to him using the name you'd made up for her. Then I suppose you took the bees to Kilgarth. You couldn't stay in your flat in town because you had to be far enough away from Holy Island that the drive seemed impossible, and be able to fake an alibi using Mary at the same time. I assume you took the bees into the basement, since you left the door unlocked."

"Did I? That was careless of me, wasn't it? Temperature is terribly important with bees, so I put them in the old playroom near the west door where I could drive the car up. One couldn't put them in the boot either, you know, not for a night drive. They'd need the warmth of the car's interior."

"So then you banged the garbage cans around under Mary's windows so she'd wake up and find you home at midnight. And then you gave her the chloral in her hot milk, which put her out like a light. You were counting on the knockout drops to make her sleep later than usual, which they did, and you wrote the note telling her you'd left the next morning at six-fifteen. It was the garbage collector's truck she heard in the morning and thought was you."

"The dustman, yes. I hoped that would happen as it did, but I obviously couldn't count on it."

"And then you drove to Holy Island, leaving sometime before twelve-thirty and arriving right around five—"

"Knowing where Jon would camp, and that he'd watch the sunrise from the ruins of the priory. He was predictable, our Jon, in his habits. He was always up between four-thirty and five. And of course we'd vacationed there as children, and when he was at university as well, so I knew where he'd go and what he'd do. Not that I relied on that. I stationed myself so I could see him come in from the dunes and follow him wherever he went."

"What excuse did you give for being there?"

"That I'd had a change in my tourist schedule, and I was to meet my Americans in Newcastle upon Tyne. I told him I'd stayed the night there, having decided to bring him breakfast. I humbly mentioned that we hardly ever had a chance to be alone anymore, knowing of course that that would make him feel guilty. I don't think he ever really cared for me as much as he thought he should. And since he was absurdly transparent in his emotional responses, it was easy to turn that to one's advantage. I asked him to take the hamper up by the Castle and get breakfast laid out, while I parked the Bentley and used the public loo."

"And Jon, being Jon, did what you wanted him to do whether he wanted to or not. If he'd heard the bees before he opened the basket, he never would've believed you'd try to kill him. So to accommodate you, he opened the basket he never would've brought and died a few seconds later."

"There was a very brisk wind that morning, luckily, and he probably told himself he'd imagined the sound of bees, or that the noise must be coming from somewhere else. I do think he heard them. He seemed to. I watched him with my binoculars from the abbey and saw it all go exactly as planned. Except for the blasted brat."

"And then you drove up to Edinburgh and met Mr. and Mrs. Harold Miller from Winnetka, Illinois at eight-ten at the North British Hotel."

"I banged straight up the coast in very good time indeed. There wasn't any traffic a'tall till I was just south of Edinburgh. It was still worrisome, though. A lorry, or a farm cart, and I would've been in serious difficulty."

"I assume you were hiding behind the trunk in the shed."

"Tonight? Yes. But putting that aside, I do have one question for you."

"Alright."

"How could you be completely unconscious one second and throw me across the room the next?"

"I was an Army Ranger, and we were trained very methodically to attack instantly with maximum strength as soon as we'd start to regain consciousness. The reaction's so ingrained, and it's so completely non-analytical, we're probably more dangerous when we're swimming back to the surface than we would be ordinarily."

Ben and Hugh both stopped and listened.

A car had pulled into the driveway. And Ben went to meet the doctor at the door and explain the situation before he led him into the living room.

He was a businesslike man, Dr. McCallam, and with hardly a look at Hugh, he pulled a footstool over to the side of the sofa and proceeded to examine Jamie MacIntosh.

McCallam was young and fair haired and serious, and after he'd finished, and was slipping his stethoscope in his coat pocket, he asked Ben if MacIntosh had "suffered a fall, which caused the abrasions and contusions."

Ben nodded. And McCallam made a note on his note pad.

"James MacIntosh is well into his seventies and has a weak heart as well. Chloral hydrate is rarely lethal, but it can be, cairtainly, in a vera large dose. I don't have reason to think he's been given a massive amount, but his heart isn't responding the way one might wish. It may be the chloral, or the fall that's set him off, but whichever it'tis, his condition is quite serious. He's been stung several times as ye can see, and there may possibly even be a systemic reaction. Either way, we shall have to get him to hospital as soon as may be. I'll give him an injection now, but I would be less than honest if I didn't tell ye that there's a distinct possibility we may lose him, with the heart as weak as it'tis."

Ben had been watching Hugh out the corner of his eye, and he saw the quick calculation and the rising hope. And while McCallam was in the hall making the necessary calls, Ben shut the door and walked across the carpet toward Hugh. "You're not going to get away with it."

"Without MacIntosh you've got precious little evidence."

"I've got the chloral hydrate, the syringe, the potassium chloride, and the ax handle you used on me."

"Without the first fingerprint on any of them, you'll remember. A case could be made that you simply planted the evidence."

"Oh? Why would I do that?"

"Perhaps you can't bear the thought of being perceived as an interfering bungler in the eyes of the police, and you've manufactured a scenario that makes you out the hero. I shall deny we've had this conversation, so it will only be your word against mine, after all. I shall never admit it to anyone again, I promise you that with complete assurance."

"I think Rory will find somebody who remembers your car or your plates."

"Perhaps. Yet that's still only circumstantial evidence. I shall produce some very good reason for why I was there, if need be, and manufacture quite a plausible explanation for why I didn't feel I could reveal it before." Hugh was smiling with his head back and his lips apart and the tip of his tongue sticking out the corner of his mouth. "No, you need MacIntosh, as you very well know. You can't even *prove* that I knew about the will! And without that, you have no motive a'tall!"

"We'll see. There's a lot of circumstantial evidence. Probably more than you realize. I've talked to your lawyer friend, Robert Whitfield. Mary mentioned him when she was describing your life in Edinburgh, and he told me that back in January you were already discussing how Kilgarth could be turned into a bed-and-breakfast, if there came a day when you needed to. You were asking him about zoning regulations and health laws that might apply."

The look Hugh gave Ben was sharp and vicious. But then he gazed at MacIntosh, at his waxy face and his slack gray lips hanging open against the sofa pillow. "I can easily explain that away without any trouble a'tall. No, you need MacIntosh, and you know it as well as I!"

CHAPTER SIXTEEN

Wednesday, May 31st

"BEN?" ALEX'S HARD-SOLED SHOES HAMMERED across the Balnagard drawing room's old wooden floor, then stopped on the oriental rug.

"I'm in the library, Alex!"

Uncle Robert looked up from *The Times* like a startled dove, in soft gray tweeds, with his gray hair and mustache, and mumbled, "Steady on, old man, there's no reason to shout, you know. Alex couldn't possibly hear you from the kitchen."

"Alex just called me from the drawing room."

"Did he? It's the first I've heard of it! We both must be getting past it, right Lizzy?"

"There you are! I wondered where you'd gotten to." Alex trotted straight toward the long trestle table where Ben sat in the middle of the library, with Robert behind him at a bookcase-desk that jutted into the room, and Lizzy in front at the same sort of carved medieval desk.

"I was just—"

"We were driven out of the dining room, rather unceremoniously *I* thought, on a pretext of tourists in the public rooms."

Robert tore a buttered croissant and pushed half of it into his mouth.

"I am sorry, Uncle Robert, but they will start through quite soon, and we're all running a bit late. I've only just finished fitting room descriptions into the wooden stands in the public rooms."

"What was it you wanted to tell me?" Ben moved a large leather-bound book away from where he sat and then poured himself a cup of coffee.

"I've found the key to the muniment room. What it was doing in my father's stud box I can't imagine. Yet there you'll find the family records—the deeds, the grants, and the architectural drawings." Alex dropped two keys (one large and wrought iron with a heavily scrolled end) onto a patch of table Ben hadn't covered with books. "The muniment room is directly above the tower sitting room, and it opens out onto the battlements. The smaller key unlocks the outside door, which sticks terribly, so don't abandon the effort too soon. It's a lovely view. One can see miles in every direction. You've got the key to the attics have you?"

Ben nodded.

"And everything you need for finishing up here? Excellent! Then I shall scramble upstairs and get to work."

"Papa, you've stuck your glasses on the top of your head again."

"Have I? Thank you very much indeed, Lizzie! You're a very observant child." Alex felt for the small gold glasses and dropped them in the side pocket of his moth-eaten cardigan. Lizzy was grinning up at him. And Alex took her head in his long strong hands and kissed the top of her forehead right at the center part, where her two blond braids began. "When will you be done, Ben?"

"Four-thirty or five, maybe."

"Shall we take a ride then? Up past Perach to the top of the moors?" Alex had just taken hold of the rope banister on the stone wall of the turret stairs, when the small, studded, courtyard door opened behind him and caught him in the center of the back.

"Oh Alex, I'm so sorry! I had no idea you were there!"

"I'm fine, my dear. Perfectly alright."

Jane Chisholm, her pale blond hair swirling away from her head as she turned and kissed her husband's chin, smiled after him as he ran up the narrow stone stairs. "He's very pleased with work at the moment. He was desperate for a really clever villain, and last night a terrifically repellent Maxwell pushed himself into the plot while he slept."

"Is this the novel about the Celtic monk?"

"Yes, seventh century, with a checkered past." Jane dropped the wooden bar across the door and then worked to turn the key in the lock. "All of us absolutely *must* keep this door fastened. The library is not to be included in the tour, and they will try to bash their way in. Now, Lizzy and Robert . . Lizzy, put down the Narnia book and listen to me, please. You must have the last of your things in the car and be ready to be packed off to the farm before our visitors start through at ten. Which is now less than an hour away. John's already in the gift shop, and David's helping set the tea room to rights, and it's not too much to ask that you and James gather the last of your things. Has anyone seen James?"

Lizzy explained why she couldn't be ready.

And Jane said, "There's no choice in the matter anymore. You must be down at the postern gate by half-nine. Take your dishes into the kitchen as you go, please. I shall scour the house for James."

Lizzie and Robert had started toward the drawing room, when Ben said, "James was—"

"I'm sorry, Ben, I almost forgot! A call came through from your secret'ry last night after you'd gone up to Perach. She'd forgotten the time difference, and it wasn't an emergency, so I told her I'd have you ring her at your university this morning. I'm afraid the kitchen telephone will be the only one available. The outside world will be swarming through the other rooms that are fitted out with phones." Jane froze and looked at Ben with worry between her eyebrows and her lips tensed together. "What if they don't swarm through? What if we've gone to the expense of converting the storage rooms into a tea room, and no one buys the first bun? There are only three or four houses like ours that serve food or drink. Perhaps there's a very good reason."

"No, it's a great idea and you've done it beautifully. I'm sure people are going to like it."

"Let's pray they do, shall we?" Jane was looking down at her hands, her long white fingers just touching the dark polished table. "I don't know if Alex has mentioned it, and I'm not a'tall sure I should, but we're so stretched financially, Ben, we could lose everything if things don't come right soon. I don't wish to burden you, but I'd like to talk to someone who's a bit more distanced than I. For what would happen to the Camerons, and the Douglases, and all the other estate workers and their families? There's no industry up here a'tall, and there're very few estates, and those there are are well fixed for workers already. These families have lived here since anyone can remember, rent free, of course, even now. And if we fail them, and they have to be uprooted, I don't know what they'd do."

"Jane, it'll be alright. Believe me."

"You sound like Micawber on his way to debtors' prison.

'Something will turn up!' Dickens did do a wonderful job with him, didn't he?" Jane stirred the potpourri in a blue and white porcelain bowl and glanced around the room without looking like she noticed a thing. "We have done what we've known to do. And yet, it's not up to us, at the end of the day, is it? And that, in itself, really is a relief, when I force myself to think about it properly. Anyway, I must dash. You haven't seen James have you?"

"He was just starting into the east woods with a fly rod when I was walking down from Perach a little before seven."

"Was he, indeed! He was supposed to feed the dogs first thing, and they're both milling about the kitchen like they haven't eaten in memorable history. Oh, well. Why am I surprised?" Jane started toward the drawing room door, and then said, "How's your evaluation of the ancestral odds and ends coming?"

"Well, I think. I should finish quite a bit today."

Alex had his feet out of the stirrups as he sat Malamaze, a dark bay seventeen-hand hunter, who was standing in a mossy patch at the edge of Loch Skiach. They were both staring at the lake that lay like a deep blue fiord in a ring of irregular hills. There were a few rock outcroppings, but no trees or shrubs on those hills, for this was the grouse moor, a land of low green heather in the spring, and yellow flowering gorse.

Ben was on Alex's left (on the big-boned chestnut with the white star), his aviator sunglasses shielding his eyes from the wide blue sky, as he looked north across the windblown lake to the Highlands—the sharp snow-covered mountains that stood like another world high behind the huddled hills.

Neither Ben nor Alex had said a word since they'd stopped by the loch. But as Alex dropped his reins to let Malamaze drink, he squinted his eyes against the western sky and asked, "Who was it on Holy Island who recognized Hugh's car?"

"A ten-year-old boy named Dickie Doughton. He went out to get the milk off the front step and saw the Bentley drive by toward the causeway. He's an excellent witness. He told Rory's reporter the number of the license plate before he was asked." Ben's horse, Matthew, picked his head up and sniffed the wind, then sighed and dropped it toward his knees again.

"I still feel such fury when I think of it."

"I know. Forgiving Hugh won't happen overnight."

"Thank God Jamie MacIntosh has survived the assault."

"Yeah, and he almost didn't."

"I still haven't taken it in, you know. I've known Hugh all my life to be a quiet, polite, self-deprecating gentleman of absolutely unquestionable character."

"It was a very consistent persona." Ben pulled his coat collar up against the wind that was scouring the moor. Then watched it ruffle a hundred acres of water into rows of ridges that bobbed up and down and against each other, on their way to the northern rim. "He wanted to be the 'laird' who's looked up to by the neighborhood. The one who sets the tone and hosts the village fete. Can you imagine how insufferable he'd have been if he'd been born in your position? But then at least we would've seen what he was."

"It seems so strange to me. Jon and his parents had no pretensions to social prominence. They never gave that sort of thing a thought."

"What kind of fish was that?"

An unusually long thin silvery one had jumped way out of the water, and they watched the circle widen on the surface.

"Couldn't tell, I'm afraid. We've stocked it with pike and

trout as part of our attempt to make the old place self-supporting. You know, fishing parties in summer, hunting parties in winter. Would you mind if we started back? I ought to tidy the stables before we walk to the farm."

They turned around beside the bothie (the low stone hut that had sheltered deer hunting thanes and their transport ponies for more than a hundred years), following a narrow track through the heather and gorse that wound across a flat stretch before it dropped down toward the valley. Alex was in front, whistling something Ben didn't recognize, before he looked over his shoulder. "Why do you think Hugh has turned out the way he has?"

"Any kind of answer would be pure speculation."

"I know, but I feel at such a loss."

"Well. He has an overdeveloped sense of self-importance. Maybe the stories about the family, the Fosters of Bamburgh or whoever else, made him feel superior to everyone else. He definitely likes thinking his family is more important than most. And that the old family 'glory' ought to be restored."

"An unsavory sort of romanticism run amok?"

"Maybe. And materialism too. The 'I am what I have' syndrome. *You* must have made him feel very uncomfortable, since your family was far more 'elevated' and you never seemed to care."

"Oh, I've cared, sadly enough. Even though I was raised to know better. And yet I am quite hostile, you know, to those with inherited titles who abuse the privileges and exalt the honors they would've been incapable of earning themselves. For it's standards of behavior one must meet, when one's own time comes. The responsibility one has to one's retainers and dependents. That's the sort of thing my parents attempted to hammer home. And why they refused to send me to boarding school, where contrary influences often seem to abound."

"Contrast that with Hugh, who made quite a point of telling me that Bamburgh Castle is much bigger than Balnagard. It was just like a little kid saying, 'My father can beat up your father.'"

"It's pathetic, Ben, it really is."

"Yeah, but isn't that the essence of what's wrong with all of us? We *want* to set ourselves above everybody else. And it's not just pride in a house, or a professional title, or the way we look. It can be a talent for training horses, or finding the best bargains, or baking an apple pie. Or being able to classify a wide range of artifacts."

"Yes, not to mention one's literary style!"

"Talent and intelligence can be a real liability. Because they help us arrange our lives so we don't see what we are."

"Although spiritual pride can be terribly insidious too. In memorizing Bible verses, and not drinking alcohol, or smoking tobacco, or saying the first rough word. One may even be tempted to feel rather smug at possessing spiritual truth. You know what I mean. At having 'proper' insights, and doing good works as well. It's a pharisaical sort of pride."

"And worse than any other."

The land had begun to fall away toward the Tay, where the fir forests grew on either side of the heather—huge tracks, planted by Alex's father and grandfather, about a quarter of a mile away. There was a hawk circling the woods on their left, and they halted the horses to watch him soar.

Alex let Malamaze walk after a minute, and then he looked back at Ben, who was patting Matthew on the neck. "Do you think Hugh felt any personal animosity toward Jon?"

"I think he was jealous of him. He never felt like he was properly appreciated. Though I'm not at all sure any amount of attention would have seemed like enough to Hugh."

"I must have been hoodwinked in that as well, for I thought Hugh idolized Jon. He even seemed a bit put out when Jon came back from the army and went right off to get his divinity degree. I remember thinking he was jealous of any work that took Jon away from him."

"Maybe. A lot of people end up hating their own idols."

"But, really, you know, there was far more talk in the family circle about what Hugh needed, and what he might like, and how they could help him, than there ever was about Jon, who was terribly independent and didn't need special attention."

"And yet Hugh saw himself as the outcast watching everyone admire Jon."

"That's not the way it was a'tall! It's so unfair, it really is. Mr. and Mrs. MacLean went out of their way to draw Hugh out and encourage him to develop his interests. That was the primary reason his father bought the boat even though it was a financial strain. Sailing was the one sport Hugh seemed able to attempt."

"Hugh also resented the fact that Jon was liked and admired for being straightforward and direct and not covering up his own defects."

"It is true that if Jon was angry, as a child, you did know it instantly. But then it was over. There were no grudges held or wounds licked."

"And people liked Jon's spontaneity, which Hugh thought was beneath him. Right?"

The trail was too steep to talk, where it twisted around the bottom of the woods between stone walls and sheer drops, and Ben lengthened his reins so Matthew could pick his own way on the stony path. But when it had leveled again and widened by Castle Perach, Ben said, "I think Hugh thought that hiding what he felt gave him power over all the stupid people who didn't appreciate his superiority. So while he pretended to be the unobtrusive, polite, self-effacing gentlemen he was taught to be, he could feel a gratifying contempt for those who were dumb enough to fall for the facade."

"I still don't understand how he can continue to profess his own innocence now, in the face of MacIntosh's testimony *and* yours."

"I'm not too surprised."

"But it's hopeless, isn't it?"

"I don't think he stands a chance legally. But I bet he'll say he's innocent to the end, and take pleasure in the fact that there'll be some people who'll think he's been framed. He really does believe he's far more intelligent than the rest of us, and misleading people appeals to his sense of power."

"That's a very twisted way of seeing the world. But then he is twisted, isn't he?"

"Even though he was raised with the same values as Jon."

"Ah. Environment versus genetics."

"As well as the role of will."

"So you'll be staying to testify, will you?"

"I'll have to stay after the trial too, for awhile. I talked to my secretary this morning, and my university's been given quite a valuable collection of medieval manuscripts by an American family of Campbells. They're distantly related to the Campbells of Cawdor, and they'd like some genealogical work done while I'm here, so I'll do that for the university before I go back. You still have the death penalty in Scotland?"

"Yes, though for how long I don't know. There's quite a movement afoot to abandon it."

They were just below Perach, picking their way through a large majority of Balnagard's pheasants, who for some unknown reason were attracted to the land around Perach. They sat in the lower branches of oaks and ash trees or they shuffled and darted across the lawn, and the cackling and the flurry of them flapping their big heavy bodies into the air made Matthew and Malamaze skitter and shy. And yet Ben and Alex both laughed as they pulled them up and made them walk around the last switchback down toward Balnagard.

They crossed the road and took the south arch through the high stone wall, passing the maze on their left and the castle draw-bridge on their right, before trotting sedately between the east and west halves of the formal gardens, past the tea room outbuilding beside the castle and the low-walled orchards on their left.

When they got to the stables, Alex looked at his watch with the same smile James had had when he'd asked Alex days before if he had time for a sword fight. "It would be great fun to gallop the bottom land, don't you think? The cows will have gone in, but we've still some time before dinner."

They walked their horses down through the north woods, in a cool green tunnel of evergreens and fern, and stepped out into the light of the broad grassy pasture that rolled along the river. They stayed on the edge beside the hill, the strip of land outside the fences that was used by the farm trucks and the Land Rover. They trotted a hundred feet, and then set the geldings into a can-ter that took them beyond Balnagard. It was Matthew's best gait, as it turned out, even when it grew into a hand gallop.

But they had to turn back and cool the horses before they put them in their stalls. And they brought them back to a trot, and then made them walk toward home.

That was when Ben remembered the list in his jacket pocket. "Tell me how you got the tapestry that's hanging in the hall by the tower room."

"My father bought it in Russia a year or two before the Revolution. He was on the Ambassador's staff then, and there were quite a few noblemen who saw what was in the wind after the August uprising of 1914. One of them told Father he intended to emigrate, and asked if he'd be interested in the family art. I don't think my father really cared much for the hanging, but he admired the Count, and I suspect Papa bought it to accommodate the poor man."

"You've never had it appraised?"

"You *are* referring to the garden scene?"

Ben smiled to himself and nodded.

"Not that I know of, no."

"It's a Gobelin, and it was woven sometime around 1640 or '50. There's an almost identical one hanging in the Cleveland Museum, amazingly enough. The only difference is that one section of background is narrower in yours. It's probably worth three quarters of a million dollars. Or about four hundred thousand pounds. Especially if you sell it on the continent, which Sotheby's can do through their Paris office. I could arrange to sell it for you myself, if you want me to, which would save the commission, but would take quite a bit longer."

"How very odd! I've always thought it rather uninteresting. Although the income would certainly be welcome! Yes, that's wonderful news indeed!"

"Now, the blue Flemish tapestries in your bedroom—"

"The ones of Noah and the ark? And Moses crossing the Red Sea? Now, those I would miss."

"Well, then what about the gun collections? The grouping on the square stairs and the one on the north wall in the gun room?"

"They're nothing I couldn't do without. I never hunt, now that we have paying guests to thin the populations."

Ben handed Alex a folded typewritten piece of paper and began humming quietly to himself.

"What's this?"

"A list of artifacts I think you could sell in a reasonably logical order to get the estate on an even keel."

Alex halted Malamaze at the foot of the path that led up straight into the woods. And as he read, a dark red flush spread up his neck and swept across his face. He dropped the hand that held the paper on his pommel and stared over at Ben. "Are you sure of this? How could ten guns be worth a million pounds!"

"Quite easily, actually. Two silver mounted flintlock holster pistols by Barbar of London dated 1675. One early Highland flintlock pistol by Thomas Caddell of Doune, dated 1700. A matched set of five pieces—a skeet gun, an over-under 20 gauge, a 20 gauge for firing ball at deer, a 30-30 rifle, a 370 magnum rifle for big game—all hand made to specifications for the Fourth Earl in the late eighteenth to early nineteenth century. Add any two others of similar value—and there are many from which to choose—and you've easily got a million pounds."

Ben saw the struggle that was taking place on Alex's face and kept himself from laughing. "Now, if you wanted to sell the whole collection, and I've counted eighty pieces, some inlaid with ivory, some with gold wire, quite a number with chased barrels or silver stocks—if you sold them all as a unit, you could probably get fifteen million pounds—"

"Fifteen million pounds! FIFTEEN MILLION POUNDS!"

"And then, of course, there's the porcelain. One of your ancestors put together an extremely fine collection. And the snuff boxes. And the books. You'd rather sell porcelain, wouldn't you, than the family tomes?"

"Absolutely! I can hardly bear to think of parting with any of the books, but I never thought for a moment that I'd have any choice."

"You have a choice, Alex. Without doubt. I've only just started in the library and the muniment room, but there're some really wonderful things. There's an illuminated book of hours from the fifteenth century—"

"I know, and it's breathtakingly done."

"And a handwritten sixteenth-century codex."

"My Great-grandfather William bought that in Rome."

"An herbal, handwritten and illustrated, from the late seventeenth century, executed meticulously by a female Argyle ancestor."

"It would be an absolute travesty to lose any of those."

"You won't have to. Not in the next hundred years. Depending, of course, on what your parliament decides to do to you next. Tell me again why we let governments profit from our deaths? They tax every cent we make the whole time we're alive, and then do it to us again to keep our kids from inheriting the family farm."

"I know! It really is a travesty."

"Anyway, I would like to study your books and papers, to segregate them by age and language, and catalogue the really interesting ones for my own amusement."

"Oh yes! Please. I'd greatly appreciate your sorting them out in whatever way you'd like." Alex folded the paper and put it in the inside pocket of his tweed jacket. He still looked stunned and vulnerable, as though he were forcing himself not to be too emotional. "I simply don't know what to say. I had absolutely no idea about the guns!"

Alex laughed suddenly and then held his head in his hands. "It's amusing, really, when one stops to think. We've been trying to live so frugally. I never throw away any of my typescript. We turn all the sheets over and use them by the telephone or for writing lists. We never turn on the central heat unless we have guests. We've been coasting down hills for years to conserve petrol. Our bank overdraft gives me palpitations, and we're mortgaged within an inch of our lives because we've been trying to refurbish the estate cottages, the Camerons' and all the other farm workers'. The work has been going terribly slowly because of the financial struggle." Alex looked blankly at Ben and then smiled as he picked up his reins.

"Well, things are going to be easier soon."

"I bought five thousand blasted pheasants this last fall to make us a bit more attractive to hunting parties, and I had to sell the rights to my Churchill book to do that! And the roof! The whole thing needs to be re-slated and re-leaded and we've had no hope of even beginning. You know we have a tutor? Jane and I both refuse to send the children away to public school, and he lives rent free in one of the cottages. Three other families send their children here as well, and they share the expense, and yet we've been terribly afraid we couldn't keep him on. The children's university education is going to cost the earth, and I can't tell you what a relief this is! I don't know how to thank you, Ben. We never seemed able to afford a comprehensive appraisal and neither of us had a clue."

"What I've done doesn't begin to be comprehensive."

"Of course, taxes will take three quarters at least. But think of the good that could be done if one were finally solvent! The foundation sort of thing Jon was hoping to set up. Wouldn't it be wonderful to begin one in his name?"

"Yes. Absolutely."

"I can hardly wait to tell Jane. She's been so good, and so

practical. Much more than I really, if the truth were known."

They were almost to the stables, and Jake, the boxer, flew out of the woods and leapt in front of the horses, who panicked immediately and jumped straight up off the ground.

"Jake, down! Settle down right now! He's supposed to be up at the farm, of course. No! Down!" Jake was trying to restrain himself. And he turned, finally, toward the stables and trotted off ahead. "Good, Jake. That's a good boy. This is his first year, moving to the farm, and it may take him awhile to get used to the idea."

"So what will happen to Kilgarth?"

"Didn't I say? The maiden aunts in Ballinluig will inherit the insurance, the house, and the contents as well. They expect to make their home there, with Mary Atwood, thankfully, and they'll be moving in straightaway. Jane spoke to them yesterday when they called to get the name of the minister who preached Jon's service. They're thinking of using the house for some sort of charity work. Something for young people. Summer retreats perhaps. Or a refuge for unwed mothers. They're talking to their own minister too, but they wanted Donaldson's thoughts as well. It's Jon's idea for the foundation that's spurred them to do something similar with whatever's come to them from him."

"That's great."

"Yes, Jon and Ellie would both be pleased. So what will you do when you finish here? And I shall pay you, by the way, for your work. Handsomely, now that I can."

"Oh no you won't! I've enjoyed it."

"That's neither here nor there."

"We'll talk about it later."

"We shall indeed!"

"I think I'll go up to Cawdor. Rory and his daughter are driving up to pack Ellie things, and Rory has asked me to stay for a day or two. I also want to see Hamish MacDonald. I don't know what I'm going to say to him, but before he dies he needs someone to go out of their way for him who'll talk to him about substance instead of form."

"You won't be leaving right away will you? You'll stay with us for a few days at least?"

"I could go and come back, I guess. It'll take me awhile to go through your books, and they've yet to set the date for the trial."

"You see, Jane and I were talking last night…" Alex had just dismounted and was unbuckling Malamaze's girth, standing in the gravel court in the center of three stone stables.

Ben thought his voice sounded strangely ill at ease, and he looked deliberately in Alex's direction as he led Matthew toward his stall in the center stable. "And?"

"Well . . Jane's sister will be coming up to visit next week. Now, I know you've never met her, but Jane and I were hoping . . well, that is to say that we were thinking that perhaps you'd enjoy each other. And it would be an absolute shame if you'd left us before she'd arrived." Alex's face was red and strained again, and his eyes were beginning to looked hunted.

Ben leaned down and rubbed Jake's ears, while he said, "I see," in a noncommittal voice.

"Jennifer has just finished her veterinarian degree, actually, and she was a great favorite of Jon and Ellie's, and we thought that it might brighten things up a bit if you were both to have someone to talk to." Alex looked mortified. As though he knew he'd bungled. As though his handling had been elephantine when great speed and lightness had been required.

"I've got the genealogy to do too, you know, so with the trial and the trip to Cawdor, I guess my plans are kind of up in the air."

Alex looked crestfallen and terribly embarrassed.

And Ben Reese took pity on him. "Okay, Alex. I'll stick around. Or I'll come back. Whichever's easier for you."

"Good! I don't think you'll regret it, I really don't."

"Don't you?" Ben patted Mathew's flank as the big gentlemanly thoroughbred walked carefully past him into his stall. And then he laughed as he shut the door.

"Who is it you've invited to dinner tomorrow?"

"The two elderly sisters who were on my train from Edinburgh."

"Ah, the dog fanciers. We should be organized enough by then to make them feel at home. The farm's quite cozy, you know. The corridors aren't so long, and there's a wonderful arbor off the kitchen. We eat all our meals there when the weather's suitable. I'll go with you when you pick them up and help you find the house."

"Yeah, I'm sure you'll be a big help."

"I don't think I like your tone!"

Ben and Alex both laughed, while Alex washed a water bucket and Ben threw hay into Matthew's stall.